McCaleb climbed into the back of the wagon, finding barely enough room to stand. He took the ten-stick bundle of capped and fused dynamite from the saddlebags and shoved it between two wooden cases near the floor of the wagon bed. After setting all but a dozen feet of fuse, he hunched down, took a match from his oilskin pouch and popped it alight with his thumbnail.

The fuse caught, sputtered and died. From somewhere in the Indian camp came the exploratory yip of a dog. Time and luck were running out for McCaleb. He lighted a second match, and when the fuse caught, swung off the wagon's tailgate. The dog now yipped excitedly, and McCaleb knew they were in for it.

An arrow whipped out of the darkness, slashing into McCaleb's right thigh. Goose caught his arm and pulled him down a creek bank. No sooner had they dropped to their knees in the water than a fusillade of rifle fire shattered the silence, the deadly slugs whipping the air barely above their heads.

McCaleb drew his Colt. At least he would find the Comanche position. Where *was* that explosion? . . .

THE GOODNIGHT TRAIL

Books in the Trail Drive Series
by Ralph Compton
from St. Martin's Paperbacks

THE GOODNIGHT TRAIL
THE WESTERN TRAIL
(Coming in December 1992)
THE CHISHOLM TRAIL
(Coming in 1993)

THE
GOODNIGHT
TRAIL

RALPH
COMPTON

ST. MARTIN'S PAPERBACKS

This is a work of fiction, based on actual trail drives of the Old West. Many of the characters appearing in the Trail Drive Series were very real, and some of the trail drives actually took place. But the reader should be aware that, in the developing of characters and events, some fictional literary license has been employed. While some of the characters and events herein are purely the creation of the author, every effort has been made to portray them with accuracy. However, the inherent dangers of the trail are real, sufficient unto themselves, and seldom has it been necessary to enhance their reality.

THE GOODNIGHT TRAIL

ISBN: 0-312-92815-7

Printed in the United States of America

St. Martin's Paperbacks edition/August 1992

10 9 8 7 6 5 4 3 2 1

To Nancy Wilson,
principal of the St. Clair County
High School in 1954

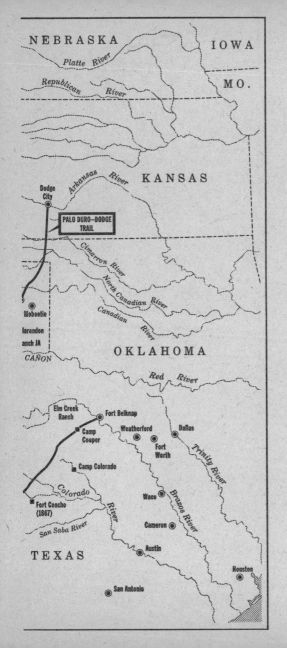

Author's Foreword

*I*n 1821, Mexico declared its independence, ending forever any Spanish claim to the American West. William Becknell, a trader from Missouri, was already near the border, preparing to trade with the Indians. Instead, he drove his pack mules to Santa Fe and returned to Missouri, his packs bulging with silver dollars. He made another trip four months later, this time with three loaded wagons. His wagon route became the Santa Fe Trail.

In 1822, the Rocky Mountain Fur Company began sending trappers up the Missouri to the Yellowstone River country. Avoiding hostile Blackfeet and Arikaras Indians, the trappers crossed the Rocky Mountains into a friendly Wyoming. South Pass, as they named it, was to become the Oregon Trail.

By 1840, the beaver hat had gone out of style and the country had been trapped out. Grizzled mountain men put their knowledge of survival and Indian lore to use by guiding wagon trains across the prairies and mountains. West of Independence, Missouri, the trail divided. The Santa Fe swung off to the southwest, to Texas and New Mexico. The other route, going northwest, was the Overland—or Oregon—Trail.

Before the Civil War, and again in 1866 and 1867, the Shawnee Trail was the principal route used by Texas cattlemen seeking northern markets. The trail crossed three hundred miles of Indian Territory—which is now eastern Oklahoma—and after moving into Missouri, bore almost exactly northeast to Sedalia. Immigrants from Missouri and other points north and east of there referred to it as the Texas Road.

After the battle of San Jacinto—which assured Texas independence—cattle were driven to New Orleans, Shreveport, and New Iberia, to be shipped north by boat. During the forties and fifties, small herds were trailed into many midwestern states. Some were driven to Chicago, and at least one herd was taken as far north as New York.

For all its notoriety, the Chisholm Trail didn't become a cattle trail until 1867, when the railroad reached Abilene. This was more than a year after Goodnight's first herd of longhorns had blazed a new trail to Denver.

Four long years of war had left the southern states not only destitute of cattle, but bankrupt. But Texas had an advantage: There were millions of wild longhorns. Goodnight believed Texans would lose no time in getting them to market. In doing so, he expected them to converge on the old trails established prior to the war, so he avoided these trails, driving through eastern New Mexico and into Colorado. There, on unspoiled range and lush graze, he established ranches where he could "hold" his herds at the end of the drive until he was ready to sell. He found a ready market; it was mining country, untouched by the ravages of war, and the miners had money to buy. On the Chisholm Trail many a Texas herd was confronted with a problem that Charles Goodnight had already foreseen. There was simply no grass on which the longhorns could be fattened after the long drive.

Goodnight's mother and stepfather moved to Texas' Brazos River country in 1845, when Charlie was nine years old, and he rode bareback all the way. By the time he was thirteen, he was riding a mustang and hunting with the Caddo Indians. At twenty he went into the cattle business, and at twenty-four he served the Confederacy as a scout for the Texas Rangers. Before he was fifty, Goodnight was dominating almost twenty million acres of range country. He possessed an "edge" that most of his Texas counterparts lacked. He rode with the daring of Fremont and with a knowledge of the frontier equal to that of Jim Bridger and Kit Carson. Fighting Indians, outlaws, and cattle thieves, he blazed the Goodnight Trail across two thousand miles of untamed, uncharted frontier and into the pages of the history of the American West.

PROLOGUE

$\mathcal{B}$enton McCaleb kicked out of his blankets and sat up on his hard bunk. The first gray light of dawn crept in through the musty room's one window. Fully dressed except for his boots, he swung his bare feet onto the cold dirt. He shivered as the chill December wind found its way through the cracks and crevices of the old Fort Belknap barracks. Fully awake now, he listened. Something had awakened him.

Whap! It came again, sounding like an alarmed beaver swatting the waters of Hubbard Creek with its broad tail. But the agonized scream that followed could have been human. McCaleb upended his rough-out mule ear boots and shook them. Dragging them on as far as he could, he stood up and stomped his feet the rest of the way into them. From a peg on the wall at the head of his bunk, he snatched his wide belt and holster. He kicked the flimsy door open and, on his way out, buckled the rig around his lean middle, the .44 Colt revolver riding butt forward on his left hip.

At first the sight that met McCaleb's eyes made him sick to his stomach. And then killing mad! Shag Oliver was beating a horse! The chestnut mare had been snubbed to a heavy corral post. Oliver had doubled a rawhide lariat and then doubled it again, and in his huge left hand it was a formidable weapon. Welts crisscrossed the trembling flanks of the terrified mare.

McCaleb caught the burly arm on its backward swing and threw Oliver flat on his back in the dusty corral. For a few surprised seconds Shag didn't move. Then he crabbed around until he faced McCaleb. He weighed three hundred pounds. Tangled, crow-black hair covered his ears and a shaggy beard hid most of his face. He had little pig eyes, like a grizzly. He had his pistol half drawn when McCaleb's boot smashed into his hand, sending the weapon skittering away in the dust. Bawling like a fresh-cut steer, Oliver lurched to his knees, swinging the doubled rawhide at McCaleb's head. Stepping back, McCaleb caught the lariat, dragging the big man toward him. His right knee smashed Oliver under the chin and again he was thrown flat on his back, raising a cloud of dust. This time he didn't get up. Behind McCaleb, the cocking of a pistol seemed unnaturally loud in the Sunday morning stillness.

"Leave him be," said a cold voice. "I'll drop the first man that pulls a pistol."

Slowly McCaleb turned. Scoggin and Kincer stood facing him, their hands hovering near their holstered pistols. Behind them stood the scout, Charles Goodnight, his Colt cocked and ready. With him were two other Rangers, prepared to side him. Scoggin and Kincer lifted their hands shoulder high. Shag Oliver sat up, blood dribbling from the corners of his smashed mouth. McCaleb had his back to the fort, but he knew who and what was coming. He could see it in the faces of the other Rangers; even Scoggin and Kincer. There was amusement and disgust, but no respect. Their commander, Lieutenant Colonel A. T. Obenchain had arrived.

"Mr. Goodnight," snapped Obenchain, "holster your weapon. If you men can find nothing better to do with your free time than brawl among yourselves, perhaps it will be better spent in close-order drill. I will speak to First Lieutenant Woolfork about it. Your lack of discipline and the total absence of respect is appalling and I won't tolerate it. By God, I will court-martial the next man who creates an unwarranted disturbance in this camp!"

Scoggin and Kincer boosted Shag Oliver to his feet. He spat blood and bits of broken teeth, glaring at McCaleb with all the hatred he could muster.

"Nex' time," he snarled, "when it's just me an' you, I'll kill you."

McCaleb said nothing. He stood six feet four and weighed two hundred pounds. He had pale blue eyes and his sandy hair curled down over the collar of his denim shirt. The other Rangers, following the Obenchain outburst, had drifted away. Only Goodnight remained. He spoke.

"I'm Charles Goodnight. My friends call me Charlie. It's Sunday, so I can't tell you what the *others* call me."

He offered his big hand and McCaleb took it. Goodnight's smile began in his eyes and worked its way down to his lips. He was a bear of a man with a neatly trimmed dark beard and short hair, topped with a wide-brimmed, high-crowned gray Stetson. He wore moccasins instead of boots. Benton McCaleb had grown up on the Texas border fighting Indians, outlaws, and other thieves. So had Charles Goodnight. McCaleb found himself liking the man.

"I'm Benton McCaleb. Nobody ever called me 'Benton' except Ma. Everybody else calls me Bent, or just McCaleb."

"Pleased to meet you," said the scout. "I've been out since Thursday. Had to ride one of the old man's dispatches to Captain Joe Ward at Victoria Peaks. Rode in late last night."

"I rode in the day you left," said McCaleb. "I've been with the detachment at Hubbard Creek, but the commander asked for another scout. Me and him just seemed to rub one another the wrong way. Now there's Obenchain. That fracas with Oliver won't help my chances here, but I can't abide a man that mistreats a horse."

"Neither can I," said Goodnight. "You should have

let him clear leather and then gut-shot him. If I'm any judge, he's the kind that'll lay up in a thicket and back-shoot you at the first opportunity. I've had my doubts about that trio since they rode in. You ever seen them before?"

"No, but I'm going to remember them. I'm obliged to you for buying in."

"I like your style, Benton McCaleb. If I'd gotten there ahead of you, I'd have done exactly what you did. Come on; I want you to meet a pair of Texans you can trust with your life."

Federal troops had abandoned Fort Belknap in 1857, and in March 1862, Ranger Company B had taken it for a main camp. Rangers, for the sake of mobility, carried bacon, coffee, salt, flour or hard biscuits. Each man made his own meal, boiling his coffee and broiling his bacon over an open fire. Goodnight led the way to a clearing where his friends already had a fire going. On two sides of it a forked stick had been driven into the ground, and by its bail, from a cross-member, a huge blackened coffeepot hung over the fire. The two Rangers hunkered down, drinking coffee from their tin cups. McCaleb recognized them as the friends who had stood ready to side Goodnight against Scoggin and Kincer. They rose to their feet as Goodnight and McCaleb approached.

"Boys," said Goodnight, "this is Benton McCaleb. McCaleb, meet Brazos Gifford and Will Elliot. When you're on the trail scouting, with Obenchain in command, you'll need them to watch your back. I swear, a Kiowa could steal that man's horse from under him before he suspected a thing."

These Rangers were the same caliber of men as Goodnight himself, and as McCaleb shook their hands, he felt a kinship with them. Brazos Gifford was redheaded and green-eyed. He wore a gray flat-crowned hat, denim shirt, Levi's pants, and rough-out, high-heeled boots. Will Elliot had curly black hair and gray eyes. Except for a wide-brim, pinch-crease black Stetson, he wore the same garb as Brazos. Each man wore a tied-down .44 Colt low on his right hip. They were all big men—over six feet—and McCaleb judged the three of them to be, more or less, within a year of his own age of twenty-eight. He and Goodnight had brought their own tin cups, and after downing some of the scalding black coffee, set about broiling strips of bacon skewered on long sticks over the hot coals.

"I hope," said Brazos, "Obenchain was just blowin' off his mad, with that talk about close-order drill. Take a Texan off his hoss, put him to walkin' in high-heeled boots, and you'd just as well take a pistol and shoot the poor bastard, 'cause he ain't gonna be no account to nobody."

"I ain't one to desert after I'm committed," said Will, "but damned if I'm spendin' another two years fightin' Indians, bandits, and rattlers just so's that old fool can play soldier. This military stuff he's always yellin' about—court-martial, formations, drillin'—don't mean nothin' out here on the border. What *really* gets my goat is when he says it's 'undignified' for an officer—meanin' him, of course—to associate with his men. Wait'll he's surrounded by two or three hundred screechin' Indians; *then* he can decide which he'd rather part with—his dignity or his hair."

"Thank God," said Goodnight, "we haven't had any real Indian trouble since he's been in command, but it's coming. Obenchain's a Virginian; he doesn't understand the frontier or its people. God only knows why he was assigned this command; politics, I suspect. Unfortunately, he isn't the only misfit. Noble as it sounds, this Frontier Regiment—the Rangers—has become a means for some men to avoid conscription. Men like Shag Oliver and his two gun hands. Are we *really* serving the Confederacy, camped here on the Texas border, while other men are being shot to doll rags by the Union Army?"

"I didn't join the Rangers to serve the Confederacy *or* to avoid the draft," said McCaleb. "There are some men

I have to kill, and I don't expect to find them wearing Yankee blue."

They observed him in silence. An unwritten code entitled them to know only as much about him as he was willing to reveal. Poking a stick under the suspended coffeepot, he tilted it enough to refill his cup. They waited, willing to hear him out if he chose to continue. He finished his coffee, put down his cup and got to his feet. The only sound was the sigh of the wind in the cottonwoods and the cawing of a nearby crow. Finally he spoke.

"One of the men I'm after is Cullen Baker. Know anything about him?"

Will Elliot whistled long and low.

"He's a curly wolf," said Brazos, "and the pack ridin' with him is every bit as bad as he is."

"He's a disgrace to the Confederacy in general and to the state of Texas in particular," said Goodnight. "He's using the war as an excuse to loot and kill. He's mighty sudden with a pistol. The Cass County sheriff says he's the fastest man alive, that nobody's his equal."

"I am," said McCaleb.

Afterward, none of the three could swear they had seen him draw. His Colt spoke once, and twenty yards away a cloud of crow feathers drifted from the upper branches of a cottonwood. Later, when Brazos Gifford and Will Elliot found the dead bird, its head had been shot away clean.

Benton McCaleb holstered his Colt, refilled his coffee cup from the big pot and hunkered down to face his three friends.

"Cullen Baker is my cousin," he said, "on my mother's side. He taught me to draw and shoot."

"So you aim to track him down and kill him," said Goodnight.

"I have my reasons," said McCaleb. "Personal reasons."

"Suppose you find Baker and kill him," said Goodnight. "What do you aim to do then? What plans do you have?"

"None, I reckon," said McCaleb.

"Benton McCaleb, you're too good a man to waste your young years tracking a no-account bastard like Cullen Baker. I'd be the first to admit he *needs* killin', but let somebody else do it."

On the frontier, a man didn't involve himself in another man's business, nor did he offer advice without being asked. Goodnight had stepped over the line, and they all knew it. Brazos Gifford and Will Elliot said nothing. Their eyes were on McCaleb. A man's natural inclination would be to tell Goodnight to mind his own damn business. But Goodnight cared about his friends, and something in his blunt appeal got through to Benton McCaleb. When he spoke, it was without a trace of anger.

"I won't be out of the Rangers until 'sixty-five, Charlie. Neither will you. What plans do *you* have? What *does* a man do with his young years, when the war's tore everything to hell and gone?"

"Once I'm out of the Rangers," said Goodnight, "I aim to rope and brand me a herd of Texas longhorns."

"For what purpose? Even if the war hadn't closed all the trails north, the tick fever would have."

"I aim to blaze a new trail," said Goodnight, "to the west, into New Mexico and Colorado Territories. It's mining country, untouched by the war, and the miners will have money to buy. I look for rivers with quicksand, hostile Indians, outlaws, and stampedes. If you crave to live dangerously, riskin' your fool neck every day, what more could you ask?"

"Hell's fire," chuckled Will, "but for the quicksand and stampedes, we're *already* doin' that."

"It don't pay worth a damn," said Brazos. "I ain't makin' enough to buy shells for my Colt."

Goodnight grinned at their bitching, but his eyes were on McCaleb.

"I like the sound of it, Charlie," said McCaleb.

"No more vengeance trail, then?"

"I reckon I'll swap that for a cattle trail," said McCaleb.

ON THE TEXAS FRONTIER. DECEMBER 5, 1861

CHAPTER 1

*I*t was May 31, 1865, two weeks after the burial of the assassinated Abraham Lincoln.

"The first day of June 1861," said Brazos Gifford, "was when I joined the Rangers. If the Confederacy—and Texas—had hung on, tomorrow would have been the end of my enlistment."

"Your enlistment," said Will Elliot, "ended the fifteenth of last month, at Appomattox, along with mine. When I joined, I got paid for the first six months, and I ain't been paid since. Sixty dollars. Fifteen dollars a year. My God, this soldierin' don't pay enough to keep a Digger Injun alive."

"I don't aim to hang around any longer," said Benton McCaleb. "If the state of Texas has any final orders for me, it'll have to track me down. I figure the next orders we'll get will come from politicians in Washington, and whatever they have in store for us won't be pleasant. The rest of the country might have been a mite sympathetic to us, but not after that fool gunned down the president. Come mornin', I say we ride for the brakes and brand us some wild cows."

The night wind fanned the coals of their tiny fire, the resulting flame lighting the narrow confines of the coulee in which they had camped. Charles Goodnight wrapped his bandanna around his hand and reached for the coffeepot, refilling his cup before he spoke.

"I expect Bent's right. God only knows what's going to happen here in Texas. Within a year—maybe sooner —I'm looking for the South to be fully occupied by Union soldiers and camp followers."

"Maybe you got the right idea, Charlie," said Will, "takin' a herd of Texas longhorns north. But it's been five years. You reckon there's still enough of your herd to make a drive?"

"I left a hundred and eighty head when I joined the Rangers," said Goodnight. "I figure, after five years of natural increase, I'm entitled to at least fifteen hundred head. Maybe more."

Brazos chuckled. "That's some hell of a natural increase."

"An unbranded cow or calf is a maverick," said Goodnight, "and when a cow's three or four years old— natural increase or not—who can say that unbranded critter belongs to him? Texas is broke, but by God, we've got longhorns by the millions. There's enough for every cowboy in Texas to have a herd, if he's got the sand to take 'em."

"I reckon," said McCaleb, "if me and Will and Brazos throwed the little cash money we have into the pot, we'd come up with enough to feed ourselves for a while. Charlie, you've trailed with us enough to know we don't start anything we can't finish. If it suits you, we'll raise a herd and join your drive."

For a moment Goodnight said nothing. These were men to ride the river with; yet they seemed to accept the leadership of Benton McCaleb without a qualm. How many times had these two stood with him and fought to the finish against outlaws and Indians? They were closer than brothers. He offered his hand to Will, to Brazos, and then to McCaleb. Only then did he speak.

"I expect you'll still be fighting bandits and Indians, but the wages ought to be considerably better. By this time next year, we should be on the trail. It'll take that long for a decent gather."

"We could rope and brand enough—maybe three or

four hundred—for a drive this year," said Brazos. "That would get us some quick money for a bigger drive next year."

"Too late for that," said Goodnight. "By the time we get to the brakes, the trails to Kansas and Missouri will be crowded with small herds. Texans won't waste any time getting these cows to market. Suppose you fight the swollen rivers, Indians and rustlers, but when you reach trail's end you find the price has dropped from fifteen dollars a head to five? Or four? You don't dare hold out for better prices, because there's other herds behind you, there's no graze for your cows, and as more cattle arrive, the already low prices may go still lower. So what do you do?"

"Take what you can get," said Brazos.

"Precisely," said Goodnight. "I aim to avoid that trap by driving west into New Mexico, north to Fort Sumner, and as far as Colorado Territory, if I have to. I want money, but I want range too. We'll be blazing a new trail into virgin territory, to a range untouched except by antelope, buffalo, and elk. We can hold our herds for a year if need be, fattening them on new grass. Colorado is mining country. Men lusting after silver and gold don't have time to raise cows, but they have to eat. And they have money to buy."

"You purely know how to start a man's blood pounding," said Will Elliot. "I'd sooner be shootin' Indians and thieves in New Mexico and Colorado as here on the Texas border. Especially if the wages is better."

"At least," said Brazos, "we don't have to cross the Red River."

"No," said Goodnight, "but with the route I have in mind, we'll ford the Pecos twice; once at Horsehead Crossing and again at Pope's Crossing, somewhere in southern New Mexico Territory. While we don't know what dangers may be awaiting us, I doubt we'll encounter anything we haven't faced here on the Texas border."

"Unless somebody has a better idea," said McCaleb,

"I'd say let's head for the brakes along the Trinity. All those mavericks on the Brazos belong to Charlie."

They laughed, Charles Goodnight the loudest of them all.

CHAPTER 2

*J*une 1, 1865, Benton McCaleb, Brazos Gifford, and Will Elliot rode out at dawn on a southeasterly course that would take them to the headwaters of the Trinity River. Goodnight's trail herd would move out in mid-April 1866, allowing them ten months to complete their gather and meet Goodnight near Fort Belknap on the Brazos. Each man was armed with a sixteen-shot .44-caliber Henry rifle and a pair of Ranger-issue .44-caliber six-shot Colt revolvers.

"Once we hit the Trinity," said McCaleb, "it's maybe two hundred miles to Cold Spring, the county seat of San Jacinto County. There's a post office and a store or two, and when we get there, we're just a day's ride from Jake Narbo's horse ranch. Jake's half Comanche, living with a full-blooded squaw; that's why he's alive and still wearin' his hair."

"I ain't got a drop of Comanche blood in me," said Brazos. "Are you on good enough terms with this half-Injun horse trader to keep his full-blooded kin from liftin' our scalps while we chase longhorns?"

"Who knows?" said McCaleb. "I'll have to talk to him. When you deal with the Comanches, nothing is for dead sure."

"More'n likely sure dead," said Will with a grim chuckle. "And I thought all we had to worry about was them varmints in New Mexico and Colorado."

"We'll need extra horses," said McCaleb, "and whatever you think of Jake and his Comanche kin, he's got the best Indian-gentled horses in Texas. We don't have the time to break horses, and even if we did, that's not the best way. Ride a horse into the ground, break his spirit, and you'll have an unwilling animal that will hate the sight of you. While we can't be sure of *anything* as far as the Comanches are concerned, it can't hurt for them to know we're buying our horses from Jake Narbo."

"I'm in favor of that," said Brazos, "but we got maybe two hundred dollars amongst us. Can we deal with this Comanche horse trader, keep ourselves in grub and ammunition until next spring, and *still* come out with enough to pay our own way in Charlie's trail drive?"

"I'm gambling that we can," said McCaleb. "What *choice* do we have? I doubt we could raise another fifty dollars cash money if we sacked the whole state of Texas. Like Charlie said, the state—the South—is broke. Our only hope lies in getting four or five hundred cows out of the brush and on the trail to market."

They continued south, following the Trinity. Just before sundown of the sixth day, they rode in to Jake Narbo's ranch. The house, a rambling adobe, had a mud-and-stone chimney. There were several less than imposing additions that had enlarged the original hut. The barn, built of cottonwood logs, had a split-shake roof and an adjoining breaking corral four rails high.

The most imposing thing about the old man who came out to meet them was the .52-caliber Spencer he held in the crook of his arm. He wore dirty overalls, an elbows-out denim shirt, moccasins, and a used-up black hat with a hole in its tall crown. McCaleb and his companions reined up, dismounting only after their host had nodded his approval.

"McCaleb," he said.

"Hello, Jake. These are my pardners, Will Elliot and Brazos Gifford. We're of a mind to rope and brand some wild maverick cows for a drive to market. We'll be needin' some gentled horses; a remuda."

"Gold," said Jake. "No trade. No Confed'racy scrip."

McCaleb flipped a coin to the old man, the setting sun winking gold off the double eagle. Deftly, Jake shifted the Spencer, neatly palming the money. Treating them to a toothless grin, he turned away without a word, shouldered aside the cowhide serving as a door and disappeared into the gloomy, windowless adobe.

"Hospitable old coot," said Brazos. "Not a scrap of hay for our horses or even a cold biscuit for us. Anybody but a damn Indian would have asked us to supper and offered to let us bed down in the barn, anyhow."

"Don't push your luck," said McCaleb. "We'll camp by the spring. He's a half-breed livin' with a Comanche woman and he's got at least two sons, yet none of them showed. The best we can expect here is an uneasy truce."

"He's almighty skittish," said Will. "I got an idea that if we get out of the brakes with a herd of longhorns and our hair still in place, we won't owe any thanks to Jake."

"We *still* need horses," said McCaleb, "and we'll take our chances with the Comanches. Jake knows we have gold, but he's not sure how much. He'll try to keep us around until he gets his hands on all he safely can, even if he has to offer us bed privileges with his squaw."

"I purely don't trust Indians," said Will. "No way I'd ever spend a night in that adobe. Got throwed in the Waco jail once, and I swear, compared to that Injun adobe, the *juzgado* looked like home sweet home."

"Jake wants our gold," said Brazos, "but he doesn't trust us. That makes it easier for us, because we can be just as suspicious as he is. Nothin' rubs me the wrong way any quicker than some hombre killin' me with kindness so's he can kill me for real, soon as my back's turned."

"That's the kind of thinking," said McCaleb, "that keeps a man alive on the frontier. We'll build just enough of a fire near the spring to boil our coffee and cook our bacon. As soon as we've eaten—after dark— we'll move back in the brush and spread our blankets there. Keep your pistols loaded and at hand. While I don't expect any trouble from Jake, I'm not so sure about the Comanches. Maybe—because of Jake—they'll hold off until they see what we're up to. But we can't count on that. Some Indians won't attack at night, but that's never bothered the Comanche. They're as ready to kill at midnight as they are at high noon."

"That's what I dislike most about plains Indians," said Will. "They were the first to have horses, and distance means nothing to them. They're the kind of bastards who'll trail you for three days if they have to, just waitin' for the right time and place."

"I'm glad we cut back on grub instead of ammunition," said Brazos. "I can stand havin' my belly lank lots better than I can stand havin' it shot full of Comanche arrows. Thank God for Captain Jack Hayes. If we ever whip the Comanches for good, it'll be all to his credit. Texas ought to build a monument to him and his company of Rangers for provin' the worth of the Colt six-shooter."

McCaleb was wide awake and he listened, wondering what it was that had awakened him. Heat lightning danced across a cloud bank far to the west and thunder muttered in the distance. Finally he relaxed and slept undisturbed until a rooster crowed just before first light.

"Chickens!" exclaimed Will. "That means eggs!"

Brazos chuckled. "Not for us. We'll be lucky if that old Injun don't want more gold than we got, just for some extra mounts."

Jake Narbo stalked into camp just as they were finishing their meager breakfast. He still carried the Spencer. He also had a tin cup, and without a word, helped himself to coffee from the pot. McCaleb had to stifle an impulse to laugh. He knew what Will and Brazos were thinking: before the month was gone, they'd be out of coffee. Jake ignored their looks of disgust and sipped his coffee. The silence dragged on, neither party wishing to seem too eager. Jake tilted the coffeepot and drained it to the grounds. Brazos fished out his half-empty sack of Durham and spilled a little of it sparingly into a sliver of brown paper, expertly rolling his smoke with one hand. Jake had dropped his empty cup and had fixed his eyes on the tobacco sack. Brazos grudgingly passed it to him, along with the thin packet of papers. Jake, using twice as much of the tobacco as Brazos had, twisted his quirly and lit it with an ember from the fire. Instead of returning the Durham and papers to Brazos, he stuffed them into the bib pocket of his dirty overalls. McCaleb caught Brazos's eye and his hand halted just short of the butt of his Colt. Finally Jake Narbo spoke.

"*Caballos.* Many?"

"Six," said McCaleb, holding up a finger on his right hand and the five fingers on his left.

"Fi'teen dolla," said Jake. "*Una.*"

"Whoa," said McCaleb. "Where *are* the horses? *Caballos?*"

"Coulee," said Jake.

"Take us there," said McCaleb.

Jake treated them to his toothless grin and set off on foot. He headed toward the adobe and then veered off to the right. The coulee was but a few hundred yards beyond the adobe and was actually the dry bed of a lesser river that had once emptied into the Trinity somewhere to the south. At the lower end—the deepest part —thick cedar posts had been planted, supporting a six-rail, wall-to-wall fence. The other end, similarly barricaded, had rails positioned so they could be dropped for entrance or exit. They halted on the embankment. Below them, two dozen broomtails were crowded. A third of them, those yet to be gentled, crowded against the farther wall, rolling their eyes in fear. The others eyed their visitors curiously. For a brief time, McCaleb, Will, and Brazos forgot Jake Narbo, focusing their attention on the horses. There were sorrels, bays, buckskins, chestnuts, browns, roans, blacks, grays, and grullas. They were stocky, deep-muscled, sturdy-legged. They had thick necks and broad, short heads. Their withers were low, their chests deep, and their hindquarters looked powerful. McCaleb managed to conceal his excitement. He judged most of them to be a little over fourteen hands and their average weight maybe a thousand pounds. *They were perfect!*

"Ten dolla," said Jake.

"Fifty dollars for all six," said McCaleb. "Our pick."

"Gold," said Jake.

"You got twenty dollars yesterday," said McCaleb. "You get thirty more."

Jake's grin disappeared and in its place was an uncomprehending frown. Brazos and Will had moved up beside McCaleb, their thumbs hooked in their pistol belts near the butts of their holstered Colts. After an uncomfortable silence, Jake held out his hand.

"Deal."

Silently McCaleb dropped an eagle and a double eagle into his palm. Jake pocketed the money and his good humor was quickly restored.

"We'll work with them three at a time," said McCaleb, holding up three fingers. "When we're ready for the last three, you'd best remember you've been paid for them. *Comprender?* No more gold!"

"*Comprender*," said Jake.

McCaleb chose a bay, Brazos a roan, and Will a grulla. They watched Jake approach the grulla, carrying only a blanket. He held out his hands to the horse as one might welcome a friend, and while they couldn't hear his voice, they saw his lips moving. The grulla's ears went up, but the horse stood its ground. The animal seemed to relax under Jake's touch. Once he had spread the blanket on the grulla's broad back, he extended his arms across the blanket and lifted his feet off the ground, putting his weight on the animal's back. Again the horse stood its ground, unflinching. Jake hooked his arm around the grulla's neck and it followed him to the end of the fenced coulee. McCaleb and Brazos let down the rails, replacing them when Jake and the horse had passed through. The grulla snorted when Will approached, but he followed Jake's example and the horse accepted him. Jake quickly brought McCaleb the bay and Brazos the roan. Without a word, he left them.

"I'll give the devil his due," said Will. "The man knows his horses."

"Now," said Brazos, "the fun begins. We get to teach these broncs all *we* know about ropin' and brandin' wild twelve-hundred-pound critters that ain't particularly anxious to *be* roped and branded."

"We'd as well spend the next few days right here," said McCaleb, "working with these horses. Then we'll ride downriver and set us up a camp."

Jake, aware that his source of gold was soon to depart, showed up at their supper fire with half a dozen fresh eggs and a jug of moonshine. He made the rounds, filling their tin cups. McCaleb didn't consider himself a drinking man; he could take it or leave it alone, and mostly he left it alone. On a Texas frontier infested with hostile, marauding Indians and quick-triggered outlaws, a man was a fool to fog up his mind with whiskey. He watched Will and Brazos, realizing he hadn't the slightest idea as to whether or not they drank. In the service as part of the Frontier Regiment on the Texas border, they'd been far removed from any such temptation. Brazos took a sip and gasped.

"My . . . God! What *is* it?"

"Snakehead," said Jake.

Thirty-six gallons of pure grain alcohol. Add two pounds of gunpowder, four plugs of chewing tobacco for color, and one rattlesnake head to give it "bite."

Without tasting his, McCaleb poured the contents into the fire, where it flamed up a brilliant blue. He turned to Jake.

"Where, Jake? Where'd you get this poison?"

"York Nance. Him, son, young squaw. *Vagabundos.*

Snakehead make *Indios loco, malo.* Nance say hunt *vaca,* pay him dolla. *Una vaca, una dolla.*"

"York Nance," said McCaleb. "Where do we find him?"

"Fi' mile," said Jake, pointing downriver.

"He sells us horses to hunt cows," said Brazos, "and now he tells us some old moonshiner named York Nance aims to charge us a dollar a head for the privilege of draggin' them wild cows out of the brush."

Will chuckled. "More surprises than Christmas. Not only does this old buzzard want money for unbranded wild cows, he's supplyin' Comanches with whiskey. I ain't ropin' the first cow until we ride downriver and teach this pilgrim the error of his ways."

"That's the way I see it," said McCaleb. "We're not taking anybody's cows as long as they're identifiable, but we've as much right to unbranded cattle as anybody. I doubt we can stop him from supplying the Indians with whiskey, though, and that bothers me. The only thing worse than a hostile, bloodthirsty Comanche is a *drunken,* hostile, bloodthirsty Comanche. We may end up choosing between a herd of cattle and our hair."

"*Indios,*" said Jake. "*Malo.*"

"Tomorrow, then," said McCaleb, "we serve notice on York Nance that we won't honor his claim to unbranded cows, not even if he holds legitimate patents on every inch of land from here to the Gulf."

"After we show him how the cow eats the cabbage," said Brazos, "let's start pullin' some cows out of the brush. Nance would need an army to stop us, and I doubt he's got one."

"No *soldados,*" said Jake. "*Indios. Malo Indios.*"

He twirled a finger around his graying hair. He didn't smile. The trio of ex-Rangers watched him disappear in the gathering dusk on his way to the adobe hut. Old Jake's words were disturbing, ominous. Suppose York Nance *was* sided by an "army" of whiskey-loyal Comanches?

Immediately after breakfast the following morning,

they rode out for their confrontation with York Nance. Jake Narbo had grudgingly consented for them to leave their three newly acquired horses in the corral adjoining his log barn. Cattle trails were well-defined along the Trinity, and at some points the sandy banks had been caved in by animals seeking water. It had been a dry spring and there were stretches where the river ran barely hock deep. They reined up, watching half a dozen cows splash out of the shallow water, up the bank and into the brush.

"Four-year-olds," said Brazos, "and not a sign of a brand. I reckon we can rope two thousand by the time Charlie's ready to trail the herd."

"You're forgettin' something," said Will. "We'll likely spend some of that time preventin' the Comanches from taking our scalps."

"I'd settle for five hundred cows and my hair," said McCaleb. "While we don't know how much truth there is to what Jake told us, I don't like the sound of it. I have no respect for a man lowdown enough to sell rotgut whiskey to hostile Indians. I expect we're going to tangle horns with this York Nance, and with the Comanches as well, if he has influence with them. If we have to face them, I'd as soon know it goin' in; I don't like surprises where Indians are involved. I want to know how the stick floats, and I expect we'll have some better idea after we talk to Nance. Keep your Colts handy when we ride in, but no shooting unless they start it. Let them open the ball."

Warily they rode, but there was no Indian sign. As every Ranger knew, that was the time to worry; in a matter of seconds you could be surrounded. Each man carried his second Colt next to his belly, tucked behind the waistband of his Levi's, and in his pocket rested a fully loaded extra cylinder that would interchange with either Colt in a matter of seconds.

Somewhere ahead, a horse nickered. McCaleb's horse answered and they reined up, listening. There was no other sound and they rode on. Rounding a bend in the river, they could see a log barn in the distance. Within an adjoining pole corral, a dozen horses milled restlessly about. They were almost to the barn before they saw the house. It stood on a treeless knoll a thousand yards from the west bank of the Trinity. They reined up, regarding the place in silence. Brazos said what all of them were thinking.

"What kind of damn fool builds his barn and corral on one side of the river and his house on the other?"

They paused midway in the shallow stream, allowing their horses to drink before riding on to the house. It proved to be nothing more than a log hut, as unimposing and as uninviting as Jake Narbo's adobe. Each end of the roof overhang that served as a porch was supported by an unskinned cottonwood pole. There was a mud-and-stick chimney and the place was roofed with cedar shakes. What might have been a window was shuttered. The gaps between the logs had been mud-chinked; the mud, baked brittle by the merciless Texas sun, had long since crumbled and had not been replaced.

The door swung open on rawhide hinges, and the young man who stepped out couldn't have been more than twenty-one or -two. He wore down-at-the-heel cowman's boots, Levi's pants, and a much-washed faded blue shirt. His old flat-crowned black hat was tilted over his eyes, and on his right hip, in a tied-down holster, rode a Colt revolver. He hooked his thumbs in his pistol belt and kept his silence, a half smile on his lips. Clearly, he wasn't going to invite them to dismount. It was an affront, an insult, but McCaleb ignored it.

"We're here to see York Nance," said McCaleb. "Get him."

"And if I don't?"

"Then I'll bend a pistol barrel over your head and get him myself."

"That won't be necessary," said a voice from the gloom of the cabin.

He filled the small doorway, a big man gone to fat. He might have been fifty, with white hair, moustache, and the florid, lined face of a drinking man. He wore a not-too-clean white shirt, black string tie, a white linen suit, and gaiters. A gold watch chain was draped across his ample belly. An enormous diamond sparkled on the ring finger of his left hand.

"Step down, gentlemen. Allow me to apologize for Monte's total lack of courtesy. Young hell-raiser; one of these days somebody's goin' to kill him."

"Ain't nobody fast enough to kill me," bawled Monte. "I'll—"

The old man's huge fist silenced him, catching him on the point of the chin and slamming him against the log wall of the cabin. Monte slid down to a sitting position, his head slumped forward. Ignoring him, the old man again turned to them.

"Come in. I've been expecting you."

They followed him into the gloomy interior of the cabin, and to their surprise, it was neat and clean. Little care had been devoted to the outside, but the inside was something else. There was a stone fireplace and hearth, hewn log walls, and a smooth, split-log floor. There was an eating table with benches, several backless, three-legged stools, and a pair of crude, wooden bunks. A cow hide hung over the door to another room. A coal oil lamp flickered on the table, its meager flame wrestling with the shadows.

"Be seated, gentlemen. A bit primitive, but livable, thanks to the diligence and civilizing influence of my daughter. I believe I know why you're here, but it would be uncivil of me not to hear you out. Proceed."

"I'm Benton McCaleb. My partners are Brazos Gifford and Will Elliot. We're here to gather a herd of un-branded maverick cows for a trail drive. Jake Narbo tells us you're making some kind of claim on these cows to the tune of a dollar a head. Well, we don't recognize whatever claim you have or think you have. You'll have to justify it, if you can."

"You are a very direct young man, McCaleb, but you've been misinformed. I make no claim to any cows except those wearing my Box N brand. As far as I'm concerned, you're welcome to as many as you can catch. I believe the 'dollar a head' Jake mentioned is for my assurance that the Comanches will allow you safe passage with your newly acquired herd *and* your scalps."

"I reckon you've said enough, Nance. We've sampled the rotgut poison you're using to buy Comanche friendship."

"Don't be a fool, McCaleb. That's how life is; you have to trade something another party wants to get something *you* want."

"I wouldn't pay you *one* dollar for every damn cow on the Trinity River. We'll protect our own cows *and* our scalps!"

Benton McCaleb got up, kicking his stool out of the way, furious. Will and Brazos, nearest the door, went out ahead of McCaleb. He had barely cleared the porch when, to his left, from the corner of the cabin, the challenge came.

"Draw, you bastard!"

A blur of motion, McCaleb turned and fired. Monte's pistol had barely cleared the holster when McCaleb's slug flung him against the cabin wall. There was a dark patch of blood on the right sleeve of his faded blue shirt, just above the elbow. Through gritted teeth he cursed McCaleb.

"Next time—"

"Next time," McCaleb interrupted, "I'll kill you."

York Nance stood in the doorway, saying nothing. McCaleb holstered his Colt. Will and Brazos mounted first, backstepping their horses away from the cabin, covering McCaleb as he swung into the saddle. They forded the Trinity, reining up on the east bank for a last look at the Nance cabin.

"Well, I reckon that splits the blanket," said Will. "Now he knows we ain't buyin' his shakedown, I reckon he'll loose them pet Comanches on us."

"Maybe," said Brazos, "we should've kept him in the dark and let him think we'd pay up after the gather. Worst he could have done is sic his Injun army on us at the finish. Now we'll likely be fightin' Comanches with one hand and ropin' cows with the other."

"He's the kind to demand an advance," said McCaleb. "What would you have used for money? Besides, I don't ride under false colors. Get in the mud to wrassle with a hog and you never come out clean."

They were no more than two miles from the Nance cabin when they heard the drum of hoofs on the trail behind them. They reined up, turning their mounts to face the oncoming rider. The horse was a young mare, solid black except for a blaze on her forehead. The rider was a girl dressed in scuffed, rough-out boots, faded Levi's pants, and a red-and-white checkered blouse. Black hair curled to her shoulders, and a floppy old gray hat rode the nape of her neck, secured by a leather thong under her tilted chin. Reining the mare to a lope, she rode up to McCaleb. She had a three-foot rawhide quirt in her hand and fire in her green eyes.

"Are you the damn skunk-striped gunman that shot my brother?"

"Your brother's a hotheaded young fool," said McCaleb, "and the way you're pawin' the ground, I won't be surprised if it runs in the family."

When she swung the rawhide quirt at his head, McCaleb dodged, seizing the startled girl by the arm. He snatched the quirt with his right hand, dragged her bodily out of the saddle with his left and flopped her belly down in front of him. Ignoring her screams, he swatted her well-rounded bottom with the quirt. Then he loosed his hold and she slid off, raising a small cloud of dust when her backside met the ground.

Brazos chuckled. "My God, ain't he got a way with the ladies?"

"Ladies don't swear and wear britches," said McCaleb.

That did it. With a shriek that would have raised the

hair on the head of a dead Indian, the girl sprang to her feet and ran to the mare. Instead of mounting and riding furiously away, she dragged a Spencer .52 from the saddle boot. When she had it free and McCaleb was sure he wouldn't hit the mare, he drew and fired, splintering the weapon's walnut stock. The force of the blow ripped the rifle from her hands and its heavy octagonal barrel broadsided the mare's flank. The horse reared, neighing in fear and pain, and then lit out for home.

"I once saw a dancing bear in a traveling medicine show," said Will, "but it couldn't hold a candle to *this*."

It wasn't over. Wearily, McCaleb braced himself for the next attack. This time she launched herself like a timber wolf, caught one hand in his pistol belt and hung on. McCaleb tried to dismount, but she had come at him on the offside, the weight of her body trapping his right foot in the stirrup. He freed his left foot, allowing her to drag him from the saddle.

They slid to the ground in an ignominious tangle of arms and legs. McCaleb's horse, alarmed at such peculiar antics, backstepped. Will caught the reins before it could run. For a few confused seconds, like puppets with strings cut, McCaleb and the girl sat facing one another. There were tear tracks on her cheeks and fury in her eyes. Suddenly, with all the strength she could muster, she slapped McCaleb. A trickle of blood ran from his nose across his lips, dripping off his dusty chin. Without a word, he got up and helped the girl to her feet. She drove the toe of her boot into his shin just above his boot top. Barely did he recover from the shock of that in time to avoid the knee aimed at his crotch. He caught her around her slender waist and hoisted her into his arms like a disobedient child. While she kicked, screamed, scratched, and clawed at his face and eyes, McCaleb carried her to the bank of the Trinity and pitched her into the knee-deep water. Without a backward look, he took the reins from Will, mounted his horse, and led out toward Jake Narbo's.

"You bullying bastard," screamed the girl, "I'll kill you for this!"

"McCaleb," said Will admiringly, "you purely got that female's full and undivided attention. She's sweet on you, and you didn't even ask her name. Before she's done, she'll stir up more trouble than all the Comanches in Texas."

"The pretty ones are always poison mean," said Brazos with an exaggerated sigh. "That's why they pass up gentle hombres like me and throw themselves at bullying bastards like McCaleb. I can hear weddin' bells already, and my God, they're more fearsome than Injun war whoops."

Will chuckled. "Wait'll Charlie Goodnight hears about this."

"A word of this to anybody," growled McCaleb, wiping his still-bleeding nose, "and I'll gut-shoot the both of you!"

They found that most of Jake Narbo's friendliness had departed. Again he accompanied them to the coulee. McCaleb chose a sorrel, Will a gray, and Brazos a black. Jake led the horses out of the coulee corral and departed without a word. They spent the rest of the day making friends with their new mounts. Taking supper early, they doused their fire well before dark. As Rangers, they had eaten cold biscuit and drunk creek water when they dared not light a fire. After their falling out with York Nance, they could be no less cautious.

"Somebody's got the word to Jake," said McCaleb. "He values that greasy scalp of his more than the gold coins we've been feedin' him."

CHAPTER 3

*J*ake Narbo soon confirmed their suspicions. The morning after their return, he showed up at their breakfast fire with his Spencer and without any show of friendliness.

"Take *caballos*," he said. "Vamoose."

Without another word, he walked away. They watched him disappear into the adobe hut.

"Wherever he stands," said Brazos, "it ain't with us. Let's take our broomtails and ride. We'll be as well off in the brakes as we are here."

Each of them leading two extra horses, they started downriver to an area McCaleb remembered from his boyhood.

"Maybe twenty miles south of the Nance place," he said, "the Trinity kind of curves back on itself and forms a small lake. In dry years, when the river's low, there's always water in this lake area. There's a blind canyon a couple of miles west, and at the head of it there's a big spring. Runoff feeds the lake at the bend of the Trinity."

"We can use a blind canyon," said Will. "How big?"

"Big enough to hold five hundred head," said McCaleb. "Maybe more. It's shaped kind of like an Indian canoe; narrow at the front, gets wider near the middle, and becomes narrow again at the blind end. When I was just a boy, I was there with my pa and some other riders on a wild horse hunt. A thirty-foot fence at the entrance will be all we'll need."

"We'll need grass," said Brazos. "How long can we hold five hundred cows without starvin' 'em?"

"One thing at a time," said McCaleb. "It's been fifteen years since I was there. If it's been recently used, overgrazed, we may have a problem. But with the state at war the past four years, I doubt our canyon's had many visitors, except for varmints and maybe some of these wild cows we're looking for. If we catch so many cows that graze becomes a problem, we may have to scout the brakes for a second holding pen."

There was no sign of life at the Nance cabin. The horse corral was empty and not a sound came from the barn. How had Nance disposed of *that* many horses in less than twenty-four hours?

"I wonder what her name is," said Brazos innocently.

"Ride over there and ask her," said McCaleb. "We'll wait for you."

"Since we had a fallin' out with her daddy, and her brother's so almighty gun happy, I'll just wait till she comes lookin' for you again. A man could get a real education around that woman; she cusses like a bull whacker."

McCaleb said nothing, just kicked his horse into a lope, leading out. Despite their apparent levity, an uneasiness rode with them. Someone was waiting, watching . . .

The box canyon was as McCaleb had described it, and to their relief, the graze was virtually untouched. They found only deer, antelope, and cougar tracks on the banks of the stream created by the runoff from the big spring.

"They don't have to depend on the spring for water," said McCaleb, "with the river so near. Let's ride the length of the canyon."

They picketed their extra mounts and jogged a little more than a mile to the blind end, where the spring was. It was delightfully primitive. The box end of the canyon had eroded down to bare rock, and a miniature water-fall cascaded down its face to splash into a pool a dozen feet below. A forest of young willows shaded the pool, and through two feet of clear water they could see the gravel bottom. Some long-ago rock slide had left the area a jumble of boulders that had mossed over, and from a thin covering of accumulated soil, a profusion of wild violets had grown in purple majesty. Along one bank of the stream there were the fragile, fluted pink blooms of wild honeysuckle. From the stream bed itself, cattails raised their furry heads. Nothing broke the silence except the chug-a-rum of a bullfrog.

"The Garden of Eden!" said Brazos. "What a shame to waste all this on a bunch of wild cows."

"Forget about the spring," said McCaleb, "and take a look at the rest of it. This could change from the Garden of Eden to hell in the wink of an eye."

Will shuddered. "Ain't it the truth? Put Injuns on them walls and we're buzzard bait."

"We *could* move our camp every night," said McCaleb, "since we have no pack mules, no wagon . . ."

"And no supplies," said Brazos.

"There's turkey tracks," said Will. "Deer too. One of us can lay out here before daylight, along this spring branch or close to the river, and we'll have meat."

"I just wish we'd brought about fifty pounds of coffee," lamented Brazos. "I purely *hate* bein' without coffee."

"We've got enough for two more weeks," said Will. "The Comanches might have your scalp by then."

"If you two are done cheerin' each other up," said McCaleb, "let's go have a closer look at the neck of this canyon and get started building us a gate. We've got a pick, a shovel, and an ax. One of us can cut posts and rails and the other two can dig post holes."

"Shakespeare was right," said Will. "There's small choice in rotten apples."

"That ain't fit work for a cowboy," said Brazos. "I'll

wrassle cows from can till can't, but this is dirt farmer work. When Goodnight moves his herd out, we'll still be workin' on this damn fence."

"It goes with the territory," said McCaleb cheerfully. "Before you get too het up over the fence, let's walk downcanyon a ways. Done right, this can be more than just a fence to keep the herd in the canyon."

He paused fifty yards into the canyon, where the west wall reached a height of forty feet or more. High above their heads a lip of rock reached out over the stream, shading them from the westering sun.

"Thirty feet from here," said McCaleb, pointing back toward the mouth of the canyon, "is where we build our fence. Then we're going to finish what nature started, and hollow out that wall for a shelter. We dig back just a few feet and we'll have protection on three sides and plenty of water within reach. The only way the Comanches can get at us is from that east wall."

"If we're going *that* far," said Will, "let's build us a breastwork along the front of the shelter, between us and the stream. We can start with logs and posts, fortifying them with the dirt we dig out of the canyon wall."

"I'm glad *you* brought that up," said McCaleb. "I'm with you. Now convince our redheaded pardner it's a good idea."

"Aw hell," growled Brazos, "I hate the work but I like the idea."

"Good," said McCaleb. "The Comanches will be after our scalps and our horses. A few days' hard work now can save us grief later. When we're done, we can post one man behind the barricade and cut down any Comanche coming near our fence, and with it in place, there's no way they can come down the canyon walls and stampede our horses and cows."

"That's exactly what they'd do," said Will. "One bunch would pull down the fence while a second party would come down the walls and stampede the stock from upcanyon."

"First," said McCaleb, "we'll dig out the canyon wall

and build a breastwork. There's no point putting up a fence until we can protect it. Once we have our barricade in place, we can always picket the horses close enough to protect them, even without a fence. In the morning, since we have only one pick and one shovel, two of us will begin work on the canyon wall while the other rides downriver and scouts the area. We could use another canyon like this one. I'll stay and dig; one of you can scout."

"This territory's more familiar to you than to us," said Will. "I'd as soon stay here and dig; there'll be a blessed plenty for all of us."

"I'll dig too," said Brazos. "At least we'll be in the shade. When you get back, that ax will be all yours."

The following morning, McCaleb rode half a dozen miles farther downriver without encountering anybody or anything except more unbranded cows. In places, the sandy banks of the Trinity had been eroded, allowing the water to eddy out into rock-bottomed pools. One such pool, in a shaded bend of the river, tempted him. It appeared to be about waist deep, with head-high bushes and underbrush offering seclusion. McCaleb dismounted, half-hitched his horse's reins to a young oak, pulled off his boots and slipped out of his dusty, sweaty clothes. He regretted having no soap; it was one of the many things they lacked. He ducked his head, splashing about, enjoying the cool water. His horse watched him with interest. Suddenly the animal raised its head, listening. McCaleb stiffened. His pistol belt with his Colt hung from his saddle horn. The horse relaxed, but for McCaleb the magic was gone, replaced by the caution that had kept him alive on a turbulent frontier. He waded out of the water and, without waiting to dry, got into his sweaty shirt and Levi's. He had on one boot and was reaching for the other, when he froze. She stood looking at him through the branches of a young cottonwood, a sparkle in her green eyes and an impish half smile on her lips.

"You'd be almost handsome, McCaleb, if you weren't a bullying bastard."

"How long . . . have you been . . . there?"

"I was here when you rode up. I dared not say anything; you're so da—darn quick with a pistol, I was afraid you'd shoot me."

"You . . . you . . ." He was unable to look at her. So flaming red was his face, neck, and ears, he might have been a child again, suffering from his first sunburn. She laughed.

Painfully close to him, she sat down on a rock outcropping, crossing her shapely legs. She wore Indian moccasins, a tan blouse, and a pale yellow divided skirt.

"I wanted to see what kind of man you *really* are, McCaleb; without a pistol in your hand, without your anger . . ."

"And without my clothes," he snarled. "Who are *you* to judge *me*? You swear like a mule skinner, you're as brash as a St. Louis whore, and you couldn't be a lady if . . . if . . ."

He paused, recalling the clawing, spitting wildcat she could become when her temper got the best of her. But something happened. She turned from him, burying her pale face in her hands. And she cried. They were great, heart-wrenching sobs that frightened McCaleb's horse, causing him to backstep in alarm. McCaleb, feeling like the heartless brute she'd branded him, sat there in helpless silence. Her tears disarmed him as her fury never could have.

"I'm sorry," he said. "I had no right—"

"You had *every* right," she wailed, turning to him, tears welling from her eyes.

Finally she rubbed her reddened eyes with the heels of her hands and, except for an occasional sniffle, became calm.

"I always make a fool of myself. If I don't do it one way, I do it another. I shamed you before your friends and left them thinking I'm . . . I'm what you just . . . called me."

"Ma'am," said McCaleb desperately, "if we're going to talk, then for God's sake, let's talk about somethin' else. Do you have a name?"

"Rebecca. But Daddy's always called me 'Beck.' I think he's ashamed of me. My mama died when I was just five, when Monte was born. I've had to watch out for him, and when you . . . you . . ."

"He drew on me, Rebecca. The boy needs to learn the cold, hard facts of life—that if you pull a gun, you can die. I could have killed him; I hit what I shoot at. It's kept me alive."

"He was killing mad at first; that's what fired me up, why I came after you. You left me sitting in the river, afoot. When I finally got back to the house, Daddy had the decency to tell me that Monte pulled first, that you could have shot him dead. He said he'd never seen a man draw as fast as you, that you're not the kind to miss. Monte was just what you called him: a hotheaded young fool. He wanted to go looking for you; I had to shame him into admitting he was in the wrong, that he owed you his life."

McCaleb said nothing.

"I have a confession to make, McCaleb. If you want to call me brash and unladylike, I guess I deserve it, but I came looking for you. I saw you head downriver, taking your time, and I got ahead of you."

"How did you know I—"

"I didn't know you'd do what . . . you did. Like I told you, after what I did—scratching, kicking, and cussing—I didn't think you'd much want to see me. With daddy's da—darned Indians on the prowl, I wasn't sure you wouldn't shoot me if I startled you. I didn't feel safe until you took off your gun."

"And my clothes," said McCaleb, half angry again.

"Damn it, McCaleb, put that out of your mind!" She stood up, hands on her slender hips. "Do you reckon I'm going to ride the length of the Trinity, telling every cow, every Indian, and every brush-popping cowboy that I saw the mighty McCaleb with his pants off, taking a bath?"

"I reckon not," said McCaleb, relenting only a little. "Why'd you come looking for me?"

"I wanted to thank you for not killing my brother. Once I realized you could have—and that it was his fault—that he provoked you . . ."

"Is that all?"

"No."

He said nothing, waiting. She came a step closer, her eyes pleading.

"When you leave here, McCaleb, take me with you."

"Take you where? We're joining Charles Goodnight's trail drive north to Denver. It's no place for a girl; there'll be outlaws, Indians . . ."

"They won't be any worse than the outlaws and Indians around here. I'm not asking you to take me along for nothing, McCaleb. I'll help you with your roundup. I can rope and ride. Who do you think roped and branded the cows wearing the Box N brand? Me and Monte. Daddy's never lifted anything heavier than a shot glass since I was born. Couldn't you see that? Why, back in Missouri, when him and Uncle Walt was rustling mules—"

"Rebecca," said McCaleb, exasperated, "thanks to your Daddy's foolish arrangement with these heathen Comanches, we'll likely have to fight them before we're done. How long do you think York Nance is going to sit back and let you work *with* us when he's *against* us? I ain't denyin' we could use some help, but you're in no position to offer it."

"McCaleb," she said, again in tears, "just listen to me. Just please let me have my say. If you *still* won't help me, then I won't bother you ever again."

He waited for her to subdue her tears.

"My mama was from Virginia, McCaleb, and she was a real lady. She came from a good family. Daddy's from Kentucky, one of five boys. The rest of them have already been shot or hung. Mama's family disowned her when she ran off and married Daddy. He killed her, McCaleb, as surely as if he'd put a gun to her head and pulled the trigger. He dragged her from one town to another, usually just one jump ahead of the law. She was so tired, she never recovered after Monte was born. When she died, although I was only five, I took her place. For twenty-one years I've been Daddy's housekeeper and cook. I begged and stole so we could eat. Monte, as soon as he was old enough, helped me swipe roasting ears from neighbors' cornfields and grub potatoes in the dark. York Nance has made his way in the world by cheating and hurting others. Three years ago we left St. Joe, Missouri, in the middle of the night, me and Monte driving the wagon while Daddy hid under a sheet. Do you know why? Because Daddy and my Uncle Walt—Daddy's last surviving brother—had been caught rustling mules. While the lynch mob went after Uncle Walt, we sneaked out of town and came here. How can a man sink lower than that, McCaleb, stealing his neighbor's stock?"

"By selling rotgut whiskey to heathen Indians," said McCaleb.

"Can't you see that's why I must get away from here? Someday they'll turn on him. Dear God, McCaleb, I don't want to die here in this sandy river bottom with those filthy Indians mutilating me!"

"Does Nance have *that* much control over these Comanches, that they'd come after our scalps if he asked them to?"

"I don't know. That's what *he* claims. Last fall, four riders were ambushed and killed, and they were roping brakes cattle, like you plan to do. I don't know if Daddy had anything to do with it or not."

"Rebecca, you're asking me for help, but you're not leveling with me. This 'dollar-a-head' foolishness Nance is bandying about just doesn't ring true. Even if he *could* provide protection from the Comanches, we don't have the money to pay, and neither does anybody else. The whole purpose of gathering and driving a herd to a northern market is to put some honest-to-God money in our empty pockets. Having us ambushed and killed— even if Nance *can* do it—won't fatten his wallet. He can't afford to keep Indians in whiskey in return for ambushing and killing; they've been doing that for centuries, without any help from the white man's poison."

"You're right, McCaleb. If I tell you all of it, will you help me?"

"If Will and Brazos agree, you can throw your herd in with ours. I'd not expect anybody to work a gather for nothing."

"Daddy takes horses in trade for whiskey," said the girl, "and he sells them for whatever he can get. Sometimes that's as little as five dollars a head. But it's with no bill of sale and no questions asked."

"Who's he selling to?"

"A beady-eyed little Frenchman from Shreveport. All I've ever heard him called is Pierre. He almost didn't take the last bunch of horses. Him and Daddy had an awful cuss fight. Pierre said all twelve horses had South Texas brands. When Daddy first started trading with Blue Feather's tribe, they were stealing horses in Mexico. Daddy said Texans didn't give a damn if the Comanches stole every horse in Mexico, but it made a big difference when those same Indians stole Texas horses. Brands don't mean anything to Indians; they steal from Texans, Mexicans, and each other."

"That's the God's truth," said McCaleb.

"The Comanches are demanding more and more whiskey for fewer horses, and Daddy refuses to reduce his price. He's threatening to *increase* his price if they keep bringing him horses with Texas brands. These Indians show up half drunk and mean; except for a few Spanish words, I don't know what they're saying. I can't understand their words, but I can tell from their shouting and screeching, they're angry. They're going to kill him, McCaleb. I can see it coming."

"You know where the box canyon is, with the spring, about three miles west of that big bend of the Trinity?"

"Yes."

"Be there in the morning. Early. I'll want you to re-peat to Will and Brazos most of what you've told me about Nance's receiving and selling stolen horses. Right now, I'm not nearly as concerned that he'll send the Comanches after *us* as I am that they'll get drunk enough and mad enough to kill *him*, and then come after *us* on their *own*."

CHAPTER 4

After Rebecca Nance had ridden away, McCaleb scouted the brakes for the rest of the day without discovering anything except the former campsite of the unfortunate riders the girl had told him about. There was the ashes and charred wood of an old fire, the morbid, bleaching skeleton of a horse, and four grassed-over graves. He took a different route returning to the canyon holding pen, riding the east bank of the Trinity. There were numerous cow tracks, but there were other tracks as well. Tracks of unshod horses . . .

When he reached the canyon, he found Will and Brazos stripped to the waist, ducking their heads in the stream. They had dug an enormous amount of dirt from beneath the canyon overhang.

"We need those logs and posts in place for the breastwork," said Will. "The dirt's in the way that we've already dug. You'd best roll out about daylight, grab that ax and get busy. Did you find anything?"

"Somebody to help us with the gather," said McCaleb.

"I hope he ain't Injun," said Brazos. "What's his name?"

"Rebecca," said McCaleb with a straight face.

Will slapped his leg and whooped, startling McCaleb's horse.

"Aw, he's bullyraggin' us," said Brazos. "He ain't

limpin', his nose ain't bleedin', and there's no claw marks on his face."

"This here thing is sure enough gettin' serious," said Will solemnly, "and there ain't a preacher within two hundred miles."

McCaleb could only laugh with them, ill concealing his embarrassment. "Enough," he finally said. "Let's get supper out of the way, and then we've got some talking to do."

When they had eaten, McCaleb told them of his meeting with Rebecca Nance. Without mentioning the embarrassing first minutes, he shared with them her reasons for wanting to join the gather. He sensed their reluctance.

"I can't imagine that fire-eyed filly bein' scared of anything," said Brazos. "She'll have to convince me."

"I believe her," said McCaleb. "I saw the fear in her eyes. That's why I'm having her come here later this evening. I'll let her tell you about the violent quarrels Nance is having with the Comanches."

"I reckon she's got a right to be afraid," said Will. "Sooner or later, a white man dealin' with Indians is goin' to lose his hair; even when he's honest. I heard my daddy tell about an old trader from Missouri that first come west with Becknell in 'twenty-one, when they first opened a Santa Fe trade route. This ol' trader—feller named Crandon—set up a post on the Colorado, north of San Antone. He liked the territory; give away lots of stuff to the Comanches, and thought they was his friends. One Sunday morning, before daylight, his 'friends' rode in and murdered him, his wife and kids. I'd say this Nance girl knows what she's talkin' about. Her ol' daddy's a fool."

"Fool or not," said Brazos, "he still may hold enough sway to bring this band of Comanche war whoops down on us; especially when he finds out his own daughter's throwed in with us."

"As far as Nance's foolish deals with the Indians are concerned," said McCaleb, "her working with us won't make any difference. The girl's had enough of Nance's vagabond existence. Jake was right when he referred to them as *vagabundos*. When it comes to do or die, she'll break with Nance. I believe the most immediate problem we have is keeping those red devils from snatching our horses. Starting tonight, we'll stand watch in four-hour shifts, dusk to dawn."

"Tomorrow, then," said Brazos, "before we chase any cows, let's burn our 3-R connected brand on every horse we got. If they end up missing, I expect we'll know where to find 'em. If we find our mounts in Nance's corral and we string the old bastard up for horse stealin', I reckon the girl ain't goin' to like it."

"You can warn her about that yourself," said McCaleb. "A little later. Like I said, starting tonight, we'll make it risky—and almighty expensive—for any Comanche coming after our horses."

Rebecca Nance rode up to their evening fire dressed exactly as she had been earlier. Her curly black hair had been brushed until it seemed to sparkle. As she swung out of the saddle in her divided riding skirt, she had the *undivided* attention of the three ex-Rangers. If that hadn't been enough, she carried a cloth-wrapped pan in which she had baked a blackberry pie. In a flour sack looped to her saddle horn there was a batch of fresh, Dutch oven biscuits.

"My peace offering," she said as the riders gathered around.

"Ma'am," said Brazos, doffing his hat and bowing, "you just feel free to slug McCaleb anytime you like."

"My God," said Will, "I ain't seen blackberry cobbler since before the war. Where in tarnation did you get the sugar?"

"Sorghum molasses," said the girl. "We were too poor to have sugar, even when it could be had."

McCaleb said little, allowing Will and Brazos to direct their questions at the girl. He found himself admiring the way she conducted herself. She was in no way coy or deceptive; she established eye contact and held it. He could see her winning them over, but while she answered their questions in a direct and honest way, she didn't volunteer anything. He realized that he'd seen a vulnerable side of her that she wasn't going to reveal to Will and Brazos. He felt an elation, a quickening of the heart, that he could not have explained. So caught up was he in this new emotion, he wasn't immediately aware that she was speaking to him.

"What about it, McCaleb? Have I passed the test, or do you have some more questions?"

"Just one," said McCaleb. "Where are you going to stand when Nance learns you're gathering a herd with intentions of pulling out?"

She got up, walked over to where he sat, and stood looking down at him.

"I'm a woman, McCaleb, but despite the fact my daddy's a shiftless old scoundrel and a bad influence, my mama came from a good family. I grew up around men whose word meant something; they'd make a commitment and stick to it till Hell froze over. I can ride, I can rope, and I can shoot. When I throw in with you, I'll side you against anything or anybody, including my father and every damn Comanche in Texas!"

Her eyes flashed with the green fire he'd come to know. Will and Brazos chuckled delightedly. Woman though she was, she thought and spoke as directly as a man would have. She had gotten through to them.

"You'll do, Rebecca Nance," said McCaleb. He got up and put out his hand. She took it, and woman though she was, hers was the callused hand of a cowboy.

"One thing more," she said. "I can't leave my brother here. I want to take him with us. After he . . . Is that going to be a problem?"

"I'll let you answer that," said McCaleb. "Despite what you think of me, I've never gunned anybody who didn't draw first."

"I believe you," she said, "and I can promise you Monte won't be laying down any more challenges. You scared hell out of him, and it was exactly what he needed. A less considerate man would have shot him dead and would have been within his rights. Unfortunately, I didn't understand any of that until I'd already made a fool of myself. Monte's young, but he'll work, and so will I. This is the first opportunity we've had to get away from here."

She shook hands with them all. Will and Brazos watched in admiration as she mounted and rode out.

"My God," said Brazos reverently, "I'd give her part of the gather just to have her around to do the cooking."

"Brazos don't care what they look like," said Will, "just so they can cook. He's in love with his belly. Me, I'd grab a handsome filly like her if she didn't know corn bread from cow pie. You sure can pick 'em, McCaleb."

McCaleb said nothing, but in an odd sort of way, he was pleased.

They stood watch from dusk to dawn, Brazos taking the last one. He had a fire going and coffee boiling when Will and McCaleb rolled out.

"They come by and scouted us," said Brazos. "Comanche sounds more like a coyote than a coyote does, if they could get rid of the echo."

"I heard 'em," said McCaleb. "We'll get as much of that breastwork done as we can and unroll our blankets behind it tonight. We'll picket all the horses near enough to keep an eye on them from our cover. Tomorrow we'll start on the fence. When it's done, one of us will have to be here all the time, for the sake of the fence *and* our extra horses."

They were branding their horses when Monte and Rebecca Nance rode into their camp. The girl stepped down immediately, but Monte remained in his saddle. He slumped awkwardly, apparently unarmed. McCaleb wondered if that had been *his* idea or Rebecca's. Finally he dismounted and slowly, reluctantly, almost painfully, lifted his eyes. Clenching his teeth in grim determination, he gripped McCaleb's extended hand.

"I done a fool thing," he said. "I won't do it again."

Each of them was acutely aware of the boy's embarrassment, but nobody quite knew what to say. Rebecca broke the uncomfortable silence.

"McCaleb, since we're joining *your* gather, we'll take orders from you. What do you want us to do first?"

Brazos caught McCaleb's eye, nudging a branding iron with the toe of his boot. McCaleb turned to the girl.

"I want both of you to take a good look at the 3-R connected brand on the left flank of these horses. We had Comanche coyotes yipping around here last night. They may come after our scalps later, but for now, I expect they're after our horses. How you manage it is up to you, but I'm asking the two of you to convince York Nance it'll be damn unhealthy for him if any of these horses show up in his corral. Do you still want to ride with us, after I've strung up your daddy for horse stealing?"

Before Rebecca could speak, Monte stepped forward, his hand out.

"I'll ride with you to Hell and back. By God, McCaleb, you're a man! I'll take him the word myself. Rebecca's wanted to break out of here, but I've been no help to her. I couldn't see any way, but now I can. I'm goin' to stand up on my hind legs and fight!"

Again McCaleb shook the boy's hand. Will and Brazos chuckled while a silent Rebecca stared at her brother as though seeing him for the first time.

McCaleb spoke to her. "As for the gather, do what you've been doing; work as a team. How many cows have you marked with the Box N brand?"

"Maybe a hundred. We got discouraged and quit."

"No sense in it," said Monte, "after the old man started making whiskey and gettin' friendly with the Comanches. There was no way, no hope, of the two of us ever gettin' a herd to market, and they're worthless here."

"They won't be worthless in Denver," said McCaleb. "We'll be trailing with Charles Goodnight, and we'll drive all the way to Cheyenne, if we have to. When we rope one of your Box N cows, we'll trade it to you for one of your unbrandeds. Keep a tally of how many unbranded cows you bring in. We'll take a day at the end of the week and brand that week's gather. I've ridden downriver another ten miles without finding anything we might use for another holding pen. We've started a shelter here; I reckon we'll make the best of this box canyon."

"You didn't ride far enough," said Monte. "The Trinity does a horseshoe with the loop to the east and the whole loop is a canyon. Walls are sixty feet high in places. The whole thing is maybe five miles long. Some stretches there's not much grass, just water and sand. Some wild hosses in there, and we'd have to fence it at both ends."

"My God," squawked Brazos. "Fence the Trinity? *Twice?*"

"Twice," said Monte, enjoying Brazos's incredulity.

"Sounds like a great place for an Indian ambush," said Will.

"It is," agreed Monte cheerfully. "I found some human bones and rusted Spanish armor. If I could spend maybe a month in there, I'd come out with some Spanish gold."

"You'd come out facedown on a travois," growled Brazos, "with your hair gone and your butt shot full of Comanche arrows."

Embarrassed by his slip of the tongue, Brazos cut his eyes to Rebecca. To his total dismay, the girl smiled at him and winked.

"I think we'll leave this bone-littered, gold-studded canyon alone," said McCaleb. "Even if the Comanches weren't a threat and we had the *time* to fence the Trinity twice, we'd be fools to try it. Sand, Monte. The bed of the Trinity is nearly all sand, and you'd never set the posts deep enough. Even if you did, the first high water would tear them loose. We'll start on our fence this morning, but we're a mite short on tools. We have an ax, a pick, and a shovel."

"I can bring a second set," said Monte, "and be back with 'em before dark. I got to go back to the house anyhow, and tell the old man to keep his hands off your hosses."

"Go get whatever you aim to take," said McCaleb, "and come prepared to stay. How about extra horses?"

"That's where we're lacking," said Rebecca. "We have to fight to keep a saddle horse apiece. Daddy sells them as fast as he gets his hands on them."

"We'll manage, then," said McCaleb. "Bring whatever weapons you have."

"All I had was a rifle," said Rebecca. "You ruined that."

"Then you can use mine," said McCaleb.

"Look!" cried Rebecca.

On the east wall of the canyon overlooking their shelter, half a dozen Indians sat their paint ponies in silence. One of them carried a lance.

"That's Blue Feather," said Rebecca. "The one with the lance. It's him I'm most afraid of. When he comes to the house, he looks at me like he's . . . got plans for me." She shuddered.

"Well," said Brazos, "why don't I just cancel all his plans with some slugs in the gut?"

"Not yet," said McCaleb. "There's five of us, but we've got weapons, ammunition, and grub for only three. As Captain Jack says, 'Don't worry about the Indians you *can* see; it's the ones you *can't* see who are going to cause all the trouble.' There may be another hundred of them waiting to see which way we'll jump."

"I doubt I'll have to say anything to the old man," said Monte. "Old Blue Feather hates my guts. That's likely why he's here; he saw me and Rebecca ride out, and he's followed. I won't feel safe as long as that Indian's alive."

"There they go," said McCaleb.

The Indians vanished as suddenly as they had appeared.

"We'd better get back to the house," said Rebecca, "and get our things together. Like Monte says, Blue Feather *looks* for ways to pick a fight with Daddy. I won't be surprised if he *forbids* us to gather cows with you. I suppose we'd better get ready to move out with what little we have that's worth the trouble."

"Come on," said Monte impatiently. "Let's get it over and done."

"That bunch may have just pulled back out of sight, waiting for you to ride out," said McCaleb. "Want one of us to ride with you?"

"I doubt he'll bother us as long as the old man's alive," said Monte, "but once they have their last big fight, I don't expect to live until sundown. I'm glad Rebecca made me see this was our only chance of getting out of here alive. I just hope our bein' here won't bring the Comanches down on the three of you."

"I reckon we'll tangle with them whether you're along or not," said McCaleb. "If this Blue Feather's got a big mad on for you, then don't disappoint him. Go get your pistol and ammunition."

When they rode away, Brazos was the first to speak. "I hate to see them riding alone, with old Blue Feather lurking around. That girl deserves better than bein' a squaw to some heathen Comanche."

"I kind of like the kid too," said Will. "A mite impetuous, but he's got sand in his craw. That pair must have a lot of their mama in them, and they'd ought to thank God every day they ain't like their daddy."

"Let's try to finish the shelter and breastwork while they're gone," said McCaleb. "We'll need the tools they're bringing to dig post holes, and with another ax, two of us can cut posts and rails for the fence. Wouldn't be a bad idea to snake down some dead pine and cedar for firewood."

Along the open front of their shelter they built a double wall of cottonwood logs lashed to cedar posts.

Each wall was head high, and the two were four feet apart, back to back. They filled the space between with dirt, and heaped more dirt against the outside wall that faced the stream. There was just room at each end of the log abutment to get into and out of the shelter. Brazos snaked dead pines into the canyon while Will and McCaleb took turns with the ax, reducing them to firewood. Their horses were all picketed within sight of their open-faced shelter, and by sundown it was as secure as they could make it. The fence would have to wait until tomorrow. It was dark when Rebecca and Monte rode in. They brought a Dutch oven, an ax, a shovel, two gallons of sorghum molasses, a bag of coffee beans, a sack of flour, half a sack of salt, a tin of baking soda, and a lidded gallon pail of sourdough. Monte wore his Colt, and they each had bedrolls tied behind their saddles. Both were in a somber mood.

"Brought as much as we could," said Monte, "because I doubt we'll be going back. Something's bad wrong. I told the old man what you said, that you'd make it hot for him if any of your hosses showed up in his corral. He didn't say a word; it was like he didn't even hear me. Then I told him that me and Rebecca was goin' into the brakes to rope wild cattle, and he acted like he didn't care where we went, what we did, or if we ever came back."

"I'm afraid to go back to that house," said Rebecca. "I don't believe he'd lift a hand to save me, the way he is now, if that Indian took me."

"You didn't see the Indians after you left here?" inquired McCaleb.

"No," said Monte.

"That bothers me," said Rebecca, "them just showing up here and riding away. Whatever they have in mind seems to involve us all, because I don't know that they've ever trailed me or Monte, until we came to your camp."

* * *

They were done with breakfast by first light, ready to start building their fence.

"I'll start digging post holes," said McCaleb. "Brazos, you and Will begin cuttin' the posts. Monte, you drag them down. Remember, eight cedar posts ten feet long and a dozen rails fifteen feet long. Rebecca, you stay here; I have some more questions about that trouble-some Indian."

Brazos and Will kept straight faces, but the twinkle in their eyes made him just a little uncomfortable. Brazos and Will each took an ax while Monte loosed his lariat and began uncoiling it. McCaleb took the pick and shovel to the point where they had decided to build the fence to close off the open end of the box canyon. Once the three riders were out of sight, he turned to Rebecca. Fledgling tears in the corners of her green eyes told him she was about to confirm his suspicions.

"You haven't told me the worst of it, have you?"

"No," she sobbed, burying her pale face in her hands. The trickle of tears became a flash flood. He said nothing more, waiting.

"Dear God, McCaleb, I'm as bad as my daddy, shifting my troubles to your shoulders because I'm too weak to stand up to them myself. I had no right to ask your help without you knowing what he . . . what I'm so afraid he's . . . done to me."

"Is that why this Comanche—Blue Feather—is trailing you? Has York Nance promised you—sold you—to him?"

She only cried the harder. Exasperated, McCaleb took her by the shoulders and shook her. Angrily, she tore herself from his grasp and dried her tears.

"I don't know for sure, McCaleb. I just don't know. That Indian acts like he has some . . . claim on me. When he'd come to the house, I . . . I had the horrible, creepy feeling that he knew something I didn't know . . . that he was just waiting, savoring what lay ahead. Daddy's made some kind of deal with that . . . that savage, and it involves me!"

"My God, girl, would your own daddy sink low enough to *sell* you to a thieving, bloodthirsty Comanche?"

"He's a weak, whiskey-drinking, compulsive gambler, McCaleb. He'd sell his soul to the devil if he got the chance. He gambled away my mama's wedding ring. It was all I had left that was hers, and he lost it on the turn of a card. He has no conscience; nothing is sacred to him."

"Not even your honor? Your soul?"

She placed her hands on his shoulders. Her tears were dry. She was beyond them. In her green eyes there was a deep sadness, a wild sorrow, that shook him to his boots. With a sigh, reluctantly, she spoke.

"My mama died in 1844, McCaleb. I've had to be a mother to Monte since the day he was born. From the time I was five years old, all I've known is drunks, gamblers, and outlaws. Would you leave your five-year-old daughter and newborn son with a whorehouse madam while you went upstairs to enjoy the favors of one of the girls? My daddy did."

McCaleb was silent. He knew she was about to reveal something that York Nance had done, some foul deed from her past that had left its scars on her.

"He tried to make a whore of me, McCaleb, when I was twelve years old. Before God, I've never told this to anybody. I've been ashamed to. Daddy had gone broke in a poker game. It's the one thing he's genuinely good at. He'd lost his watch, his cuff links, even half a box of cigars. None of the other gamblers would stake him; they knew him too well. He would have even gotten on his knees and begged them if it would have helped. All he had left was me; a skinny twelve-year-old with one faded dress, no socks, and not a thread of underwear. So he offered me—promising that I'd go to bed with any man that wanted me—for twenty dollars. One man was an outlaw and killer, the rest, no-account, seedy gamblers; but they were *decent* men, McCaleb, and they refused his offer. Not only that, they beat him within an inch of his life, booted him out of the saloon and warned him never to come back."

"They should have cut him like a bull, gut-shot him, and then strung up what was left," said McCaleb bitterly.

"They were going to hang him, but I begged them not to. I wondered, in the years that followed, if I'd made a mistake."

McCaleb's mind's eye peered back over the years to that frightened child she had spoken of, and he found himself not just disliking York Nance, but hating the man. Suddenly he was sure that Nance *had*, indeed, promised this girl to a drunken, murdering Indian! That was why they hadn't been molested and their horses stolen. The Indian was stalking the girl. But why hadn't he simply taken her while she and Monte had been alone? What was he waiting for? Had the Indians' presence been a subtle warning to McCaleb and his friends to shy away from Rebecca?

"Please," said the girl, "don't ever tell . . . what I've just told you. You don't know—nobody could ever know—how much it . . . it hurt me."

"You have my word," said McCaleb. "Any man in this camp would gut-shoot Nance, and they'd have to do some hard ridin' to get there ahead of me. But we can't undo your hurt after all these years; it would solve nothing. We must devote our attention to these Indians. I can promise you *one* thing: despite what Nance may have promised that Comanche, he won't have you as long as I'm alive."

She hadn't removed her hands from his shoulders, and she was uncomfortably close. When his eyes met hers, his heart leaped like a sun-fishing bronc. Of all the precarious situations in which he'd found himself, none had been the equal of this! She threw her arms around his neck, kissing him long and hard. When she drew away, her cheeks were rosy, there was a smile on her lips and a twinkle in her green eyes.

"You said I was brash and unladylike, so I reckon I've

lived up to your expectations. But I'm not used to kindness from men. Despite being neck deep in ego, and mule-stubborn, you're a decent man, McCaleb."

McCaleb, at a total loss for words, stood there in silence, feeling his neck, ears, and face going red. Suddenly he was aware that Monte was within sight of them, snaking down his first posts. Had he been close enough to witness the girl's embrace? He would tell Will and Brazos, and none of them would ever believe he hadn't planned to be alone with Rebecca with just such a result in mind. But Monte seemed not to notice them, loosing his catch rope from the posts and riding back. McCaleb cut his eyes to Rebecca and she flashed him a devilish wink, obviously enjoying his discomfiture. She *knew* what had spooked him, and it rankled, having her understand him so well.

The ground—even the stream bed—was flint hard, and Monte, Will, and Brazos had the posts and rails cut long before McCaleb had even the first hole dug. They threw all their efforts into building the fence, and by sundown it was finished, standing six rails high, reaching from one canyon wall to the other. The cedar posts had been "doubled," standing side by side, creating an enclosure for the rails so they could be easily lowered and just as quickly replaced. While they worked, Rebecca had set up her Dutch oven in their newly established camp. Her sourdough biscuits laced with sorghum molasses was, as Will and Brazos declared, the best supper they'd had since before the war. As McCaleb reached for another biscuit, his eyes met hers and again she winked at him. He quickly averted his eyes, and the others were startled by the girl's merry laugh. It was the first time he'd heard her laugh. He marveled at the change in her. And in himself . . .

CHAPTER 5

$\mathcal{T}$he day after the fence was completed, before they could begin their cow hunt, a violent storm blew in from the west. Lightning—yellow, orange, and then blue-green—blazed jagged trails across lead-gray skies. Even the runoff from the spring became a roiling muddy torrent. They were comfortable in their sheltered, protected camp.

"This is wonderful," said Rebecca. "Without it, we'd be spending a wet, muddy, miserable day."

"Best get used to that," said Brazos. "I talked to some riders that went up the Shawnee Trail to Sedalia, back in the fifties. They spent fourteen hours crossin' the Red, stripped down to their drawers and boots."

Monte, Will, and McCaleb laughed. Rebecca's face colored, but she was game.

"I'm going on this trail drive, Brazos Gifford, if every cowboy there, including you, strips down to the bare hide!"

Monte, Will, and McCaleb whooped, not at what the girl had said, but at Brazos. His face had turned a brighter shade of red than his hair, and it was a while before he could manage a sheepish grin.

"Starting tomorrow," said McCaleb, "four of us will ride into the brakes and start the cow hunt. One of us will have to stay here and watch over our extra horses, grub, ammunition, and the fence."

"Rebecca," said Monte. "She makes the best biscuits."

"Leave *me* stuck in camp every day," snarled Rebecca, "and I'll see that you *never* get another biscuit. I'm sick of being a cook to ungrateful men who never think beyond their bellies!"

"All right," said McCaleb. "We'll take turns in camp, but I'm warning the lot of you: I don't make biscuits worth a damn."

By September 2, 1865, they'd roped and driven 275 longhorns into the canyon. It was Saturday morning, and they had begun branding their week's gather. Two irons—one the Box N and the other a 3-R connected—heated in the small fire. Their next candidate for the 3-R connected iron was a bawling, kicking three-year-old that Will and Brazos had thrown and hog-tied. McCaleb and Monte, catch ropes horn-looped, were dragging another struggling animal toward the fire. One of their horses nickered and all activity ceased as they watched the mouth of the canyon. Four horsemen appeared, riding single file, the last one leading a pack mule. McCaleb looked at Will, then at Brazos, and they fanned out in the Ranger formation they'd used so often when facing unknown danger. Will took his position a dozen feet to McCaleb's left, while Brazos moved an equal distance to his right. Twenty yards away the four reined up. Their horses looked sleek, grain-fed. A towheaded kid had no weapon in sight, but the other three wore well-used, slick-handled Colts in tied-down rigs.

"Step down," said McCaleb affably.

The three foremost riders dismounted, but the kid leading the pack mule didn't move. Except for the leader's gray Confederate officer's coat, they all wore range clothes, run-over boots, and used-up gray hats. They had shaggy, unkempt hair, and except for the kid, were unshaven. They wasted no time on formality. The apparent leader—the man in the Rebel coat—spoke.

"I'm Captain Nathan Calvert, of the Independent

Rangers. In the name of the Confederacy, we're confiscating four of your extra horses."

"Mister," said Brazos coldly, "it purely don't make a damn to us if you're Robert E. Lee, with papers to prove it. Lay a hand on just *one* of our horses and *you'll* be as dead as the Confederacy."

"You are defying my order, then?"

"We are," said McCaleb. "We don't recognize the Confederacy *or* your 'Independent Rangers.' Who is your commander?"

"Colonel Cullen Baker."

"Cullen Baker is scum," said McCaleb, "a deranged killer. All you'll get from us is a chance to mount up and ride."

"Take them!" bawled Calvert, going for his gun.

They were his last words. So swiftly did McCaleb draw and fire, the roar of Colts to his right and left might have been the echo of his own. His slug took Calvert in the chest, driving him back against the flank of his gray horse. The animal snorted and pranced away, allowing its dying master to slide to the ground, his unfired Colt in his hand. Both Calvert's companions were down, neither having fired a shot. The towheaded kid had released the mule's lead rope and sat with his hands shoulder high. McCaleb, Colt in his hand, beckoned him down and the kid dismounted.

"One of these pilgrims is still alive," said Brazos.

The man lay on his back, the front of his Levi's already blood-soaked from the wound just above his belt buckle. His eyes, dull with pain and the knowledge of impending death, met McCaleb's.

"I'm . . . hard hit," he muttered. "Can't you do . . . nothin' . . . fer me?"

"We have plans for you," said McCaleb. "Brazos, you and Will get your catch ropes and make us a pair of renegade neckties. We'll ride this pair of skunks far enough back into the woods so's they don't stink up the canyon and decorate a cottonwood with 'em."

"My God, McCaleb! No!"

Rebecca Nance stood there, fisted hands on her hips, sparks of green fire flickering in her eyes.

"He's just a boy, McCaleb, and he didn't lift a hand against you. Why can't you just let him go?"

"I believe," said McCaleb, his voice dripping sarcasm, "you promised to take orders from *me*, since this is *my* gather. Now shut up! *That's* an order!"

Will and Brazos said nothing. McCaleb half expected Monte to side with his sister, but the boy remained grimly silent. Finally, McCaleb turned to the towheaded kid.

"What's your name, boy, and how old are you?"

"Tom Calvert. It ain't none of your business how old I am."

"Related to Nathan?"

"He was my brother," said the kid sullenly.

"Your brother was a fool, boy. Can you give me one good reason why we shouldn't string you up and let the crows pick your bones?"

"I won't beg!" snarled the kid. "Whatever it pleasures you to do with me, then do it an' be damned!"

"Mount up, then," said McCaleb with a grim smile, "and you'll soon be shaking hands with the devil."

Brazos tossed a coiled, forty-foot rope and McCaleb caught it. Deftly, he tested the thirteen-knot noose, assuring himself that it would slide freely. Turning, he sought out Will Elliot.

"Where's the other noose, Will?"

"Won't be needing it. The jaybird that was gut-shot just cashed in."

"Well, kid," said McCaleb, "looks like you'll swing alone."

"McCaleb, please . . ."

Exasperated, he whirled to face her, but his angry response died on his lips. Big tears rolled down her dusty cheeks. From the corner of his eye he caught Will and Brazos casting less-than-tolerant looks at him. Angrily, he turned on the towheaded little renegade responsible for this dilemma.

"Kid, if I let you ride out, will you go home and *stay* there?"

"I ain't promisin' you nothin', 'cept I'll kill you if I can!"

To everybody's surprise, Rebecca slapped him. Hard.

"You little fool!" she snapped. "You make that promise and you keep it. If you don't, I'll put that rope around your neck myself!"

"Yes, ma'am," the kid gulped. "I'll do it. I'll ride!"

He adjusted the offside stirrup. Going to the near side, momentarily shielded by the horse, he drew a Colt from beneath the folds of the too-big shirt. Dropping to his knees, he fired under the belly of the buckskin. The slug burned a fiery path across McCaleb's left hip, just above his pistol belt. But McCaleb had been ready for him; stepping to his right as he drew, he fired once. His shot caught the kid in the belly, seeming to lift him to his feet, and then flopping him to his back. The skittish buckskin reared, nickered, and galloped away. McCaleb returned his Colt to its butt-forward position on his left hip. Monte lowered his eyes, ashamed that his sister had brought about a near tragedy. There was a shocked silence. The very last thing McCaleb needed or expected was a new outburst of anger from the girl, but she didn't spare him.

"You're always right, aren't you, McCaleb? Why can't you be a little more human and a little less like the Texas answer to God Almighty?"

McCaleb ignored her and peeled off his shirt. He hunkered down at the stream, soaked his bandanna and used it to wash away the blood from the angry wound just below his rib cage. He was bleeding like a stuck hog and it looked far more serious than it was.

"McCaleb . . ."

She was at last aware that he had been shot, and he experienced a grim satisfaction from the concern in her voice. It was *time* she worried about somebody besides no-account renegades! He slapped his bloody bandanna to the ground. He got to his feet, drawing as he turned to face her. Flipping the Colt, he caught the weapon by its barrel, offering it to her butt first.

"Take it," he growled in disgust, "and finish what you started."

"McCaleb," she said timorously, "I . . . I didn't know he . . . shot you."

"There's just too damn *many* things you *don't* know," he snapped.

He snatched the soggy bandanna; holding it against his still-bleeding wound, he turned to the others. Monte regarded him seriously, worry in his eyes. Will and Brazos had relaxed, sheepishly aware that he was dealing the headstrong girl a deserved reprimand and not faulting him for it.

"Unsaddle their horses and unload the pack mule," said McCaleb, "and then take those four scum outside the canyon somewhere and bury them. But nothin' fancy; drop 'em in a coulee and cave in the banks. When you're done with that, empty their packs and their saddlebags with an eye for food and extra ammunition. Be damn sure you take their gun rigs, and go through all their pockets before you plant 'em."

"Aren't you going to take their boots and clothes?" snapped Rebecca.

"Yeah," said McCaleb grimly. "Take their boots and clothes too."

Will and Brazos turned quickly away before the girl saw their grins.

With a clang, McCaleb kicked the branding irons away from the fire and put on some water to boil. He removed his gun rig; from his saddlebags he took a little jar of salve and an old undershirt. When the water had heated, he sloshed some of it on the wound, wiping it dry with part of the old shirt. He coated the angry gash with salve, and as best he could, folded the rest of the shirt into a thick pad, wrapping it around his lean middle and tying the ends together. The girl watched in silence until she could endure it no longer.

"You'd die before you'd ask for help, wouldn't you?"

"God Almighty don't need any help," said McCaleb.
"I'm sorry; I shouldn't have said that."

"Then why did you?"

That rekindled the fire in her eyes. Without another word, she went stomping off down the creek, and McCaleb chuckled to himself. He didn't see her again until Brazos, Will, and Monte returned from their grim task, leading four riderless horses. The pack mule had wandered away and grazed a few yards down the canyon. The three dismounted, strangely subdued. Brazos took something from his pocket and approached McCaleb.

"Nothin' much in their pockets," said Brazos, "except for Calvert, the leader of the pack. Found this on him; reckoned you'd want it."

In McCaleb's hand he placed a little golden locket on a thin gold chain. For a long moment McCaleb stared at it, his face pale, his mouth a thin, hard line. Brazos stood there in embarrassed silence. Rebecca stood beside him, her curiosity having gotten the better of her.

"What is it? What's wrong?"

McCaleb took her hand, placed the locket in it, and walked away. He followed the creek, disappearing into a stand of young cottonwoods. Rebecca looked at the locket in her hand and then at Brazos.

"Open it," he said.

With trembling fingers she found the clasp, opening the locket like a tiny book. There were two photographs; in the left frame, that of a pretty, dark-haired girl; in the right, that of a much younger Benton McCaleb.

"His . . . wife?" inquired the girl.

"I expect so," said Brazos. "Whoever she was, it's reason enough to gut-shoot Cullen Baker if he was a party to this."

"Then they took this . . ."

"Off her dead body," said Brazos.

The girl turned toward the cottonwoods where they'd last seen McCaleb. At first she walked slowly, hesitantly. It was as though she were drawn by a force only she could feel. Her pace quickened, and by the time she reached the cottonwoods, she was running. Brazos turned back to his companions, saying nothing. He had no idea what was about to take place, and didn't want to know. He would side McCaleb to the death against outlaws, thieves, or hordes of screeching, hostile Indians, but *this* time, Benton McCaleb was on his own.

Rebecca found McCaleb at the very end of the canyon, at the spring. He sat on a mossed-over rock staring into the pool. There was no sound except the never-ending splash of water cascading down the stone face of the canyon. She seated herself on the rock beside him without a word. After a long, painful silence, it became apparent that he didn't intend to speak to her. It would be up to her. She sighed.

"A western man dares not ask another man about . . . himself," she began, "but I'm not a *man*, McCaleb. What are the rules . . . for western . . . women?"

"They stay out of a man's business," said McCaleb gruffly.

"All right!" she flared. "I told you I didn't know how to be a lady, and that's the truth. But I . . . I'm a woman, and sometimes I . . . I let my heart get in the way."

"Like this morning," he growled.

"Yes," she sighed. "You're never wrong, McCaleb, so you don't know how it feels, standing up for something —or somebody—and making a complete fool of yourself. My daddy's never had the . . . the sand . . . to stand up for anything, and as hard as I try *not* to be like him, I . . . I play the fool as often as he does."

She became aware that he was watching her from the corner of his eye and that the hard lines of his face had softened. In a brief rise of fury, she thought he was going to agree with her unflattering self-appraisal, but he didn't.

"*You* decided that I'd never been wrong," he said.

"I've been wrong and I have the scars to prove it. I added another this morning."

"Thanks to me. You might have been killed."

"I've never been *that* wrong. While I was wrong in *not* stringing up that little sidewinder, I was *right* in my certainty he was going to try and kill me. It's a sixth sense that's kept me alive."

"How did you . . . ?"

"In Texas, ma'am, when a man vows he's going to kill you, believe him. Especially when he's ridin' with a band of cutthroats like this Baker gang. I knew, when he raised his offside stirrup, he'd pull a gun when he had the horse between us. A man just out of the saddle after a long ride don't need to bother his stirrups. The kid was buyin' time, needin' an edge."

He spoke softly, patiently, realizing it was just about the first time he had spoken to her without anger, almost the first time either of them had spoken without shouting. His voice died away; his eyes were on the locket she held in her hand.

"Will you tell me about her . . . and about Cullen Baker?"

He was silent for so long, she thought he wasn't going to answer. He seemed to be fighting a battle within himself, and she held her breath. If he didn't talk to her now, she feared he would remain trapped forever within the past, where she couldn't follow. With a sigh, reluctantly, he spoke.

"Her name was Laurie. I gave her the locket the day were were married, in New Orleans. The pictures were taken there. We had been married barely three months. I hired on to boss a herd to Shreveport, where they would be shipped north by boat. Our nearest neighbors were ten miles away. I wanted her to stay with them, but she wouldn't. She had chickens to feed, cows to milk, and we had some new calves. She was stubborn and headstrong, like . . . like . . ."

"Like I am?"

"Like you are," he said. "That was the one thing I didn't like about her. That, and the fact she never believed the tales about Cullen Baker."

"Do you *really* believe that he . . . Baker . . . ?"

"I believe he did it or had it done, although I have no proof. He's the kind who enjoys seeing living things suffer. She had been stripped, raped, tortured, and finally gut-shot, which is the slowest, most painful way to die. But that wasn't enough. Her body had been mutilated with a knife."

"Dear God! Perhaps Indians—"

"No," said McCaleb. "They ransacked the place, taking things Indians wouldn't bother. Such as a little gold I had put away. When the neighbors got worried and went to see about her, every track they found was left by a shod horse. Just as a posse was about to ride, a storm came up and rained out the trail. I learned that some of the Baker gang had been seen within a few days after I'd moved out with the herd. That's all the proof I need. Cullen Baker's my cousin, and I have every reason to believe he's responsible."

"But why?"

"Because she rejected him and married me. He vowed he'd see her dead, but Laurie didn't believe me. She just laughed and said I was jealous. I know for a certainty what I only suspected then: Cullen Baker is nothing but a cold-blooded killer. I was born in eighteen thirty-seven, two years after Ma and Pa left Tennessee. Cullen's family came here in eighteen thirty-nine, when he was four years old. Ma tried her best to keep me away from Cullen. He's from her side of the family, and she's always been scared to death of him, even when he was just a kid. Anyhow, he could pull pistol like hell wouldn't have it, and it was him taught me how to draw and shoot."

"This man, Nathan Calvert, is dead. Can't you forget Cullen Baker?"

"I *have* forgotten him, damn it, as far as killing him's

concerned. I thought if I killed *him*, I could put her memory to rest. Charlie Goodnight convinced me I was a fool for trailing Baker, and by the time we were discharged from the Rangers in 'sixty-five, I thought I could forget. I jumped into this trail drive up to my ears, and drove Cullen Baker from my mind. I won't *ever* stop hating the bastard, but I stopped *thinking* about him.''

"You've forgotten Baker, but you haven't forgotten . . . her.''

"Killing Baker a hundred times wouldn't help me,'' said McCaleb. "It's not *how* I lost her, but the *losing* of her, that haunts me. If only I could forget her, put her memory to rest, then maybe *I* could rest. It's hard to look to the future, when I'm chained to the past.''

When McCaleb and the girl reached the mouth of the canyon, they found the branding fire going, the irons ready. Silently their three companions watched them approach, relaxing when they could see no evidence of battle. They had removed the pack and pack saddle from the mule and were spreading the contents of the pack on a blanket.

"My God,'' said Will, "them jaybirds carried enough artillery and shells to start a war. This is what the kid pulled on you.''

He tossed the weapon and McCaleb caught it.

"An 1850 Colt pocket revolver,'' he said. "Don't see many of these. Four-inch barrel, .31 caliber, nine inches long. That's almost a sleeve gun. Here,'' he said, handing the pistol to Rebecca. "Be a mite easier for you to handle than a .44 Colt.''

"Thank you,'' said Rebecca. She tucked the weapon under the waistband of her Levi's.

"We got two more Spencer .52's and a needle gun,'' said Brazos. "It's a genuine U.S. Army Schroeder carbine, .53 caliber. It'll fell a buffalo from a mile away. We picked up three more Colt six-shooters, and the daddy rattler had a poke with two hundred dollars in double eagles. Mostly grub on the mule. That bunch must of robbed a trading post. There's two sacks of coffee beans, salt, flour, two sides of bacon, some airtights of peaches, tomatoes, and condensed milk. In a saddlebag there's a dozen sticks of dynamite with caps and fuses."

"We now have fifteen horses and a mule," said McCaleb. "That's enough to whet the Comanche appetite. I look for them to try pulling down our fence while a second bunch comes down the canyon wall to spook our horses. Monte, one of these extra Spencers is yours; Rebecca, you take the other. Tonight and every night, we'll watch that fence. Whoever's on sentry, sing out at the first sign of Indians."

McCaleb sat up, reaching for his Henry in the dark. Brazos peered over the breastwork toward the shadowy bulk of the fence. He hadn't awakened them; the Comanches had done that.

"Comanche coyotes out there," said Brazos.

"I heard 'em," said McCaleb. "Cut down anybody near the fence, but don't forget there's likely another bunch upcanyon. They may try using some of the horses for cover, getting as close as they can. Be sure of your targets before firing upcanyon, lest you hit a horse or cow."

Suddenly an arrow thunked into the breastwork. In quick succession there were three more.

"They're on the other wall of the canyon," said McCaleb, "right in front of us. They may try getting our attention while another group drops loops over our fence posts. Hold your fire until you have a target."

The Comanches came at them from three directions. They came down the east wall of the canyon like shadows. Upcanyon, others spooked the horses and some of the captured longhorns, sending them in an uneasy trot toward the fence at the lower end of the canyon. A horse galloped past, a Comanche clinging to the offside. Using the animal for a shield, he flung a lance under the horse's neck.

"Keep to cover," shouted McCaleb. "Use your Colts. Hold your fire and make them come to us."

The rush came when the attackers who had slid down the opposite wall of the canyon tried to come over the barricade to get at the defenders. Colts roared and as suddenly as it had begun, it was over. McCaleb used his hat to fan the powder smoke away so that he could breathe.

"Thank God for this wall!" cried Rebecca. "It's all that saved us."

"Is anybody hurt?" McCaleb asked.

There were no injuries.

"I cut down a couple of 'em at the fence," said Will, "but I think we lost a horse or two, either to gunfire or arrows."

"Come first light," said McCaleb, "we'll have a look. I doubt they'll try anything else tonight. Rest of you get what sleep you can; I'll watch for the rest of the night."

They found only two bodies the following morning.

"They came back for their dead," said McCaleb. "They had to leave these two because they didn't want to come under our guns again."

Will and Brazos returned, having gone to see about the horses.

"Couple of the horses have arrow wounds," said Brazos. "With some salve to keep the blowflies out, they'll be all right. The mule's dead. Poor little bastard took an arrow in the throat."

"I'm not surprised," said McCaleb. "They like mule better than beef. If you can find a gully deep enough and close by, take your catch rope and snake the carcass into it. Drop those two Comanches in there too. Then cave in the sides good and deep. Will, you and Brazos have seen the signs. How many did we kill?"

"Two at the fence," said Will, "and maybe five more from that bunch that tried to come over the wall. That's a hell of a loss, not to have counted coup or taken even one scalp. That might be enough bad medicine to spook 'em into stayin' away from here."

"Maybe," said McCaleb, "but that won't help us while we're in the brakes ropin' wild longhorns. They won't forget this."

CHAPTER 6

$\mathcal{M}$cCaleb, expecting trouble in the brakes, was sorely tempted to leave Rebecca in camp. He caught her covertly watching him, as though suspecting just such a move. He was getting tired of this aggressive female's demands, so he left their arrangement alone. Anyhow, the day following the attack was Rebecca's turn in camp; that allowed him a little time to study the situation. Right after breakfast, he had some words of caution for them.

"From now on, whoever's in camp *stays* in camp; no wandering upcanyon to the spring or anywhere else. We came here to gather wild longhorns, not to fight Indians, but the choice is no longer ours. Dodging these Comanches is like trying to hide from a prairie fire. God knows how many we're up against, so they have us by the short hairs when it comes to strength. We have to finish this gather *and* keep our hair. After last night, we know we have a camp we can defend. The Comanches know it too. I'm looking for them to come after us while we're in the brakes, roping longhorns. If either team gets in trouble—Indian trouble—fire three quick shots. Any questions?"

There were none. The rest of them rode out, leaving Rebecca to defend the camp. McCaleb tried to relax. Their camp was safe and they had repulsed an Indian attack, inflicting heavy losses. What *else* could go wrong?

But something could and did. Sunday, while they were branding their week's gather, York Nance rode in.

Nance dismounted without an invitation and didn't beat around the bush. He was disheveled, his personal attire showing the lack of Rebecca's care. The girl and Monte said nothing, waiting.

"McCaleb, we need to talk. We *must* talk."

"I have nothing to say," said McCaleb. "My position hasn't changed."

"Unfortunately, mine has," said Nance. "Thanks to you."

"Would that have anything to do with us cuttin' down on your Comanche friends when they made a run on our horses?"

"It would," said Nance. "I have three of your animals. If you are prepared to listen to reason, you're welcome to them."

"I'm not prepared to listen to anything *you* consider reasonable," said McCaleb. "You just keep the three broomtails; it's worth that to me, just to get your measure. Now mount up and ride."

"I'll have my say, McCaleb. You've lured my son and my daughter into your camp, and I demand that you release them. I forbid them to remain here another day."

"Forbid and be damned," snarled Monte, "and don't go layin' this on McCaleb. Me and Rebecca asked to join his gather. We're buildin' us a herd, and when McCaleb moves out, we're ridin' with him. We're in this to the finish!"

"Then so be it," said Nance curtly, "but you won't *like* the finish, boy. It don't matter that you're forted up in this canyon. It don't matter if you catch a thousand cows or five thousand. What *does* matter is that you're three hundred miles into Comanche territory. Not one of you will live to see the end of the drive."

"I've been ashamed of you before," cried Rebecca,

"but never so ashamed as I am now! It's a poor excuse for a man who would send Indians to murder his own flesh and blood."

Nance paled, swallowing hard. When he finally spoke, his voice shook.

"It's out of my hands, girl. The Comanches don't want white men comin' here. Blue Feather's no fool; if he allows this gather—this drive—to succeed, there'll be more. I tried to discourage you, McCaleb, just as I have discouraged others, because this is my last chance for a stake. My life has been just one busted flush after another. The moonshine, the horses, just pocket change. There's one hand left to play, and I aim to win, even if I have to side with thieving, murdering Comanches. There's something *they* want and something *I* want; God help anybody that gets caught in the middle."

Without another word he mounted and rode out. There were tears sliding down Rebecca's cheeks. Monte's lips were a thin angry line. Will and Brazos stood with their thumbs hooked in their pistol belts.

"I reckon that tears it," said McCaleb. "Monte, you and Rebecca are free to pull out if you don't like the way the stick floats."

"I told you I'd ride to hell with you," said Monte, "and I will."

"And so will I!" snapped the girl, knuckling tears from her eyes.

"I wonder what kind of trade he's cooked up with them Injuns," said Will. "He thinks *he's* using the Comanches and *they* reckon they're using him. My God, if *that* ain't the makings for the biggest double-cross since Cain bushwhacked Abel!"

"He's asking for it," said McCaleb, "and there's *nobody* more capable of seeing that he gets it than the Comanches. They'll take him for what they can get. Then they'll take his hair, stake him out and build a fire in his crotch."

"One thing he told us—if we can believe him—is that our real danger will come *after* the gather," said Brazos.

* * *

The winter was mild in southeast Texas, and by December 1, 1865, they had eight hundred longhorns. But the very success of their gather created two serious problems. As the herd grew, so did their risk. The more wild cows they caught, the fewer they found near the safety of their camp. With each passing day they rode farther downriver. Finally the limited graze within the canyon forced them to move the herd to open range. Contrary to McCaleb's prediction, branding and confining the cows to the canyon hadn't tamed them much, if at all. It took all of them, riding hell-for-leather, to keep the ornery brutes in line as they drove them to open range at dawn. To their dismay, they found dozens of old bunchquitters with no purpose in life except to return to the chaparral. The five riders spent the entire day swinging doubled lariats, popping flanks, convincing the deserters they belonged with the herd. Come sundown, forcing the unruly herd into the narrow mouth of the canyon was the most difficult part of an unbelievably trying day. Exhausted, they slumped around the supper fire drinking coffee. Nobody had the strength to prepare anything more elaborate. Brazos spoke.

"I reckon we might as well end this gather right now. It don't matter that we're still four months away from the start of Goodnight's drive. If we start tomorrow, I ain't sure we can have these damn stubborn cows at Fort Belknap in time."

"He's got a point," said Will. "A good half of this herd, if they don't change their ways, we'll have to rope the bastards and drag 'em to Belknap one at a time."

Nobody laughed. Tiredly McCaleb got up, poured himself some coffee and hunkered down. Finally, with a sigh, he spoke.

"I reckon we got our work cut out for us. But if we can't handle these brutes *here*, how can we ever trail 'em through that two thousand miles of wilderness Goodnight's talking about? As for adding to the gather, we'll lay off for a few days, until we're able to control what we have. After the day we've just had, I'd say we can't spare even *two* riders for cow hunting."

"I'd like to catch two hundred more," said Monte. "That would be an even thousand. If we can tame this eight hundred, we can tame two hundred more."

Everybody, including Rebecca, just looked at him.

"That's *after* we tame the bunch we already got," he added quickly.

The second day was no better than the first. By the fifth day, the herd seemed more content to graze and there were fewer bunch-quitters. By the eighth day, the moving out at dawn, the grazing, and the return drive at sundown had become routine.

"From here on out," said McCaleb, "we're going to protect the herd we have, even if it means a smaller gather. Starting tomorrow, we drive *all* the longhorns *and* the extra horses to open range. At noon, we move them back into the canyon and spend the rest of the day increasing our gather."

He said no more, allowing them to digest this information, awaiting their response.

"We've been lucky gettin' by with just one of us to protect the camp," said Will. "If the Comanches showed up in three groups, like before, they'd overrun the place. Just one of us, even with a Colt in each hand, couldn't defend it."

"That's why only *three* of us are going into the brakes," said McCaleb. "Monte and Rebecca will be here behind this breastwork, ready to cut down any Comanches with devilment on their minds."

"Why me?" howled Monte. "Ain't I good enough to rope cows?"

"McCaleb," said Rebecca, her temper flaring, "I *told* you—"

"*Stop it!*" said McCaleb, his voice cold and brittle. "I'm going to level with both of you. There's more at stake than roping cows. I'm talking about Indian savvy. Will, Brazos and me, we're Texas-born. We grew up on the frontier and spent the past four years with the Rangers, fighting Indians. I won't say we're perfect, but we're *never* all wrong at the same time. I'd bet my boots and saddle there's not an Indian alive that can get *past* the three of us. That's all of us will go; two will rope long-horns while the third scouts the area for Comanches."

He said no more. Rebecca remained silent. Monte came around first.

"I reckon that makes sense," he said. "If we get just two cows a day, we'll still hit a thousand head before we move out."

"We can shoot for that," said McCaleb. "One more thing. When we move the stock to and from open range, only *four* of us will go. We've been pushing our luck. I hate to have just one of us guarding the camp under any circumstances, but there's the necessity of getting the herd out to graze and then moving them back into the canyon."

"Sooner or later," said Rebecca, "I knew you'd figure a way to leave me here behind this wall during the graz-ing *and* the cow hunt. If I'm not good enough to pull my weight, why did you take me in?"

"Because you agreed to follow my orders," said McCaleb. "The order I've just given you and Monte is for the good of the outfit. It's not your fault you're not a born-and-bred Texan with Indian savvy, but it *is* your fault when I've explained the reason for an order and you choose to disobey or just ignore it."

He hadn't become angry and shouted at her. He hadn't even raised his voice. She felt like a disobedient child and fought down the urge to say something spite-ful in retaliation. She surprised herself as well as McCaleb.

"I'm sorry," she said. "I *do* owe you a lot for taking me and Monte in. I'll do whatever you . . . want me to do."

After that, Rebecca made a conscious effort to im-prove her attitude toward McCaleb, and it was a rare day she didn't treat them to Dutch oven biscuits.

As the wild longhorns became less numerous, they

rode downriver as far as ten miles. Since they didn't know for sure where the Indian camp was, they became more watchful than ever. Despite the added risk of greater distance, never did they ride in with less than two cows. Sometimes there were more. Their method was simple. The lead rider got his loop over the cow's horns while his partner roped the hind legs. While the second rider held his mount steady, the lead rider moved forward, throwing the longhorn off balance and forcing the cow to the ground. With both horses holding, catch ropes taut, each rider piled out of his saddle. With piggin' string they tied the longhorn's front and back feet, loosed their catch ropes, and went looking for another cow. Hog-tied, unable to get up, the animals thrashed about until they were exhausted. Finally, weak and wobbly-legged, they could be led with a horn loop.

Their next fight with the Comanches took place on December 21, 1865. As they had expected, it happened along the river, during a cow hunt. It was a fight they could have avoided, and the outcome was as strange as the incident that led them to become involved.

"Smoke," said Brazos. "Could be Comanches."

They dismounted.

"They're downwind," said McCaleb, "but let's leave the horses here. Something tells me there won't be any cow hunt today."

Each man carried two Colts, a fully-loaded extra cylinder, and his sixteen-shot .44-caliber Henry. They crept down a cedar-lined arroyo that almost paralleled the Trinity. The arroyo grew shallow, and they dropped to hands and knees until they were close enough to hear the babble of voices.

"Comanche," said Brazos.

"How do you know, this far away?" asked McCaleb.

"Can't understand a word they're sayin'," said Brazos. "Remember, I'm from South Texas. There's Apaches, Alabamas, Delawares, and Cherokees south of San Antone, along the Medina River. The Spanish once had missions all over South Texas, and most Injuns learned a little Spanish. I even learned some Apache myself. I talk Spanish better'n a full-blood Mex. But these heathen Comanches, they got a gibberish all their own."

Will chuckled. "He can say 'go to hell' in Apache."

Brazos cast him a black look and they crawled on. The arroyo virtually played out before they reached a point where they could see. McCaleb counted a dozen Indians. While he didn't understand their guttural speech, their laughter was obvious enough. They seemed pleased with whatever was about to take place. And then McCaleb saw the man they had lashed to a tree.

He, too, was Indian, but dressed differently than his captors. He wore only buckskin leggings. His bare torso was crisscrossed with bloody knife cuts and he appeared to be on his feet only because his arms had been rawhided behind him with the tree for support. His head hung forward until his long hair hid his face. McCaleb smelled roasting meat, and at first that appeared to be the reason for the fire. As their merriment increased, one of the Comanches brought dead leaves and small dead branches, heaping them at the feet of their unfortunate captive. When they finished eating, they were going to burn him alive!

"Won't make no difference to him," said Brazos. "If the poor bastard ain't already dead, he's close. They've had him awhile; been starvin' him. You can count his ribs. That's why the heathen devils are cookin' and eatin' before they finish him. He's half starved and they mean to torture him with the smell of cooking food."

"Dead or alive," said McCaleb grimly, "I'll not allow them the satisfaction of burning what's left of him."

"Amen," said Will. "He's Injun too, but if he's enemy to the Comanches, then I'm on his side. Let's make *good* Injuns of them Comanches!"

"Formation, then," said McCaleb. "Give them the same chance they gave that poor devil and the same break they'd give us. Let's cut 'em down!"

They stepped out with Colts blazing. McCaleb's clicked on empty and he palmed the second Colt with a border shift. But it was over. So great had been their surprise, not a man escaped. After the thunder of their Colts, the silence was all the more intense. Brazos walked among the fallen, nudging them with the toe of his boot.

"We're a mite rusty with the pistols," he said. "Three of 'em still alive."

"Shoot them," said McCaleb, "and then search the camp; see if there's anything we can use. Will, take one of their best horses and loose the rest. We'll need one for this poor fellow if he's still alive."

He slashed the rawhide bonds and caught the Indian before he fell. The man's back had been gashed and slashed repeatedly, the blood having dried in long red-brown furrows.

"He's wearin' Apache moccasins," said Brazos. "What're we gonna do with him? He looks nearer dead than alive."

"I reckon he is," said McCaleb, "but he *is* alive. He's some kind of man to have survived what he's been through. Since we've gone this far, we'll take him back to camp. He may be too far gone to take the ride, but there's nothing we can do for him here."

"I'd as soon lay off the cow-hunting for a while," said Brazos. "I got an idea this bunch was on their way somewhere, and when they don't show, then their friends will come lookin' for 'em. Personal, I don't aim to be around when them friends view the remains."

McCaleb and Brazos lashed the blanket-wrapped Indian to the paint pony. Will collected an armful of knives. Bows and arrows were piled on the fire.

"They'll trail us," said Brazos as they rode out.

"I expect them to," said McCaleb, "but it'd be a waste of time to try and hide our trail. They'll know it was us. I don't expect Blue Feather to swallow this. It might be just the thing to blow the lid off whatever York Nance is cooking up. The old fool's goin' to learn *muy pronto* you don't cozy up to rattlers without gettin' bit."

They rode into camp without any cows and with what appeared to be a dead Indian. Will and Brazos lifted him off the Indian horse and carried him into the shelter. Rebecca took one look at the bloodied body and shrieked.

"My God! What have you *done* to him?"

"Took him from the Comanches," said Brazos, "before they hurt him."

The girl took charge, boiling water, washing away the dried blood from the many cuts and lacerations. There was little they could do, for they had no medicine except the jar of salve in McCaleb's saddlebag.

"He's burning with fever," said Rebecca. "There's infection somewhere."

And there was. They found a far more serious wound in his lower left side, beneath the waist of his buckskins.

"Stuck him with a lance," said McCaleb. "Pour about half that quart of rotgut whiskey in there. If *that* don't finish him, he's got a chance. Snakehead's poison enough to kill whatever poison is in that wound."

For three days and nights they watched the Indian fight his way back from the very brink of death. Brazos shot a deer and they fed the half-starved Apache thick venison stew. Stubbornly he hung on; the cuts on his chest and back scabbed and his fever diminished. The grievous wound in his side began to heal. One night after supper he sat up and looked around. So long had he been silent and still, Rebecca yelped like a startled puppy.

"*Quien es?*" said Brazos. "*Apach'*?"

"*Apach',*" said the Indian. "*Lipan. Ganso.*"

"*Ganso?*" said Brazos, pointing to the Indian. The Apache nodded.

"He's Lipan Apache," said Brazos. "Lipan, an Apache chief, defied the Comanches and built a village on the Medina River, south of San Antone. The Lipans and Comanches are bitter enemies. This feller's name is Ganso. In our lingo, that's 'Goose.' "

"*Comanch'*!" spat Goose venomously. "*Bastardos! Pagano asesinos!*"

Brazos chuckled. "He says the Comanches are pagan killers."

Brazos tried the few Indian words he recalled, without a response from the Apache. Then he tried some Spanish and suddenly the Indian spoke.

"*Treinta veranos.*"

"*Usted?*" said Brazos.

"*Ganos treinta veranos,*" said the Indian.

"Thirty summers," said Brazos. "He's thirty years old."

Goose grew stronger and began to eat. With signs and the Spanish words the Indian knew, Brazos pieced together what had taken place.

"Fifteen Comanches," said Brazos. "They attacked his village and killed everybody except him. He killed three of them and that's why they took him alive. They respected his bravery and wished to torture him. He says we saved his life and now he belongs to us."

"My God," said McCaleb. "Just what we need; a homeless Indian."

"You're right," said Brazos. "He's exactly what we need. Captain Jack Hayes swore by Lipan Apaches as scouts. Flacco, one of Captain Jack's scouts, was commissioned a captain in the Rangers. Governor Sam Houston gave him a captain's rank and pay."

Goose stayed, and despite his limited Spanish, he had many talents. He could ride, he could rope, and as a scout he had no equal. His undying hatred for the Comanches seemed to give him an edge the rest of them lacked. When they returned to the brakes to rope longhorns, Goose went with them, scouting the area. McCaleb had given him the Indian pony, a bowie knife, one of the extra pistol belts, and a Colt revolver. Slowly but surely the Lipan Apache became a part of their outfit, and it was an addition none of them ever regretted.

CHAPTER 7

*M*cCaleb had a feeling, a nagging premonition, that time was running out. In mid-January 1866 he made his decision.

"We're moving out the first day of February. Two more weeks. I don't care if we reach Belknap a month early. We'll find some graze and fatten these brutes until Goodnight's ready with his herd. For the next two weeks we'll send two teams to the brakes. Brazos, you'll work with Goose, and I'll work with Will. We don't dare leave Rebecca in camp alone, so Monte will stay there with her. I don't know how or when it's coming, but there's goin' to be trouble. We must be prepared."

The following Sunday, while the rest of them branded the week's gather, McCaleb sent Goose to scout the Trinity as far north as Jake Narbo's and then downriver to York Nance's place. The Indian had already been over the area on his own, and with just such a purpose as this in mind, Brazos had made him familiar with Narbo and Nance. Goose rode out at noon, returning an hour before sundown. They waited for him to speak or give sign.

"*Dos carros*," said Goose.

"*Donde?*" McCaleb asked.

Goose hunkered down and with his finger began to draw in the dust. A long, winding line was the Trinity. A crude, stick-legged horse represented Jake Narbo's horse ranch. A square in the dust on each side of the Trinity placed the Nance cabin and barn. Following the winding line that was the river, Goose used four fingers. He passed the Narbo ranch, proceeding to the Nance barn, on the east side of the Trinity. From there, using only two fingers, he made deep tracks to the southeast, away from the river.

"*Uno carro,*" he said.

Brazos slapped the Indian on the back in appreciation.

"Whatever Nance is swapping, the Comanche required two wagons," said McCaleb, "but only as far as the Nance barn. One wagon was left there."

"*Despoblado carro?*" said Brazos to the Indian. "*Vacante?*"

"*Un despoblado carro,*" said Goose. "*Vacante.*"

"One wagon left behind," said Brazos. "Empty. If they needed a *pair* of wagons to get it to the Nance place, how can it be hauled away in *one*?"

"Who knows the Comanche mind?" said McCaleb. "Likely not that far to their village. What *is* that load? What's *in* that heavily loaded wagon? Brazos, you understand Goose better than I do. Ask him if he can trail that wagon *into* the Comanche camp, find out what its load is and get out alive."

"Can you imagine," said Will, "what would happen to *one* Lipan trapped in a village of God knows how many Comanches?" He chuckled. "This may be *your* chance to learn 'go to hell' in Apache."

"You may be right," said McCaleb. "That's asking an almighty lot."

But they had underestimated the Indian. When it came to Comanches, he had made their cause his own. With the Spanish words he understood, some sign language and some finger-drawn symbols in the dust, Brazos was able to convey McCaleb's question—and request—to the Lipan.

"He'll go tonight," said Brazos, "after moonset. Be back before dawn."

None of them slept. Finally, without a word, Goose

vanished into the darkness of the canyon. Briefly they heard the soft thud of his horse's unshod hoofs and then there was silence. McCaleb looked at the starlit sky; the position of the dipper told him it was after midnight. It was Rebecca who spoke for them all.

"I know he's an Indian, but he's a *good* Indian. Dear God, please don't let them get him. . . ."

McCaleb sat hunched by the fire nursing a cup of coffee, unable to sleep. Even *he* didn't hear the Indian ride in. He awoke with a start, only then aware that he'd dozed. He'd spilled his coffee, and the empty cup hung from one finger. Goose hunkered on the other side of the fire, a .52-caliber Spencer across his knees. Seeing McCaleb awake, the Indian grinned and tossed him the Spencer. It was brand new and had never been fired. He felt the protective coat of grease applied to all weapons before they left the factory. The others were awake; grimly, he passed the Spencer to Brazos. Words were unnecessary; they all knew what it meant.

"*Cuantos?*" said Brazos.

Goose held up both hands, fisted. He opened and closed his hands four times. He then opened his left hand and held up three fingers on his right.

"My God!" said McCaleb. "Forty-eight cases of Spencer repeaters!"

"That's twelve to a case," Will said, musing. "Put them rifles in the hands of five hundred and seventy-six Comanches, and them bastards could take on the entire Union army!"

"*Usted*," said McCaleb. He passed the Spencer to Goose, butt first. "It's yours; God knows, you're going to need it!"

The Indian took the weapon, but he wasn't finished. He pretended to load the rifle. He didn't know the word for ammunition, but every one of them—even Rebecca —knew what he meant.

"*Cuantos?*" said Brazos.

Goose raised both fisted hands and opened them,

spreading his fingers. He then dropped his left hand, raising two fingers on the right.

"A dozen damn cases," groaned Brazos. "Them Comanches can take Texas and then go after Mexico! Nance knew what he was talkin' about; I reckon *none* of us will get out of here alive."

"*Tormento*," said Goose. "*Na-Na-Nance. Tormento.*"

McCaleb cut his eyes to Rebecca, but it was too late to shield her from the terrible truth. Her face had gone white and she sat with her eyes downcast, clenching and unclenching her fists.

"*Donde?*" McCaleb asked.

"*Carro*," said Goose.

"Well," said Brazos in disgust, "the old fool's come up with another busted flush. They got him, enough Spencers and ammunition to take over the world, and the only thing we don't know is *why* he's still alive."

"I reckon we know that too," said McCaleb, looking at the girl. "I—We—Rebecca thinks that the Comanche —Blue Feather—wants her. She fears that Nance, whether he intended to go through with it or not, may have led the Indian to think—"

Seeing the unbelief and disgust in their faces and the tears streaking the girl's cheeks, he couldn't go on. But enough had been said. Monte got to his feet, stumbling out into the canyon.

"I'm *glad* they've got him!" he shouted. "*Glad!*"

Will and Brazos said nothing. The girl's tears continued unabated. Although McCaleb had expected some macabre scheme on Nance's part, he was shocked that the old reprobate had come up with something of this magnitude. For a minute he forgot their precarious position, watching Goose. His eyes were on the girl, knowing the message he had brought was the reason for her tears.

"*Comanch' bastardos!*" he said.

McCaleb got up and stepped out into the canyon. Fifty yards away, Monte Nance stood on the bank of the stream, his head down, looking into the water.

"We've got some talkin' to do," said McCaleb. "You still with me?"

Monte walked along the bank of the stream until he faced McCaleb.

"Yeah," he said, "I'm with you if we have to fight ever' damn Injun in Texas!"

Rebecca had dried her tears, built up the fire, and had a fresh pot of coffee boiling. Monte seated himself next to Goose, and McCaleb remained standing. He walked to the very back of their shelter, picked up the saddlebags they had taken from Nathan Calvert's horse and returned to the fire.

"This is the end of the gather," he said. "We're moving out *muy pronto*, but we can't outrun the Comanches. I have a surprise for them, but they'll come after us; I want us to have the protection of this camp until we take some of the fight out of them. Come dark, with Goose to guide us, I'm taking Will and Brazos on a visit to Blue Feather's village."

"Why can't I go?" growled Monte.

"Same reason as last time," said McCaleb impatiently. "Besides, we're not attacking the camp. The fewer there are of us, the safer we'll be. I want to sneak in, defang this rattler and be gone before they know we're there. We'll need *someone* here to guard our camp, same as before."

"What *are* you planning to do?" Rebecca inquired anxiously.

"I'm planning to take Nance out of there," said McCaleb, "if he's still alive. And then I'm going to make use of the dynamite the Baker gang left us. I aim to scatter that wagonload of Spencers from Hell to breakfast."

"My God," said Brazos. "Twelve sticks of dynamite and a dozen cases of ammunition! When *that* lets go, it'll rattle the windows in New Orleans! There'll be Spencer barrels and wagon wheels fallin' for forty years!"

"Why don't we take a packhorse," said Will, "and bring back some of that Spencer ammunition? If we've got to snatch Nance out of that wagon, why not take one more minute and get something that's useful to us?"

"No," said McCaleb. "Just a saddled horse for Nance. No more."

"Amen," said Brazos. "Let's go in there with nothin' on our minds except grabbin' Nance, scatterin' that wagonload of rifles all over Texas, and gettin' the hell out with our hair in place."

"Just blow the wagon where she stands," said Monte callously. "Let the old fool go up with it. He got himself into this mess. He deserves it!"

"Monte!" cried the girl.

"Nobody deserves being in the hands of the Comanches," said McCaleb. "Not even York Nance. You saw what they did to Goose."

They saddled an extra horse for Nance, using one of the saddles left by the Baker gang. Goose, beginning to think like a cowboy, had already taken the best one for himself. Nobody talked. Foremost in their minds loomed the potential consequences of their after-dark visit to the Comanche village.

They rode out at moonset, Goose taking the lead. Will Elliot led the saddled horse intended for York Nance. Brazos had carefully explained their mission, and when the Apache had learned they were going after the much-hated "Comanch'," his joy knew no bounds. McCaleb carried the saddlebags with the dynamite. Having had experience with the explosive, he had carefully capped two sticks, cutting a thirty-second fuse for each. The remaining ten sticks he capped and tied in a bundle, attaching the rest of the fuse—maybe fifty yards—to the center of it. They forded the Trinity at the Nance barn.

In the starlight they could see the shadowy hulk of the abandoned wagon, its hooped canvas top a ghostly gray-white. McCaleb estimated they had ridden no more than five miles from the Nance place when Goose reined up. Brazos nudged his mount alongside for a whispered conversation with the Apache. Brazos then spoke to Will and McCaleb.

"They're liquored up on Nance's rotgut whiskey. Only one guard on the wagon with Nance and the guns. Goose wants us to take a look."

They came to a creek, following it upstream for maybe a hundred yards before Goose halted them. It was the last decent cover they'd have before entering the clearing in which the Indian village stood. The fire had long since died to a bed of coals. A fitful breeze flirted with a still-red ember, raising a few sparks quickly swallowed by the darkness. The canvas-topped wagon had been left with its tailgate next to the creek, and the bank was high enough that a man on hands and knees might reach the wagon unseen. McCaleb touched the Indian's shoulder, pointing back the way they had come. When they had reached the horses, McCaleb spoke in a whisper.

"All of us will go to the wagon. Will, you and Brazos keep below the bank of the creek. Goose will go into the wagon and I'll follow. If Nance is still there, we'll cut him loose and boost him out. Get him back to the horses if you can. He gives you any trouble, bend a pistol barrel over his head and rope him to the saddle. I'll give you a slow count of fifty before I light the fuse; after that, we'll have maybe five minutes before the big charge blows. You should reach the horses ahead of me and Goose; mount and ride for camp. If there's pursuit, we'll cover you."

On hands and knees, Goose leading the way, they crept along the bed of the shallow creek. So slowly did the Indian lead them, pausing often to listen, there was no betraying sound of their movement. In McCaleb's shirt pocket there was an oilskin pouch of matches, and he'd slung the saddlebags around his neck to protect the dynamite. Finally the wagon stood above them and Goose lifted his hand, bidding them halt. The Apache had tied a rawhide thong to the haft of the bowie McCaleb had given him, allowing the formidable weapon to hang down his back. Starlight glinted dully on the foot-long blade as the Indian drew the knife and melted into the shadows beneath the wagon's tailgate.

There was a soft grunt and then silence. For what seemed an eternity they waited, hardly daring to breathe. Then the grisly thing that descended upon them from the darkness startled even McCaleb. Goose dangled the dead Comanche over their heads, holding him by the ankles. With Brazos's help, McCaleb lowered the macabre burden into the creek. When he touched the Indian's head, his hand came away bloody. Goose had taken his first scalp from the hated "Comanch'." Just as McCaleb was wondering how many more there might be, the Apache climbed to the tailgate. There had been only one guard. Slowly McCaleb rose to his feet, the water dripping from him sounding unnaturally loud as it pattered into the creek.

The wagon was a huge Studebaker, but it was stacked to the bows with wooden rifle and ammunition cases. By the time McCaleb had moved up beside Goose, the Indian had cut Nance's bonds. McCaleb wrinkled his nose at the stink. Nance had been there maybe three days, and the Comanches obviously hadn't loosed him even long enough to tend to his personal needs. He took one of Nance's arms while the Indian took the other. Nance grunted.

"Quiet!" hissed McCaleb. "You bring them down on us, and we'll leave your stinking carcass right here among 'em!"

Taking every precaution, they lifted Nance out of the wagon and down into the creek. Will and Brazos steadied him and they all waited, listening. There was only the sigh of the wind. McCaleb lifted his hand, starting his count. Will and Brazos moved slowly, half dragging Nance between them. They had thirty yards to go before leaving the creek; until then they could be seen from the Comanche camp. Could they get the old man to the horses in time? He stopped the count, watching them out of sight before turning to his task of placing the dynamite. Goose touched his arm and he froze. The

Apache gripped the bowie in his right hand. The Comanche rounded the wagon box, and Goose, like a striking rattler, had his left arm around his enemy's throat. A violent, deadly thrust to the belly silenced the Comanche. Goose withdrew the bowie and stood there, his head up, like a lobo wolf keening the wind. Finally he touched McCaleb's arm.

McCaleb climbed into the back of the wagon, finding barely enough room to stand. He took the ten-stick bundle of capped and fused dynamite from the saddlebags and shoved it between two wooden cases near the floor of the wagon bed. For a few seconds he stood there mentally cursing himself. For all his careful planning, he had overlooked something! He could not string the fuse on the ground! A heavy dew fall had wet the grass, and a damp fuse would just sputter out. Barring that, a watchful or restless Comanches might see the fiery trail in the darkness. He dared not shorten the fuse, lest the charge blow before they were safely away. How in tarnation was he going to unwind fifty yards of dynamite fuse in the cramped confines of the wagon? It must not "overlap" or cross itself in any way, lest the fire take a shortcut and the explosion come too quickly. He found he could reach two of the wooden bows supporting the wagon canvas, and he spiraled the fuse around them like a vine. It was painfully slow going, working by feel and the meager starlight that crept in through the canvas pucker. Needing more space, he stood on the two-foot-high side of the wagon box, stretching to loop the fuse across the front of the wagon's load. He dragged down one of the long wooden cases into the small area where he'd been standing. With a dozen feet of fuse remaining, he wound it lengthwise around the box, careful to keep each turn separated from the last. Finally, when there was nowhere else he could stretch the fuse without it crossing or touching itself, he reached the end of it. He hunched down, took a match from his oilskin pouch and popped it alight with his thumbnail. The fuse caught, sputtered and died. From somewhere in the Indian camp came the exploratory yip of a dog. Goose gripped his arm with an urgency McCaleb could feel. Time and luck had run out. He lighted a second match, and when the fuse caught, wasted precious seconds until a yard of it had been consumed. Again the curious dog yipped, and by the time McCaleb swung off the wagon's tailgate, he knew they were in for it.

He followed Goose's lead, dropping quietly into the creek. They had maybe a few seconds before the Comanche pinpointed the reason for the dog's excited yipping. As they moved away from the wagon, the creek bank sloped to a height of less than three feet; poor cover if they had to make a stand. Discovery came quickly. An arrow whipped out of the darkness, slashing into McCaleb's right thigh. Goose caught his arm, pulling him down to the meager protection of the creek bank. No sooner had they dropped to their knees in the water than a fusillade of rifle fire shattered the silence, the deadly slugs whipping the air barely above their heads. *All* the Spencers weren't in that wagon; some of them had been broken out for use!

Gritting his teeth against the pain, McCaleb snapped off two thirds of the arrow's feathered shaft, getting it out of the way. They would have to make a run for it, Spencer-armed Comanches or not. Drunken as they probably were, he had little doubt the Indians were already crossing the creek to the north of them and that they'd soon be trapped in a deadly cross fire from the opposite bank. But there was a clock ticking in McCaleb's mind, warning him of a far more imminent danger. In three minutes the dynamite would blow, scattering them all over Hell and half of Texas!

McCaleb drew his Colt. At least he would find the Comanche position. Keeping his head down, he fired twice in the direction from which the first Comanche volley had come. The response was instantaneous. There was a muzzle flash from half a dozen rifles, closer this time. Then in answer, like an echo, came the most beautiful sound McCaleb had ever heard! Maybe fifty yards to the south, from the brush on the opposite side of the creek, two Henry rifles laid a devastating fire on the Comanche riflemen! It was all the opportunity McCaleb and Goose needed, and more than McCaleb had dared hope for. Splashing through the shallow water of the creek, they ran for the sheltering darkness of the cottonwoods.

Will and Brazos! Despite his pain and their predicament, McCaleb was elated. He'd given them specific orders to take Nance and ride. Silently he thanked God that Rangers *and* ex-Rangers never let "orders" stand in the way of doing what necessity demanded. Their horses had been brought much nearer, and McCaleb sighed with relief. He and Goose pulled the slipknots and swung into their saddles, pain a fiery reminder in McCaleb's thigh. At the sound of horses coming hard, they drew their Colts. Brazos rode in first; Will followed, with Nance's horse on a lead rope.

Not a word was spoken. Goose led out, followed by Will and Nance, with McCaleb and Brazos bringing up the rear. McCaleb listened, hearing nothing. Where *was* that explosion? After the Comanches had discovered them, had they become suspicious and found the burning fuse? He didn't think so; it would be unlike the Comanches to put *anything* ahead of pursuit. Suddenly the earth trembled, reminding McCaleb of a long-ago buffalo stampede. It began slowly, rose to a sustained rumble and then faded, like the angry mutter of faraway thunder. They reined up, listening. McCaleb felt blood soaking the leg of his Levi's; his wound hurt like seven shades of Hell.

"I hope that loudmouth dog was under the wagon when it went up," said Brazos. "Hadn't been for him, that blast might've took all them war whoops off our trail in a bunch."

"No chance of that," said McCaleb. "Soon as you and Will let up with the rifles, I'd bet every brave old enough to fork a pony lit out after us. After the blast, I don't look for them to trail us tonight. It got some of them, and I reckon it'll draw the others back to camp to have a look at the damage. But come tomorrow—and from now on—we'll have a fight on our hands."

When they rode into camp, Rebecca stared in fascinated horror at the two grisly Comanche scalps Goose had thonged to the waist of his buckskins. York Nance all but fell out of the saddle, surly and silent. The girl regarded him in tight-lipped anger while Monte pointedly ignored him.

"Monte," said McCaleb, "will you stir some life into that fire and put on some water to boil? Brazos, I'll need you and Will to help me take out this arrow."

"McCaleb," snapped the girl, "I'm not going to bite you; why won't you let me help?"

"Because you don't know how," said McCaleb. "They do."

Monte took the fire-blackened bucket off the coals; the water was boiling. Will Elliot took his own bowie and cut away the right leg of McCaleb's Levi's at the hip, slitting the fabric down to the arrow shaft to expose the angry, purpling wound. Without a word, Rebecca brought McCaleb the quart jar with what was left of the whiskey. He twisted off the lid and regarded the vile stuff without enthusiasm. It was a poor excuse for painkiller, but all they had. There was maybe a third of the original quart, and he downed half of that. It had about the same effect as swallowing a handful of live coals. When he recovered from a fit of coughing and wheezing, he sleeved the sweat from his eyes. When at last he could breathe, he took the rest of the fiery liquid, enduring a second siege of choking and coughing. Brazos and Will chuckled. The Apache had a half grin on his usually stolid face; this he understood. Monte and the girl weren't watching McCaleb's unwilling performance; their eyes were on York Nance. Nance eyed the jar of moonshine hungrily as McCaleb drained it. For the first time since his arrival, he spoke.

"McCaleb, you're a glory-seeking damn fool! Why

didn't you take your herd and go, while you still had a halfway chance?"

McCaleb wiped his still-sweating face on the sleeve of his shirt and turned grim eyes on Nance. Through gritted teeth he spoke.

"Because we've never had anything even *close* to a halfway chance, thanks to your greed and stupidity. If six of us against God-knows-how-many Comanches armed with Spencer rifles sounds like decent odds to you, it's no wonder your life's been one busted flush after another. If you aim to spend the rest of the night in this camp, then get out there to the branch and wash the stink off yourself."

Nance was unable to meet McCaleb's grim blue eyes. He got up and disappeared into the darkness of the canyon.

Will allowed enough time for the whiskey to take hold. To cauterize the wound, two bowies lay with their blades in the coals. McCaleb, sweating, clenched his teeth on a rimfire cartridge. He nodded to Will. Everybody, except for Monte and Rebecca, knew what was coming. Will drew his Colt and twirled it, gripping the barrel. With his left hand he steadied the broken shaft of the arrow and with his right he swung the Colt, bringing the butt down on the protruding wooden shaft. McCaleb grunted in pain and there was an involuntary cry from the girl. Sweat dripped off McCaleb's chin and pain turned his eyes to blue ice. Again he nodded to Will and again Will swung the Colt. Despite the cartridge clenched in his teeth, McCaleb cried out. There was a splattering of new blood as the head of the arrow emerged from the flesh. Brazos took hold of the barbed tip, pulling the broken shaft through the wound and out. A white-faced Monte watched, but the girl had turned away.

"The easy part's over," said Will. "You ready to finish it, pardner?"

"Finish it," said McCaleb, through still-clenched teeth.

Will took one bowie from the fire and Brazos the other. The foot-long blades, glowing red, were allowed to cool slightly, to a silver-gray. Will held his hot blade an inch away from the angry wound where the arrow had entered; Brazos held his blade near the wound where the arrow head had been driven out. Will nodded and they moved as one, pressing the flat of their blades to bloody flesh. With an anguished cry McCaleb lay back, his eyes glazed, unconscious.

"My God!" cried Rebecca. "Did you have to be so . . . so brutal? Is there no other way?"

"Reckon there is," said Brazos grimly. "We could of saved him some hurt now and cost him a leg next week."

They salved the wound. Rebecca built up the fire and put the coffee on to boil. It was a good four hours to first light, but nobody slept. Their eyes were on McCaleb. Despite the cooling night wind, there were patches of sweat on his denim shirt. Coming out of it, he blinked his eyes. Struggling mightily, he tried to rise to a sitting position. Knowing him, Will and Brazos made no move to help; wisely, Monte and the girl followed their lead. Goose sipped his coffee in silence, his face expressionless. Hands on the ground behind him, McCaleb, like a huge crab, backed up until his back was to the wall of their hollowed-out shelter.

"Coffee," he muttered.

Silently Rebecca handed him a tin cup of the scalding brew. His hands trembled and he used them both to steady the cup. Still nobody said anything. None of them paid the slightest attention to York Nance when he stalked back into their shelter and flopped down against the wall as far from McCaleb as he could get. McCaleb held out his cup and Brazos refilled it. McCaleb's hands no longer trembled. He spoke.

"I'll keep watch until first light; the rest of you, get what sleep you can. God only knows what we'll be up against, come morning."

* * *

McCaleb sat before the graying embers of the fire, hat tipped over his eyes, Henry rifle across his knees. The others slept, except for Rebecca. The girl sat on the other side of the fire, silent. York Nance snored to the extent that McCaleb wondered how anyone else slept. What were they to *do* with the old fool? He was ample excuse for the Comanches to murder them all at first opportunity, and if *that* wasn't enough, that dynamited load of Spencer rifles would be.

"McCaleb," said the girl, "why don't you let me keep watch? You need sleep yourself."

McCaleb said nothing. The girl's temper flared.

"Here you sit," she snapped, "drunk on rotgut whiskey and in pain, but you *still* won't turn loose. You hurt, you bleed, you . . . Damn you, Benton McCaleb, when are you going to . . . to . . ."

"Don't you swear at me," growled McCaleb. "Next time I take a quirt to you, I'll lay it on a mite harder."

He tipped his hat still lower, but try as he might, he couldn't ignore her. His eyes felt gritty, like he'd been through a sandstorm. He took off his hat, wiping his still-sweating face on his shirtsleeve. And then, for some reason he didn't understand and against his will, he looked at Rebecca and found her watching him. She wore that disturbing little half smile that left him with the uneasy feeling that she knew something about him that even *he* didn't know and likely didn't *want* to know. He remembered the time she had shamelessly watched him bathing jaybird naked in the Trinity, and felt his cheeks, neck, and ears going red. He was thankful for the darkness surrounding them, and as the night wind brought new life to the dying fire, he again tipped his hat over his eyes.

CHAPTER 8

$\mathcal{D}$awn brought McCaleb some fever, but still no sign of the Comanches. It was a strange game and he hadn't the faintest idea what kind of hand they might draw next. The very last thing he expected was the predawn appearance of Jake Narbo. The sun was barely pinking the eastern horizon when the old half-breed rode into their camp. Hands shoulder high, he reined up, silent. McCaleb, despite the pain in his thigh and a giddiness as a result of the fever, hobbled out to confront Narbo.

"Get down, Jake."

But Jake Narbo remained in his saddle. His hard old eyes touched them all, remaining the longest on York Nance.

"Many die," he said. "Now you die."

In the dust at McCaleb's feet he dropped a gold eagle and two double eagles. He reined his horse around, kicked it into a lope and rode away.

"They've purely scared hell out of him," said Will. "He wants no part of us, not even our gold."

"And *he* lives with a Comanche woman," said Brazos. "That don't say much for *our* chances, does it?"

The morning passed without any attempt at retaliation by the Comanches. Despite their fortified camp, McCaleb had expected them to make *some* show, if only to fire on their mud-and-log wall from the opposite rim of the box canyon. But there was no attack. Within minutes after Jake Narbo had ridden away, however, a Comanche brave appeared on the east rim. He sat his mustang for a minute or two and then vanished as silently as he had come. An hour later, almost to the minute, he appeared again. The strange ritual continued, never varying, until darkness hid the canyon wall.

"If he shows in the morning," vowed Brazos, "I'll put a couple of Henry slugs right under his wishbone."

"No use," said McCaleb. "I was afraid of this. They're playing a waiting game and time's on their side. They know we'll soon be forced out of this canyon. There might be enough graze to last another week, but no more. After moonset, I'll send Goose to scout their camp; it's time we found out how many we're up against."

"Don't be a bigger fool than you've been already, McCaleb," said Nance. "Leave the cattle, saddle up and ride out; it could save your life."

"And yours?" snarled Monte. "*You're* the cause of this, and now you're expectin' us to give up our cows and get you out of it!"

"We're not giving up our herd," said McCaleb. "You're the fool, Nance. With or without the cattle, we'll have to fight. While we've done enough on our own to bring the Comanches down on us, thanks to your foolish promises, they want *more* than just our scalps."

"If McCaleb won't spell it out," said Rebecca, "I will. You promised *me* to that Indian, didn't you? They're just waiting for us to leave here, and when we do, with or without the herd, they'll strike. McCaleb means to fight for *me*, something that would never cross *your* mind!"

"I ought to gut-shoot you," snarled Monte. "You promised my sister to Blue Feather; that's why the greasy, low-down son's been follerin' us around like he's staked a claim!"

"But I *didn't* promise her!" cried Nance, finally showing some emotion. "I just . . . I didn't . . ."

"You didn't *promise* him," said McCaleb, "but you

didn't say no, did you? You allowed him to think what he wanted to think, using her to sweeten the pot. We've cost Blue Feather his Spencer rifles; if he takes our hair in revenge, that leaves Rebecca as the only chip in the game. Blue Feather aims to finish us and then take her. She'd be better off dead."

"If he takes *her*," said Nance, "he might—"

McCaleb knew what was coming. He caught Nance by the front of his dirty shirt, lifting him off the ground, choking off his words.

"You double-dealing old skunk," he gritted, "don't you even *think* of such a trade!" Furious, his face a mask of disgust, he flung Nance to the ground.

Supper was a painfully silent meal. Nance had again become surly and mean, his eyes flickering malevolent daggers at McCaleb. Monte didn't eat; just stared at Nance with undisguised hate. The girl kept her head down, biting her lip, saying nothing. McCaleb nodded to Brazos and the two of them stepped out of the camp, into the canyon.

"Get with Goose," said McCaleb. "He can ride any-time it feels right to him. I want to know how many there are and where they are."

His wound bothering him, unable to sleep, McCaleb took first watch. Fed up with Nance's snoring, he slipped out of camp, hobbling to the fence. He hunched down to sit on the third rail, taking his weight off the still-hurting right leg. The moon had just slid beyond the horizon, and with only the starlight, the world seemed a pit of blackness. He could see nothing, and though the footsteps were soft, McCaleb was ready. When the girl spoke, he eased the hammer down and holstered his Colt.

"Do you always expect an enemy, never a friend?"

"I reckon I have more enemies than friends. It keeps me alive."

"Your wound's bothering you, isn't it?"

"Hurts some; fever's down. It'll heal."

"What are we going to do? We can't stay here much longer."

"We're moving out," said McCaleb. "When Goose returns, we'll know how many there are and where they are. Indians are superstitious; they're likely to see the loss of a battle or anything unusual as bad medicine. Many a tribe has ended the fight with the death of a chief."

"They might think of the explosion as bad medicine?"

"I'm counting on it," said McCaleb. "If some of them were killed, it might buy us a little time. But we'll have to fight; Nance has seen to that."

For a long moment she was silent. She stood facing him, so close he could hear her breathing. When at last she spoke, her voice was soft.

"McCaleb?"

He said nothing, waiting.

"Thank you," she said, and then she was gone.

Goose rode in an hour before dawn. McCaleb had slept little. He built up the fire and, with the exception of York Nance, they gathered around to learn what the Apache had to report. Brazos began his patient interpretation, and by the time Rebecca had the coffee ready, he had the information McCaleb wanted.

"They've moved the village upriver to within a mile of Narbo's place," said Brazos. "Goose believes twelve or more were killed when the wagon went up, and that's why they moved. Bad medicine. He reckons there's fifty of 'em at the village. He found nine more in a camp between here and the river, where we've been grazing the herd. There's four staked out on the canyon rim to keep us nervous."

But the Apache wasn't finished. With his finger, he drew in the dust his familiar twisted line representing the Trinity. A stick horse became Narbo's ranch, an arrow the Comanche village, and dots on the east and west banks of the Trinity placed the Nance buildings. To the south, paralleling the river, he drew a second line with an arrowhead at the end. Then he held up both hands, fingers extended.

"Comanch'," he said. *"Comanch' bastardos!"*

"Ten Comanche ridin' south," said Brazos. "I purely don't like the looks of *that*."

"Neither do I," said McCaleb. "God knows, there's enough of them without going after reinforcements, but that's what they've got in mind."

"I don't believe that," said Monte. "There'd be more than seventy of 'em, if what the Indian says is true. Why do they need more than *that* just to come after six of us?"

"There's a hell of a bunch you don't know about the Comanches," said Brazos with a hint of contempt. "They don't understand dynamite; way they see it, there's just a few of us, but we're makin' powerful medicine. They plan to hit us with a bigger war party, just on the chance we got some more of that strong medicine. Right now they're uncertain; a little scared of us."

"That's our only ace," said McCaleb, "and we're going to play it. God help us if we're readin' the wrong sign, but it's the only chance we have of leavin' here with the herd *and* our hair. We're movin' out within the hour."

They broke camp swiftly, making good use of the double-rigged pack saddle the unfortunate mule had left behind. The crucial time had come when they must drive the unwilling longhorns to open range and head them north to Fort Belknap on the Brazos. Two hundred of the brutes had been in the box canyon less than a week, not nearly long enough to become accustomed to any degree of captivity. These unruly ones would become bunch-quitters, breaking madly away at the slightest opportunity, determined to return to the chaparral from which they'd been unwillingly taken.

In silence they reined up at the head of the canyon. It was a critical moment; once they moved the herd to the open prairie, danger—and perhaps death—would be riding with them.

McCaleb spoke. "The first four or five days will be hell on the flank and drag riders. These newest ones—the wild ones—with ideas of quittin' the herd, will be breakin' to the flank or the rear. Until they decide to trail with the others, I reckon we'll be almighty busy. I expect the Comanches to trail us, so I'm keeping Brazos and Will with me, ridin' drag. When they attack, it will likely be from the rear. Monte, you take the right flank, Rebecca the left. While I'm looking for the Comanches to hit us from behind, we can't gamble on it. Goose will be riding point, and I'm depending on him to warn us of trouble ahead. Especially Comanche trouble. Once we're past their village and Narbo's place, we can pretty well follow the Trinity. Whatever it takes, I'd like to get beyond that Comanche village before their reinforcements arrive. It'll be a long, hard twenty-five miles."

Until York Nance spoke, McCaleb had forgotten him.

"Am I to ride with you, or would that only encourage them to attack?"

"They'll attack whether you're with us or not," said McCaleb, "and you know why. If you aim to ride with us, stay with the drag and don't cause more trouble than you already have. There's a pair of extra .44 Colts on the packhorse, if you're of a mind to arm yourself."

McCaleb swung his lariat, popping the knotted end against a longhorn flank. With a startled bellow the cow lurched into a trot. McCaleb's cowboy yell echoed down the canyon and the drive began.

The first day was a nightmare of confusion, more difficult than any of them had imagined. At every opportunity the latest additions to the herd—the wild ones—lit out like hell wouldn't have it, bound for the brakes. By the time—or before—they headed one bunch-quitter, there was another. One troublesome old cow—twelve hundred pounds of brindle fury—refused to turn, almost goring Rebecca's roan. Had it not been for the girl, McCaleb would have shot the ornery beast.

Rebecca tried to head the brute as it broke from the herd, but the longhorn wouldn't yield. She wheeled her horse, escaping a savage horn, but not quickly enough to spare her roan a wicked cut along its left flank. Furious, recovering quickly, she pounded after the wayward longhorn, uncoiling her lariat. She heard but ignored McCaleb's shouts. Angrily he slammed his Henry into the saddle boot and lit out after her, readying his own loop, praying he reached her in time to spare her the consequences of the fool thing she planned to do.

Hanging off the side of her horse like an Indian, the girl galloped alongside the brindle, catching the brute's hind legs with an underhand loop. She had double-dallied her lariat around the horn, and when the rope went tight, the roan stood fast. When the brindle cow hit the end of the line, the ornery brute went down in a cloud of dust. But one catch rope wasn't enough. The long-horn came up fighting the rope, killing-mad. The valiant roan stood fast, seconds away from the lethal horns, when McCaleb's loop snaked out. The steeldust back-stepped, snugging the horn loop while Rebecca's roan kept a tight loop on the longhorn's hind legs. Rebecca had dismounted and used her handkerchief to swab the bloody gash on the horse's flank. She appeared not to notice the furious McCaleb as he threw himself out of his saddle and came after her. Roughly he grabbed her shoulder and flung her around to face him.

"*Nobody* with the brains God gave a Texas jack would rope a wild cow without a backup rider!" he shouted.

"I *had* a backup rider," said the girl mildly. "You."

"*Nobody*," bawled McCaleb, "but a mule-headed female Missouri tenderfoot!"

"I saved us a cow."

"*No* cow is worth havin' a horn shoved through your own gut or gettin' your horse gored! You little fool, you could have been killed!"

"Ah reckon Ah could," she said, mimicking the Texas drawl. "Would it have bothered you, McCaleb, if Ah *had* been?"

"Yeah," he gritted, "it would. We'd be even *more* short-handed."

Without another word he went to his saddle and snatched off the yard-long rawhide strips they used for piggin string. He grabbed the flailing front legs of the ornery old brindle cow and tied them securely. After tying the hind legs in similar fashion, he loosed Rebecca's catch rope and then his own. He coiled his loop and swung into the saddle, but try as he might, he was unable to avoid the girl's eyes. She had controlled her temper while he had lost his. Even now she wore that enigmatic half smile that bothered him. Why hadn't she cussed him, kicked his shins or slapped his face? *That* he could have understood.

A good day's drive with a seasoned herd would have taken them ten miles, but when sundown forced them to a halt, McCaleb judged they hadn't traveled even half that. Theirs had been a perfectly wretched day, and the night promised to be no better. Goose had scouted the area before and guided them to a low-banked willow-shrouded section of the Trinity where the herd could be watered. Will and Monte rode back and loosed the brindle bunch-quitter. Having been hog-tied and helpless for three hours, the troublesome brute was exhausted and had no objection to being led back to the herd. McCaleb dared not leave the restless herd unattended, even for a few minutes; they ate their meager supper two at a time.

"No sleep for any of us," said McCaleb, "until they bed down. When they do, three of us will sleep while the other three stand watch. Brazos, when the herd quiets down, have Goose scout our back trail."

Not until after midnight did the herd finally settle down. McCaleb and Monte took first watch; Goose vanished quietly into the night, riding south. The Apache returned two hours later. McCaleb wasn't surprised to find Will, Brazos, and Rebecca awake, awaiting the Indian's report. Even York Nance appeared interested.

"Seguir," said Goose. He spread both hands, then clenched his fists and raised three fingers.

"Thirteen of them," said Brazos. "That means the four from the canyon rim and the nine that was staked out where we used to graze the herd."

"That's an unlucky number," said Rebecca. "Thirteen."

Will Elliot chuckled. "Any number's unlucky when you're dealin' with the Comanches. But that's good news; they don't aim to jump us until the reinforcements arrive."

"The longer *that* takes," said McCaleb, "the better our chances. We're *still* twenty miles south of the Comanche village, and I want us past that before they attack us. We need the time and the miles to teach this herd some trail manners. Right now, one blanket-waving Comanche could scatter them to Hell and gone."

The second day was a little better. Some of the cattle seemed caught up in the spirit of the drive, and it affected the others; even some of the bunch-quitters. But not old brindle. The troublesome longhorn again made a run for it. Rebecca, riding a quick little bay, successfully headed the brute, popping her on the flank with the knotted end of a lariat. McCaleb didn't seem to notice when the longhorn fled bawling back into the herd. Just before the sun dipped below the western horizon, Goose again led the thirsty herd to the river. Will jogged his black up alongside McCaleb's steeldust.

"Yesterday," said Will, "I reckoned it was just luck, but it ain't. That red pilgrim's leadin' them cows to the river where the bank's low on our side and high on the other side. They can get to the water easy and drink, but they can't climb up the far bank and make a run for it. That Apache's considerably more than just a good scout. He's a cowboy."

"He's an Apache, a scout, *and* a cowboy," said McCaleb, "in that order. Don't forget those Comanche scalps he wears thonged around his middle."

Goose again scouted their back trail, reporting the continuing pursuit of the thirteen Comanches. They rode night herd in pairs, circling the bedded herd in opposite directions, their rifles ready. The night passed without incident.

"Two days," said Brazos, "and all they've done is follow us at a distance. I'm as nervous as a squirrel in a treeful of bobcats. Why don't they jump us and get it over with?"

"The herd's settling down," said McCaleb. "We'll be almighty close to that Comanche village by tonight. Get with Goose; we'll have to water the herd *before* we reach it or we'll have to drive beyond it. I can't see us driving the herd to the river in plain sight of the Comanche camp."

"I have the strange feeling," said Rebecca, "that they don't intend for us to drive beyond that village. I believe they'll come after us tonight."

"Tonight," said McCaleb, "I want Goose to scout that bunch on our back trail *and* that Comanche village."

Tension ran high; the same premonition that stirred Rebecca affected them all. Again they rode night herd in pairs, nobody sleeping, each of them awaiting the Indian's return. There was no moon, and the stars seemed unusually dim and far away. Soundlessly the Apache returned. McCaleb eased the hammer down on his Colt, returning it to its butt-forward position on his left hip.

"*Comanch' bastardos!*" hissed Goose. "*Muchos!*"

His next move was grimly prophetic, something he had never before done. He carried the Spencer rifle and, getting to his feet, looking toward the south, he held the weapon over his head. The words he muttered, not even Brazos understood.

"Build up the fire enough for us to see," said McCaleb, "and break out the picks and shovels. I reckon all of you know what a buffalo wallow looks like. We're going to dig one, or something similar to it. We'll dig as deep as we can, piling the dirt up around the edge. They'll expect us to be in the open, unprotected, and while they may hit us from the south, we can't be sure of that. Rebecca, gather up all our canteens; take Goose with you, go to the river and fill them. We don't want to be pinned down here without water."

The girl gathered up nine canteens. She held one of them up in the firelight, pointing to Goose and then to herself. The Apache understood, scooped up the remaining canteens, and Rebecca followed him into the darkness toward the river. The activity had awakened York Nance. The old man lay with his head on a saddle, unkempt, uncaring.

They were in a low-lying area which in time of flood might have been underwater. The soil was loose and sandy and they reached a depth of three feet without encountering rock or other obstacles. It was twenty feet across, more square than round, but offered some protection where there had been none. They took their places an hour before dawn.

"I hope they don't stampede the herd," said Rebecca. "All that work for nothing."

"If they come from the south," said Brazos, "we'll be *between* them and the herd, so they'll have to kill us first. If that happens, the herd won't be important to us."

"They don't care a whoop about the herd," said McCaleb. "They could have hit us on the open range, when we drove the cattle out to graze. They want our scalps."

In the darkest hour, just before dawn, the Comanches struck. The cowboys had no warning except the pounding of unshod hoofs. An arrow whipped into the banked dirt above McCaleb's head, showering it down on him. To his left Goose fired his Spencer. McCaleb opened up with his Henry, raking the area. Brazos and Will followed his lead. There was the bark of Monte's Colt and the spiteful pop of Rebecca's .31-caliber pocket pistol. Amid this volley there was a continuous *thunk* of arrows and lead plowing into the banked dirt in front of them and into the bank behind them. Somewhere in the darkness a horse screamed. It ended as suddenly as it had begun. There was a silence that seemed all the more intense for the bedlam it replaced. Cautiously McCaleb got to his feet and immediately stumbled over a body. His exploring hand encountered the stubbled face of York Nance.

"Reload," said McCaleb. "They may be back. Anybody hit?"

"Damn close," said Will. "My left earlobe's gone forever."

"Nance may have caught a bad one," said McCaleb. "It'll be light in a few minutes. We'll stay put until then."

First light revealed two dead Indian ponies. The dead and wounded—if any—had been taken away under cover of darkness. York Nance lay on his back. Just above his belt buckle a Comanche arrow was buried two thirds of the way into his massive belly.

"My God!" said Brazos. "All he had to do was lay low!"

"He got up to run," said Monte bitterly.

Rebecca said nothing. She kept her head down, biting her lip, tears streaking her dusty cheeks. McCaleb took Nance's limp wrist and found a weak pulse. If he were still alive at sundown, it would be a miracle. Goose looked from the weeping girl to the mortally wounded Nance.

"*Comanch' bastardos!*" he said.

"We're moving out in ten minutes," said McCaleb.

"We can't just . . . leave him," sobbed Rebecca.

"You can," said Nance in a weak, raspy voice, "and you will."

Brazos brought a canteen; the old man drank long and noisily. Finally he lifted his slitted, pain-filled eyes until he found McCaleb.

"Will you . . . leave me a full canteen . . . and a . . . loaded pistol?"

"A full canteen," said McCaleb, "and *two* fully loaded Colts."

"Eleven . . . for the . . . bastards," gritted Nance, "and one . . . for me . . ."

"No!" cried Rebecca. "No!"

"Girl," begged Nance in desperation, "for once . . . you listen to . . . me. . . . And Monte . . . where is . . . ?"

McCaleb virtually dragged the white-faced Monte close enough for the old man to see him.

"Both of . . . you," gasped Nance, "are like your mother . . . not like . . . me. She was a . . . a . . . lady, too good for the likes of . . . me. Both of you . . . go . . . go and forget you ever knew me. I can buy . . . you . . . a little time, slow them down . . . some. I know I ain't lived . . . like a . . . man . . . but by God, I . . . I aim to die . . . like one. Don't . . . don't deny me . . . that."

Monte helped the weeping girl to her feet and tried to lead her away, but she broke loose and fell on her knees beside the old man. She took one of his hands in hers and kissed his dirty, stubbled cheek.

"Good-bye, Daddy . . . good-bye."

McCaleb loaded two of the Colts that had belonged to the Baker gang, placing them and a full canteen of water within Nance's reach. Despite the trouble the old man had caused, there was a lump in McCaleb's throat. The herd was already moving out; as he turned to go, Nance spoke.

"McCaleb . . . take care of . . . her."

They pushed the herd. After the before-dawn attack, McCaleb expected the Comanches to follow. He listened, expecting to hear the faraway blast of Nance's Colts, knowing it would mean the Comanches had taken their trail. For Monte and Rebecca Nance there would be a more sinister meaning, with every shot like the ticking of a deadly clock, measuring the final minutes of York Nance's misspent life. . . .

Suddenly there were three quick shots. Nance's Colt! McCaleb reined up, listening. There was the heavy bark of a rifle, followed by two more shots from the Colt. The rifle spoke again, the Colt three times. The others had halted, listening. The Colt blasted once, twice. Two rifles opened up and the Colt answered. Eleven times the Colt had spoken. McCaleb turned his eyes to Rebecca, finding her slumped in the saddle, her face buried in her hands.

For the twelfth and last time the Colt spoke, and Rebecca Nance's cry of anguish tore at McCaleb's heart.

York Nance had drawn his last busted flush. . . .

Sundown caught them not quite ten miles north of the Comanche village. McCaleb had Goose lead the herd to the Trinity for water, and afterward they drove the weary brutes a mile west and bedded them down. Every rider was exhausted. McCaleb looked at their grimy faces, knowing their weariness was reflected in his own. Theirs had been a brutal day, pushing the herd since first light. They'd had no sleep the night before, with yet another night of vigilance and uncertainty ahead, unless something was done to improve their lot. McCaleb made a decision and called them together.

"Brazos, soon as it's dark enough, put Goose on our back trail. I want to know how many there are and where they are, and we'll attack *them* before they come after us. If they want a fight, then by the Almighty, they'll get one. But it'll be on our terms, not theirs. Then we're driving this herd to the Brazos. From there to the high country, it's the Goodnight Trail!"

CHAPTER 9

*T*he westering sun slipped behind a massive cloud bank, painting it bloodred. Swallows dipped out of the graying February sky, riding a west wind that brought a freshening promise of rain. There was a distant grumble of thunder and an almost imperceptible flicker of lightening.

"We're in for a bad one," said McCaleb. "With those thunderheads moving in, the night will be black as the underside of a stove lid. Brazos, get with Goose. When he thinks it's dark enough, have him scout our back trail. I want to know how many are after us and where they are. Right on the heels of the storm, we're going to hit that Comanche camp with everything we have. Blue Feather is going to die; that ought to be a big enough dose of bad medicine to rid us of them."

"*Must* we attack them?" cried Rebecca. "There's so *many* of them."

"It's our only chance," said McCaleb. "Not once in the history of the world has *any* battle been won on the defensive. By the numbers, we're dead. We're going to attack, take them by surprise and shoot to kill."

"One more good reason," said Will, "is that we can't overlook the chance they might use the storm as cover to hit *us*. The herd will be spooky enough; mix a few Comanche war whoops with all the thunder and light-

ning and them longhorns won't stop runnin' till they hit
Galveston Bay."

"That's a chance we'll have to take," said McCaleb.
"I'm counting on Indian superstition and common
sense. We all know of riders who have been killed by
lightning, and I'm gambling the Comanches have had
some experience with that."

"If we *all* go," said Rebecca, "that means the herd—"

"Will be on its own," said McCaleb, "until we get
back. Remember, we have no idea—yet—how many
Comanches we'll be up against. We'll need every gun
and we'll go in shooting. You're welcome to stay with
the herd, if it'll make you feel better."

"McCaleb," said the girl defiantly, "I can shoot as
good as any man here, and come hell or high water, I'm
ridin' with you!"

The rising wind was whipping the first raindrops into
their faces when Goose returned. His report was short
and without preface. He held up both hands fisted and
opened them palm out, spreading his fingers. He repeated the procedure three more times.

"My God," said Brazos, "that's better'n six to one!"

"All the more reason to take them by surprise and
shoot to kill," said McCaleb. "We can end it pronto if we
can take Blue Feather out of it; the others will run. But
that comes later; right now, we have another problem.
Let's get out there and sing to the cows. If they start to
run, try to head them, start 'em milling. The one direction we *don't* want them running is south. If they're hell-
bent on running, we'll head them toward the Trinity.
For three quarters of a mile, the east bank's steep
enough to stop 'em cold. Now let's ride!"

The storm-bred wind slapped rain in their faces with
such a force that it stung like sand. They still wore their
hats only because they'd been tied in place with piggin
string. Thunder became a veritable drumroll of sound,
that which was the farthest away seeming but an echo
of that nearest at hand. Lightning spider-webbed the
rain-swept skies, striking somewhere with such an in-

tensity that the very earth shook beneath their feet. Somewhere in the herd a cow bawled and, like coyotes, others joined in. So continuous had the lightning become, McCaleb saw the first old longhorn get to her feet. He could have sworn it was that old brindle fool that had been a bunch-quitter since their first day on the trail. The charge was set; a single spark and all hell would break loose. And as though on cue, it came. There was an explosion rivaling anything McCaleb had ever heard. His steeldust reared, nickering in fear. On the ridge a hundred yards to the west, a tree burst into flame, an eerie torch in the storm-swept darkness. As though it were the signal they'd been waiting for, the spooked herd was off and running. McCaleb rode hard, preparing to head them if they stampeded south.

"Hieeeeeyah!" he whooped. "Hieeeeeyah!"

The lightning still flashed continually and McCaleb saw two riders on the north side of the herd, pounding toward the river. He slowed his mount, knowing the longhorns would begin milling when they hit the Trinity's steep east bank. Thunder had faded to a distant rumble, and the driving rain had slacked to a drizzle. McCaleb twisted in his saddle and in the next lightning flash found Goose and Rebecca trotting their mounts a few yards behind. He reined up, waiting for them.

"They're headed for the river," said Rebecca. "Now what?"

"We leave them where they are," said McCaleb. "There's enough grass in the river bottom to hold them until we're ready for them. Just as soon as we can get with Monte, Will, and Brazos, we're going to hit those Comanches."

"*Comanch' bastardos!*" said Goose. "*Matar!*"

Nobody appeared any the worse for the stampede except Will. His horse had fallen and the animal limped. Will was muddy, bruised, and furious.

"That old brindle cow," said Will, "just charged right into us! Soon as I saddle another horse, I'm trackin' that old hellion and puttin' a Henry slug right between her beady eyes!"

"No," said McCaleb, "just as soon as you saddle another horse, we're going to end this Comanche threat once and for all. There's three times as many of them as when they attacked us before; if we don't take every advantage and hit them *first*, we're dead."

Goose led out and they followed in single file, McCaleb bringing up the rear. They didn't ride due south but crossed immediately to the east bank of the Trinity. There was no moon, and although the sky was clearing, the starlight wasn't sufficient to betray them. McCaleb found the dipper and judged it wasn't even ten o'clock. He had no doubt the Comanches had waited out the storm, chuckling as their herd stampeded. The Comanches loved to spook a herd, and when the riders and their mounts were dead tired as a result of the stampede, attack. Many a herd had been driven right through a cow camp, forcing the sleeping cowboys to run for their lives. More often than not they found themselves weaponless, afoot and facing—on the heels of the stampeding herd—a band of screeching Indians. This, McCaleb believed, would be the best possible time to attack. It would be the very last thing the Comanches would expect as they waited for the riders to exhaust themselves and their mounts pursuing the stampede. When Goose reined up and dismounted, the others followed suit. McCaleb judged they had ridden six or seven miles.

Leaving the others with the horses, McCaleb followed the Apache along the bank of the Trinity for almost a mile. The rain-freshened night wind still came out of the west, and McCaleb smelled smoke. That meant they were downwind from the Comanche camp. Goose touched his arm and he stopped, waiting. The wind brushed a coal in a dying fire and it glowed red in the darkness, like a malevolent eye. Again the Apache touched his arm and they advanced to the point where they were directly across the river from what remained of the fire. In times past, high water had undercut the Trinity's west bank, leaving an overhang. On a wide sandbar, the Comanches had taken refuge from the storm, the overhang sheltering them from the wind-driven rain. From the west bank the Comanche camp would have been impossible to locate; more than ever, McCaleb was impressed with the Lipan Apache's skill. Dimly, in the starlight, he could see blanket-wrapped forms strung out beneath the overhang on each side of the dying fire. He touched the Apache's arm and they silently made their way back to the horses. Although the wind still favored them, he spoke in a whisper.

"They're rolled in their blankets next to the water, under an overhang of the west bank. I know we can't get them all, but we can take enough of them out of the game to convince the others that we're bad medicine. We'll be within twenty yards, so this calls for Colts. Brazos, Goose had just the one Colt; see that he has extra cartridges. Rebecca, make every shot count; all the .31-caliber shells we have is what the kid carried in his pockets. Goose will take the lead. We'll position our-selves ten paces apart so we don't all end up shooting at the same targets in the dark. I'll give you a minute or two before I open the ball; it's dark beneath that over-hang. Will, you and Brazos empty both your Colts but hold your extra cylinder in reserve, like I plan to. That's where we retreat. Before they're able to shoot at our muzzle flashes, we'll be gone."

They returned to the point where McCaleb and Goose had observed the Comanches and found it silent and unchanged. McCaleb proceeded down the river bank to the farthest position. He counted to a slow one hundred, checking his Colts, giving the others time to adjust to the darkness beneath the opposite bank's overhang, twenty yards away. Reaching the end of the count, he drew his Colt and began firing. The others opened up, and almost immediately there was return fire. McCaleb fired at a muzzle flash and the weapon was silenced. He counted just four more shots from the besieged side of the river, and when the fire was returned, the Comanche weapons spoke no more. McCaleb's second Colt clicked on empty. It was time to go!

"Move out!" he shouted.

Brazos and Will dropped back to help McCaleb cover their retreat. But there was no pursuit. Had their fire been so devastating that the survivors—if any—were unable to pursue? McCaleb didn't think so. Far more likely that most of them, although taken by surprise, had slipped away in the darkness. Those directly in the line of fire hadn't been so fortunate, but how many below or above their ambush had escaped? Had their losses been high, had Blue Feather been seriously wounded or killed, they might see it as bad medicine and forsake the fight. But McCaleb had a nagging suspicion they hadn't done nearly as well as he'd hoped, and a premonition that this wasn't going to end until somebody put a slug between Blue Feather's eyes or a bowie in his gizzard. They had reached the horses before McCaleb realized the Indian wasn't with them.

"Goose is missing," he said.

"He was next to me," said Monte. "When you hollered 'move out,' he dropped back and I reckoned he was joining you. His Colt must've been empty; he holstered it and pulled his bowie."

"We have to help him!" cried Rebecca.

"We're getting out of here," said McCaleb. "Goose is taking scalps. If the live ones who escaped headed for the brakes, he'll be all right, but if they return for their dead, there'll be roast Goose for breakfast. He's on his own; let's ride!"

They found their supplies intact and their extra horses grazing peacefully. But there wasn't a cow in sight. Clouds had again moved in from the west, and in the absence of the starlight, the darkness seemed more intense than ever. Still damp from the soaking rain, a chilling west wind had their teeth chattering.

"I'm goin' to have me a cup of hot coffee," said Brazos, "if I have to fight every damn Indian in Texas."

"Let's move to the north side of that ridge," said McCaleb. "They can smell a fire forty miles away, but we'll at least keep them from seeing it. I could use some coffee myself, and the stronger the better."

They cut some limbs from the underside of a fallen pine and soon had a fire going. Rebecca put a double handful of coffee beans in an old four sack and crushed them with a butt of her Colt. Gratefully they sipped the strong brew. It was just two hours from first light when Goose returned. Rebecca's joy at his return was marred by the gruesome trophies he'd brought with him. Tied with a piggin string, he held the bloody, hairy bundle over his head.

"*Comanche,*" he said triumphantly. "*Muchos muerto!*"

"*Cuantos?*" inquired Brazos. "*Cuantos muerto?*"

Goose held up both hands, fingers spread. Then he fisted the left hand, leaving the right open, fingers extended.

"Fifteen of them!" shouted Monte. "Maybe now they'll leave us be!"

"Don't count on it," said McCaleb. "We're going after the herd at first light; anybody wants to sleep, you've got maybe two hours. I'll keep watch."

McCaleb sat cross-legged like an Indian, his back to the dying fire, facing south. His hat tipped low, Henry rifle across his knees, he might have been asleep. By now the girl knew better. She sat on the opposite side of the fire sipping coffee, and apparently, as far as McCaleb was concerned, she might not have existed. Finally she spoke.

"Before I do anything else, McCaleb, I'm riding far enough upriver to take a bath."

So long was he silent that she became angry, convinced he was asleep or ignoring her, suspecting the latter. When he finally responded, there was a hint of amusement in his voice that further irritated her.

"You've just been through a frog strangler of a storm. There's another cloud bank buildin' in the west. Be another storm by the day after tomorrow."

"McCaleb," she said in a pitying tone, "it's not the same. I haven't had these clothes off in more than a week."

"If you've got the sense God gave a tumbleweed," said McCaleb, "you'll not take them off until this Indian trouble's behind us."

She said no more, but she didn't need to. She would do it now if for no better reason than to prove to him that she could. He sighed.

When they neared the river, McCaleb was relieved to find what appeared to be the biggest part of their herd, grazing peacefully in the river bottom. Rebecca didn't waste any time. She trotted her horse a few yards upriver and then reined him around to face them.

"I'm going up there around the bend to take a bath," she said, "and I'd better not be disturbed."

"Tell that to the Comanche," said Brazos. "Don't let her go, McCaleb."

"McCaleb knows I'm going," said the girl. "I'm taking my pistol; the first man—red or white—that pokes his nose out of the bushes, I'll shoot him like the sneaking coyote he is!" She rode angrily away .

"Reminds me of one of them Greek stories," said Will. "This feller was out hunting, and accidental like comes up on this pretty girl, Artemis, who's taking a bath. It ain't even his fault, but she gets a real mad on and turns him into a deer. Then his own dogs jumped on him and killed him."

"Good thing our little filly ain't got that power," said Brazos with a grin. "McCaleb would be wearin' the biggest pair of antlers in Texas."

McCaleb didn't join in their laughter. While their eyes were on the departing Rebecca, McCaleb watched the Apache. Like a lobo wolf keening the wind, Goose canted his head toward the south. In his right hand he held the lethal bowie knife and when he kneed his horse around to face them, McCaleb didn't like the bleak look in those obsidian eyes.

"Ten minutes," said McCaleb. "If she's not within sight of us, I'm going after her."

"Not me," said Brazos. "Not while she's . . ." His voice trailed off as he caught the look in the Apache's eyes and saw the bowie in his hand.

McCaleb pointed to Goose, then to himself, and then in the direction the girl had gone. The Indian nodded his understanding.

"I'm taking Goose with me," said McCaleb. "The rest of you hold fast. If she's all right, no use in all of us getting shot." He tried to grin but didn't quite make it. "Goose believes something's wrong, and when it comes to the Comanches, I'll take his feelings over my own. If you hear just one pistol shot, come a-running."

They rounded the bend in the river and there was no sign of the girl or her horse.

"Rebecca!" shouted McCaleb, "where *are* you?"

But there was no sound other than the sighing of the wind and the distant cawing of a crow. They quickly located the secluded little pool to which the girl had gone. On a huge flat stone at the shallow end, they found her hat, her boots, her Levi's, and the faded old blue shirt of Monte's she'd been wearing. Goose quickly found the trail. The faint tracks of an unshod horse led upriver, followed by the plainer tracks of Rebecca's shod roan. McCaleb drew his Colt and fired one shot. Goose swung into his old saddle from the off side and kicked his horse into a run.

"*Matar!*" he shouted. "*Matar!*"

McCaleb was right behind him. The others would have no trouble following. He hoped they would have the sense to do what he had failed to do, and bring the girl's clothes. Had the fool Indian dragged her away stark naked? Her embarrassment would be nothing, McCaleb decided, compared to whatever the Comanches had in store for her. He had no doubt they were after none other than Blue Feather, but why had he done this alone? Had their devastating ambush of the night before been more bad medicine than Blue

Feather's band was willing to swallow? If it had come down to a personal vendetta on Blue Feather's part, then all they had to do was kill the troublesome bastard and the threat from this particular band of Comanches would be over.

McCaleb grew more and more anxious. Why hadn't they sighted the fleeing Blue Feather? He had no more than a ten minute start and he couldn't travel as fast with Rebecca's horse on a lead rope. What did the Comanche have in mind? There was no way he could escape, unless McCaleb was reading the wrong sign. Suppose he and his little group was riding into a well-planned ambush? But Goose still pounded ahead; even in his zeal to kill the hated "Comanch'" it would be unlike him to overlook such a possibility. On a ridge less than a mile ahead, McCaleb saw them. Angrily he slid his Henry back into the boot. The range was still too great.

McCaleb hadn't ben following Blue Feather's trail; he simply kept Goose in sight, trusting the Apache's unerring skill. Finally it occurred to him what Goose was doing. The Lipan was veering to the east, toward the river. At some point Blue Feather must cross to the east bank of the Trinity and work his way back toward the Comanche camp. When he did, Goose meant to be there waiting for him! McCaleb slowed his mount, sparing the animal, and splashed across the river right behind the Apache. Goose reined up, listening. McCaleb drew his Henry, jacking a shell into the chamber, but Goose shook his head. He lifted his own Spencer from the boot, letting it slide back. *He* meant to take the Comanche himself! Goose raised his right hand over his head, brandishing the huge bowie.

They waited in a pin oak thicket until their quarry was close enough for McCaleb to hear the thud of the horse's hoofs. Without warning, Goose kicked his horse into a run, carrying the huge bowie in his right hand like a cavalry saber. McCaleb was right behind him.

Blue Feather's horse was done. The Comanche dropped the lead rope and drew his own knife.

McCaleb kicked his own mount into a run and caught Rebecca's roan, calming the tired and frightened horse. Rebecca had been roped belly down across the saddle. Rawhide thongs had been looped about her wrists and they passed beneath the horse's belly, securing her ankles with the other end. She was wrapped from head to toe in an Indian blanket. He cut the thongs and, doing his best to keep the blanket in place, lifted her off the horse. Suddenly she exploded into a kicking, clawing fury that resurrected vivid memories of a time, when just a boy, he'd tried to free a young bobcat he'd managed to catch. The blanket went flying and in the next instant the furious girl made two startling discoveries. The first, that she was *not* fighting the hated Blue Feather, and second, that she was *stark, jaybird naked!*

McCaleb freed himself of her, appearing not to notice her as she lay sprawled on the ground. He slapped his hat against his thigh, freeing it of dirt and leaves, and then placed it carefully on his head. Gingerly he felt his nose and his hand came away bloody. There was a salty taste of blood on his tongue. There was a trio of livid bleeding scratches extending from below his left eye to the collar of his shirt. He felt like he'd been pawed by a cougar. Still doing his best to ignore her, he looked around. The horse Blue Feather had ridden stood with its head down, spent. Goose's mount was calmly cropping grass. The fight had shifted into the brush and both the combatants were afoot. Rebecca Nance refused to be ignored any longer.

"Damn you, McCaleb, where are my clothes?"

"Why shucks, ma'am," said McCaleb in that exaggerated drawl she'd used on him. "Ah reckon Ah doan' know."

In the next few seconds McCaleb discovered that Rebecca Nance had an even larger vocabulary of unladylike words than he'd suspected. With his fists or his guns, he'd have killed a man for what she called him.

He'd had more than enough of her sharp tongue. Grimly he took a piggin string from his belt, doubling the yard-long rawhide strip. It wasn't a quirt but it would serve his purpose. The girl's angry tirade lessened as she realized what he intended to do. She tried to roll away from him but wasn't quick enough. He caught her wrist, lifted her up, and flung her belly down over the saddle to which she had so recently been tied. Startled, her horse sidestepped and looked around at him; had McCaleb not been so angry, he'd have laughed at the look of patient disgust in the roan's eyes. He moved up against the horse, trapping the girl's flailing legs with his body. With his left hand across her shoulders so she couldn't throw herself backward, he laid the rawhide across her bare backside, raising some satisfying red welts. She couldn't have screeched any louder if Blue Feather had scalped her. Finally McCaleb turned her loose and stepped away from the horse, allowing her to slide off and fall on her bare bottom. He picked up the Indian blanket, flapping it to free it of leaves and dirt. He was listening for approaching riders; Brazos, Will, and Monte would be coming.

"McCaleb," she snapped, "if you don't give me that blanket, when I get my hands on a gun, I'll shoot you. I swear to God I will!"

Carefully, deliberately, McCaleb folded the blanket and put it under his arm. When he spoke, it was in that infuriating Texas drawl.

"Ma'am, Ah been needin' a new saddle blanket and Ah reckon this'll do. Old Blue Feather ain't gonna need it and you don't really *want* it, else you wouldn't of flung it away when Ah helped you off youah hoss."

Her face paled and she turned her back to him, drawing her knees up under her chin. He grinned to himself, enjoying her predicament. But she couldn't bear it; she began crying, great heart-wrenching sobs. Then came the sound of approaching riders. Brazos, Will, and Monte! She turned to him, arms outstretched like a repentant child, forgetting everything except her need.

"Please . . . oh, please, McCaleb! The blanket . . . please! Don't let them see me . . . like this!"

"Do you promise not to take any more baths in Comanche country?"

"Give me the da—the blanket, McCaleb, and I promise I'll *never* take another bath anywhere within a hundred miles of you!"

"What are you going to do about my broken nose and my face? I feel like I've been in a knife fight and everybody had a knife except me."

"I'm . . . sorry, McCaleb. I thought you . . . I thought it was . . . him . . . when you took me off . . . the horse. Please . . . give me the blanket. Must you shame me before the others? Before my brother?"

McCaleb heard the horses splashing across the river. She stood before him so dejected, so defenseless, he did what he'd planned to do at the start, if she hadn't cussed him. He draped the blanket over her shoulders, allowing her to wrap herself in it. She dried her eyes with the heels of her hands and then she smiled.

"Thank you, McCaleb. Now we're even; for that day at the river."

The three riders dismounted, their concern turning to grins. Brazos was the first to speak.

"They've been at it again, and we missed it! My God, they *are* serious! Goose had to fight the Comanches while *they* fight each other!"

"I once knowed a prize fighter," said Will, "that never won a fight, and he had a better-lookin' nose. Goodnight's got to hear about this!"

"If he does," snapped Rebecca, "I won't make another sourdough biscuit from here to Colorado Territory. I was wrapped in this blanket and I . . . I couldn't see. When McCaleb cut me loose, I thought it was the Indian. I was afraid. I'm sorry. . . ."

"Where's Goose?" Monte asked.

"Taking another scalp," said McCaleb. "I planned to put a couple of slugs in the Comanche, soon as I got close enough, but Goose wouldn't have it. They've hurt Goose more than they've hurt us, so if Blue Feather had to die, I thought Goose had earned the right to handle it his way. I just hope he's not cut too bad; they finished it with knives."

Goose was a fearful sight. His bare arms, his upper body—even his face—had been splattered with blood. But most of it wasn't his own. He wore yet another scalp thonged to his waist, and the grisly thing dripped fresh blood as he walked. Rebecca shuddered.

"*Comanch' bastardo,*" said Goose through a rare grin. "*Muerto!*" From his waistband he took the .31-caliber Colt, handing it to Rebecca butt first.

"I thought you were going to shoot whoever followed you," said Monte.

"He threw a blanket over my head," said Rebecca. "I suppose I'm not very good at protecting myself. Thanks to all of you for coming after me."

"Wasn't us," said Brazos with as straight a face as he could muster. "It was McCaleb. He ain't *never* had a woman that was fool enough about him to bust his nose twice!"

Except for McCaleb, they all laughed. Even the Indian.

"Let's get those cows ready for the Goodnight Trail," said McCaleb.

Monte had brought Rebecca's clothes, boots, and hat. They waited while she made her way to dress in a nearby thicket.

They rode out, following the Trinity's east bank until they reached the point where the stampeding herd had hit the river. Just as McCaleb had hoped, the east bank had been steep enough to double the herd back on itself and start them milling. They found no tracks on the east side of the river. By sundown the herd was again pointed north. To everyone's surprise, that troublesome brindle cow gave up her bunch-quitting ways and decided to lead the herd.

"That's my brindle," said Rebecca smugly.

"I reckon that's what you expected all the time," said McCaleb dryly.

"Of course," said the girl just as dryly.

McCaleb waited until after supper to say what was on his mind.

"There'll be a moon tonight, and we're going to drive as far as we can before moonset. I mean to leave this part of the country behind as quick as we can."

CHAPTER 10

"*I* figure we're a hundred and twenty-five miles south-east of Waco," said McCaleb. "Maybe a twelve-day drive if there's no more Indian trouble and no bad stampedes. We'll find Goodnight's outfit along the Brazos, somewhere north of Waco."

"I hope there's a store or trading post in Waco," said Rebecca. "I'd swap a cow for a little piece of soap."

"It might take that," said McCaleb, "and more. I look for just about everything to be in short supply, especially ammunition. I expect every town to be occupied by Union soldiers by now."

"I don't know as they'd bother occupying Waco," said Will. "It wasn't that much of a town last time I was there. A pair of general stores, five saloons, a livery, a jail, a barbershop, and a whorehouse . . ."

He blushed, remembering Rebecca. The others laughed.

"I don't care *what* it is," snorted the girl, "if it has an honest-to-God bathtub. It wouldn't hurt the rest of you to spend some time in it. The tub, I mean."

They bedded down the herd at midnight. McCaleb estimated they were at least twenty-five miles north of the Comanche camp, and while he expected no more trouble from that quarter, he had to be sure.

"Brazos, ask Goose to scout our back trail. Starting tomorrow, we'll be more concerned with what's ahead of us. Once we leave the Trinity, we'll be driving cross-country. To bed the herd down near water, we may be facing some sixteen-hour days. Maybe some dry camps if the next creek or water hole is too far away."

Goose returned, reporting no Comanches on their back trail. McCaleb thought the Apache seemed a little disappointed. They moved the herd out at dawn. Well-grazed and watered, they moved readily along, following their self-appointed leader, old brindle. McCaleb trotted his mount to the point position, riding alongside Goose. He held up his canteen, pointed in the direction they were traveling and then pointed to the Indian.

"*Agua*," said Goose.

"*Paradero agua*," said McCaleb.

Without another word the Indian kicked his horse into a lope and was soon swallowed up in a stand of cottonwoods on the ridge ahead. McCaleb remained in the point position. To his surprise, Rebecca trotted her roan up next to his bay.

"You're supposed to be riding flank," said McCaleb.

"Will moved up to cover for me; the herd's moving well and I wanted to see where Goose is going."

"To look for water," said McCaleb. He said nothing more. She had something on her mind, but he had no intention of making it easy for her.

"I rode all of yesterday and until we bedded down the herd last night," she said, "standing in my stirrups. My legs feel like I've walked all the way."

"If I'd had a real quirt instead of that piddling strip of rawhide," said McCaleb, "you'd *still* be standing in your stirrups this morning."

He expected that to set off her hair-trigger temper, but she fooled him; she laughed. He kept his head down, fighting a grin. Despite all his resolutions to the contrary, he looked at her and that was his undoing. There was laughter—and something else—in her green eyes, which was irresistible. He found himself laughing with her, yielding to the knowledge that it had taken her abrasive nature to spark his interest. While he would never forget the dark-eyed girl he'd married in New Orleans or her brutal murder, there was something within him yearning to let her go, to allow her to become the memory that was all she could ever be. He was no less determined to avenge her death if and when he could, but would even that vengeance cleanse his heart and mind? For five long years bitterness and hatred had sustained him, but he felt a release, a letting go. How long had it been since he had laughed? The sound of his own laughter seemed strange, unfamiliar.

"I didn't know you could laugh," she said.

"I've never had much to laugh about."

"McCaleb, I . . . I just want to say I'm sorry for . . . a lot of things. I was being honest when I told you I . . . that I didn't know *how* to be a lady. Those things I said to you . . . I . . . oh, what can I do? I can't unsay them, but will it help if you know *why* I . . . I said them?"

He rode with his eyes straight ahead, as though fascinated by the ears of his bay. Finally he looked at her and nodded.

"I'd made a fool of myself, McCaleb. Again. I deserved a quirting, or worse. I deserved whatever that Indian had planned for me, but you saved me from that. When you cut me loose, I truly thought it was *him* and I was going to make him pay dearly for whatever he did to me. I closed my eyes and just scratched and fought. When I found it was you, that I'd smashed your nose again, bloodied your face, I . . . I blamed *you*, like it was *your* fault I was in such an embarrassing mess. I said those . . . mean things . . . called you what I . . . those names because I . . . I *hated* what I'd done. I simply couldn't bear having you think worse of me than you already did. . . ."

McCaleb said nothing.

"It's terrible to speak ill of the dead, McCaleb, but my daddy never cared what I did. I could have forgiven all his faults and weaknesses, but not that. Why do you think Monte was strutting around with a tied-down

Colt, trying to be a man and not knowing how? Why *shouldn't* I swear like a mule-skinner? My daddy didn't care. My mother died when I was so young, I don't even remember what she looked like, McCaleb, but do you know what I treasure, what I remember as though it was yesterday? She whipped me when I did wrong. She cared enough to punish me. Do you know what it's like, growing up without anyone to care what you do, what you say, what you think?"

"Don't you reckon you're a mite old to be looking for a man to take your daddy's place, to be what he ought to have been?"

She was silent for so long, he thought he'd gone too far. She reminded him of a deceptively calm outlaw horse just before it exploded. When finally she spoke, her voice trembled, but not with anger. She bit her lower lip as big tears rolled down her dusty cheeks.

"I just . . . want someone . . . to care. Someone to care . . . what I do . . . what I say. You never seemed to . . . to notice me . . . unless I . . . did something so . . . so foolish . . . so childish . . . you had to . . . to punish me. My God, I felt like . . . like Lot's wife after she'd been turned to a pillar of salt. I had to . . . to swear at you . . . disagree with you, scratch your face, knowing you thought me less and less a . . . a lady. I had to . . . to forsake . . . everything else . . . to get you to see me as . . . as a woman."

"I've never doubted you were a woman," said McCaleb. "If I'd had any doubts about that, what you did yesterday would have put them all out to pasture. Since you've left nothing else to my imagination, why don't you tell me the rest of it? And this time, tell me the truth!"

She kept her head down, seeming intensely interested in her saddle horn. The tears dripped off her chin, splashing on the backs of her clasped hands.

"I'll tell *you*, then," said McCaleb. "You've told me enough that I can get a handle on the rest. If it matters so much what I think, how I feel about you, I reckon it's time you learned that I've *never* been as put out over what you've *done* as I have when you've lied to me."

She forced herself to look at him, but the words wouldn't come.

"Yesterday morning, you insisted on going upriver to take a bath," said McCaleb, *"knowing* that Comanche was dogging us. And you knew why. You also knew that despite all you said about us staying away, that I'd be after you if you stayed too long. You planned for *me* to get impatient and walk up on you, but the Indian got there first. That troublesome Comanche fell into the trap you set for *me*."

"I wasn't setting a trap for you," she cried in anguish. "I . . . only . . ."

"I reckon," said McCaleb, "if I'd followed you, found you standing there jaybird naked, you wouldn't have yelled your head off?"

"No," she said in a small voice, "no."

"That wouldn't have bothered you," said McCaleb, "but when I found you wearing only a blanket, tied belly down on an Indian pony, you tore into me like a wounded catamount when I cut you loose."

"I thought it was him. . . ."

"That Indian hadn't had a bath since the flood. I could smell the stink fifty feet away. So could you."

"What are you . . . going to do . . . with me?" So softly did she speak, he barely heard her over the thump of the horses' hoofs and the plodding herd.

"If you *ever* lie to me again—about anything—I'm done with you. You can swear, fight, anything. I'll wash my hands of you for good!"

"What about the . . . other?"

"What you did," said McCaleb, "don't bother me near as much as the way you went about it. It was a damn fool thing to do, knowing we had that Comanche stalking us, knowing he had his eye on you."

"But we'd shot up their camp, killed so many of them . . ."

"You never take *anything* for granted where the Comanches are concerned. You did accomplish one thing; you lured that troublesome Indian within our reach, but I'd never have allowed you to take that risk."

The sharpness had left his voice. She knuckled the tears from her eyes. She still didn't look at him, and when she spoke, it was sadly, resignedly.

"You once said I was brash as a St. Louis whore; now that I've lived up to your low opinion, are you going to ignore me again?"

Again she studied her saddle horn, afraid to look at him. The silence dragged on. Finally, impatient and half angry at his lack of response, she lifted her eyes and her heart skipped a beat. There was a grin on his face and a twinkle in his eyes.

"Rebecca Nance, after you chucked that blanket away, I couldn't ignore you if you *were* a St. Louis whore! You've plumb got my attention. Are you satisfied?"

"Ah reckon Ah am," she said with a timid smile. "Ah reckon Ah'll do until you can find you a lady."

He took a pair of piggin strings from his belt and began slapping the rawhide thongs against his thigh. When he spoke, he still wore the grin.

"Ah reckon Ah'll have me a lady, time we get to Denver," he said, "even if you have to stand in your stirrups every jump of the way."

They drove the herd until after dark to reach the creek Goose had found. The banks of the stream were heavily wooded, and they bedded down the herd on an open plain where the graze was better. Far to the west there was an occasional flicker of lightning, showing gold behind a cloud bank.

"Likely another storm by tomorrow night," said Brazos. "This time we can't run them up against the high bank of the Trinity."

"Maybe they won't spook that easy," said Will. "So far they've been a steady bunch. They've had time to get used to the trail since that run to the river."

"They'll run," said McCaleb, "if the lightning strikes close by. Sometimes it don't have to strike; just let it take to the ground in balls of fire as big as wagon wheels, bounding about like tumbleweeds. Until the worst is over, we'll all stay in the saddle on stormy nights. Quiet nights like tonight, when the herd's resting easy, we'll ride in teams of two for three hours at a time."

"I'm ridin' with Goose," said Monte.

"I got to ride with Brazos," said Will, "elsewise I don't get any sleep. I have to sleep when he does or his god-awful singin' keeps me awake; sounds like a moose in pain."

McCaleb knew what they were doing. A cowboy sense of humor was never very subtle. They would fight to the death for him against hostile Indians or outlaws, but they'd laugh their heads off as he stumbled to his feet, bruised and bleeding, after being piled by an outlaw horse. Perfectly aware of his stormy relationship with Rebecca Nance, they would seize every opportunity to pair him with the headstrong girl. He grinned in the darkness. The joke might be on them!

"The herd's so quiet," said Rebecca, "can't we dismount and sit for just a while on something softer than a saddle? My bottom's still sore in a place or two."

"Not bad," chuckled McCaleb, "when all I had was a piggin string."

"First impressions are the truest; the first time I saw you, I said you were a bullying bastard."

"Still got some of that salve in my saddlebag," said McCaleb, "but I reckon we'd best save that for more serious wounds."

They had taken the first watch, and by the stars McCaleb judged they had two more hours. They sat on a mossed-over oasis beneath a huge red oak, their backs against its trunk. Their ground-hitched horses cropped grass nearby. Somewhere an owl hooted.

"McCaleb, what are you going to do when we get the herd to Colorado?"

"Sell, if the price is right; hold them if it's not. When

we sell, I might come back to Texas, put some money into breeding stock, drive them to Colorado and start a ranch. It's new range. That's what Goodnight plans to do."

"You have lots of confidence in him, don't you?"

"His ideas are sound. That's why we're driving through eastern New Mexico Territory to Colorado. Texas is broke, and Texans don't have anything to sell except cows. Northern trails will soon be glutted. There'll be no graze along the trail and none at the end. The range will look like its been hit with a grasshopper plague. Herds will have to be sold on the spot, for whatever they'll bring. Charlie believes we can throw our herds on this Colorado range and hold them for a year, if need be, until the price is right. For a few years—until the Yankee radicals in Washington get tired punishing us—I reckon a ranch in Colorado wouldn't be a bad idea."

"If Texas is occupied by Federal troops, what does that mean to us? Will we be allowed to just . . . go?"

"I don't know what to expect. I won't be surprised if the South-haters in Congress haven't come up with some laws earmarked especially for us. I reckon we may get some idea of what's been done when we reach Waco. With or without Goodnight, I'd not hesitate to take a herd to Colorado Territory. But I believe—and he agrees—that combining our herds will improve our chances against whatever we encounter: Union troops, outlaws, or Indians."

"Since you were Rangers like Goodnight, why didn't you, Will, and Brazos go partners with him?"

"Wouldn't have been fair to him," said McCaleb. "He already had the makings of a herd dating back to before the war, while we had nothing. With his natural increase, he's likely *got* a herd, if he can round 'em up. Charlie Goodnight's as close as a brother, and never, during my four years with the Rangers, did we face any situation we couldn't handle. But we don't always agree on everything; I feel a bit easier, more my own man, sided by Will and Brazos. They feel as strong about Goodnight as I do, but in some ways he's a lone wolf. So am I. But for his sake as well as ours, we'll trail together. We're facing lots of unknowns, and we'll be stronger facing them together."

He felt her shudder. Her hand had found its way to his shoulder without his being aware of it. Again there was a loosening of the band of hate and bitterness that had so long gripped his heart. They were of the same mind at the same time, and seemingly, without any conscious effort on the part of either of them, their lips met. He drew away first, and she spoke, softly.

"What are you thinking?"

He laughed. "I'm thinkin' this is the closest I ever got to you without endin' up cougar-clawed and bleeding."

"Do you want me to scratch your face and smash your nose, just so you can feel more natural with me?"

He failed to respond as she had hoped, and she could have bitten her tongue. Why hadn't she said something more in keeping with this newly discovered gentle mood of his? She still sat close to him, her hand in his, but he might as well have been in Waco. Despite his apparent acceptance of her, there was still a gulf between them, an uneasiness of which they were both aware. It seemed they had nothing to talk about, and the silence grew long and painful. The one thing she yearned most to ask, she dared not. She was uncertain as to how far she could go without risking the little she had won. But had she won *anything*? There was a nagging suspicion that her kiss, rather than drawing him closer to her, had instead triggered painful memories of his dead wife. Even now, as he sat beside her, she feared that he was retreating into those dim, lonesome corridors of the past, seeking to sustain a memory of that which was lost to him.

"I reckon we'd best mount up and finish our nighthawkin'," he said.

The interlude was over, and after the prolonged silence, his words had startled her. She felt let down, unsatisfied, but what had she expected of him? He got up and took her hands, helping her to her feet. The movement seemed to have brought him back to her, and her heart leaped at his reluctance to let her go. Suddenly he drew her to him and took her breath away with a hard kiss. When he spoke, it was almost a whisper in her ear.

"You're a beautiful woman, Rebecca Nance; you'll take some gettin' used to."

The darkness hid her smile. And her tears.

Dawn broke with a patch of blue sky overhead and ominous gray clouds bumping shoulders from horizon to horizon. Sunrise was limited to a faint pink glow in the east, while a west wind brought the unmistakable feel of rain.

"I purely don't like them clouds," said Brazos. "That's 'Indian sign'; cloudy all around, and when them clouds meet in the middle, it's Katy-bar-the-door. For sure we'll get wind, rain, thunder, and lightning, and I won't be surprised if there's sleet, snow, and hail throwed in."

"I look for it about midday," said McCaleb. "It's close enough that I'd bed them down and wait it out if we had any kind of shelter, any chance of preventing a stampede. But we're on open range and one place is as good as another. At least we'll have daylight in our favor. We'll move 'em out and hope we find us a canyon before the thunder and lightning starts."

They came upon dry creek beds and buffalo wallows, but nothing suitable to shelter them from the impending storm. At first the rumble of thunder was so distant it was almost imperceptible. As it drew closer, in keeping with the horizon-to-horizon cloud formation, it seemed to come at them from the four corners of the earth. A spectacular golden blaze of lightning sprang to life on the western horizon, zigzagging its way in giant steps to the east before flickering out.

"Might as well bed 'em down," said McCaleb, "and prepare for the worst. Wherever the lightning strikes, look for 'em to run the opposite direction. When they start to run, our only chance is to get ahead of them and turn the leaders, forcing them to circle. Push 'em, from the flank. For God's sake, don't let them overrun you and trap you in the stampede. If your horse goes down, you're done."

McCaleb knew they were in for it when the herd refused to bed down or graze. They just stood there lowing mournfully, waiting for the moment when something set them off. Strangely enough, it wasn't the storm that started them running. Goose had tied a blanket behind his saddle, as he often did, with the idea he might use it to turn the stampeding herd. Making ready, he loosed it. The rising wind caught one end of the colorful blanket and billowed it out. Bawling in terror, the herd lit out.

Goose was nearest the leaders to the north, but they veered southeast, putting Monte Nance closest to the front of the stampede. The others, including McCaleb, were to the rear of it. They lit out, hell-for-leather, but if the herd was turned, it was up to Monte or Goose. Monte had the advantage as the herd swerved toward him. Overconfident, he did the very thing McCaleb had warned against. Pulling his Colt, he rode directly into the path of the charging herd! Lightning struck somewhere close, shaking the earth. Monte's horse reared, stumbled, almost fell. McCaleb heard Rebecca cry out somewhere behind him as the kid was piled out of the saddle a hundred yards ahead of the stampeding herd. His frightened horse was off and running. McCaleb kicked his bay all the harder, fighting the sickening realization that there was nothing he could do except watch it happen. But no! There was the Apache pounding ahead of the herd on the upper side. He had the blanket tied around his middle, trailing behind. He leaned out of the saddle, reins in his teeth, guiding the horse with his knees. He was going to try and grab the kid before the charging herd cut him to ribbons!

But the thundering herd cut a hundred-yard swath,

too wide for Goose to snatch the fallen Monte before they both were lost in a sea of lethal horns and pounding hooves. McCaleb heard his own anguished voice crying out over the fury of the storm and the thunder of the herd. What happened next, none of them ever forgot. Goose reached the kid, but instead of attempting a rescue, loosed the Indian blanket he'd tied about his waist. Even amid the thunder from the heavens and the thunder of the charging herd, McCaleb heard the whooping of the Apache. He held the blanket by two corners and the storm-bred wind did the rest. Slowly but surely, the herd split around the fearful apparition. McCaleb rode wide, firing his Colt and yelling himself hoarse. Old brindle led the half of the herd that had split his way. Seeing him pounding beside her, the brute continued to turn until she was heading in the direction the frightened herd had come. When the herd had split, it had also slowed, allowing Will and Brazos to head the other half.

McCaleb slowed his bay; the thunder had diminished, and although there were brilliant displays of lightning on every horizon, it was no longer striking. The wind was whipping the rain into his face so that it stung like sand. Rebecca trotted her roan up alongside his bay. Her face was chalk-white and he was sure her tears were mixing with the driving rain. The girl slowed her horse and McCaleb looked back. Goose again had the Indian blanket knotted about his waist, and Monte sat behind him. McCaleb reined up and waited for them. They both wore foolish grins, reminding him of a pair of kids who, having barely escaped being victims of their own folly, now expected praise for having survived.

"By God," said McCaleb grimly, "I ought to shoot both of you. Him for starting the stampede, and you for getting caught in it!"

They swallowed their grins and Rebecca glared at him in amazed anger, but he didn't care. He kicked his bay into a lope and followed the now slow-moving herd.

CHAPTER 11

*I*t was a perfectly miserable day. Darkness would come early and be all the more intense because of the storm. Despite their good fortune in turning the herd, they had lost some cows. Come daybreak, McCaleb intended to double back and round them up. With that in mind, as well as their need for shelter, he didn't plan to travel much farther. They followed what had but hours before been a dry creek bed. It now ran bank-full, the brown water rolling on its way to join the Trinity somewhere to the south. McCaleb hoped by following the stream to a higher elevation they might discover some natural bulwark—perhaps a ridge or bluff overhang— that would provide some shelter from the storm.

The perverse mood of the herd seemed inspired by the elements. Cattle normally drifted with a storm, tails to the wind, and driving them into it was so difficult it bordered on the impossible. Constantly they broke away. McCaleb headed one bunch-quitter on the very bank of the creek. The sodden bank crumbled, the bay went down, and McCaleb was piled head first into the dirty brown water. Despite the fact that he had ridden four hours in the cold driving rain, he came out of the creek with his teeth chattering, his hands, face, and ears numb and hurting. He stomped about, trying to restore feeling to his half-frozen body. Brazos loped his horse along the creek, leading McCaleb's bay. He tried to mount, and at first was unable to do it. Gritting his teeth, trembling with exertion and cold, he swung into the saddle.

"We've played out the string," said Brazos. "We got to bed down these critters and find some shelter, if it's nothing but a stand of cottonwoods. We're less than an hour from full dark and there's snow on the way. This creek has to start *somewhere*, and I'm bettin' there's a ridge or shelving rock at its head. I sent Goose to look around."

"Get to the others," said McCaleb through chattering teeth, "and start the herd milling. No sense in pushing them any farther unless there's some hope of shelter. We'll hold them until Goose returns."

McCaleb was all too familiar with the winter storms that blew out of the Texas Panhandle. There was, indeed, a feel of snow in the air, and with such a dramatic drop in temperature, it would likely last until the storm blew itself out. That could take three days. The driving rain changed swiftly to sleet and just as quickly to snow. The ground and the backs of the longhorns wore a coat of white by the time the Indian rode in. Goose held up two fingers and pointed to the west, into the worsening storm.

"Move 'em out!" shouted McCaleb, the wind whipping his voice away.

Each of them had anxiously awaited the Indian's return, and they were already on the move. Once halted, the herd had little desire to resume the drive. Most of them stood with their tails to the storm and would freeze in that position unless forced to move. The men swung doubled lariats against snow-whitened flanks, their cowboy yells seemingly unheard, swallowed up by the howl of the wind. Monte swatted old brindle until the brute, bawling, lunged ahead into the storm. The exertion restored some life to McCaleb's numbed body. He groaned through clenched teeth. What a blessed relief it would be if only he could remove his sodden boots and rub some feeling into his frozen feet! But there was no time. Time was their enemy. Time and the deepening snow . . .

It seemed like an eternity of wind-driven sleet and snow before the shelter they sought loomed ahead of them. The wet-weather stream they had followed was the overflow from a larger, more permanent creek that ran due south along the foot of a ridge. Even in the gloom of twilight and swirling snow, they could see the cottonwoods and willows lining the banks of the creek. They swatted the lagging longhorns all the harder with their lariats, driving them into the protection of the brakes. The ridge, their bulwark against the fury of the storm, seemed to tame the wind. McCaleb breathed a long sigh of relief. It was infinitely more than he'd hoped for!

At one point the creek swung forty feet away from the ridge, ovaling around a flat stone outcropping that was the west bank. High above, like the prow of a sailing ship, was a stone overhang. In the dry, protected area beneath it was the months-old remains of a fire. There were even a few chunks of dry wood, and with a wind-blown accumulation of dried leaves, they soon had a fire of their own. Goose, Monte, Will, and Brazos immediately began searching for more wood. They insisted that McCaleb, having been piled in the creek, remain by the fire. He didn't argue. Rebecca began breaking out the contents of the pack saddle.

"We don't have a dry blanket among us," she said, "or you could get out of those wet clothes. We'll just have to build a big fire, if there's enough dry wood."

"There is," said Monte, returning with a load, "but if there's Comanches, they'll see or smell our fire."

"I don't care," snapped Rebecca. "Let every Comanche in Texas see *and* smell it. We were all half frozen. I'd as soon fight Indians as freeze."

"I'd have to agree with that," said McCaleb. "There's a good stand of trees in this creek bottom, so I reckon it won't be seen. As for the smoke, the force of the wind will scatter it. Some things in life are worth whatever risk is involved. This fire is worth an Indian attack."

The storm continued until almost noon of the following day. They went into the cottonwoods and pines along the creek, spending the morning gathering wood. Even when the storm blew itself out, the next several days would be abysmally cold. Having lived so far to the south, Monte and Rebecca were not prepared. Neither of them had a coat.

"We'll stay here another night," said McCaleb. "New cloud bank in the west. Don't *ever* trust a Texas blue sky when there's clouds building and the wind's cold. Besides, I aim to back-trail to where the herd split at the tag end of the stampede. We lost some cows, and we can use this snow to track them. We'd best recover what we can, while we can. It's a long trail to Colorado, and I reckon we'll lose some stock."

Despite the passing of the storm and patches of blue sky, there was still a cold west wind. McCaleb, Will, and Brazos rode out, back-trailing to where they had broken up the stampede by splitting the herd.

"Just one thing wrong with this idea of yours," said Will. "It's been twenty-four hours since them cows cut and run. You know how they drift with a storm. They may be back on the Trinity by now. And there won't *be* any tracks in the snow unless we trail 'em to the place where the storm passed them. Up to there, the tracks will be snowed over."

"You're right," said McCaleb, "if they drifted with the storm until it died. But even a fool cow gets tired, and I'm counting on them sheltering in some thicket until the snow stopped. From there on, they'll be leaving tracks."

Their search was rewarded and McCaleb shouted triumphantly when they found fourteen of their herd forlornly awaiting salvation or starvation, whichever came first. McCaleb twisted around in his saddle and found the sun had already dipped behind a cloud bank.

"God knows how far we'll have to ride to round up some more," said Brazos, "and there may not *be* any more."

"If these fourteen pilgrims get troublesome," said Will, "we'll be doin' right well if we get 'em back with the rest of the herd before dark."

"I'd have to agree with both of you," said McCaleb. "With our luck, all fourteen of these brutes may be bunch-quitters. We could be until after dark getting them to camp, if we start now. Even if we had the daylight, it wouldn't make any sense to go hunting *more* cows when we're not sure there are more to be found. We'll take what we're sure of and ride. In the morning, I'd say let's make a rough tally and see how close we are to the nine hundred and eighty we started with."

They found that in their absence Monte and Goose had shot a young buck and were broiling venison steaks. Rebecca had heaped hot coals on top of the kettle and they could smell the sourdough biscuits. Coffee bubbled in the blackened pot. It was the only decent camp they'd had since leaving the box canyon near the Trinity.

"This is a beautiful place," said Rebecca. "It saddens me to think we may never pass this way again, that I'm seeing it for the first and last time."

"Aw hell," said Monte callously, "you felt like that when we sneaked out of St. Joe. We nearly starved to death there, and half the town was tryin' to hang the old man."

"It's a shame and disgrace," snapped Rebecca, "to speak ill of the dead. He was your daddy."

"He was also a no-account old scutter who would of been hung for mule rustling if he hadn't run out while the mob was hangin' his brother. Him bein' dead don't change none of that. Them Comanche arrows don't sanctify a man, do they, McCaleb?"

McCaleb had been half listening, enjoying the good food and warm fire. Suddenly everybody's attention was focused on him. Damn the kid for dragging him into a fool situation that might further antagonize the girl!

"I reckon," said McCaleb deliberately, "before he died, your daddy faced up to the poor showing he made in this world. We had our differences, but he died like a man, and I respect him for that."

Right after breakfast Will and Brazos went into the brakes along the creek. Taking separate counts, they tried to decide if they were missing enough cows to justify another search.

"I reckon," said Brazos, "we're within fifteen head of what we started with. That's close enough for me."

"I figure it within twenty head," said Will, "give or take a few."

"It's time to move out, then," said McCaleb.

Despite the continued presence of clouds to the west, the day turned pleasantly warm and the sun made muddy slush of the snow. They crossed the herd at the south end of the ridge and headed them northwest. McCaleb took the point position, again sending Goose to scout the country ahead. He wasn't too surprised when Rebecca trotted her roan alongside his bay. He only hoped *this* visit would be more pleasant than the last, when he had confronted her with her deceit and lies.

She spoke. "The cows look terribly thin, don't they? You can see their ribs."

"You're seeing the effects of the snow. They haven't grazed since the day before the stampede. Horses will paw through the snow to get at the grass underneath. Cows won't. Cover the grass with snow and a cow will stand there and starve to death. I've sent Goose to find water, but we'd be better off in a dry camp tonight, if there's good graze for the herd."

"McCaleb?"

He allowed himself a cautious look at her from the corner of his eye. She wore that strange little smile that always bothered him.

"Thank you for last night, McCaleb. It was kind of you to say what you did. Monte looks up to you, despite the way he acts and talks. What you said to him after the stampede, that cut him deep."

"I aimed for it to," said McCaleb. "I don't praise a man after he's done the very damn thing I've warned him *not* to do. A rider trapped in a stampede on the Shawnee wasn't so lucky. Do you know what was left of him? They found his Colt and the heel from one of his boots."

She shuddered. What he had said was all the more frightening because he had stated it matter-of-factly, without anger.

"You were right, then," she said, "but don't you think you were a little unfair to Goose? Even if he didn't understand your words, the meaning got through to him. We owe him so much. The herd was going to run; it was just his bad luck the wind took hold of the blanket and finished what thunder and lightning had started."

This time he looked directly at her. He was silent for so long, she was afraid he wasn't going to respond. Still she saw no anger in his eyes; only what might have been tired resignation. Finally he spoke. Quietly.

"I was hard on Goose for the same reason I was tough on Monte. I care what happens to them. While the rest of you were crowing because they came out of it alive, I was thinking of what *might* have happened. Suppose the herd hadn't turned, had just kept running? I reckon I had my mind on those unmarked graves we might have left behind us on the prairie. It's almighty hard staying alive when you do everything *right*, without making fool mistakes that can get you killed. I didn't want either of them forgetting that."

The Indian's scouting expedition took longer than usual, and when he returned, he had a surprise for them.

"Fish!" cried Rebecca. "Fish for supper!"

Goose grinned at everybody, even McCaleb. They had no idea how he'd caught them. There was a dozen or more, strung on a rawhide thong, and he presented them to the girl. Goose led them to a grassy knoll where the snow had been burned away by an enthusiastic sun, providing graze for the herd. Just as McCaleb had hoped, normally dry water holes and streams were full as a result of the storm, so water was plentiful. He estimated they'd covered ten miles. They spent a pleasant hour around the supper fire, drinking hot coffee and eating broiled trout.

"We'll be in Waco in another week," said McCaleb, "if nothing *else* goes wrong. Will, what day is this?"

Will Elliot had kept track of the days and months by tying knots in a piggin string. Each week ended with a double knot representing Sunday. He retired a string at the end of the month, starting a new one.

"This is February twenty-first," he said.

While at night there were faraway signs of lightning, there were no more storms or stampedes. On the seventh day they bedded the herd on the east bank of the Brazos River, a few miles south of Waco. They were near their appointed rendezvous point with Goodnight and his cattle. At a low point in the river—a crossing—they found tracks of unshod horses. Goose hunkered down and studied them.

"*Indios*," he said, looking at McCaleb. "*Muchos Indios.*"

"Maybe it's just a herd of wild horses," said Rebecca hopefully.

Goose looked at her pityingly, as though he understood her words. He shook his head. With his left hand he pointed toward the setting sun; he fisted his right hand and then held up two fingers.

"These horses had riders," said McCaleb. "Depth of the hoofprints says that. Unshod horses tells us they're Indians. Goose says the tracks are two days old. Twenty or more riders. I reckon that's bad news for somebody. We'll continue our night watch, two riders in three-hour shifts. Still an hour of daylight; I'd feel better knowing which way that bunch is riding."

He pointed to Goose, to the tracks, and then across the river, where the two-day old trail led. The Indian nodded, took his Spencer and waded across the waist-deep Brazos. Sunset was near; with darkness approaching, it would be a short trail, easier followed afoot. His nose to the ground like a hunting wolf, the Apache was soon out of sight.

They kept their supper fire small, concealing it in a fire pit. There was no wind, and the branches of the cottonwoods that lined the Brazos would dissipate the smoke. Goose didn't return until after dark, and he brought bad news.

"*Comanch' bastardos,*" said the Indian. "*Matar.*" He pointed due west, then held up three fingers.

"*Muerto?*" questioned McCaleb, holding up three fingers.

"*Muerto,*" repeated Goose.

Realizing his limited Spanish was inadequate, the Indian hunkered down and brushed away the dead leaves. Pointing to the river, he then drew a line representing it. He drew a square a short distance from the west bank of the Brazos, and within the square made three side-by-side vertical marks. From the square he drew a line back to and across the river, representing the trail he had followed.

"*Casa,*" he said, pointing to the square he'd drawn.

"*Muerto en casa?*" asked McCaleb, holding up three fingers.

The Indian nodded. He then drew a series of lines fanning out from the square, pointing west. He again held up two fingers.

"Three dead," said McCaleb, "not more than two or three miles west of here. Happened just a little while after they crossed the river. Goose says two-day old tracks lead away from the house, to the west."

"Some of us will be riding over there in the morning, then," said Will. "They'll need burying."

"Yes," said McCaleb, "it's the least we can do. We'll lose another day, but those poor souls likely have kin somewhere who need to be notified. We can take the news to Waco. It's the nearest town; somebody there's bound to know them or know of them."

It was a grisly scene. They found the bodies of the man and his wife in the three-room cabin. Their son—in his teens—lay on the ground outside, near the front steps. They had all been scalped and mutilated. The men's privates had been cut off and stuffed in their mouths. The woman's breasts had been hacked off and a stake, made from the splintered leg of a kitchen chair, had been driven through her lower belly. The three of them, naked and mutilated, were bloated horribly. The boy had been further mutilated by coyotes or wolves, the flesh having been torn from his arms and legs. The stink was unbearable. With bandannas over their noses and mouths, the men threw feed-sack sheets and threadbare blankets over the bodies. Each was rolled in bedclothes, like a cocoon, and one at a time the macabre bundles were lowered into their graves.

McCaleb left Will and Brazos to fill in the graves while he searched the cabin. Going through the family's meager possessions, he found little that would be helpful in reaching their next of kin. There was only an old letter with an Ohio postmark. Will and Brazos returned to the house. Will swung open the sagging back door and beckoned to McCaleb. The bushes and brush behind the cabin were startlingly white, like they'd been through a snowstorm. Feathers! Thousands, maybe millions, of white feathers!

"Fool Comanches ripped the feather beds open," said Will. "They even hauled the poor woman's home-canned goods out there and busted every jar."

"This kind of thing," said Brazos, "makes me want to give up hunting cows and go hunting Comanches. I'd like to track down every one of the murdering sons and roast them alive over a slow fire."

"We may be tangling with them before we reach the Pecos," said McCaleb. "When they rode out of here, they headed west. Once we join Goodnight, we will be taking the trail west. I found very little to identify these folks. Not a sign of a weapon; not even a pocket knife. There's nothing more we can do except take the news to Waco. Let's ride."

Before the trees hid it, they paused, looking back at the desolate little cabin. Nobody spoke. It was something each of them had experienced before, but it never got any easier.

It was dusky dark when they bedded down the herd just south of Waco. The sun had set red behind a cloud bank, and the wind blew cold from the north, bringing to them the persistent yipping of a dog. Except for the Indian, they all relaxed. Goose seemed more apprehensive than ever. Was it the proximity of town, of people, or was it something else? McCaleb watched and wondered. They would approach the town cautiously.

"In the morning," he said, "will be soon enough to ride into Waco. Three of us will ride in and three will stay with the herd. Will, I want you with me; you spent some time here before joining the Rangers. Might be some folks here who'll remember you."

"I hope one of 'em ain't the sheriff," said Will. "He's likely to lock me in the *juzgado* on general principles."

"Take Rebecca with you," said Brazos. "She's been doing the cooking, and if there's anything to be had, let her choose. Includin' the two hundred we took from the Baker gang, we got better than three hundred dollars in gold coin."

"Hard as the war's been on everybody," said McCaleb, "I doubt we'll find anything to buy, even with gold. Times being what they are, we'd best keep that gold out of sight for a while."

McCaleb, Will, and Rebecca rode into Waco when the sun was an hour high. It was an unimposing little town strung out along the Brazos River. The first buildings they came to—log huts—had been boarded up.

"The jail's at the other end of the street," said Will. "Can't see it from here. Street kind of follows the curve of the river. The old storekeeper Daugherty might remember me; he knew my pa."

The store was a big, square slab-sided building whose false front had once been painted white. The paint had peeled, taking with it most of the once-imposing black foot-high letters that had spelled "Daugherty and Sons." An old hound lay under the roof overhang that served as a porch. He opened one eye as though considering announcing their arrival, decided they weren't worth the effort, and stayed where he was.

The old man sat in a rocking chair by a potbellied stove. His spittoon was a gallon bucket, and the brown splotches on the floor were mute testimony to his inaccuracy. He showed no surprise, greeting Will as though only days had elapsed since they had last met.

"Howdy, Will. Been ten year since I seen you. Your mammy and pappy still livin' up t' Mineral Wells?"

"Yeah," said Will. "How're things with you, Virg?"

"Gone to hell in a hand basket. Lost both m' boys in the war. Nothin' keepin' me here, 'cept I'm too damn old an' stove-up t' ride out."

The nearly bare shelves attested to the truth of what he had said. His pitifully small supply of merchandise was either homemade or home-grown.

"Virg," said Will, "this is Benton McCaleb and Rebecca Nance. We have near 'bouts a thousand longhorns from the Trinity River brakes. We're going to Fort Belknap and from there to Colorado Territory, with Charlie Goodnight. We're almighty short on supplies, especially ammunition."

"Wisht I could he'p you, Will. Most of all, by God, wisht I was able t' saddle up an' ride alongside ye. Cain't offer you nothin' 'cept some good advice. Git away from here quiet as you can, take them cows an' cut a wide swath around this town. We got our own deetachment of blue-bellies. The tall hog at the trough is a second lieutenant named Sandoval. Besides him, there's a sergeant an' five privates. But that ain't the worst of it. We got us a bran' new *appointed* sheriff."

"That's terrible!" said Rebecca. "Can they *do* that?"

Daugherty seemed to notice Rebecca for the first time. He combed his fingers through his thinning gray hair and shifted his tobacco to his other cheek. He spat, missed the can, and then he spoke.

"They can an' they have. Some Federal judge made th' appointment. What does *he* know, sittin' on his fat haunches in New Orleans?"

"Who *is* this appointed sheriff?" questioned McCaleb.

The old man again shifted his cud of tobacco, fired a stream at the can and missed. Then he turned to McCaleb.

"He's a no-account, whiskey-soaked son of a bitch— beggin' your pardon, ma'am—named Shag Oliver. He's so poison-mean he'd kill a dog just to see it die. Compared to him, the soldiers ain't half bad. Was him I had in mind when I said you ought to of took your herd an' moved on."

"We've met," said McCaleb, "and from your description, if he's changed, it's for the worse. Unfortunately, we have some information that'll have to be turned over to him if he's sheriff, appointed or not. I reckon a dozen miles south, maybe two miles west of the Brazos, we buried a man, his wife, and their son. Comanche killings."

"That'd be the Mathisons. They was a standoffish family. He was right good at findin' an' cuttin' bee trees. Brung in a dozen quarts of wild honey onct, an' I traded him out of it. Still got three fourths of it."

"I reckon we've avoided him as long as we can," said Will. "His highness is headin' this way."

Shag Oliver had changed very little, except for the gap where McCaleb had removed three of his upper teeth, and the size of his ponderous belly, which now seemed bigger than ever. He came stomping in, his little pig eyes glittering in fiendish anticipation.

"Well, now, if it ain't Mr. High-and-Mighty himself," said Oliver with a smirk. "Got me a score to settle with you. Downright obligin' of you to show up, seein' as how I got a nice empty jail waitin' fer you."

He struck what he considered a threatening pose, his hand on the butt of his Colt. McCaleb made no move. He spoke quietly, calmly.

"Oliver—"

"That's *Sheriff* Oliver to you!"

"Oliver," said McCaleb deliberately, "yesterday, a dozen miles downriver, we buried a family killed by Indians. Mr. Daugherty tells us they were the Mathisons. This old letter is the only thing we found that might help locate their next of kin."

Oliver snatched the letter from McCaleb's hand. Swiftly he drew and cocked his Colt.

"Indians, huh? How do I know you didn't kill 'em yourself? I reckon I'll lock the three of you in the hoose-gow till I figger what I can charge you with. Git going!"

"Sheriff," said Virg Daugherty, "you can't jail a lady."

"Haw, haw," chortled Oliver, "an' why not? What's jail to some saloon slut—"

Until the day he died, Virg Daugherty never tired of telling about the day when Benton McCaleb bested an outlaw sheriff who had the drop. McCaleb's left hand drove Shag Oliver's gun hand toward the ceiling and the Colt sent a slug harmlessly through the roof. McCaleb then snatched his own Colt from its butt-forward position on his left hip, and with all his strength laid its barrel just above Oliver's left ear. The blow would have felled a full-grown grizzly. The building shook and the stove pipe jumped loose where it had joined the potbellied stove. Shag Oliver lay flat on his back. The hound on the porch, startled out of his slumber, began to bay. Soot from the disconnected stove pipe began to sift down and Rebecca sneezed.

"I reckon," said Will, "we might as well get back to

the herd. Sooner or later we'll have to kill this jaybird. But if he's the Union army's pet coon—"

"Don't blame *that* on us. We had nothing to do with his appointment."

The young second lieutenant stood in the open door, the inquisitive old hound behind him.

"I'm Lieutenant Martin Sandoval. I believe I'm due an explanation."

McCaleb again recounted, as briefly as he could, their burying the murdered Mathison family. He told of Oliver's unfounded accusation, of the threat of jail, and finally, the insult to Rebecca.

"You did nothing to provoke him, then," said Sandoval.

"Not today," said McCaleb. "Four years ago I stopped him from beating a horse. He promised the next time we met, he'd kill me. This was the next time. I had no idea he was here. We're driving a herd of longhorns north and had hoped to replenish our supplies here."

Shag Oliver sat up, blinking his eyes. His hand went to his holster, and finding it empty, he began looking furtively around, seeking the missing weapon. Lieutenant Sandoval spied the fallen Colt, retrieved it and stuck it under his belt.

"Damn you," bawled Oliver, "gimme that pistol! I'll gut-shoot that bastard if it's the last thing I ever do!"

"Then I'll personally *see* that it's the last thing you ever do," snapped Sandoval. "I'm in charge here. My commander-in-chief is the president of the United States. He outranks the Federal judge that appointed you. I'll have no more trouble!"

"They're Rebs!" snarled Oliver. "Th' law says they ain't even supposed to have guns. Mebbe I'll turn you in, kid, fer not doin' yer duty."

"That's not fair!" cried Rebecca. "If the government takes our guns, we'll be at the mercy of every murdering Indian and outlaw in Texas! You won't do that . . . will you?"

"He's right about that," said Sandoval. "The Reconstruction Act of 1865 authorizes me to confiscate weapons."

"You ain't even in the United States," growled Oliver, "an' mebbe we won't never let you back in. Them cows ain't gonna do you no good if you can't get 'em out of Texas. Johnny Rebs can't leave th' state. Tell 'em, sojer boy!"

"No," said Sandoval, "I'm going to tell *you* something, mister. It was Mr. Lincoln's dream that the Union would again be one nation, and it *will* be. He wanted to build, not destroy. Legally, we *can* confiscate your arms and confine you to the state during the period of reconstruction, but you can get around both these restrictions with one simple act."

"I reckon," said McCaleb, "you're going to tell us what that is."

"I am," said Sandoval. "You must take an oath—in writing—that you will never again take up arms against the United States of America."

"We never done that in the first place," said Will. "We was fightin' Comanches and outlaws on the north Texas border."

"Nevertheless," said Sandoval, "Texas *did* secede and take up arms. You are Texans, so you'll have to take the oath. I'm headquartered at the jail. I'll join you there shortly, and the three of you can sign. Then return to your herd, and have the rest of your riders come in and sign. When you've done that, take your herd and move out. I want no more trouble."

"Take a couple of quarts of wild honey with you," said Virg Daugherty.

Sandoval didn't follow them immediately. McCaleb reckoned Shag Oliver was just low-down enough to grab a rifle and shoot him in the back, and he suspected Lieutenant Sandoval had the same opinion of the "sheriff."

When McCaleb, Will, and Rebecca returned to the herd, Brazos, Monte, and Goose rode in to take the oath.

The Apache was allowed to sign with an "X", and Sandoval witnessed it.

They crossed the herd to the west bank of the Brazos, bypassing Waco. Scarcely three miles north of town they found more Indian sign, just hours old. More than fifty unshod horses had crossed the river, heading east. It was still early afternoon, but McCaleb halted the drive. With *that* damn many Indians in a bunch, all of them obviously of one mind, you could bet your last pair of clean socks they planned to raise some hell.

"Still two hours till dark," said Brazos.

"I know it," said McCaleb, "but I want Goose to trail that bunch. If they keep riding east, fine. But they could swing wide, double back to the south and come at us from behind. Or they could ride a day to the north and be lying there waiting for us. I don't like Indian surprises. They always end up being the hair-raising kind."

Goose didn't return until almost sundown, so they bedded down the herd for the night. The wind was from the south, and they were still near enough to Waco to hear the yipping of the town dogs. Goose hunkered down and drew his familiar map. One long line represented the Brazos, while a circle on the east side marked the town. Then east of Waco, paralleling the river, he drew many lines which passed the town and continued south.

"*Comanch'*," he said. "*Muchos.*"

"They can't be doubling back after us," said Will, "or they'd have cut back toward the river between here and Waco. What do you make of that?"

"Wouldn't bet my saddle," said McCaleb, "but I have a strong hunch. It's three-hour watches, two riders at a time. When you *do* roll in your blankets, picket your horses and leave them saddled."

"Sandoval and his boys may have a fight on their hands," said Brazos.

"It's not *our* fight," said Rebecca. "They ran us out. Besides, we're low on ammunition ourselves."

"Sandoval was decent to us," said McCaleb grimly,

"and if he needs help, then I aim to do what I can. We saw what was left of that Mathison family. Knowing what the Comanches do to white women, I won't allow it to happen without a fight. If you don't think it's our fight, then think awhile on this: there are fifty or more warriors in this band. If they're able to buffalo the town, they'll come after us."

Supper was eaten in silence.

"First watch," said McCaleb. "Who wants it?"

"Me and Goose," said Monte.

"Then I reckon me and Brazos will take the second," said Will.

"I don't like the third watch," said Rebecca sullenly.

"Then sleep," said McCaleb. "I can handle it alone."

When Will woke McCaleb for the third watch, McCaleb was amused to find that the girl was up, had gone after her roan, and had brought his bay as well.

"I thought you didn't like the third watch."

"Shut up, McCaleb. Just *shut* up!"

In silence, for what McCaleb judged was an hour, they circled the herd in opposite directions. Finally, at the point where they met, she spoke.

"McCaleb."

He acknowledged her query by reining up, but said nothing. He could see her pale face in the starlight.

"I suppose you think I inherited my daddy's selfishness," she said.

"No," said McCaleb, "I think you're ornery enough to cultivate some of your own. I'm wondering how long it'll take you to grow up enough to quit blamin' your daddy for all your bad habits."

Damn it, if she was looking for an excuse to fight, he'd give her one! She sighed, perhaps in exasperation, and then she laughed.

"I'm torn between admiring you and hating you," she said. "It does me no good to become angry with you, because you don't *really* care. Do you?"

"No," said McCaleb. "You can be angry and *still* be a

lady. But not if you cuss and fight like a bobcat. If you *ever* cuss me again, I'll take the quirt to your backside."

She laughed and reached for him. He leaned out of his saddle and met her halfway. . . .

CHAPTER 12

$\mathcal{W}$ith the first hint of approaching dawn, the eastern horizon had gone from gray to pale rose. Rebecca had the breakfast fire going. McCaleb and the others had unsaddled the picketed horses, allowing the animals to roll. They would rope new mounts from their remuda for the day's drive. The wind had shifted, coming out of the west, so they almost didn't hear the shots. Goose heard them first. He pointed to the south.

"*Comanch' bastardos. Matar.*"

McCaleb held up his hand for silence. Then, sounding faint and far away, they heard the ominous crack of rifles.

"Rope me a fresh horse," said Rebecca. "I'm riding with the rest of you."

"Rifles fully loaded," said McCaleb. "Brazos, keep a rein on Goose until we're close by. If they've surrounded the town, where we hit them won't make much difference, but if they're attacking from the south, we can circle around and catch them in a cross-fire. Let's ride!"

McCaleb led them down the west bank of the Brazos, halting less than a mile north of the besieged town. He pointed to Goose, then toward the sound of shooting.

"*Comanch',*" said McCaleb. "*Paradero. Muy pronto.*"

Goose nodded his understanding. Taking his Spencer, he dismounted and quickly disappeared into the brush along the river. The rifles had momentarily gone silent, but suddenly there was a new burst of firing.

"Soldier rifles," said Brazos. "These war whoops may be all bows and arrows."

"Won't it be better for us," asked Rebecca, "if they don't have rifles?"

"Not necessarily," said Will. "Them Comanches can nock and loose an arrow about as quick as I can cock and fire a rifle. Most of them are god-awful accurate."

From his saddlebag McCaleb took a slender parcel, unwrapping the oilskin to reveal the last two sticks of the Baker gang's dynamite. With his bowie, he nipped off two thirds of the fuse from each of the sticks.

"Less than ten seconds left," he said. "This was bad medicine to the Comanches before; maybe it can be again."

Goose returned with disturbing news. His quick drawing indicated that although the Comanches had attacked from the south, part of their force had been deployed to the east and west in a horseshoe pattern.

"Fire and brimstone," snorted Brazos, "why didn't they split the band into quarters and just *surround* the town?"

"Because the soldiers are camped at the north end of town near the jail," said McCaleb. "They've crept in on the three unprotected sides, using the buildings for cover. Soon as Sandoval and his boys are concentrating their fire on Indians they *can* see, some of those from the flanks will slip into the brush and launch a surprise attack from the north."

"Dear God," cried Rebecca, "there's so few of us; what can we do?"

"Hit them with a surprise attack of our own," said McCaleb. "I reckon we'll have just about enough time to move in *behind* these flankers as they begin to sneak in from the north. We can cut them down before they know what's hit them, if we play our cards right."

Brazos fed the instructions to Goose with a series of quick drawings in the sand. He drew lines to indicate movement of the Comanches from east and west flanks to create an attacking force from the north. He then pointed to Goose, to himself, and to each of the others, drawing a series of lines taking them behind the Comanches advancing from the north. He looked at Goose and the Indian nodded. Brazos brought his Henry into firing position and simulated the firing of it. He then pointed to Goose, to himself, and to each of the others, drawing six lines *away* from the scene of the attack, to the north.

"*Comanch' bastardos*," grunted Goose. "*Matar*." He understood.

"We advance together and retreat together," said McCaleb. "Let's go."

McCaleb was tense. Would the Comanches split their forces, expecting to converge on the soldiers from the north? Common sense told him the Indians would send a few of their number from the band to the east of town and a few from the force to the west, creating a fourth attacking force from the north. McCaleb and his outfit had only to wait until this band had gathered, and to fall in behind them. With Sandoval's soldiers ahead of them and McCaleb's outfit behind them, the Comanches would be caught in a cross-fire. It might well eliminate a fourth of the attackers without risk to the defenders. Goose raised his hand and they halted, waiting. The Apache pointed west. They hunkered down in a thicket, watching seven Comanches advancing eastward in a stealthy line.

"My God," whispered Will, "if there's seven more coming from the east flank, that means there's maybe sixty in the band."

It was poor odds. Once the seven had advanced past their position, Goose led them carefully ahead. Again Goose raised his hand, halting them. Silently, swiftly, the seven Comanches from the east flank appeared, joining their comrades from the west.

"Fourteen of them," said Brazos, "and they'll move

fast. We'll have to hustle if we're leavin' ourselves room to retreat."

"Come on, then," said McCaleb. "Let's not lose sight of one another. See that scrub oak thicket ahead? Once they pass through it, we'll use it for cover. Fire when I do. Keep firing until they're all down."

McCaleb's outfit moved into the thicket as their quarry left it.

"Now," said McCaleb, "while they're without cover, cut them down!"

Six Comanches fell with the first volley and five with the second. The twelfth, wounded, tried to crawl away; Will fired once and the brave didn't move again. The last two had fled toward the town, vanishing into the nearest concealing brush. Goose was already after them.

"*Retirada*, Goose," shouted Brazos. "*Retirada!*"

But there would be no retreat. Monte Nance went down with a Comanche arrow in his side. There was a yelp of terror from Rebecca. *Behind them*—God alone knew how many—was yet *another* party of Comanches!

"Move ahead," shouted McCaleb. "It's our only chance!"

Rebecca helped the wounded Monte as best she could. Goose looked back and Brazos waved him on. Then, as though on command, he and Will dropped back to join McCaleb. Each of them had a sixteen-shot Henry, and they would try to buy enough time for the others to reach Sandoval's position in or near the jail. By now, McCaleb suspected, the Comanches had begun flanking movements. By falling back, the trio had greatly increased their danger of finding Comanches before and behind them. Rebecca screamed. A hundred yards ahead Goose was locked in a fight to the death with one of the Comanches who had escaped their attack. Knives flashed in the early morning sun as the combatants circled, each seeking an advantage. With a spiteful bark, Rebecca's .31 Colt spoke and a second Comanche staggered to his feet behind Goose. He lunged at the Apache's back and coolly the girl fired again. The

Indian fell and lay still. Goose had a bloody knife slash across his bare torso and some lesser cuts on his brawny upper arms. There was no more time for hand-to-hand fighting. Just as McCaleb was about to shoot the Comanche, Goose made his death thrust. Despite their predicament, the Apache took time to scalp his victim.

"Go on!" shouted McCaleb.

The Comanches closing in from behind had drawn closer. One arrow whipped through McCaleb's shirt-sleeve, ripping the flesh above his left elbow. A second one whispered past his ear. McCaleb, Will, and Brazos continued to advance, pausing to fire at their pursuers. Suddenly a rifle slug thunked into a cottonwood trunk above McCaleb's head. In quick succession there were two more shots.

"Sandoval," shouted McCaleb, "hold your fire! We're coming in!"

There was no vocal response, but McCaleb received his answer. While the firing continued unabated, none was directed at them. Goose, Rebecca, and Monte were far ahead and had vanished into a dense thicket of young pines.

"Come on," said McCaleb. "We're close enough to make a run for it!"

They ceased firing and ran for the sheltering thicket, a shower of arrows falling around them. They caught up to Goose, Rebecca, and Monte just as the trio emerged from the thicket. Thirty yards away was the rear of a squat adobe building. On each side of a heavy oak door was a barred window, and from each window protruded the muzzle of a rifle. The first voice they heard belonged to one of the riflemen behind a barred window.

"Halt and identify yourselves. If that savage is your prisoner, why is he armed?"

"He's Apache," said McCaleb, "and part of my outfit. Lieutenant Sandoval knows me; get him."

"Hello, McCaleb," said Sandoval. The heavy oak door swung open.

"Don't know how many are chasing us," said McCaleb. "We ambushed a war party sneakin' up on you, but when we tried to retreat, there was another bunch right behind us. Left us no choice except to join you. One man's been hit; don't know how bad."

"Come on in," said Sandoval. "Private Hardesty is a medic."

Rebecca led Monte in first. Goose refused to enter the building. He held the Spencer over his head and pointed back in the direction they had come.

"*Comanch' bastardos. Matar.*"

"I'll stay with him," said Brazos. "With that thicket so close to hide 'em, four of us won't be a bit too many."

That was gospel. That thicket, providing abundant cover to within a few yards of the jail, worried McCaleb too. Put enough Comanches out there, and half the Union army couldn't root them out. Up till now Sandoval's small force hadn't had to defend the vulnerable rear of the jail, but that was about to change. The jail had four cells and an outer office that boasted a battered desk and half a dozen ladder-backed, cane-bottomed chairs. McCaleb wasn't surprised to find only Sandoval's sergeant and all five of his privates defending the jail. It would be impossible to defend the entire town, with it strung out along a single street that meandered along the river. Suddenly there was a burst of fire somewhere to the south of them. McCaleb looked at Sandoval.

"They took us totally by surprise," said the lieutenant. "There's only a few townsmen; it was their firing that alerted us. I sent three men to investigate and they were driven back. Best we can tell, everybody else is forted up in Virgil Daugherty's store. The devils have taken over some of the unoccupied buildings. See that old saloon building out there with the high false front? They're on the roof, and any man stepping out that front door takes his life in his hands. We have the worst position in town, with the jail at the very end of the street, and woods on both sides and behind us. In front, as I've already told you, is that false-fronted building with God knows *how* many of them camped on the roof."

There was a window on each side of the heavy oak door. The oiled paper that had covered them had been cut to ribbons.

"We can't remove the woods," said McCaleb, "but we *can* eliminate that old building they're roosting on."

"I've thought of that. I'm planning to fire it after dark."

"You don't *have* until dark, Sandoval. Where's that *appointed* sheriff?"

"He bunks in a cabin at the other end of town. It's possible he's dead."

"I doubt it," said Will. "Our luck's been lousy all day; why should it improve now?"

"He's sheriff," said McCaleb, "and we need every man who can fire a gun. Even Shag Oliver. His place is here at the jail."

"Couldn't none of us stand the bastard," said Private Hardesty.

"That will be enough, Private," said Sandoval.

Will grinned. Hardesty said nothing but continued cleansing Monte's wound. Monte, his shirt off, lay belly down on the desk. The arrow had left an angry bloody wound where it had gone in. It had then struck a rib, tearing its way out of the flesh, leaving an equally bloody gash. It was serious enough but had missed his vitals. Whatever else went wrong, thought McCaleb, at least the kid had medicine and medical attention.

Sandoval spoke. "Then you don't believe we can make it until dark?"

"No," said McCaleb. "Do *you*?"

He sighed. "No. They'll overrun us. The Alamo was under siege for thirteen days. Without a miracle, we won't last thirteen *hours*."

Ridding themselves of the Comanches lurking behind the roof parapets of the abandoned saloon wouldn't solve all their problems, but they had to begin some-where. McCaleb turned to Sandoval.

"Put two riflemen at each window to cover me. I'm going out there and flatten that buzzard perch."

McCaleb unbuttoned his shirt, removing the two sticks of oilskin-wrapped, capped, and fused dynamite. He ripped off a strip of the oilskin, using it to bind the two sticks of explosive together. He twisted the two short lengths of fuse together, tying them tight with another strip of oilskin.

"I reckon this will bring the building down," said McCaleb, "and when it does, cut down on any of them that come out of it alive. In fact, Sandoval, leave my two men to cover the rear of the building, and station all your men with rifles at the windows. Rebecca, when that building comes down, swing the door open. You men cut them down; don't let any of them out of there alive."

Sandoval brought the two soldiers who had been stationed at the rear of the jail. Briefly, McCaleb told them what he planned to do.

McCaleb clenched his teeth on the stems of half a dozen sulfur matches. He judged the old saloon was maybe sixty or seventy yards away. The closer he got to it, the more difficult for the defenders on the roof to loose their arrows at him without revealing themselves to the men who would be covering him. He took a deep breath and opened the big oak door just enough to squeeze through. Clutching the dynamite in his left hand, he lit out in a zigzagging run. Behind him the rifles roared. An arrow cut through his Levi's just below the knee, falling away when it struck the leather of his boot top. Ahead of him the body of a Comanche toppled from the roof, crashing into the dust with a thud.

Twenty yards. Thirty. Forty. Fifty! He drew up to the building and whipped a match against the rough fabric of his Levi's. Nothing! His second and third attempts were similar failures. Had his matches gotten wet through their oilskin pouch? Two Comanche arrows thudded into the dirt at his feet. His fourth and fifth matches failed. With his heart in his throat he tried the last one. With a sputter it caught, almost died, then leaped to life. He touched it to the dynamite fuse, and when the sparks told him it had caught, he flung the explosives in an arc that would drop them on the roof of the old saloon. Then he ran toward the rear of the building, but away from it, taking himself out of the line of fire when the structure came down and the riflemen began shooting the survivors.

When the dynamite blew, he couldn't resist turning to witness the result of his handiwork. The old saloon came down in a clatter, dust rising like smoke in the morning sky. From the jail the firing continued, and he hoped, despite the dust, they were finding some targets. He shied away from the front of the jail, approaching it from the east side. Suddenly from the brush came a deluge of arrows. Two of them came close enough that he felt the wind of their passing. He drew his Colt and fired three quick shots into the brush. Drawn by the roar of rifles and the explosion, Brazos and Goose saw his predicament and opened up with their rifles. With their fire covering him, he made his way around to the rear of the adobe jail.

The firing from the jail ceased. Inside, the main room in front reeked of powder smoke.

"McCaleb," said Sandoval, "that was as neat a maneuver as I've ever seen. I don't suppose you have more dynamite?"

"No," said McCaleb. "But the Comanches don't know that. They won't know what hit them, and they'll take what just happened as bad medicine. They'll learn from their mistakes, and I doubt we'll find them using these buildings for cover; especially the rooftops. Any idea how many we just took out of the fight?"

"Six," said Sandoval, "including the one that was shot off the roof before you threw the dynamite. There might be others who didn't survive the blast."

"I doubt it," said McCaleb. "Six of them could have pinned you down until dark and overrun your position. Have you fought Indians before?"

"No. I saw action with Sherman at Atlanta. What do these savages *want*, McCaleb?"

Will Elliot stepped away into the corridor and headed for the back door, lest the Union soldiers witness his look of extreme disgust. Monte and Rebecca eyed McCaleb. It was a moment before he trusted himself to speak.

"They want your horses, your weapons, and your hair, Lieutenant. Don't take it personal; they hate all white men. Texans have been fightin' them a century before we ever heard of Santa Ana. Welcome to the party."

"I won't be intimidated," said Sandoval. "While they are demoralized, I'll take some men and—"

"Get your gizzard shot full of arrows," said McCaleb. "There is no such thing as a demoralized Comanche, Sandoval; just one more cautious. And dangerous."

"I'm in command here," snapped Sandoval angrily. "I—"

He was interrupted by a burst of fire from the rear of the jail. With a startled cry, Private Hardesty went down, an arrow through his shoulder. McCaleb swept Rebecca to the floor, drew his Colt and dropped beside her. Despite his wound, Monte crouched behind the battered desk, his Colt ready. Three more arrows whipped through the tattered remnants of oiled paper that had covered the front windows. McCaleb fired twice and there was a roar behind him as the soldiers opened up with rifles. The attack ended as suddenly as it had begun. Beneath Sandoval's left ear, an arrow had cut an angry gash. The wound bled profusely, soaking the front of his blue tunic. Ignoring his own wound, the lieutenant turned to the fallen Hardesty.

"Kenton," he snapped, "you and Dennis get Private Hardesty into one of the cells and see to his wound." He then turned to McCaleb, who said nothing, reloading his Colt from his diminishing supply of cartridges.

"We got another one!" shouted Monte.

"We picked off two more," said Will, emerging from the cell corridor, "but Brazos is hit."

"Bad?" inquired McCaleb.

"Damn bad," said Will. "Help me bring him in."

"Where's Goose?"

"He's gone into the brush after the bastard that cut down Brazos."

"McCaleb," said Lieutenant Sandoval, "I—"

But McCaleb was gone. He had followed Will into the cell corridor and out the back door. Brazos lay on his back, eyes closed, teeth gritted. McCaleb caught his breath. The arrow had gone in just under the breastbone. Hunkering down, he listened to Brazos's breathing, praying there would be no telltale bubbling sound and no bloody froth on his lips. God, if it had pierced a lung . . .

Gently as they could, they carried Brazos into one of the empty rear cells and placed him on a hard bunk. Silently they removed their hats and stood looking down at their friend. White-faced, Monte stared through the bars. Behind him, unashamed, Rebecca wept. Brazos opened his eyes.

"Hurts like . . . nine shades of . . . Hell. Will it . . . come . . . out?"

"It'll have to," said McCaleb.

"You and Will," said Brazos. "Not them."

"They won't touch you," said McCaleb, "but they have medicine. Maybe some laudanum. I'm going to find out."

There was a shriek of pain from the wounded Hardesty. McCaleb found privates Kenton and Dennis attempting to withdraw the barbed arrow from the anguished young man's right shoulder, just above his collarbone.

"You don't *withdraw* an arrow," said McCaleb grimly. "You'll have to drive it on through."

"No," screamed Hardesty. "No!"

"Then it'll have to stay where it is," said McCaleb. "I've got a man who's been hit harder than you, and I need the use of your medical kit. Do you have laudanum?"

"We have," said Lieutenant Sandoval from the corridor. "Do you know how to remove that arrow, McCaleb?"

"I do," said McCaleb.

"Then do it," said Sandoval, "and you're welcome to whatever we have for your man."

"Give him a heavy dose of laudanum," said McCaleb to the pair of pale privates. "While it's taking hold on him, I want some of it to begin preparing my friend."

They had three bottles of the tincture of opium, and McCaleb watched as they forced a massive dose of it upon the unwilling Hardesty. They also had, McCaleb noted, alcohol and iodine. Brazos would be spared the hot irons.

"Brazos," said McCaleb, "we've got laudanum. We'll need a little time for this to take hold. Then me and Will can get that Comanche toothpick out of you. Hang on, pard."

McCaleb waited until the wounded Hardesty was snoring noisily. Will had remained with Brazos. Lieutenant Sandoval stood grimly by, having posted the remainder of his men at the front and rear of the jail.

"This won't be pretty," said McCaleb, "but if you aim to spend some time on the frontier, it's something you need to know."

He broke the shaft of the arrow, leaving enough of its length to drive the barbed point through the flesh. With the butt of his Colt he struck the broken end of the shaft. It advanced, but only a little. Hardesty, unconscious, grunted. Sandoval gritted his teeth as the butt of McCaleb's .44 slowly but surely drove the thing through the young private's flesh. Sweat dripped off McCaleb's chin when finally he was able to grasp the barbed point and withdraw the broken shaft from the bloody wound. Breathing a long sigh, Sandoval clasped his hands to hide their trembling. McCaleb grinned at the ashen lieutenant.

"Now," said McCaleb, "pour some alcohol into the wound, and after that use plenty of iodine where the barb entered and where it came out. You'd best do it right; if you don't, he can die from infection."

Sandoval started to speak but thought better of it, proceeding to do as McCaleb had ordered. He said nothing when McCaleb took a bottle of alcohol, a bottle of iodine, and some bandages from the medical kit. To McCaleb's surprise, Goose had returned and for the first time had entered the adobe jail. Slung on his shoulder was a quiver of arrows, and he carried what had to be a Comanche bow. The grisly thing he gripped in his right hand could be only a Comanche scalp. He held it over Brazos and shook it.

"*Matar*," he said. "*Comanch' bastardo. Matar.*"

Carefully he placed the bloody scalp on the floor at the head of the bunk where Brazos lay. He then unfolded it to reveal the terrible payment he had exacted. It held the Comanche's bloody, severed privates! Rebecca gasped. Goose took that for approval and gave her a satisfied grin. He then turned to McCaleb, a question in his eyes. McCaleb held up the empty laudanum bottle. Then, with the butt of his Colt, he pretended to strike the arrow's protruding shaft. Goose understood and nodded. Still carrying the Comanche bow and quiver of arrows, he went out.

"For God's sake," cried Rebecca, "do something with . . . *that*!"

Goose had left the bloody scalp and gory appendages for Brazos. With the toe of his boot, McCaleb kicked the brutal evidence of Apache retribution under the bunk. Despite the girl's horrified reaction, it was a touching tribute to Brazos, and McCaleb would see that he was aware of it.

"We'd best get it done," said Will. "He's in pretty deep."

It was the worst moment of McCaleb's life. His palms were already wet with sweat, although his hands were cold. His was an agonizing fear that, although the arrow hadn't struck a lung, it might yet pierce one as he drove it out. The very attempt to save Brazos might kill him!

"Everybody out," said McCaleb, "except Will. He may have to spell me."

McCaleb was afraid for Brazos's life, and he knew Will shared that fear, but he didn't want the others sensing it. They had enough trouble already. He broke off the feathered end of the shaft, leaving only enough length to drive it through.

"You want me to do it?" asked Will.

"No," said McCaleb. "You've ridden more trails with him than I have. If this is where his ends, it'll be as tough on you as it will on me."

There was nothing more to be said. McCaleb knelt beside the bunk and began. The Colt's barrel became slippery in his sweaty hands. When the barb finally emerged, he was exhausted.

"Finish it, Will."

Will Elliot completed the grisly surgery and bound the wound. They could do no more. Brazos's breathing was labored but steady. He groaned.

"He'll make it," said McCaleb, "if he can fight off the infection."

"I reckon these blue coats mean well," said Will, "but they don't know doodly about fightin' Indians. Here we sit, with a Comanche behind every tree and bush, with Sandoval on the prod because he reckons you're stealing his thunder. Just as sure as the wind rolls a tumbleweed, if we're here past sundown, them Comanches will rush us."

"That's why we're going to rush them first," said McCaleb. "I want to know if Sandoval's more concerned with his status as commander than in saving his hair. If he throws in with us, he'll fight our way."

The laudanum was wearing off and the wounded Hardesty was groaning. Lieutenant Sandoval looked questioningly at them as they stepped through the door into the crowded room. Monte sat on the desk, Colt in his hand. Sandoval's sergeant and four unhurt privates stood near the windows, their rifles at the ready. Rebecca sat in a chair, its ladder back tilted against the wall.

"Lieutenant," said McCaleb, "you're pushing your luck. Who's watching that pine thicket that's just two jumps from the back door?"

"Your Indian's out there," said Sandoval. "My men aren't comfortable with him."

"They're going to be even *less* comfortable with the Comanches unless we make our move before dark. When we've whipped these murdering devils, you can go back to being the commander, but just this once you're going to fight like a Texan. If you want to come out of this alive, that is. Do you want to win with our tactics or lose with yours?"

Sandoval puffed up like a toad but the wind went out of him as he read fear and uncertainty in the eyes of his men. The siege had scarcely begun and already one of their small number lay wounded and bleeding. Anguished moans from the wounded Hardesty were more devastating than McCaleb's words had been. None of them doubted the truth of those words, and to a man they believed their commander's decision would seal their doom or give them a fighting chance.

With a sigh, Sandoval spoke. "You've fought these devils, McCaleb. We haven't. We'll do it your way. Tell us what you have in mind, what you'd have us do."

"Since this is a federally occupied town, I want your word as an officer and a gentleman that we won't be held responsible for damage to buildings."

"You have my word."

"We're hurting for ammunition, Sandoval. I know you can't help us with the Henrys, but three of my outfit have Spencers. Like yours."

"I'll issue each of them a hundred rounds."

"Hardesty can't fight; we have a need for his Spencer."

"Take it, then," said Sandoval. "What else?"

"Do you have any coal oil?"

"Only what's in the lamp. The globe's broken but the rest of it's under the far end of the desk."

"Do you have a needle gun and a sharpshooter who can handle it?"

"Yes, on both counts. A .53-caliber Schroeder. Sergeant Nelson is a dead shot. It has a range of almost a mile."

"There are eleven of us able to fight," said McCaleb. "We'll leave four to defend the jail and our wounded. Choose two of yours and I'll pick two of mine. The rest of us are going out and teach these Comanches how the calf ate the grindstone. Rebecca, load Hardesty's Spencer for an extra. I want you and Monte here at the jail with a pair of Sandoval's men."

There were no arguments.

"Privates Kenton and Dennis," said Sandoval, "you'll remain here at the jail. Privates Stanzer and Jacobs, you'll accompany me and Sergeant Nelson."

"Lieutenant Sandoval," said McCaleb, "we're going to do the *last* thing these Comanches will expect us to do. We're going to form a skirmish line and attack *them.* The very boldness of it will give us the advantage. The buildings that hide *them* can also hide *us.* We'll fire the vacant buildings where they're holed up, if that's what it takes. I know they'll flank us, and as soon as we're far enough from the jail, they'll fall in behind us. Sergeant Nelson, that's where you come in. Fill your pockets with shells. While we advance, you'll be our rear guard. The needle gun has a far greater range than their arrows. Indians are superstitious; they're likely to regard as bad medicine a gun that can kill at such a distance."

"Brilliant strategy," said Sandoval, "up to a point. Six of us will be advancing to the south. If we can assume these savages have formed four attacking parties, then six of us will be attacking only a fourth of their total number. How long can Sergeant Nelson stand off seventy-five percent of their attacking force? Eventually they'll overrun him. And then us."

"Sandoval," said McCaleb, a touch of exasperation in his voice, "I don't aim to spend *that* much time advancing. This won't be an *orderly* battle to be fought by rules. While Nelson protects our flanks and rear, we'll be able to concentrate *all* our fire on maybe one fourth of these hellions. Once we've advanced as far as Daugherty's store, we can join forces with the defenders who are holed up there. Then, with our combined strength, we will turn on those Comanches that Sergeant Nelson has held at bay with the needle gun. Once we've cut down all opposition to the south and have added the guns at Daugherty's store to our strength, this bunch will be wondering if their attack was such a good idea after all. Before they get enough confidence to challenge the sergeant's needle gun, we'll turn on them and give them the biggest dose of bad medicine they've ever had."

"Texas," said Sergeant Nelson, "it's a good plan. I'll put the fear of God into them with the Schroeder .53."

"Will, send Goose in here and have him bring that quiver of arrows with him."

McCaleb went into one of the cells and took a thin blanket from the bunk. Goose came in the back door and down the corridor. McCaleb beckoned him into the cell. He took six arrows from the quiver and pointed to the blanket.

"*Flecha de fuego*, Goose."

The Indian nodded. He sat on the floor, took his bowie and began slashing two-foot strips from one end of the blanket. Goose then wrapped a woolen strip around the barbed ends of the arrows, making each of them a fist-sized torch, when soaked with coal oil. McCaleb took the globeless lamp from beneath the desk and found it half full of coal oil. Without a word to anyone, he returned to the cell where Goose was busy at his task. Rebecca followed McCaleb and stood looking through the bars.

"What's Goose doing?"

"Making fire arrows," said McCaleb. "Once he's done, six of these arrows will have wool heads. They'll make dandy torches that Goose can shoot onto rooftops or through windows."

Private Hardesty had fallen into a fitful sleep, moaning occasionally. In the cell adjoining the one where McCaleb and Goose worked, Brazos groaned. When Goose had finished with the arrows, McCaleb saturated each of the wool heads with coal oil, and the Indian placed them in the quiver heads up. He then followed McCaleb to the front of the jail, where the others waited.

"We're ready to move out," said McCaleb. "I'm expecting the Comanches to regroup and follow us. But they've outfoxed me once; I didn't expect them to send a second party and box us in after the ambush. The four of you who will defend the jail must be especially watchful; if I'm guessing wrong, they could rush you. We're cutting the defense almighty thin, but it's a chance we'll have to take. Any questions?"

Nobody spoke. Monte was buttoning his shirt. Rebecca was loading Hardesty's Spencer with ammunition Sandoval had supplied. Sergeant Nelson was filling his pockets with shells for the needle gun.

"Will," said McCaleb, "you take the east side of the street and I'll take the west. Sergeant Nelson, you're our rear guard, as planned. Sandoval, you and your other two men will flesh out the line. Goose stays close to me." He pointed to the Indian, to himself, and beckoned.

McCaleb stepped out the door. Goose followed, bow and quiver of arrows slung over his left shoulder, his Spencer at-the-ready. Without incident they reached the shambles of the dynamited saloon. Suddenly there were four quick shots from behind them. Had McCaleb guessed wrong? Were they attacking the jail? But no! There was the blast of the needle gun.

"Here they come!" shouted Sergeant Nelson.

"Hold them back as far as you can, Sergeant," shouted McCaleb.

"Not many to shoot at," said Nelson. "They're splitting into two forces. They're going to flank us. Half a dozen just broke for that brush along the river."

"Try to pin down the bunch that split to the east," yelled McCaleb. "I have plans for those who've taken to the brush along the river."

It was about what he expected. He pointed to Goose, to the quiver of arrows and then to the brush into which some of the pursuing Comanches had gone. Goose drew and nocked one of the fire arrows, flexing his massive arms and bending the bow almost double. McCaleb fired a match, cupping it in his hand until it flared into life. The wool-wrapped, oil-soaked head of the arrow burst into flame and Goose loosed it into the waist-high brush and dried buffalo grass. The fire was no danger to the town and would burn itself out at the river, but it would rob the Comanches of any cover along the west flank. They'd be driven to the west bank of the Brazos, rendering their arrows ineffective but leaving them within reach of Sergeant Nelson's .53-caliber needle gun.

They didn't fare as well on their east flank. While the side of the street nearest the river was mostly open, there were various buildings on the other side, including a deserted, boarded-up general store. Behind it the other half of the flanking force had taken refuge, leaving McCaleb and his small band of attackers in the open street. While the Comanches were unable to loose their arrows with any effectiveness from behind the store, neither could McCaleb's men find a target. Goose held up a fire arrow.

"*Fuego?*"

McCaleb shook his head. Firing the building would do little good; the Comanches would simply move to the next nearest one, perpetuating the standoff. They couldn't torch the whole town.

"Sandoval," said McCaleb, "take your two men to that saloon just beyond the store. Using the saloon for cover, move in behind that bunch and we'll either cut them down in a cross-fire or run them so far into the brush they won't be a threat to us."

McCaleb, Will, and Goose held their ground until they were alerted by firing from Sandoval's position. Then they charged the back of the abandoned store, to find their quarry had fled into the woods. The way was clear and McCaleb's men moved ahead to join Sandoval.

"They were expecting us," said Sandoval in disgust.

"I reckoned they would," said McCaleb, "but we needed them out of the way. We know where *they* came from and where they are. Where are those we should be encountering from the south?"

As though in reply, there was sporadic firing somewhere ahead of them.

"They're attacking Daugherty's store," said Sandoval.

"That's why we haven't met with any resistance from them," said McCaleb. "Before the flank groups can get organized, we'll have time to jump that bunch attacking Daugherty's place. Let's go!"

Daugherty's store stood at the southern end of the winding dirt street, and well before they reached it, they could see activity on the flat roof. They heard the unmistakable sound of someone using an ax, but the high false front of the store kept them from observing what was taking place.

"Sergeant Nelson," said McCaleb, "we're not within range, but with the needle gun, *you* are. I want you to swing out far enough to the east so that you can see what's going on atop Daugherty's store, behind that false front. I reckon those red devils are using an ax to chop through the roof. We'll cover you, should those we just chased into the brush decide to attack. I want you to use that needle gun and pick them off the roof."

Leaving the main street, they trotted toward the woods into which the Comanches had recently fled. The false front of Daugherty's building stood head high, but the front-to-back parapet on the sides sloped down to roof level before reaching the rear of the building. They immediately spotted three Comanches on the roof, one of whom was vigorously swinging an ax. There was a blast from the needle gun and the ax wielder faltered in mid-swing. The ax clattered to the flat wooden roof. Wilson's next shot caught a second Comanche, but the third vanished over the farthermost edge of the roof. There was the twang of Goose's bowstring and a faraway grunt. The Comanche who had ventured out of the nearby brush lay on his back, an arrow driven deep into his belly.

"Come on," said McCaleb. "It's time we went on down to Daugherty's and combined forces with whoever's been doing the shooting."

They approached Daugherty's store so that they could observe the rear of it from a distance. From there they made their way along the south side to the front. There were two separate pools of dried blood on the ground near the front door.

"Virg," shouted Will, "is anybody hurt? Who's in there with you?"

"That you, Will? Nobody hurt. Four of us old mossyhorns in here, an' we're almighty low on shells. Got some women an' kids too. Who's out there with you?"

"Me and two of my outfit, along with Lieutenant Sandoval and a couple of his men. We just shot a pair of Comanches off your roof."

"Heard 'em up there," said Daugherty. "We bored two of th' bastards when they kicked th' door open. You comin' in, er you want us t' come out?"

"Virg, this is Benton McCaleb. We've hurt them. Sergeant Nelson has a needle gun and we've got them running scared. I reckon you'll be more useful out here where they can see you. Even if you're low on ammunition, the Comanches won't know that. If you have Spencers, I reckon we can spare you some shells."

"Look!" shouted Sandoval.

On the west bank of the Brazos, half a mile distant, two dozen Comanches sat their horses, watching.

"They're either giving us up as a lost cause," said

McCaleb, "or they're gathering for some war talk with their medicine man. Maybe we can convince them their medicine is bad. They reckon they're out of range of our rifles. If that's the bunch we drove across the river when we set fire to the brush, they haven't tasted the needle gun. If they had, they wouldn't be so near. Sergeant Nelson, can you pick off a specific target at this distance?"

"I can," said Nelson. "Walkin', runnin', flyin' or standin' still."

"You have two choices," said McCaleb, "and either will serve our purpose. See that one wearing the headdress and the one next to him wearing buffalo horns?"

"I can get either one," said Nelson.

"The one with the mess of feathers is the chief," said McCaleb, "and I'd say that buffalo horns is probably the medicine man. Bring down either of them and this attack will be over."

"Get the medicine man," said Will. "He's the bastard that fires them up for the attack, promising them they'll count coup and take lots of scalps. Drop him and it'll put the fear of God into them. They're so superstitious, they'll shy away from here forever."

Following the ominous blast from the needle gun, nobody spoke. On the distant river bank there was pandemonium, horses milling, dust swirling.

"Damn it," said Sandoval, "I can't see a thing. Is he down?"

"He's down," said Sergeant Nelson, aggravated. "I *hit* what I shoot at."

"The sergeant's right," said Will. "That's why we can't see anything. They're purposely milling the horses, using the dust as cover so we can't drop any more of them while they recover the body of their medicine man. They won't leave him. They'll hightail it away from here."

"I reckon," said Virg Daugherty, "we can all git back t' doin' what we was doin' b'fore that bunch of red coyotes interrupted us."

"I don't suppose," said Lieutenant Sandoval, "you've seen the sheriff?"

"No," said Daugherty, "I ain't, an' th' *less* I see of him, the better I like it."

"Lieutenant," said McCaleb, "unless you have further need of us, I want to get back to the jail and see how Brazos is doing."

"Go ahead," said Sandoval. "We have to search the town for our missing sheriff. Or his body."

"McCaleb," said Will, "Goose is gone. I'd best stay with Sandoval and look around."

It was sound thinking. Goose, with bow and a quiver of Comanche arrows slung over his shoulder, might look like just another Indian to Virg Daugherty and his cronies. Since Goose spoke no English, it would be wise to have Will there to speak for him if need be.

Walking toward the opposite end of town, McCaleb could hear the shouts of children as they escaped from their confinement in Daugherty's store. It was a cheerful note that helped to dispel the gloom and lessened the ghost-town atmosphere. When McCaleb reached the old boarded-up store building the first party of Comanches had taken refuge behind, something seemed out of place. While the glassless windows had been boarded up, the door had not, and it stood partially open. He was dead *sure* that door had *not* been open when they had chased the Comanches away from the abandoned building. McCaleb drew his Colt, and when he stepped up on the dusty porch, his right foot went through the rotten floorboards. He extracted his foot and, testing the floor before trusting all his weight to it, made his way to the door. Peering into the dim interior, he could see nothing. He nudged the door with the toe of his boot, and on creaking, rusty hinges, it opened the rest of the way. Cautiously he stepped inside and a huge cobweb caught him full in the face. He sleeved it away and went on. Suddenly, between his shoulder blades, there was that creeping chill that never failed to warn him when there was danger near. The voice behind him was gloating and ugly, the Colt's cocking sound loud in the musty stillness. He froze.

"Drop the pistol. None o' yer tricks. I'll cut you in two."

"So this is where you've been hiding. Shag Oliver, you're a gutless, yellow-bellied coyote."

"But I'll be *alive* and you'll be *dead*, you self-righteous bastard. Now you drop that pistol or I'll kill you where you stand. Drop it, damn you!"

McCaleb dropped the Colt.

"Now," said Oliver with a chuckle, "you got any last words, any prayers, you'd best be sayin' 'em. On the count of five, I'm aimin' to blow you to hell an' gone. One . . ."

McCaleb weighed his odds. While his eyes had grown accustomed to the gloom, it was still dark enough that he was unable to see the Colt he had just dropped. If he threw himself to the dusty floor, he might not find the pistol at all, or if he did, not soon enough to save himself.

"Two . . ."

McCaleb, never one to fool himself, recognized his predicament for what it was. He had everything to gain and nothing to lose. He would make his desperate move at the count of four.

"Three . . ."

But the count ended there. It was the last word Shag Oliver spoke or would ever speak. The blast from a rifle was cannon-loud in the closed-up building, and in contrast, with the ringing in his ears, McCaleb barely heard the body strike the dusty floor. Slowly McCaleb turned. In the dim light from the open door stood Lieutenant Martin Sandoval. Muzzle down, he held a still-smoking Spencer rifle.

"It will be my sad duty," said Sandoval, "to inform my superiors that Sheriff Oliver died heroically during an attack by hostile Indians."

CHAPTER 13

$\mathcal{M}$cCaleb returned to the jail to find Brazos and Private Hardesty mumbling in feverish sleep. Monte, despite his lesser wound, was still unsteady on his feet. Except for the fate of Shag Oliver, McCaleb explained what had happened.

"Dear God," exclaimed Rebecca, "it's not even noon. We've only been here five hours and it seems like days. Where's Will and Goose?"

"Goose drifted off somewhere and Will's looking for him. From the look of Brazos, I reckon we'll be here awhile. We'll need to bring the herd a mite closer to town."

"Here come Will and Goose," said Monte.

"I found him on the roof of Daugherty's store," said Will. "He was takin' scalps from them two Comanches Sergeant Nelson dropped with the needle gun."

Goose had tied one of his gory trophies to each end of a rawhide thong and had looped it around the muzzle of his Spencer. Privates Kenton and Dennis looked as though they were going to be sick.

"Monte," said McCaleb, "keep an eye on Brazos while we move the herd."

Goose trotted ahead, McCaleb, Rebecca, and Will following. They saw no sign of the Comanches. Not even the dead.

"However spooked they were at Sergeant Nelson's

gulching their medicine man," said Will, "they came back and removed their dead."

They found their horses still safely picketed and the herd grazing peacefully along the river.

Virg Daugherty had or was able to get some moonshine, and the vile stuff soon had Brazos and Private Hardesty sweating.

"So *that's* how it is," said Sergeant Nelson. "Unless he's shot full of arrows, a man can't get any whiskey in these parts."

"Bullets or arrows," said Will. "A man's got to be too near dead to help himself or resist; elsewise, you can't get him to *drink* this rotgut."

Brazos was on his feet within a week. The rest of the outfit was kept busy moving the herd to new graze. They also found time to wash their clothes and blankets. When Brazos was well enough to ride, and they were about to move the herd out into the mid-March dawn, Lieutenant Sandoval presented McCaleb with a brown envelope.

"For what it's worth," said Sandoval, "it's a letter stating that you and your outfit took up arms on behalf of the Union, that you fought for the United States of America against hostile Indians. I've recommended that you be allowed to keep your arms, and in view of your willingness to pledge your loyalty to the Union, I believe my recommendation will be honored. You'll not be permitted to leave Texas without permission, as required by the Reconstruction Act of 1865, but permission will be granted. Good luck, McCaleb."

Five days north of Waco, they came upon the first of Charles Goodnight's holding pens. A dozen longhorns milled about in a small coulee whose mouth had been barricaded by horizontal cottonwood rails rawhide-lashed to heavy vertical cedar posts. Backwater from the Brazos backed up far enough into the coulee for the penned animals to satisfy their thirst.

"No brands," said Will with a chuckle. "Pretty a

bunch of Mavericks as I ever seen. We ought to hair-
brand the lot of them and throw 'em in with ours, just to
bullyrag Charlie."

"Too much work," said McCaleb. "You get a hankering to wrassle them twelve-hundred-pound varmints
for fun, count me out."

They bedded down the herd early, a good two hours
before dark. There was good graze, and McCaleb
wanted to make contact with Goodnight. Taking Goose
with him, he rode north, following the river. They had
ridden maybe ten miles when they heard the familiar
bawling and thrashing about of a captured longhorn.
McCaleb drew rein and the Indian halted beside him.

"Hello," shouted McCaleb. "Hello the camp!"

"Who might *you* be?" inquired a cautious voice from
the brush.

"Benton McCaleb, friend of Charlie Goodnight. Are
you part of his gather?"

"Might be," said the voice. "Stand down an' keep
your hands in sight. I ain't got a pile of confidence in a
white man what slopes around with a Injun. They stampeded our herd to hell an' gone las' fall. Never *did* git
'em back. Whatcha want with Charlie?"

"Got a herd ten miles downriver. Me and a couple of
my pardners were in the Rangers with Charlie. We aim
to trail our herd along with his to the high country, to
Colorado Territory. The Indian's a Lipan Apache and
one of my riders. The Lipans scouted for the Rangers
and they're enemies to the Comanches. Charlie can tell
you that."

McCaleb and Goose had dismounted, backstepping
their horses until the animals were between them and
their unseen challenger. There was a sound somewhere
to the rear, but McCaleb resisted the urge to turn. While
he had been talking, the cautious, unseen wrangler had
worked his way around behind them. Finally he spoke.

"You can turn around, but keep your hands shoulder
high."

McCaleb lifted his hands and Goose followed his lead.

He was a young man, redheaded, maybe twenty-one or -two, dressed in dirty range clothes and run-over boots. A dusty old black Stetson rode his shoulders, secured by a rawhide thong. Out of the brush behind him stepped a second man, similarly attired, except he was dark-haired and had no hat. Both men wore belted Colts, and the redhead carried a new-looking Spencer, muzzle down but still cocked.

"I'm Benton McCaleb. The Indian's name is Goose."

"That his first name or his last name?" inquired the dark-haired rider, speaking for the first time.

The pair of them broke into a fit of laughter, but it died on their lips when Goose moved closer. In his left hand, having appeared as though by magic, the lethal foot-long blade of the bowie glinted in the westering sun. The look in the Apache's obsidian eyes could only be described as murderous.

"He doesn't like being laughed at," said McCaleb.

"S-Sorry," said the redhead.

"Goose," said McCaleb.

Slowly, almost reluctantly, Goose lowered the formidable weapon until he held it at the same angle his adversary held the cocked Spencer. It was an affront that needed no words. Carefully, the redheaded young man took the Spencer off cock and eased the butt of it to the ground, holding it by its muzzle. Just as carefully, Goose returned the bowie to its rawhide thonged position around his neck and the huge knife disappeared over his shoulder. Only then did the two wranglers swallow hard and seem to relax.

"That's better," said McCaleb with a grin. "When he knows you better, maybe he'll show you his collection of scalps. Now who are *you*?"

"I'm Red Alford," said the redhead, "and this hombre is Langford Dill. His friends—what few he's got—call him Dill."

"If it's all right with the two of you," said McCaleb,

"I'd like to ride on into Charlie's camp, let him know we're just downriver, and get back to my herd before dark."

"Why don't we ride in with you," said Alford, "and show you the way? By the time you're ready to head downriver, we can ride back this far with you. By then, this old cow ought to have thrashed some of the meanness out of her carcass, so's we can throw her in with the others."

"By then," said McCaleb with a chuckle, "it'll be near suppertime and too near dark to go looking for another mossyhorn."

The three of them laughed, and even Goose looked a little less murderous. The two Goodnight wranglers mounted their horses and led out, followed by McCaleb. Goose brought up the rear. They had ridden perhaps half an hour when McCaleb smelled wood smoke. Some of the other riders had already called it a day, and half a dozen gathered around the fire over which hung a huge blackened coffeepot. Each of them dropped their tin cups and got to their feet. While somewhat reassured by two of their own outfit accompanying the strangers, they were wary, hooking their thumbs in their belts near the butts of their holstered Colts. Alfred and Dill reined up and dismounted.

"This gent hailed us downriver," said Red. "His name's McCaleb and he claims to know Charlie. The Injun's one of his riders."

None of the men around the fire said anything. Due to the continuous problem with the Comanches, *any* Indian was suspect, and they eyed Goose with undisguised suspicion. Finally one of the riders spoke.

"Charlie ain't here. Reckon he'll ride in 'fore dark. You're welcome to step down an' wait. They's coffee in th' pot."

Goodnight's men were decidedly cool, extending only the range courtesy that western custom demanded. McCaleb couldn't fault them for that, because they had no proof of his relationship with Goodnight. It wasn't uncommon for rustlers and outlaws to ride in, take the measure of an outfit, and at a time and place that suited them, gun down the crew and take the herd. McCaleb and Goose dismounted. They led their horses away from the camp until they found suitable graze, picketed them and returned on foot. The fire had died down to a bed of coals and only two of the riders remained. Alfred and Dill had gone, presumably to wrassle their captured longhorn to a holding pen. Goose knelt down, his back to a pine, saying nothing. McCaleb grew increasingly impatient at the delay.

"Bent McCaleb! You old cow thief!"

Charles Goodnight hit the ground running. His hair was longer and more unkempt than usual, and despite his being barely thirty, there was some gray in his dark hair and beard. He was a big bear of a man, and while he wrung his friend's right hand with his own, he pounded McCaleb on the back with his left. In his enthusiasm, he almost overlooked Goose.

"Charlie," said McCaleb, "this is Goose. He's a Lipan Apache, one of the survivors from Chief Flacco's tribe. You remember Flacco?"

"My God, yes," said Goodnight. "The best scout Captain Jack Hayes and the Rangers ever had. Captain Jack personally hunted down the bastards that killed Flacco, and I didn't blame him. Howdy, Goose."

Goose understood little if any of what Goodnight had said, although his eyes lighted briefly at the sound of Flacco's name. McCaleb didn't believe the Indian was going to accept Goodnight's extended hand, so long did he hesitate. Finally Goose gripped Goodnight's brawny paw and their eyes met. McCaleb had a strange feeling that Charles Goodnight was on trial, that the Indian had accepted him only because he was Benton McCaleb's friend. How strange, thought McCaleb, that Goose had been with them for months without any outward show of friendship on their part, not even a handshake. He was one of them and somehow he was not. Goodnight's booming voice brought McCaleb back to the present.

"I reckon you're stayin' for supper?"

"No," said McCaleb, "I just wanted you to know we're maybe fifteen miles south of you. Why don't you ride down to our camp tomorrow? I want all my outfit to sit in on our conversation, and it'll be easier for you to join us than for all of us to leave the herd and come here. We had a run-in with Comanches at Waco and Brazos caught a bad one. He's still weak, but we couldn't keep him out of the saddle any longer."

"Very well," said Goodnight. "See you tomorrow. *Hasta luego*, Goose."

At sunrise Charles Goodnight rode into McCaleb's camp. He greeted Goose with a lifted hand and McCaleb with a nod. He dismounted and in his bow-legged lope went to meet Will and Brazos. When all the hand-pumping and back-thumping was over, Goodnight's eyes sought out Monte and Rebecca Nance. They had approached timidly; having heard so much about Goodnight, they stood quietly before him.

McCaleb cleared his throat. "Charlie, this is Monte Nance and Rebecca, his sister. Their daddy was killed by the Comanches and they asked to throw their herd in with ours. We got out with our hair and not quite a thousand cows."

Gravely Goodnight took Monte's hand and then turned to Rebecca. She was hatless and her long raven hair curled around her shoulders. Faded Levi's hugged her slender hips, and Monte's old denim shirt, a bit too small to begin with, stretched tight across her breasts. Sun and wind had so tanned her face and neck, the freckles splashed across her nose seemed almost white. None of this was lost on Goodnight; he looked her over from head to toe and grinned appreciatively.

He chuckled. "Well, Bent. I see you haven't spent *all* your time catching longhorns."

Monte, Will, and Brazos shared his laughter, but McCaleb did not. It was cowboy humor at its worst, and he expected the girl to flare up like hell with all the fires lit. She exceeded his every expectation. Throwing her awe, timidity, and caution to the wind, hands fisted on her hips, she stalked over and confronted the big man. McCaleb had never seen her so on the prod.

"Mr. Señor Charles Goodnight," she bawled, "how *dare* you insinuate I've been roped and branded like a maverick heifer! I don't care if everybody else thinks you're nine feet tall and solid gold! I think you're just a . . . a . . . big dumb cow wrassler!"

Nobody loved to laugh more than Charles Goodnight, and he laughed loudest and longest when the joke was on himself. He threw his big hat to the ground, slapped his thighs and laughed until he could laugh no more. Brazos, Will, and McCaleb matched his unbridled mirth with their own. Monte stood there with an uncertain grin, while Goose's expression could only be described as puzzled. He hadn't understood Rebecca's words or the reason for them, but he knew anger when he heard it. His was a world of black and white, without shades of gray. Anger begat anger and then somebody died.

Quickly Rebecca's face changed from the white of anger to the red of embarrassment. How did you vent your anger on one who laughed at your insults? The man was every bit as insufferable at Benton McCaleb; no *wonder* they were friends!

"Ma'am," said Goodnight, dusting off his hat, "I meant no harm. You're a beautiful lady; even a big dumb cow wrassler can see that."

"Thank you," said Rebecca, blushing even more furiously. "I'm sorry—"

"Nothing to be sorry for," said Goodnight cheerfully. "I rode bareback all the way from Illinois when I was nine. Growed up amongst rustlers, outlaws, Injuns, and jaybirds like this bunch standin' here looking at me. So what else *could* I be, except a big dumb cow nurse? Somebody fetch me a cup of that six-shooter coffee and let's get on with our talking."

McCaleb covered their months in the brakes, dwelling mostly on their trouble with the Comanches. He mentioned none of the difficulties encountered as a result of

York Nance's skulduggery and was rewarded with the gratitude in Rebecca's eyes. He told Goose's story, praising the Apache, and finished with their part in the defense of Waco during the Comanche attack. McCaleb handed Goodnight the letter Lieutenant Sandoval had given them.

"Won't hurt your case," said Goodnight, after reading it. "God knows, we need all the help we can get. Like we figured, carpetbagger courts have come in and taken over the state, leaving us disenfranchised. A puppet legislature with carpetbaggers and scalawags pulling the strings. By the time I got home, they'd stolen every cow I ever owned, and now they're running a bill through the legislature to make it legal!"

He glared at them like a fierce old buffalo bull surrounded by wolves. Nobody said anything, and in a milder tone he continued.

"They call it the 'tallying law,' and it allows anybody to build a herd by just going out on the range and gathering everything he can find, brands and earmarks be damned! It's made official by having the herd 'tallied' by an inspector appointed by the carpetbagger court. From all I've seen and heard, these court-appointed inspectors are the most unreliable, no-account bastards to be found. Slip them a pint of whiskey or a dollar—anything to make it worth their while—and they'll tally anything you want, falsifying earmarks and brands in any manner that suits you. Then all the rustler or rancher has to do to make it legal is to record the tally at the county courthouse. The law then allows the herd to be sold, *assuming* that the original owners were paid, *assuming* that *every* man is honest!"

"Texas is broke except for cattle," said McCaleb, "and now they've come up with a legal way to rob us of them."

"Possession has always been nine tenths of the law," said Goodnight, "and we'll make that law work for *us*. But we'll do it legal and honest by taking only unbranded animals. We stand to be hurt only to the extent that thieves could take our herds, dispose of them, and disappear. We'll play by their rules and have our cows tallied by one of their 'inspectors' before we try to leave Texas."

"It's true, then," said Will, "that we need permission to leave?"

"It's the law," said Goodnight, "but like everything else in this carpetbagging administration, it can be bent hell-west and crooked, if you know somebody."

"I'm assuming," said McCaleb, "that you know somebody."

"I don't," said Goodnight, "but Oliver Loving does, and he'll be trailing his herd with us."

"I've heard of him," said Brazos. "He's been around awhile. Been up the Shawnee to Sedalia and took a herd to Illinois in 'fifty-five. I'd calculate he's a mite . . . uh, old . . . for a drive as long and hard as this."

Goodnight chuckled. "He's fifty-four, and I didn't hog-tie him, he volunteered. He's a veteran on the trail. He sold beef to the military before the war, and one of the officers he dealt with is at Austin, part of this occupation."

Having recovered her composure and self-confidence, Rebecca spoke for the first time since her confrontation with Goodnight.

"There's been a war, Mr. Goodnight, and everybody's against us. Why should this one officer feel any different?"

He groaned. "Don't call me *Mister* Goodnight. I'm Charlie. To answer your question, the military, despite this foolish occupation, *needs* beef now more than ever. Believe me, Loving knows what he's doing. Now that the war is over, more and more Union soldiers will be moving west to fight Indians. That means more forts and more people to feed. What most concerns the military right now is the more than eight thousand hungry Navajos in northern New Mexico Territory, at Fort Sumner. Other trail herds are going north into Kansas; we'll be driving near Fort Sumner. Does that tell you anything?"

"That we won't be going to Colorado," said Rebecca.

"Some of us will," said Goodnight. "Quite a bit of Loving's herd is suitable for breeding stock. Few of mine are; just beeves and dry cows."

"That's about all we've got," said McCaleb. "Can't afford to be too choosy when you're dragging 'em out of the chaparral. There's a chance, then, that we could sell our herd at Sumner?"

"I'd say so," said Goodnight. "I aim to sell off as many as I can, hit the trail back to Texas, and buy a bigger and better herd while prices are rock bottom. I reckon Colorado will still be there."

It was a drastic change from their original plan, and McCaleb wasn't at all sure he liked it. Or was he a little jealous of Oliver Loving, Goodnight's newfound friend he had yet to meet?

"That's a whole new direction," said McCaleb. "You still planning to move out in mid-April?"

"I reckon not," said Goodnight. "Mr. Loving won't be ready until June first. So far I have eight hundred and forty head; I'd like to make it an even thousand. Then we'll move upriver, joining herds with Loving twenty-five miles south of old Fort Belknap. You can wait here and we'll go together, or you can wait there for me and Mr. Loving."

"I think we'll move on," said McCaleb. Just who *was* Oliver Loving to hold up their drive for *two months* until *he* got ready?

Goodnight studied their faces, lingering the longest on McCaleb, Brazos, and Will. He knew they were impatient and unsatisfied. He'd known them too well for too long. While he liked and believed in Oliver Loving, these men had long been his friends, and he wanted their approval. He played his last card.

"I realize we're getting a later start, but we'll need time to ready ourselves for the trail. I'm having a government wagon completely rebuilt with the toughest wood to be had. Iron axles too. I'm taking twelve yoke of oxen, using six at a time. Go to the general store in Weatherford and tell Silas Moon who you are. We've made arrangements for supplies, including sufficient grain for the horses and ammunition. If you need credit, buy what you need and pay when you sell the herd."

"I never liked counting my chickens before they're hatched, Charlie," said McCaleb. "We'll pay for what we get; in advance."

Goodnight got up, tipped his hat to Rebecca and shook hands with everybody except Goose. The Indian remained where he was, dark eyes inscrutable. Goodnight swung into the saddle, lifted a big hand in silent farewell and rode out.

"Supplies," said Brazos. "Grain and ammunition. Sugar, tea, and rock candy, I expect. How in tarnation did he do that, with Texas occupied and dirt poor?"

Will chuckled. "I'd imagine, if Oliver Loving can talk the Federals into lettin' us out of Texas with three thousand cows, he can shake 'em down for grub and ammunition."

"I'm starting to despise that man," said Rebecca, "and I haven't even met him. We're not going to accept that offer, are we?"

"Why not?" said McCaleb. "We need grain for the horses and grub for ourselves, not to mention ammunition for our Colts and rifles. Where else are we likely to find what we need, at *any* price?"

"Well," said Rebecca defiantly, "if you know where we're joining herds with this . . . this Yankee-lover, then let's get our herd there ahead of his and use the best grass to fatten *our* cows while he piddles around!"

They took their time, allowing the herd to graze along the way, and arrived on Elm Creek range the first Sunday in April. It had been a wet spring and Elm Creek ran bank-full.

"It's beautiful," cried Rebecca. "So peaceful!"

"Don't let it fool you," said McCaleb. "This is about

where Charlie was holding his herd last fall when the Comanches stampeded them."

Feeding into the creek was a shallow, willow-lined stream which they followed until they found a shaded, secluded spring. The remains of several old fires were testimony to its popularity as a campsite.

"There's somethin' serious we need to take care of," said Brazos. "We been out of coffee for a week. I can eat turkey or deer if I got to, but I ain't goin' another day without coffee if I got to ride to Weatherford and get it myself."

"We *do* need to replenish our grub and get some grain for the horses," said McCaleb. "It'll take some time to get them back in shape. I reckon I'll have to go, since I'm bossin' the drive, and I'll take one of you with me. We'll take two packhorses. Any volunteers?"

"Take Rebecca," said Brazos, "unless somebody's got a better idea. I don't care *who* goes as long as we get some coffee. The cook ought to have some say-so when it comes to choosin' the grub."

"We've got time to get there and back before dark," said McCaleb, "if we start early in the morning. Is there anything the rest of you need that we might find at Weatherford? Brazos, see if you can get through to Goose."

"If I could have at least one pair of socks," said Monte, "I'd be happy."

"The same for me," said Will, "and for God's sake, some soap. It purely wasn't meant for a man to shave without soap. My face looks and feels like I been shavin' in the dark with a dull bowie knife."

"Bring us some tobacco," said Brazos, "and if they got any, a bottle of paregoric. Goose just shakes his head; what do you get for an Indian that's already got a horse, a bowie, a new Spencer, and a bagful of shells?"

McCaleb and Rebecca rode out at first light. Each led an extra horse, McCaleb's bearing the pack saddle. Weatherford, as best McCaleb remembered, was slightly to the southeast of Belknap, and since they were now some twenty-five miles southwest of the old fort, he judged they were a good forty miles from the little town.

"How much of a town *is* Weatherford?" inquired Rebecca.

"Mostly in name only," said McCaleb. "It's never been much more than a watering hole about two ax handles west of Fort Worth. I doubt it's any more substantial now, unless there's a saloon."

"No whorehouse?"

"I reckon not. Why? You tired of punching cows?"

How far dared he go with this unpredictable female? If he had fanned the flames of her volatile temper, the best he could expect would be a long silent trip, with her sulking there and back. The worst, of course, would be her backsliding and cussing him like a bull whacker. To his surprise, she laughed, her green eyes twinkling.

"Would you be my first customer, McCaleb?"

"I reckon not," he said, matching her tone. "Way you scratch and claw a man, I'd be plumb scared to get close to you with my britches off. I might end up missin' some parts I'd have trouble gettin' along without."

"Wal," she said, in that perfectly ridiculous drawl, "Ah reckon Ah'll jus' keep on a-punchin' cows."

He laughed until he cried, and she joined in. It was a milestone he'd never expected to see. Only too well did he remember her pawing the ground when Goodnight had jokingly implied that McCaleb might have some kind of hold on her. He did and he didn't, he decided. He believed he was mostly responsible for that. He had made her so aware of her unladylike behavior that the mere suggestion of impropriety prodded her into a defensive fury. Recalling the lengths to which she had gone to attract his attention and win his approval, he believed he understood her. With others she flared up at the slightest implication that she was less than a highborn lady. But with him she was an impudent, fun-loving woman.

"Who are you thinking about, McCaleb?"

"Why do I have to be thinking about *any*body? Maybe I'm thinking about the herd."

"I'd take that as an insult if I didn't know you better. You think about the herd when you're *with* the herd."

"And when I'm with you, I think about you?"

"Don't you? Sometimes?" She sounded more wistful than sarcastic.

"Ah reckon Ah do," he said, mimicking her drawl.

She laughed, pleased. Her green eyes softened. "McCaleb, on the way back, let's find a secluded creek and take a bath."

"Together? Naked?"

"Have you ever taken a bath in your entire life when you weren't?"

"In the saddle," he said, "but *never* possum-naked with a female lookin' at me. Not since I was five and my mama stood me in a washtub and scrubbed my back and ears."

"I'm not your mama; you can wash your own back and ears. Ever since I was carried away by that Indian, I . . . I'm nervous about . . . taking off all my clothes."

"But you won't be nervous if . . . I'm there?"

"No." She blushed only a little. "You care about me . . . don't you?"

"Ah reckon Ah do," he said. "If'n a Injun come along an' wanted you, Ah wouldn't take nary less'n ten ponies fer you."

He was serious enough to restore the confident twinkle to her eyes and humorous enough to make her laugh. The ride to Weatherford seemed entirely too short.

They bypassed the little town, riding three quarters of a mile beyond it to a low rambling log building without a sign of a window.

"That's it?" she asked. "Why is it stuck out here by itself?"

"That's it," he said. "Unless it's changed hands, an old coot named Silas Moon owns it. He lives in a kind of lean-to behind the place. He used to buy, sell, and trade livestock. He'd have horses, mules, cows, hogs, sheep, and goats. Most town folks don't want to see and hear the stockyards from their front porch."

There was no sign of life. They dismounted, half-hitched their horses to the rail, and McCaleb tried the front door. It was barred from the inside. He rapped on it with the butt of his Colt.

"How does he run a store with the door locked?"

"He has to," said McCaleb. "If Indians and outlaws could just walk in, he wouldn't last a week. He sells to folks he knows. Been a spell since I was here; might take Goodnight's or Loving's name to get us in."

CHAPTER 14

$\mathcal{F}$inally, after McCaleb's incessant pounding, a head-high peephole slid open in the massive oak door. Although the April sun was bright, they could see nothing, and when the man spoke, his voice sounded muffled.

"Stand away from the door so's I can see you."

McCaleb and Rebecca stepped back.

"Who are you and whatcha want?"

"I'm Benton McCaleb and we need supplies. Charlie Goodnight told us to come here. We're trailing our herd with his."

"You any kin to them McCalebs over t' Mineral Wells?"

"That's my mama and daddy," said McCaleb.

The big door swung open and they entered. Silas Moon was a thin little man with a fringe of gray hair above his ears and an equally gray goatee. His store seemed surprisingly well-stocked; boxes and crates were stacked almost to the ceiling. There was a mingled aroma of coal oil, molasses, roasted coffee beans, and smoked meat. Behind and above the counter a huge cedar beam reached from one wall to the other. On meat hooks suspended from the beam hung sides of bacon and hams. McCaleb noticed they were leaving faint boot tracks in a thin film of flour that covered the wooden floor. That *was* a surprise; flour had been as scarce as gold during the war years. Silas Moon said nothing, waiting for McCaleb to speak. Eventually he did.

"Silas, this is Rebecca Nance. She's part owner of the herd and is our best cook, so we'll let her decide on the grub. I'm concerned with grain for our horses and shells for our Colt revolvers and our Spencer and Henry rifles."

"I'm tellin' you the same as I told Goodnight and Loving," said Silas. "I got my first full shipment of goods since before the war, and I got t' get enough cash money t' restock. I ain't sellin' out t' th' bare walls on credit; not t' nobody!"

"We're not asking for credit," said McCaleb. "If the price is right, we can pay in gold."

Silas regarded them with new respect, licking his thin lips before he spoke. His watery blue eyes seemed warmer and the frown that had puckered his brow vanished.

"You always git a better price, payin' as you go. Take as much as you need of anything I got. How 'bout a barr'l of flour, t' start?"

"Too much," said McCaleb. "Make it a couple of fifty-pound sacks. We don't have a wagon."

"Might he'p you find a wagon," said Silas.

"No," said McCaleb, "we'll stick to packhorses. Our money might be better spent on shells, grub for ourselves, and grain for the horses."

"Smart thinkin'," said Silas cautiously. "Can't beat a sure-footed pack animal in rough country. Matter of fact, I got a pack saddle I'll *give* you, just to git it out of my way. Had it since b'fore th' war. Consider it a bonus for payin' cash."

Of course Silas offered the saddle! Money spent for mules and a wagon would leave McCaleb's outfit with less to spend in Moon's store.

"Thanks." McCaleb grinned, wise to the old man's motives.

McCaleb bought a thousand rounds for every rifle and for every Colt except Rebecca's .31-caliber pocket pistol. There was little demand for that caliber, and Silas had no shells. McCaleb bought six hundred pounds of shelled corn. It was far more than they could pack, but he wanted to buy while it was available.

"Silas," said McCaleb, "we'll have to come back for some of this; we have only two packhorses."

"I'll stash it away," said Silas. "It'll be here when you come for it."

Left to herself, Rebecca came up with things McCaleb wouldn't have thought of. She found bottles of iodine, alcohol, laudanum, and part of a bolt of white ticking that could be used for many things, especially to dress wounds. She came up with a small scissors, a thimble, spools of thread, cotton socks for all the men except Goose, and some quick-silvered glasses—mirrors, small enough to fit into the palm of the hand. She had bought only one thing for herself: an ample supply of soap.

Once opened, condensed milk wouldn't keep, so it came in understandably small tins. McCaleb took four dozen of them. With Brazos in mind, they took ten pounds of coffee beans. Silas opened a hundred-pound sack of brown sugar and weighed out ten pounds of that. They completed their purchases with fifty pounds of beans, two sides of bacon, a ham, two gallons of sorghum molasses, and a half gallon of moonshine.

"Not much 'shine for a whole crew," said Silas.

"It's not for the whole crew," said McCaleb. "Handy for sweatin' fever out of a man after he's had an arrow drove through him or lead cut out of him. We don't aim for everybody to get in that condition at the same time."

"Don't forget Brazos's tobacco," warned Rebecca.

"Half a dozen sacks of Durham, Silas," said McCaleb. The pack saddle Silas had given them was old but serviceable, needing only to have its leather oiled. It was double-rigged, and except for half the ammunition and half the corn, their two horses, each with a pack saddle, carried their loads handily.

Silas Moon watched them out of sight. He had four gold double eagles in his hand, a satisfied smile on his

face, and the assurance that they—and their gold—
would return.

They had made good time. The west wind was balmy,
the Texas sky the bluest McCaleb had ever seen it, and
the sun was just noon high. Rebecca had the soap in a
sack of its own, looped to her saddle horn. McCaleb had
powerful misgivings about the pair of them stripping
off jaybird naked, however secluded the area. Modesty
had nothing to do with his reluctance; God knew, they
were past that. Their four horses—two of them bounti-
fully loaded—would make a band of Comanches rich.
Besides that, a white man's scalp and a beautiful female
captive would have them dancing for joy.

"That's a nice creek just ahead," said Rebecca. "Willows are right down to the water. Nobody could see us
until they got within ten feet."

"And we can't see *them*," said McCaleb, "until *they're*
within ten feet. Make that five feet, if they happen to be
Comanches."

"Dear God, McCaleb," she shouted, exasperated,
"can't we ever do anything without the damn Indians
being in the way?"

"Not as long as we're in their territory and there's
more of them than there is of us. If you're hell-bent on
havin' a bath with that new soap, then *have* one. I'll have
one eye on you, one eye on the prairie, and *both* hands
on my Henry rifle."

She knew him well enough and the Comanches well
enough that she didn't argue. They found a break in the
willows, rode down the low creek bank and splashed
their horses across to the other side. Rebecca took the
lead, turning her mount and the packhorse upstream
where the water wouldn't be muddy from their crossing. McCaleb followed, reining up behind her when she
had found the spot she sought. She dismounted, tying
the reins of her horse and those of the packhorse to a
nearby willow. The animals immediately took to nip-
ping the freshly greened young leaves. McCaleb dismounted, half-hitching the reins of his animals to

another willow. Rebecca loosed the thong on the neck of the sack and took out a piece of the soap.

"You will . . . stay close, won't you?"

McCaleb grinned. "I wouldn't miss it for the world. I aim to see that you don't end up on an Indian pony with me tryin' to get there before some Comanche's done some things to you that can't be undone."

She sat on the new grass, held up her feet and he dragged off her boots. She stepped out of her faded Levi's and slipped off the shirt. She wore no undergarments. Her face and neck had been tanned by the sun and wind, as had her slender arms to the elbow, but the rest of her was milk-white. He gave her a low whistle of appreciation and promptly forgot his resolve to keep one eye on the prairie. She splashed into the creek, stumbled or put her foot into a hole, and fell facedown. The resulting commotion startled her horse and the animal jerked its head. McCaleb calmed it and scanned the prairie as far as he could see. Reassured, he turned his attention back to the girl. She had found a place where the water was waist deep, and was soaping her upper body. She shook herself like a dog, jiggling her breasts at him. He'd never been more conscious of her beauty, and he decided that if he were in there with her, the very *least* of their danger would be the Comanches. Finally she climbed out, leaving the shade of the willows and moving into the warm sun. She stretched, turning this way and that, more for his benefit than anything else, he decided. He grinned appreciatively, keeping his distance.

"It's your turn now," she said, laughing.

"No," he said. "Get ready and let's ride."

"You're ashamed, aren't you?"

"No."

"You're ashamed of me, because I . . ."

She turned her back to him, and he was at a loss as to what was bothering her. He put his hand on her bare shoulder and she jumped like he'd touched her with a hot iron.

He sighed. "Give me the soap," he said, "and then get your clothes on. I'm not about to get in that water until you've got yourself together and you're up here with this Henry. And promise me you'll look at the prairie once in a while."

She turned to face him with a mischievous twinkle in her green eyes and not a trace of a tear on her cheeks. She had bluffed him into doing exactly what she had wanted. Despite his anxiety for their situation, he regretfully watched her button the faded shirt and stuff the tails into her Levi's. When she had tugged on her boots, he handed her the Henry and dragged off his own boots. There were enormous holes in the heels of his socks and each of his big toes poked out grotesquely. The girl laughed.

"That's the reason I didn't want to do this," he said gravely.

He removed his shirt first and then stepped out of his Levi's. If he turned his back she would see the seat was out of his drawers, so he took the bull by the horns and got out of them, facing her. She did a fair job of repeating the whistle he had directed at her. He stretched both arms toward the heavens like a sun-worshiping Indian.

"Now," he said, "are you satisifed?"

"No. Get in the water and use the rest of the soap. Ever since I've known you, you've smelled like horses and cows with your own sweat on top of that. Just once I'd like to know what you're like underneath."

He waded into the creek until the water reached his middle. He ducked his head, soaped his hair and dunked it again. He had ridden and slept in his clothes for so long, he thoroughly enjoyed the soap and the cold water. He spent a pleasurable ten minutes in the water and climbed out, shivering, making his way into the sun. Rebecca went to her horse, untied the sack in which she carried the soap, and took out a new pair of socks.

"Shucks, ma'am," he drawled, "Ah jus' got them others broke in."

She laughed, dropped the socks and put her hands on

his bare shoulders. Slowly, she slid her hands around his neck, moved up against him, and their lips met. When she drew away, it was only enough that she could speak.

"I like you so much better this way," she said.

"The smell or the view?"

"Both. You know what comes next, don't you?"

He pulled away, shook his dusty shirt and shrugged himself into it. He methodically fastened each button, got into his faded Levi's and stuffed the tail of his shirt into them. Then he sat down and pulled on one of the new socks. He reached for the second one when she caught his hand.

"You knew what I wanted, didn't you?"

"I reckon I did," he said.

"So it wasn't just the Comanches that bothered you, was it?"

"No."

"You wanted me, didn't you? Like I . . . wanted you?"

"I reckon I did . . . do."

"Then why not, Benton McCaleb, why not?"

"A trail drive . . . it's not the time . . . not the place."

"I'm twenty-seven years old, McCaleb. I've been pawed and propositioned since I was twelve. You're the only man I've ever wanted, and you don't want *me*. *When* is the time and *where* is the place?"

"I don't know," he said.

The rest of their ride to Elm Creek range was as silent as it was miserable. Why hadn't he taken her like she wanted him to do, like he had wanted to? He had no answers for her. Worse, he had none for himself.

"I ain't going to lie around and do nothin' until June," said Brazos. "Why don't I just ride downriver and tell Charlie we're goin' ahead?"

"Because we'd be taking unfair advantage of him and Loving," said McCaleb. "Charlie's told us about the government agent at Fort Sumner and of the possibility that we might sell our herd there. It wouldn't be right for us to jump the gun, getting our herd there first. Besides, we might have some trouble dealing with the government on our own."

"While you were gone," said Will, "I did a tally on the herd. We're short at least thirty head. Charlie's camp is nearly a hundred miles south. Since we've got nothing better to do, why don't we start beatin' the bushes and add some more cows to our herd?"

"I expect Charlie pretty well cleaned out these brakes before he moved on," said McCaleb, "but it won't hurt for us to ride out and see if he missed a few. Two riders at a time, though."

"Let me and Goose take the first turn," said Monte.

"Go ahead," said McCaleb. "Where is Goose? I haven't seen him since we returned from Weatherford."

"Goose ain't been worth a damn for nothin'," said Brazos, "since he got his hands on that lookin' glass. Wherever he is, he's settin' there admirin' his ugly mug."

"I didn't know he was going to be like this," said Rebecca defensively. "It only cost a nickel; I felt guilty, bringing everybody something except him."

Rebecca slipped down to the river and found Goose. So engrossed was the Indian in what he was doing, he failed to hear her approach. She was downwind from him, and as she drew closer, she heard a low guttural sound. She pondered a moment before she realized the Indian was laughing to himself. He tilted the small mirror this way and that, using the sun to cast a bright patch of light on the water, nearby trees, and a distant boulder at a bend in the river. Under the girl's boot a dry twig snapped, and with the swiftness of a panther the Indian flung himself to the side, rolled and came up with the bowie in his hand.

"It's me, Goose!" she cried.

Slowly the Indian relaxed. He was no longer interested in her. She followed his gaze to the hard ground on which he had been kneeling. The small mirror was shattered, its tiny fragments winking like diamonds in the April sun. Slowly the bowie rose to thrust position and Goose lifted his dark eyes to meet hers. She saw no recognition, only death. She tried to cry out to him but could not. He took a step toward her and then another. Chill after terrified chill rippled through her body. Forcing herself to move, she slowly lifted her hand to the pocket of the shirt she wore. Her trembling fingers brought out her own little mirror and it caught the sun. Goose halted and slowly lowered the bowie. Death left his eyes and again they became impassive, revealing nothing. Slowly, on knees that trembled, she knelt, placing the little mirror on the ground. She almost didn't make it to her feet, stumbling backward into an oak. Goose, taken with the magic of the glass, ignored her. He knelt, testing the new mirror in the sun. Her heart pounding in her throat, Rebecca Nance turned and ran.

Halting in a thicket, she caught her breath. She must compose herself, she must think. What was she going to do? She had no doubt that the Indian had been about to kill her over a shattered five-cent trinket. Had any of the four men in camp witnessed her danger, they'd have shot Goose without hesitation. She didn't want that, but having seen this savage side of him, how far could she trust him? Up till now, his ruthlessness and brutality had been directed at their common enemy, the Comanches. Slowly she got herself under control, stilling her trembling hands and wobbly knees. How could she warn the others so that they might be prepared to defend themselves should they unintentionally arouse the Indian's savage temper, as she had? Monte had taken a genuine liking to Goose, standing watch with him, riding into the brakes after wild cows. There was no denying the Apache had turned the stampede, but suppose at some point and in some manner Monte offended Goose? She shuddered. Even tomorrow the two of them would be riding into the brakes together!

* * *

To everybody's surprise, they actually found a few cows in the brakes along the Brazos River to the south.

"Charlie wouldn't have missed this many," said McCaleb. "We're roundin' up a few of his bunch the Comanches stampeded last fall."

"I reckon you're right," said Will, "but without brands, they're just good old Texas mavericks, as much ours as his."

They stood watch in pairs every night, not daring to relax their vigilance, but there was no more Comanche trouble. While there were several spring storms, there was no thunder or lightning of serious enough proportions to provoke a stampede. By the end of the second week in May, they were riding as far as ten miles without sighting a single cow.

"We got a thousand and five," said Will, "according to my count."

"That's it, then," said McCaleb.

Charles Goodnight rode into their camp on May 21.

"Got my thousand head," he said, "and a few more."

"So did we," said McCaleb. "Found some of your old stampeded herd. Finest bunch of mavericks I ever laid an iron to."

"Better you than the Comanches," he said. "They really cleaned us out."

"When are you going to Weatherford for your supplies?" McCaleb asked.

"Tomorrow," said Goodnight. "We're out of coffee and mighty low on most everything else."

"We can spare you some coffee," said McCaleb, "and likely anything else you're hurtin' for. We've been to Weatherford once and need to go again before we start the drive."

"I'll bed down my herd alongside yours," said Goodnight, "and our riders can work together. I won't be going just to Weatherford and back. I'll go to Parker County first. Before we started our gather, I bought an old government wagon and hired a man to rebuild it like I wanted. I'll drive the wagon back to Weatherford and load up with supplies."

By sundown Goodnight had bedded down a thousand bawling longhorns just south of McCaleb's herd. Since Goodnight was low on supplies, McCaleb had invited them to supper. With the time at hand when his outfit was to join Goodnight's—and eventually Loving's —McCaleb had misgivings as to how the transition might affect Goose and the temperamental Rebecca. Suppose the Apache gutted some thoughtless cowboy with his bowie? And what of Rebecca Nance? Out of deference to McCaleb, Brazos and Will had shied away from the girl, but the Goodnight and Loving riders had no reason to be partial to his feelings. Cowboys were unpredictable where women were concerned. He had seen lifelong friends beat each other black and blue over some whore who didn't care a rap for either of them.

Rebecca outdid herself, preparing sourdough biscuits and serving them with the wild honey Virg Daugherty had given them. There was plenty of beans and bacon, and they washed it all down with cup after cup of coffee. With Goodnight's riders on short rations and hungry, introductions were left undone until after supper. As everybody nursed a last cup of coffee, Goodnight got to his feet.

"Stand up when I call your name," he said, "so these folks will know who you are. When I'm done, McCaleb will introduce his hands. Red Alford?"

Reluctantly the young man got up and stood there looking sheepishly at the toes of his run-over boots. Gratefully, he sat down, and his roping pardner Langford Dill unwillingly took his place as Goodnight introduced him.

"This ugly jaybird," said Goodnight, pointing to a grinning Negro, "is Jim Fowler. Sometimes he calls himself Jim Goodnight, but there's no truth to the story that he's my illegitimate son."

They all laughed. Goodnight continued, introducing Charlie Wilson.

"His family was run out of Arkansas in 'fifty-seven. His brother, 'One-Armed' Bill, is the best cowboy that ever worked for me. Last fall he quit, bought a few barrels of whiskey on credit, and started a saloon in Jacksboro." He pointed at another rider, and the slender young man with sandy red hair got up.

"This is Simpson Crawford," said Goodnight. "He's a fighting Irishman who'll fight at the drop of a hat. If you don't have a hat, he'll loan you his and drop it for you. His friends, when he has any, call him Simp."

There was nothing reluctant about the Irishman. He grinned good-naturedly, caught Rebecca's eye and winked at her. McCaleb scowled.

"The German," said Goodnight, pointing to a heavy-set man with a flowing moustache, "is Nath Brauner. He's cross-eyed and purely hates rattlesnakes. The old man there on the end—I reckon he's pushing thirty-five —is Wes Sheek."

Quickly McCaleb introduced his small crew, employing none of Goodnight's humor. It came as no surprise when he discovered that Goose was nowhere to be found. He did the best he could, warning them that the Apache was wary of whites but had proven himself invaluable to them in Comanche territory.

"I don't like Injuns," said Simp Crawford. "None of 'em. For his sake, you'd best keep him out of my way."

"For *your* sake, my friend," said McCaleb coldly, "you'd best stay out of *his* way."

"I'll fire the first man that starts trouble," snapped Goodnight, "and that goes for all of you. Mind your manners, and McCaleb can control the Indian. But if you provoke a wolf, don't whine when you get bit."

"Simp ain't seen *that* wolf's teeth," said Red Alford. "He's got a knife as long as a cavalry saber. He'll cut your gizzard out pronto."

Goodnight and his men returned to their camp, leaving McCaleb's outfit in a somber mood.

"I'd hoped," said McCaleb, "that Goose could scout for all three outfits, but I've changed my mind. Given a chance, with all the dust and confusion, bunch-quitting, thunderstorms and stampedes, somebody might be tempted to back-shoot Goose. It could happen without us ever knowing who did it. I'm going to ask Charlie for third position, allowing his and Loving's herds to go ahead of ours. That'll eliminate our need for a point rider, and we'll be eating the dust of three thousand longhorns."

"I don't care," said Rebecca. "It'll be more like we still have our own herd."

"We'll be giving up some advantage," said Will. "Indians or outlaws don't often strike at the point, but at the tag end of a drive, where it's the most vulnerable. The drag rider's got nobody to watch his back, and he's got the stragglers from the entire herd—in this case, *three* herds—on his hands."

"That's gospel," said McCaleb, "and a herd of three thousand longhorns could be strung out for two or three miles. I'll get with Goodnight and Loving and arrange some signals. Otherwise the drag riders can be cut down by Indians or outlaws and a big chunk of the herd stampeded before the rest of the outfit up ahead knows what's going on."

Monte snorted. "Well, if we're goin' to fight all the varmints anyhow, we should of done like Brazos wanted and went ahead with our own drive."

"We won't have the drag by ourselves," said McCaleb. "I'll see to it that Charlie has at least one rider with us and Loving another, if not more."

Nobody objected when McCaleb decided to take Goose with him on the trip to Weatherford. One reason, as they likely suspected, was that McCaleb did not fully trust the Goodnight outfit in their boss's absence. They seemed friendly enough, but when it came to Indians—*any* Indians—most Texans saw them in the same light as Simp Crawford. Crawford could provoke Goose, kill him and, except for Goodnight's threat to fire him, go unpunished. While it was gross injustice, it was the prevailing mood of the time, and McCaleb's unfailing premonition of trouble throbbed anew. Somewhere on the trail that lay ahead of them, Goose would have to fight for his life, and Benton McCaleb decided that the Indian would have more than a fighting chance. Goose was panther-quick; if he had the desire to learn, McCaleb would teach him the fast draw that his infamous cousin, Cullen Baker, had taught him.

To McCaleb's surprise, Goodnight chose Simp Crawford to accompany him to Weatherford. He could only conclude that Goodnight had sought to avoid trouble by taking the potential troublemaker with him. Goose had already roped the three animals they would use for packhorses, and was cinching the second pack saddle in place when Goodnight and Crawford rode in. Crawford tensed when he saw Goose, but the Indian ignored him. Goodnight took in the situation, shot Crawford an unfathomable look and said nothing.

"Brazos," said McCaleb, "you're in charge while I'm gone. If there's trouble, work with Charlie's outfit. Keep your guns ready, all of you, and don't stray from camp alone. For *any* reason." He had his eyes on Rebecca, and she returned his look without expression.

"I'm leaving Wes Sheek in charge," said Goodnight, "and since we're out of grub, I'm askin' permission for my boys to take their meals with you until we get back."

"Glad to have 'em," said Brazos. "I'll get with Wes after breakfast and we'll lay out a day and night watch."

Goodnight led out, followed by Crawford, McCaleb, and Goose. The Apache led one packhorse, McCaleb a second, and Crawford the third. Goose eyed Simp Crawford warily, sensing the man's hostility. The journey was mostly silent. They halted only to rest and water the horses, the last time at the little creek where McCaleb and Rebecca had taken their baths. Memories of her flooded his mind, and he found himself facing the dismal realization that she had made no further overtures toward him. Their relationship had become so strained that her spark seemed to have died, leaving only casual indifference. Try as he might, he couldn't free his troubled mind of her until they reined up at Silas Moon's store.

Goodnight pounded on the heavy oak door until Silas identified them and slid back the bar. Goose made no move to follow them into the store, and neither did Simp Crawford. Moon's eyes lighted briefly when he recognized McCaleb, but he greeted Goodnight with no enthusiasm.

McCaleb understood Moon's predicament. Apparently, Silas Moon's rich inventory, and the credit he must have needed to purchase those goods, had been the result of Oliver Loving's influence with the Federals. Moon now found himself in a position where he must extend unlimited credit not just to Loving, but to Goodnight as well. It had created an uneasy alliance, which further fueled the fires of McCaleb's misgivings about Loving's "connections." Before the war there had been rumors of kickbacks, short tallies, and of entire herds that existed only on paper. McCaleb wanted no part of the proposed sale at Fort Sumner if there was even a taint of dishonesty. He was glad he had paid for the goods he'd taken from Silas Moon's store. He listened as Goodnight intensified Moon's discomfort.

". . . all written down for you, Silas. I'm going to Parker County and get my wagon. I'll be back about this time tomorrow; be sure all this is ready. I expect you'll be seeing Mr. Loving by the end of the week."

From the look on Moon's face, McCaleb decided that Mr. Loving would be about as welcome as the Angel of Death. Goodnight had turned to go, when his eyes fell on a gun rack pegged to the wall beside the door. Two rifles rested on wooden pegs, and hanging from its trigger guard was an obviously new nickle-silvered .44-caliber Colt revolver. It had bone grips and, even in the poor light, the silvered surface of the weapon glittered.

Goodnight hefted it, border-shifting it from hand to hand. Silas Moon looked like he was about to be sick.

"Put this on my bill, Silas, along with a couple boxes of shells," said Goodnight. Without a word, Moon went into the back of the store and returned with the shells. Suddenly there was a cry of pure terror from outside that froze them in their tracks. McCaleb recovered first and flung open the heavy door. Simpson Crawford stood on tiptoe, his back against the log wall of the store. His shirt had been slashed and hung in tatters. His right arm hung at an awkward angle and his un-fired Colt lay at his feet. Goose held the glistening bowie's point at Simp's throat. A thin rivulet of blood ran down the cowboy's neck. Simp's eyes bugged out like a toad's and his face and neck were frog-belly white.

"Goose!" said McCaleb. *"Ninguno!"*

The Apache turned savage eyes on McCaleb and returned his murderous gaze to the terrified Simp. For a moment it seemed he would plunge the huge knife into Crawford's throat. Reluctantly he lowered the bowie and backed away. Crawford slumped down against the wall, moaning. McCaleb turned to Goodnight.

"Get up, Simp," said Goodnight, without a trace of sympathy in his voice.

Crawford stumbled to his feet, ignoring the Colt. He looked about, the expression in his eyes bordering on madness. McCaleb said nothing.

"Mount up, Simp," said Goodnight.

Despite Crawford's former arrogance, McCaleb felt a touch of pity for the man. Grasping the horn with his left hand, Simp made three attempts before he was finally able to pull himself into the saddle.

Goodnight turned to McCaleb. "I ought to be back here before noon tomorrow," he said.

Seeing no evidence of further trouble from Crawford, and no impending retribution from Goodnight, Goose returned the bowie to its thonged position around his neck. Like McCaleb, he waited, each of them aware that the next move was Goodnight's. It was an awkward situation, from which the man couldn't extract himself without some conciliatory act. But when it came, it was all wrong, despite Goodnight's obvious intentions. Impulsive to a fault, he extended the new .44 Colt to Goose, butt first. With his big left hand he motioned toward himself, toward the Colt and then toward the Indian. Goose accepted the weapon and then carefully, deliberately, dropped it in the dust at Goodnight's feet. Still facing Goodnight, he back-stepped to the log wall of the store, his craggy face expressionless.

Despite his rough manner and often brusque speech, Charles Goodnight was a sensitive man, and the show of contempt—without a word being spoken—cut him deep. It was the first and only time McCaleb had ever seen him so totally embarrassed, so at a loss for words. His face flamed crimson down to his beard and he seemed to shrink before McCaleb's eyes. Silently he swung into his saddle, kicking the big black into a lope. Simp Crawford followed.

CHAPTER 15

$\mathcal{A}$fter McCaleb had paid Moon, only fifty dollars of their original stake remained. The sun was a good four hours high, but with nothing better to do, they pitched camp. McCaleb had bought some tins of sardines, and they washed them down with strong coffee. Goose wolfed down the oily little fish like he'd been eating them all his life, his bronze face devoid of expression. You never knew, McCaleb reflected, whether Goose was happy, sad, or just didn't give a damn. The only thing he displayed in unbridled abundance was murderous anger. Something that had long puzzled McCaleb became even more puzzling after the Indian's confrontation with Simp Crawford. There was no doubt that Crawford had gone for his gun or that Goose had taken it away from him, breaking or dislocating his arm while doing so. The Indian had a .44-caliber Colt revolver, yet he rarely used it, preferring the bowie. He could have used the gun on many occasions at far less risk to himself. Why hadn't he? He had disdained the use of belt and holster, preferring the weapon against his belly, its muzzle tucked under the waist of his buckskins. Brazos and Will never tired of pointing out that the accidental firing of the Colt could cost Goose some vital parts of his anatomy.

McCaleb got up and the Apache's eyes followed him. In a blur, McCaleb drew his Colt and pretended to fire it. He returned it to its cross-hand position on his left hip and then pointed to Goose. The Indian seemed in doubt as to what was expected of him. Again McCaleb drew, and this time there was a drumroll of sound as he fired, striking one of the empty sardine tins. Each successive shot sent the tin bounding farther away, until the Colt clicked on empty. McCaleb punched out the empty casings, reloaded from his cartridge belt and holstered the Colt. Then he pointed to Goose and to another of the tins a dozen feet away. The Apache drew and fired four times. Only his first shot struck the tin; the last three were clean misses. McCaleb saw that his reflexes were good and his hand as swift as a striking rattler, but his draw was awkward. The Colt was in an unnatural position for a fast draw. McCaleb shucked his gun belt, took the Colt and shoved its muzzle under the waist of his Levi's at the same position the weapon normally rode in the holster. Goose slid his own Colt around on his left hip and with a faster, far less clumsy motion drew and fired twice, striking the sardine tin each time. The Colt clicked on empty and McCaleb handed him enough shells to reload. Then to McCaleb's surprise, Goose positioned the Colt butt forward on his right hip. Left-handed, he drew and fired three times. Not once did he miss!

Goose returned the Colt to its butt-forward position on his right hip. McCaleb took one of the now-battered sardine tins and tossed it into the air. Again the Indian drew left-handed, and his first shot struck the tin before it hit the ground. His second shot sent the tin bounding into the air, and the third struck it before it hit the ground! McCaleb snatched off his hat, swatting it against his thigh in delight. Drawn by the gunfire, Silas Moon stood in the doorway shading his eyes. McCaleb waved his hat, lest the old man think there was an outlaw or Indian attack coming. So limited was his vocabulary, Goose rarely said anything, and it came as a surprise when he suddenly spoke.

"Rapido?"

"Mucho rapido!" McCaleb replied.

Demonstrating with his own Colt, McCaleb was able to convey to Goose the idea that he should practice his draw without actually firing. He had witnessed the Apache's accuracy; there was little room for improvement except in his ability to get the pistol into action quickly. Practicing the fast draw wasted no ammunition. His back to a pine, McCaleb tilted his hat over his eyes and sorted things out in his mind. Everybody in his outfit was right-handed. He doubted that Goose had ever had a Colt in his hand until he had been given the one he now carried. It seemed he had adopted their custom, and finding himself uncomfortable with it, had avoided using the Colt. Goose was naturally left-handed, and only when he had been encouraged to emulate McCaleb's fast draw had he really lived up to his potential. McCaleb hadn't gone out of his way to communicate with the Apache, depending on Brazos. But today Brazos hadn't been around, and McCaleb for the first time felt he had gained some ground with Goose. The only thing diminishing his pride in the Apache's dexterity with a pistol was the sobering awareness of Goose's volatile temper. He believed, however, that Goose was more than just the bloodthirsty savage he often appeared. He could easily have killed Simp Crawford instead of disarming him and scaring him out of his wits.

Before dark, McCaleb filled the coffeepot at the spring and doused all that remained of their supper fire. They rolled in their blankets near the picketed horses, depending on the sensitive animals to sound a warning at the approach of man or beast. They slept undisturbed, had their breakfast of broiled bacon and hot coffee, and waited impatiently for Goodnight's return. The wind being out of the southwest, they heard the approaching wagon long before they were able to see it. They saddled their mounts and, leading the three packhorses, rode to Moon's store. Finally the wagon, drawn by six yoke of patient oxen, rattled into view. McCaleb wasn't

in the least surprised that Simp Crawford hadn't returned, but Goodnight wasn't alone. Two strange riders,
one of them leading Goodnight's mount, rode alongside
the wagon. Goodnight's early years as a bull whacker
served him well; he handled the six yoke of oxen expertly.

He clambered down from the wagon and swatted his
dusty hat against his thigh. The accompanying riders sat
their saddles in silence until Goodnight bid them dismount. They were Mexican vaqueros, so alike that
McCaleb couldn't tell one from the other. They wore
tight-legged dark breeches, matching dark jackets that
ended at the waist, and white shirts. Their boots were
solid black, and each wore a wide-brimmed, tall-
crowned sombrero and a Colt on his right hip. They
looked more like dandies or gunslicks than cowboys,
McCaleb thought. Each rode a big gray whose Arabian
ancestors likely weren't too many generations back. Silas Moon stood in the open door watching. Goodnight
didn't waste time.

"This is Donato Vasquez and his brother Emilio," he
said, looking at McCaleb and Goose. He then addressed
the Mexicans in Spanish, gesturing toward McCaleb and
Goose as he did so.

McCaleb nodded and the Mexican duo nodded in
turn, neither offering to shake hands. One of them—
McCaleb thought it was Emilio—looked at Goose and
then spoke foolishly.

"*Ganos? Ganos comico, comico!*"

Goose didn't think it was funny and neither did the
Mexican, once he saw the look in the Indian's eyes.
Goose advanced and his adversary backstepped, hold-
ing up his hands.

"*Ninguno*, Goose," said McCaleb. "*Ninguno.*"

Goose halted, looking directly at Charles Goodnight,
who—aware that he was already on the bad side of the
Indian—strove to make amends. He spoke rapidly in
Spanish to the offending Emilio, and McCaleb heard
Simp Crawford's name. Apparently the shaken Emilio

had just been made aware of Crawford's fate and his
reason for leaving Goodnight's drive. Emilio's face
paled. Earnestly, in Spanish, he spoke to Goose, and the
Indian relaxed. At least, thought McCaleb, the Mexican
could make amends in a language Goose could understand. Donato, who emerged as the older and probably
the wiser of the two, also spoke to the Indian in rapid-
fire border Spanish. McCaleb was unable to understand
a word. He cut his eyes to Goodnight and the big man
grinned.

"He says Emilio speaks with the voice of a donkey; a
foolish *pelado* who is unfit even to feed the goats."

The Apache's craggy face lost its hostility and he relaxed. Somewhere beyond that murderous temper
lurked a sense of humor, McCaleb thought.

Goodnight climbed back up to the wagon seat. He
swung the six yoke of patient oxen in a half circle and
maneuvered the rear of the wagon up to the front of
Moon's store. Goodnight's wagon—the very first
"chuck" wagon, and a prototype for all that followed—
was an impressive vehicle. Goodnight was proud of its
design and was quick to display its uniqueness.

"It's an ex-Army wagon," he explained. "Solid iron
axles. Stripped it down to the running gear and had
everything else rebuilt. There's a double floor of seasoned oak, both pitch-sealed so's she won't leak. Sides
of the box are eighteen inches higher than normal, also
pitch-sealed. That water barrel on the right-hand side
will hold a two-day supply of water. There on the left
side is an oversize toolbox big enough to hold a shovel,
an ax, branding irons, hobbles, extra harness, horseshoe-
ing tools, and any extra stuff the cook or hands might
need. There's four bentwood bows to support the canvas cover. Now, come around to the back and take a
look at my chuck box—the only one of its kind."

The chuck box was built onto the very rear of the
wagon, extending maybe three feet back into the wagon
and reaching almost to the top of the last canvas-sup-
porting bow. The entire face of the chuck box was cov-

ered with a door, hinged at the bottom, that swung down on a dangling leg to form a worktable. The chuck box itself was a series of compartments and drawers, each designed for a specific purpose. Across the very top of the box there were four small closed drawers, and beneath them, a row of three larger ones. Below the drawers, the rest of the chuck box was devoted to open compartments.

"Little drawers across the top," said Goodnight, "are for flour, sugar, beans, dried fruit, and coffee beans. First two big drawers are for tin cups, plates, and eating tools. That last one is the possibles drawer; I aim to use it for medicines, bandages, scissors, needles and thread, and whatever else I can think of. That biggest open space on the bottom is for a sourdough keg. The other spaces are for salt, lard bucket, baking soda, jug of molasses, coffeepots, and a jug of whiskey. Strictly medicinal, of course. On the side, over the toolbox, is the coffee grinder. There under the chuck box is a 'boot' for skillets and dutch ovens. Behind the box itself, I'll carry an extra wagon wheel, bedrolls, slickers, extra guns and shells, a jug of coal oil, lanterns, and a tin of axle grease, plus grain for the team and the remuda. The little bit of beans, fruit, coffee, sugar, and flour in the chuck box is just for the cook's immediate needs. I'll carry bulk supplies of these things in the wagon box, along with a side of beef, sides of bacon, and some hams. We might as well start loading. The barrel of flour comes first."

He spoke rapidly in Spanish to Donato and Emilio, and the Mexican riders followed Silas Moon into the store. They hauled the goods out and Goodnight hoisted everything into the wagon. Silas Moon watched, offering no assistance, Goodnight apparently expecting none.

An hour before noon they were ready to move out. The wagon would slow them down and they'd be lucky to reach Elm Creek by dark. McCaleb was about to swing into his saddle when Goodnight called him over to the wagon.

"Bent, I had some disturbing news from old man Whitt, the carpenter that built this wagon. I have a favor to ask of you. Not for me, but for an old friend of mine. Tie your horse behind the wagon and ride with me. I'll have the Vasquez boys lead two of your pack animals."

McCaleb tied his roan to the rear of the wagon and climbed over the high-sided wagon box to the seat. Goodnight waited until the six yoke of oxen had settled into their harness before he spoke.

"Remember me telling about One-Armed Bill Wilson quitting me last fall, going to Jacksboro and opening a saloon?"

McCaleb nodded, saying nothing.

"Well," continued Goodnight, "the Federals have Bill in the guardhouse at Fort Richardson, near Jacksboro. He's been accused of murder, framed. Next Monday they plan to take Bill to Decatur, where he'll be court-martialed. They say Bill's a goner if he ever goes to trial, and conviction means death by firing squad."

"I reckon," said McCaleb, "you don't aim for that to happen. How do you figure I can be of any help?"

"We'll need Rebecca's help, and I thought you—"

"Whoa," said McCaleb. "I'll do anything I can, Charlie, but we're not endangering her."

"So *that's* how it is," said Goodnight. "You and her . . ."

"That's how it is," said McCaleb grimly.

"Let me tell you the rest of it," said Goodnight. "If you're willing to ask her, and she says no, then . . ."

They didn't reach their combined camp on Elm Creek until well after dark. McCaleb, having long since left the wagon seat and straddled his roan, rode into camp leading two packhorses, Goose trailing with the third. Goodnight drove directly to his own outfit. McCaleb reckoned there would be time enough for his riders to fuss over the new chuck wagon and to meet the Vasquez brothers. He and Goose went to the fire and poured themselves cups of coffee from the blackened pot.

"Thank God you got back when you did," said Brazos. "I don't believe Charlie's ever fed that outfit a square meal. They went through our grub like a swarm of locusts."

All of them had spoken to him except Rebecca. They unloaded the packhorses, and she helped. It was a while before he was able to speak to her without the others hearing. Goodnight had sworn him to secrecy.

"Would you have felt better about me," he asked with a grin, "if I'd been mutilated and scalped by Indians?"

"Not especially," she said. "We needed these supplies."

"I'm touched by your obvious concern. I'd not bother you, except that I'm forced to ask a favor."

"Forced? I don't see anybody holding a gun on you."

"It's not for *me*, damn it. I'd rather *be* scalped by Indians than ask you to do anything for me. It's for Charlie."

"You mean *Mister* Goodnight. He strikes me as the kind of man who's real handy with his mouth. Let him ask his own favors."

Furious, he grabbed her by the shoulders and shook her till her teeth rattled. She slapped him. Hard. He drew her to him in a crushing embrace, planting a solid, lingering kiss on her lips. She almost responded, then went rigid as a fence post, following with an upraised knee that caught him where it would do the most damage. Sick, he sank down with an agonized groan.

The three tired packhorses, freed of their burdens, had been allowed to roll. Monte then led them out to graze, picketing them with the rest of the remuda. As he passed McCaleb, he stopped and stared down, surprised.

"Why are you sitting out here in the dark?"

"I reckon I'm just tired, kid. Almighty tired . . ."

Since the watch for the night had already been picked, McCaleb let it stand. The outfit's usual antics might result in pairing him for three uncomfortable hours with a silent Rebecca Nance, and he was in no mood for that. He rolled in his blankets, skipping supper and avoiding further conversation. Why had he allowed Goodnight to talk him into a "favor" involving the stubborn, unpredictable girl? They were but five days from the time of Bill Wilson's removal from Fort Richardson, and no more than ten days from the arrival of Oliver Loving's herd. His mind so occupied, McCaleb failed to notice a flicker of lightning on the western horizon, nor did he hear a faint rumble of thunder. He drifted into fitful, uneasy slumber.

"Roll out and mount up," shouted Brazos. "There's a bad 'un coming."

McCaleb sat up, fully dressed except for his boots. The west wind had turned cold, evidently forgetting it was the third week in May. The moon and stars had disappeared behind a swirling mass of thunderheads. Thunder rumbled closer, and the very earth vibrated. Uneasy, a cow bawled. McCaleb stomped into his boots, grabbed his saddle and headed for the remuda. Brazos and Will had been on watch and were already saddled. Sudden lightning spiderwebbed the sky, and a rearing horse pulled its picket pin. Brazos caught the frightened animal before it could run. Monte, Rebecca, and Goose were mounted and ready when McCaleb swung into his saddle. They began circling the restless longhorns, and in the distance, as lightning zigzagged across the murky heavens, they could see the Goodnight riders performing the same weary task. Charles Goodnight jogged his big black alongside McCaleb's roan just as the first heavy raindrops slapped their backs and shoulders. McCaleb was tying his hat in place with piggin string.

"Too much lightning," said Goodnight, the wind whipping his voice away. "Been too quiet. We're overdue for a bad one. These brutes *know* they're going to run. They're just waitin' for something to set 'em off and they'll fog out of here like a prairie fire."

"Storm's blowin' out of the west," said McCaleb. "I'm counting on them running away from it, unless there's ground lightning. Suppose I group my outfit to the north of our herds and you move yours to the south? Unless they break right into the storm, we'll have them boxed. If they run to the east, like we expect, then both outfits can ride to head them. If the lightning plays tricks on us and they break north or south, we'll still be ahead of them."

"Be almighty careful," warned Goodnight, "if they run to the east. Lots of dry stream beds and arroyos you won't be able to see in the dark. Pass the word to your riders. At the worst, a tumble into one of them could kill you and your horse. At best you might come out of it stove-up and crippled."

McCaleb moved his riders to the north of the combined herds, passing on Goodnight's warning. Somewhere to the west the lightning struck with a rending crash. There was the plaintive bawling of a cow, followed by another and then another. Lightning struck again, closer this time, the horrendous sound accompanied by a trembling of the earth and the acrid stink of sulfur. Jagged fingers of fire illuminated the stormy skies, and the herd, as one, rose to its feet.

Faint and seemingly far away there was gunfire. McCaleb didn't know if it was from his own riders or the Goodnight outfit. He pounded along parallel to the now running herd, the slashing rain and storm-bred wind at his back. The herd spread out, some of the lethal horns coming much too close. When lightning flared, McCaleb saw a rider ahead of him who might have been Goodnight; he thought he recognized the big black horse. If the Goodnight herd was running ahead of his own, and he believed they were, then McCaleb's outfit was wasting its time. The stampede would already be so strung out, his riders would never be able to head it.

McCaleb felt that however futile their efforts, they mustn't throw all the burden on the Goodnight riders. He slapped the roan on its sodden flank, urging the animal to greater effort. Suddenly the earth beneath the hoofs of the running horse seemed to fall away. There was a scream from the roan—terrifyingly human—and McCaleb heard nothing more as he was lost in a maelstrom of blinding pain. The roan had gone into the arroyo head first and lay on its side, its neck grotesquely twisted. McCaleb lay trapped beneath the horse, unable to free himself had he been conscious enough to even attempt it. There was no sound except the moan of the wind and the pattering of the cold rain. It splashed into McCaleb's face, and he was as unaware of that as of the blood mixing with it from a gaping wound just above his eyes. It was four long hours until dawn, and the arroyo was slowly filling with water. . . .

"I haven't seen Bent," said Goodnight, puzzled. "I reckoned I'd find him somewhere back here. Our bunch started to run before yours did; when yours lit out and caught up with the tail end of ours, that put the leaders of the stampede so far ahead, none of you could have turned them. I hope he didn't take a fall, maybe into some arroyo."

"We must look for him," cried Rebecca frantically. "He may be hurt!"

"I have two lanterns in the wagon," said Goodnight. "We'd better go get them. With this rain . . ."

Rebecca, Monte, and Goose took one lantern while Goodnight, Brazos, and Will took the other. Following the path of the stampede in the trampled, muddy earth, they rode slowly, unable to see more than a foot or two beyond the lantern's feeble glow.

"Deep arroyo out there a ways," said Goodnight. "Runs maybe a mile out into the prairie. When there's a storm like this, it takes the runoff into Elm Creek. This close in, the herd should have been bunched enough to miss it. A rider swinging wide to avoid getting caught up in the stampede could have run into it. Mesquite, brush, and young trees grown up along the banks; it'll be as black down there as the inside of a cow."

Goodnight carried one lantern and Monte the other. They found the arroyo and, leaving their horses, walked the length of it. Will, Brazos, Rebecca, and Goose parted the head-high cottonwoods and stomped through the underbrush so that the lantern bearers might get near the edge of the steep banks. There was a gurgle of water below them, but in the continuing rain their attempts to direct the feeble light from the lanterns to the water's surface were futile. Trudging from one end of the arroyo to the other—where it fed into Elm Creek—yielded exactly nothing except frustration, and in the case of Rebecca, a growing fear.

"Much as I hate to," said Goodnight, "we'll have to wait on first light. Darkness is bad enough, but with this continuing rain, it's impossible."

"No!" cried Rebecca. "He's down there and he's hurt. Please, let me have one of the lanterns. I'll start where the arroyo feeds into the creek and wade it; follow it to the end. I'll find him."

"Damnation!" said Goodnight. "That's what we should have already done! Come on, Rebecca, I'll go with you!"

"Me and Brazos will take the other lantern," said Will, "and start from the other end."

The cold rain on McCaleb's face restored his consciousness. Lying on his back, he tried to sit up, and found he was unable to. He was under the dead horse, pinned from the waist down! Fast running, cold water lapped at his chin. He must summon help! Twisting to the right, he worked his numb right hand to his left hip, seeking his Colt. The holster was empty. His Henry was in the saddle boot, on the underside of the roan. He had no doubt they were looking for him, but the water was rising. At best, he thought dismally, he had but a few more minutes. Somewhere, sounding far away, he thought he heard Rebecca's voice. . . .

"Here," he cried weakly, without much hope. "Here . . ."

* * *

Rebecca fell on her knees beside him, the water reaching her armpits. Goodnight drew his Colt and fired three quick shots. They came on the run, and McCaleb saw only the dim glow of the lantern on the high bank above.

"Bring the horses," shouted Goodnight, "and throw us a rope. He's under the horse, and we'll have to move it. He's alive but he's hurt."

Dawn was a rosy glow in the sky when Red Alford and Wes Sheek rolled back into camp. They brought the chuck wagon for McCaleb. Goodnight insisted that McCaleb drink half a quart of moonshine to diminish his fever. Will Elliot sewed up the ugly gash in McCaleb's forehead, sloshing the closed wound with iodine.

"After breakfast," said Goodnight, "it's roundup time."

"Not for me," said Rebecca. "I'm staying with McCaleb."

"Maybe we ought to leave Goose with you," said Brazos. "This wouldn't be a good time for the Comanches to show up."

"Their tough luck if they do," said the girl grimly. "I've had a hard night and I'm in no mood for a bunch of Indians. I have a Spencer rifle and I know how to use it. I'll shoot their ears off."

Goodnight laughed, his eyes twinkling. Benton McCaleb was a lucky man.

When the others had joined Goodnight's crew to round up the scattered herds, Rebecca put on a kettle of water to boil. McCaleb slept, probably a result of the moonshine, but there was the shine of sweat on his face. He no longer had a fever. They had stretched him out on a double thickness of blankets, his head on Rebecca's saddle. Now that he was safe and alive, she looked him over critically. He was a mess, muddy from head to toe. She tugged off his boots, peeled off his socks and found his feet blue with cold. She had a time stripping off his Levi's and shirt; they seemed like part of his skin. He was no help to her, being limp as a strip of wet rawhide. His thighs had a purplish tint, as though badly bruised, and his left knee looked swollen. He had been lucky; had the horse fallen on his upper body, his chest would have been crushed. Some of the cloth she had bought for bandages she ripped into towel-size hunks. She soaked half a dozen of them in hot water and spread them over his bruised thighs and swollen knee, replacing them with hot ones as they cooled. Suddenly his eyes were wide open and he was watching her. When he spoke, his voice sounded thick, like he was half asleep.

"Did you strip me like this before . . . while the others . . . were . . . here?"

"Of course." She giggled. "Why?"

He said nothing. To her total surprise, his face flushed —not with anger, but embarrassment. She was immediately sorry for having deceived him.

"They left you just like you were hauled out of that arroyo," she said. "I did the rest, including peeling you down to the bare hide. How do you feel?"

"No worse'n if I'd had my skull crushed with a rock and then had half a ton of horse fall on me. Can you find one more blanket to cover me?"

"Everybody's gone after the cattle, and I'll cover you before they return. You've got some bad bruises and a wrenched knee. I can't keep these hot cloths coming with you under a blanket."

"You're almighty concerned with how I feel. Last night you tried to change me from a bull into a steer. That hurt worse than bein' pitched into that arroyo on my head."

She dropped the steaming cloth she'd just fished out of the kettle, came to where he was lying and got down on her knees beside him. "I'm sorry," she said. "Truly sorry. I hated myself after I . . . I did that. Then after the stampede . . . when I was afraid you might be . . . dead . . . I . . . I wished I was dead. Whatever you say or do to me, I'll never, ever do that again. Can you forgive me?"

"Only if you promise me something and keep your promise."

"What must I promise?"

"You've had a big mad on," said McCaleb, "ever since we took that bath in the creek. You wanted something I wasn't ready to give, and when I didn't do what you wanted, you took it as a slight. Like I tried to tell you, it wasn't the time or the place and it was no fault of yours. You're truly a beautiful woman, and God knows, I wish I was ready for you, but I'm not. I want you to promise me that the *time* and *place* can be of my choosing. You said you wanted me; do you want me enough to let it be on *my* terms?"

"I don't know. I feel like a withered old maid. I don't know how much longer I can wait for that time and place. Whatever happens or doesn't happen between us, I promise not to be mean and spiteful, ever again."

CHAPTER 16

*T*wo days prior to One-Armed Wilson's removal for court-martial, McCaleb and Rebecca started for Jacksboro. Rebecca was uneasy.

"Suppose these Federals know Bill Wilson doesn't *have* a wife?"

"Not likely they will," said McCaleb. "They're Federals in name only. They're a bunch of renegade Texans that Goodnight, Bill and Charlie Wilson, and a few others run out in 'sixty-one. They went to Kansas, joined the Union army, and now they're here to get even. Charlie had nobody he could send that wouldn't be recognized."

"It just seems like a weak plan," said Rebecca.

"I agree, but it's the best we can do. You don't break a man out of a military stockade. Just be sure you tell Wilson this is Charlie's idea. Repeat back to me what you're going to tell him."

"He's to take the money Goodnight's sending him," said Rebecca, "and buy whiskey with it, but not for himself. Once he's out of the guardhouse, somewhere between Fort Richardson and Decatur, he's to get his guards drunk. Then he makes a run for it, traveling by night, until he can join Goodnight's drive somewhere between here and the Pecos."

McCaleb halted three quarters of a mile from Fort Richardson, where he could see without being seen. Rebecca rode in alone, was stopped by a sentry at the gate and allowed to enter. McCaleb waited an anxious hour. Finally he saw her exit the gate and breathed a sigh of relief. She joined him and they trotted their horses back the way they had come. Finally Rebecca spoke.

"I gave him the money and told him what Goodnight said for him to do. He said, 'I'd of thought Charlie would of sent me a pistol.' "

"Damn fool," said McCaleb. "This is his only chance, and Goodnight knows it. We can't fight the Federals, even if this particular garrison *is* manned by cutthroat Texans flying under false colors. This is all we can do, all I promised to do, and all I aim to do. Let's ride!"

June first came and went without a sign of Oliver Loving. Finally, on June 4, 1866, he rode in with ten riders and eleven hundred longhorns. He was a big man, weighing a good two hundred pounds and, despite his fifty-four years, as sturdy as a post oak. He had no gray hair and looked not much older than Goodnight. He dismounted, shook hands with Goodnight and McCaleb, but hardly cast a glance at anybody else. Three of his hands reined up behind him. They were grizzled old tobacco-chewing Texans, looking more like mountain men than cowboys. They cast suspicious, slanch-eyed looks at Goose, and when the Indian returned their stares, they shifted their eyes to Rebecca. While a certain camaraderie had developed between McCaleb's and Goodnight's outfit, Loving's riders seemed standoffish and wary. Goodnight broke the uncomfortable silence.

"Get your herd settled in, Mr. Loving; then perhaps you and your outfit will join the rest of us for supper."

But the Loving outfit seemed to have better things to do. Just before dark Goodnight rode in, speaking without dismounting.

"Mr. Loving took the time to stop at Weatherford and load his supplies. He believes we can begin the drive this coming Wednesday, June sixth."

McCaleb nodded. Nobody said anything until Goodnight had ridden away.

"Well, bless my soul," said Brazos. "I hope Mr. Loving don't decide he wants to shoot a wild turkey and celebrate Thanksgivin' before we start."

"Mr. Loving," said Rebecca, "looked like he just came from a war, or was going to one. I never saw so many guns on one man and one horse."

"In Comanche country," said McCaleb, "I reckon five guns ain't too many. But if a man can't shoot his way out with a Colt six-shooter and a sixteen-shot Henry, he's likely a dead peckerwood anyhow."

"I reckon that brace of saddle Colts ain't a bad idea," said Brazos, "but I'd draw the line at that Colt revolving six-shooter rifle. He's a braver man than me."

"Suppose it could be made to fire the same shells as the Colt revolver," said Monte. "What would be wrong with that?"

"Someday," said Will, "there'll be a rifle that will take the same shells as a Colt revolver, but it won't be a revolving rifle. Too much gas blowback and chain firing. There's got to be clearance between the front end of the revolving cylinder and the rear end of the barrel or the cylinder won't turn. Powder gas escapes through the gap; could set your shirt afire or put out your eye. Chain firing sets off not just one shell, but two or three. That's why most Texans swear *by* Colt's six-shooter revolver and swear *at* his six-shooter revolving rifle."

June fifth, the night before the drive would begin, Goodnight called them all together. He didn't waste any words.

"Benton McCaleb's outfit will be riding drag for the duration of the drive. This is the most vulnerable and probably the most dangerous position, and I'm almighty glad to have three ex-Rangers watching our back trail. I'll be riding ahead, scouting for suitable range, bed grounds, and water holes. I have asked Mr. Loving to take charge of this drive. While this trail will be as new to him as it is to me, he has taken the time to seek out and talk to several old-timers who drove the Butterfield stages half a dozen years ago. Mr. Loving, why don't you tell us what you've learned? Give us some idea as to what lies ahead?"

Since his arrival, Oliver Loving had said little, so it came as a total surprise—at least to McCaleb's outfit—when he spoke with eloquence and conviction. He had a tablet on which he had made notes.

"From here to the headwaters of the Middle Concho it's an easy drive. Beyond that, for upward of a hundred miles, there's no water. Not until we reach Horsehead Crossing, on the Pecos. We will cross the river, follow it to the Rockies and parallel them northward. While I am in charge of this drive, there will be no drinking. Any rider caught violating this rule is subject to dismissal. Any time, any place."

By the first gray light of dawn the combined herds were strung out to the west and the Elm Creek range was behind them. It was an easy drive as they followed the ruts that were the trace of the Southern Overland Mail. From dawn to dusk they rarely saw Goodnight. He ranged far ahead, doubling back occasionally to signal the point riders the direction the herd should take.

Slowly McCaleb's outfit gained a grudging respect for Oliver Loving. The man never stayed in one position more than a few minutes, pounding into the mesquite after bunch-quitters, conversing with the point riders, then dropping back to the drag. Once he jogged his horse alongside the Indian's, speaking to Goose in Spanish. Goose responded and Loving rode on. Reaching the North Concho, they crossed the divide to the Middle Concho, following it westward until it headed into the Staked Plains. They bedded down the herd at the headwaters of the Middle Concho. Ahead of them lay the deadliest, most treacherous stretch of the fledgling trail. Loving spoke to them at dawn.

"Fill every canteen to the brim," said Loving, "and let

the herd drink its fill. We'll spend the day here and move out at sunset, bedding them down late."

The point riders loped into the setting sun, the herd following. They drove until moonset, bedded down for the night and pushed on at dawn.

Alkali dust rose in clouds. McCaleb pulled his hat brim lower, trying to lessen the glare of the merciless sun. His bandanna covered his nose and mouth, but when he touched his tongue to parched lips, there was still a bitter alkaline taste. Will and Brazos, their own faces half hidden by dusty bandannas, jogged their mounts along on either side of him.

"For all Mr. Loving's experience," said Brazos, "this was a fool move. Driving makes cattle twice as thirsty. We should of drove them all night, bedded them down until dusk and drove all night again. They're used to waterin' every day, and by tonight they'll be so thirsty they won't bed down at all. By morning they'll be ready to drop in their tracks, not only from thirst, but from millin' around all night."

"I reckon you ought to talk to Charlie," said Will. "With a mixed herd, we'll be lucky to make fifteen miles a day. Closer to twelve, I'd say. If Charlie's Mr. Loving knows what he's talking about, and it's near 'bouts a hundred miles from Middle Concho to the Pecos, we're going to see the bones of this whole damn herd strung out along these alkali flats."

"I won't have to talk to Charlie," said McCaleb. "I'm reading it about the same as you. Nobody's going to sleep tonight. By morning, I think even Mr. Loving will see how the stick floats."

All night the cattle walked and milled, bawling their misery, refusing to lie down. Emilio, Goodnight's Mexican cook, kept the coffeepot full. Nobody slept. Wearily they moved out, the plaintive bawling of the cows a dirge.

"My God," said Brazos, "them cows walked far enough around in circles last night to have reached the river. They'd have been better off if we'd kept them moving; we'd be that much nearer water."

"I expect Charlie agrees with you," said McCaleb. "Here he comes."

"I'm taking charge of the drive," said Goodnight brusquely. "From here to the Pecos, no more camps. We're going to lose some, but we'll lose them all if we don't get them to water. Push them as hard as you can."

By sundown canteens were dry and there wasn't enough water left in the cook's barrel even to make coffee. They plodded on, the cattle growing weaker, the riders half blinded by dust and a growing need for sleep. Lips split open from the heat and throats were tormented by thirst and alkali. Goodnight had the point riders holding back the leaders while the drag, with doubled lariats, swatted the weaker stumbling cattle forward. Despite all McCaleb's threats and her good intentions, Rebecca cussed like a mule skinner. The bawling of the thirst-crazed cattle was a cacophony of misery. In a matter of hours their flanks had become drawn and gaunt and their ribs stuck out like roots in thin soil. As their heads sank lower, their very tongues dragged in the alkali dust. Their eyes seemed to glaze, sinking deeper into their sockets as death came ever closer. Wild-eyed and thirst-maddened, some of the beasts tried to gore anything within reach. They were cut out of the herd and left to die. Goodnight on his big black rode from point to flank to drag and back again. Oliver Loving had joined the drag riders, swatting the gaunt flanks of the bawling, stumbling cattle.

At the end of the third day, although there was no relief from thirst, welcome nightfall brought relief from the heat. Three hours before dawn they reached Castle Canyon, twelve miles from the Pecos River. The wind shifted, touching their blistered faces with cooling dampness.

"My God," shouted McCaleb, "they're going to run!"

The lead cattle thought they smelled water and lit a shuck downcanyon, but the heroic efforts of the point riders and Goodnight himself stopped them at a bend in the canyon. Slowly they closed the gap, bringing up the rest of the herd. It was but a few minutes until first light.

"Hold them here," said Goodnight. "I've heard a lot about this river, none of it good. I want a look at it. I'll fill the canteens."

When Goodnight returned and the riders had quenched their thirst, he spoke to Oliver Loving and then trotted his horse over to McCaleb.

"I'm going to take some riders and drive the strongest part of the herd to the river. When they've been watered and put to grass, we'll take the others, the weaker ones. There's just one good place to ford the river. At the nearest point the banks are maybe a dozen feet high. If we take them all at once, we can't control them. Once they smell water, they'll take the shortest route to it and there'll be hell to pay."

It made sense. McCaleb and Loving took most of the hands and blocked the canyon. Goodnight and his riders were successful in reaching the river, watering the cattle, and swimming them across. But the breeze, turning treacherous, brought the scent of water to the remaining thirsty longhorns and there was no holding them. Loving's mount was gored and the body of the kicking, screaming horse was all that saved his life. Riders literally climbed the canyon walls. The maddened, stampeding herd performed exactly as Goodnight had feared. They headed for the nearest, most inaccessible point of the river, plunging off the steep bank and taking part of the horse remuda with them. McCaleb slowed his mount, allowed Oliver Loving to swing up behind him, and they rode madly after the other riders in pursuit of the stampeding herd.

It was total, unbelievable chaos. Some of the cattle and several horses died in the fall. Some were hurt, while others, trapped under the bodies of those that followed, had drowned. A few stood in the water next to the high bank over which they had plunged, while others had been caught in the river's quicksand. Goodnight was already in the water, astride his big black, uncoiling his lariat. McCaleb reined up, allowing Loving to dismount, and then sent his bay splashing into the river. Hour after hour they worked, pausing only long enough to down the hot coffee Emilio kept ready. Again and again they plunged into the treacherous river, trying to save as many of the animals as they could. When finally it was too dark to see, they slept in their wet clothes and boots, the piteous bawling of the trapped and dying cattle invading their dreams.

The second day was even more terrible. Some of the cattle mired in quicksand had sunk deeper, sealing their doom. Others were simply beyond reach, trapped beneath unscalable banks with God only knew how much quicksand between them and their would-be rescuers. After a second day of almost fruitless toil, Goodnight made a decision.

"I've had enough. We've been a week without rest, spent two days in this blasted river, and we'll be lucky if some of us don't die from the exposure. This is just another loss on top of what we've already had to swallow. We'll rest here two or three days, tally our herds and horses and then move on."

Their tally revealed a loss of more than four hundred longhorns. Goodnight estimated that three fourths had died on the trail and the rest as a result of the disaster at Horsehead Crossing. They had lost a dozen horses, some with broken necks after their plunge into the Pecos and some with broken legs, shot in acts of mercy.

"Total damage," said Will, "is a hundred head and three of our horses."

"I expected worse," said McCaleb. "Hardest on the cows, I reckon."

"Right," said Brazos. "Nearly all she-stuff; always a problem with a mixed herd. Cows are weaker, got a shorter stride."

Goodnight rode into their camp and swung out of his saddle.

"We're having dried apple pie for supper tonight," he

said. "Everybody's invited. Kind of celebration. We'll be moving out at dawn. I'm anxious to get to Pope's Crossing and put this godforsaken river behind us."

They spent an almost festive evening gathered around Goodnight's chuck wagon. There were fried ham, beans, boiled potatoes, hot biscuits, coffee, and the promised dried apple pies. Oliver Loving's outfit was last to show up, almost reluctantly filing past the chuck wagon and serving their plates. One grizzled old rider looked around, fastening his eyes on Goose.

"I ain't about t' hunker down wi' no damn Injun," he growled.

"Me neither," vowed his companion.

Goose ceased eating, aware that it had something to do with him. Expecting trouble, McCaleb got up, but Goodnight was ahead of him. He held his big hand palm out, bidding Goose to remain where he was. He then turned, facing not only the antagonists who had spoken, but their comrades as well.

"Sorry boys. The Indian stays. Help yourselves to all the grub you want, but if you're not comfortable with everybody here, then you'll have to eat elsewhere. Mr. Loving has *his* rules; this is one of mine."

"Consider it my rule as well," said Loving, stepping out of the shadows. "Yance, you and Jake go on back to the herd and take your supper with you. If any of the rest of you share their feelings, I'd suggest you join them."

Loving then spoke to Goose in rapid Spanish and the Indian resumed his eating. The rest of Loving's riders served their plates, kneeling down to eat. McCaleb heaved a sigh when the meal was over and the outfits drifted back to their respective areas. Monte and Goose had second watch from the McCaleb outfit, along with Goodnight riders Wes Sheek and Charlie Wilson. McCaleb only hoped this unpleasant incident had served as a warning to Oliver Loving. It would be a mistake putting either of the Indian-haters on the same watch with Goose.

There was trouble during the Apache's watch, but it didn't come from the expected quarter nor was it directed at Goose. Suddenly the night came alive with gunfire and the pounding of horse hooves. McCaleb rolled out, dressed but for his boots, grabbing his rifle. But there was no moon, and in the dim starlight he couldn't tell friend from foe. One cow bawled, then another. Finally a rolling thunder of firing split the night, followed by the pounding of hooves as the herd stampeded. Wearily, McCaleb returned to his blankets, feeling around until he found his boots. The firing had ceased, leaving only the distant drumming of hoofs. McCaleb cocked the Henry; somebody was coming.

"Don't shoot! It's me. Monte!"

"McCaleb here. What in tarnation happened? Where's Goose?"

"I don't rightly know. They shot my horse from under me. I think Goose got one of them. He piled off his horse and onto one of theirs, taking the rider with him. I saw 'em go down and then the herd started to run."

"McCaleb," bawled Goodnight, "can you hear me?"

"I hear you."

"Come on to the wagon."

McCaleb headed for the wagon, Monte limping along with him. Goodnight lighted a lantern, hanging it on a hook near the top of the chuck box. In its feeble glow McCaleb saw a body stretched out on the ground. Seeing the shoulder-length black hair, he at first thought it was Goose. Drawing closer, he saw the man had a moustache and the swarthy brown skin of a Mexican. He also was dead, having had his throat cut. Goose was very much alive, holding his bloody bowie. Three of Loving's riders were there, including Yance and Jake. Their eyes were on the formidable knife in the Indian's hand.

"Mexican bandits," said Goodnight. "Thanks to Goose, we have one of them. Unfortunately, they successfully stampeded maybe half the herd. They hit the tag end and the cows are headed downriver, back toward Horsehead. The rest of the second watch—two of my riders and two of Loving's—managed to drive a wedge between the rest of the herd and the bandits. Your outfit bore the brunt of the attack, Bent. Where's Brazos and Will? And Rebecca?"

"Here," said Brazos from the darkness. "Nobody hurt except Will. A horn raked him across the backside and he won't set easy in the saddle for a while."

"I'm ridin' at first light," snarled Will. "I'll trail the bastards all the way to Juarez and pull it down on their heads, one brick at a time."

"We'll not have to ride that far to find them," said Goodnight. "If they run true to form, they'll gather as many of our cattle as they can and try to dicker with us to buy them back."

"I've never been one to dicker for something that was already mine," said McCaleb. "We'll buy them back, all right, but not with gold or silver. We'll use .44-caliber hot lead."

Goose rode out as soon as it was light enough to see and returned in less than an hour. He went to the chuck wagon for his breakfast while Brazos related the facts as best he could from what the Indian had told him.

"Eleven of 'em," said Brazos, "and they've got near 'bouts two hundred head. Ours. Moving slow, Goose says."

"Good," said McCaleb. "We won't have any trouble catching up to them. Brazos, you and Will get ready to ride. Soon as Goose eats, we'll move out."

"Hey," shouted Monte, "I'm part of this outfit!"

"So am I," said Rebecca. "*Four* of you against *eleven* of them? Come on, McCaleb!"

"That's right," said Goodnight. "We have enough riders to match them, man-for-man. Don't take any unnecessary risks."

"I don't aim to," said McCaleb, "but it was my outfit they cut down on, and we owe them. Goose is ready; saddle up, all of you. Let's ride!"

The trail was clear enough to have been followed at night if there had been a moon. Goose rode at a fast lope and they fell in behind him, single file. McCaleb turned, lifting his hand to Goodnight.

"Don't wait for us, Charlie," he shouted. "Move 'em out. We'll catch up to you."

"They're seriously outnumbered," said Oliver Loving.

"I know," said Goodnight. "Those bandits are in big trouble, but it's their own fault. They got three of the saltiest ex-Rangers in Texas on their trail."

Loving cut his eyes to Goodnight, expecting to see the big man smiling at his own joke, but Goodnight was serious. Dead serious.

McCaleb's outfit reached a point along the Pecos where the ground was flint-hard. Goose reined up, pointing southeast. McCaleb studied the ground in that direction. The trail was faint but plain. Five of the eleven had left the herd, but why? Had they fallen back, planning to move up from behind, trapping their pursuers in a deadly cross-fire? Suddenly, far to the east, McCaleb saw dust rising in the early morning sun. A dust devil? No. It continued in a straight line. Who, or what, was causing that? Certainly not those five Mexican bandits; he didn't doubt they were just waiting for the right time to fall in behind their pursuers. Well, he didn't aim to wait until they closed the jaws of their obvious trap. He turned his horse toward the river, kicking it into a lope, getting back to his outfit. They had seen the cloud of dust to the east.

"Don't know what that is," said McCaleb. "We'll face it when it gets here. Five of those Mex rustlers have fallen back, likely planning to move up behind us when the time's right. But we're going to catch up to those with the herd, dispose of them, and then turn back to meet the others."

He led out at a gallop and the others followed.

"Ride them down," shouted McCaleb. "Shoot to kill!" With an almost military precision, rifles were drawn from saddle boots and shells jacked into firing chambers. They galloped in a six-rider skirmish line, a dozen feet apart, their mounts even. The sun was less than an hour high, but every rider's shirt was dark with patches of sweat, as were the flanks of their horses. McCaleb looked back, expecting a telltale cloud of dust, but saw none except their own. What had become of those five riders who had left the herd? If back-shooting had been their intention, where *were* they? The dust cloud to the east had grown, but distance and shimmering heat waves prevented them from seeing who or what had caused it.

"Whoever that is," shouted Brazos, "they're headin' for the crossing."

Horsehead Crossing was less than a mile distant. These outlaws with their stolen cattle were about to run headlong into whoever or whatever was rapidly approaching the crossing from the east. Slugs began kicking up dust a dozen feet ahead of their horses before they heard the gunfire. They were still out of range. McCaleb reined up.

"They're forted up behind those rock outcroppings where the river bank begins to rise," he said. "They must be holding the cattle somewhere near the crossing. We could flank them on the east, work our way south and come up behind them, but I reckon we'd best not be in any hurry. Whoever's been raising all that dust to the east is at the crossing by now. Comanches maybe. Let's hold our fire until we know who they are and where they stand in regards to these Mex rustlers."

They sat their horses, waiting. No more shots were fired. Finally, around the bend of the river, skirting the rock-strewn, mesquite-shrouded knoll where the rustlers had taken refuge, came the strangest procession any of them had ever beheld. First there were eleven riders, obviously Mexican, hands held shoulder high. Behind them lumbered three canvas-covered, mule-drawn wagons. There were two outriders for each wagon, each armed with a rifle. They all rode slightly to the rear of the outlaw band, three on each side. They all wore Mexican garb, including the high-crowned, wide-brimmed sombreros. So did the two men on the box of the first wagon, but only the driver was Mexican. The other wore cowman's boots, blue serge pants, white shirt, and red suspenders. He had an ample belly, a black beard, piercing blue eyes, and a Henry rifle across his knees. McCaleb kneed his horse far enough to the side to read the sign on the lead wagon's canvas. In foot-high red letters, ovaled like a rainbow, he read: JUDGE ROY BEAN. Beneath that, in a straight black line, were smaller letters reading: *The Law West of the Pecos.*

McCaleb's outfit stood its ground, rifles cocked and ready. Finally, Red Suspenders loosed a stream of tobacco juice and spoke.

"Who might you be?"

"Benton McCaleb. Last night a bunch of ladinos stampeded and stole some of our herd. We're fair-to-middlin' sure it was this bunch standin' here in front of your wagon. How do you figure into this?"

"Judge Roy Bean, late of San Antone. Run into five of these gents, all ridin' hell-bent-fer-election an' waggin' rifles. Reckoned I'd better take 'em into custody 'fore they hurt theirselves er somebody else. Seen all th' dust foggin' up near th' crossin' an' a couple hunnert cows millin' about. Then we come up on half a dozen more of these fellers layin' up there in th' mesquite shootin' their rifles an' actin' downright hostile. So I brung th' lot of 'em along. Reckoned I'd git your side. Felipe Mendoza is segundo fer this outfit; he claims they aimed t' sell these cows to you folks. He further claims you took th' stock, wouldn't pay fer 'em, an' that you was tryin' t' kill him an' his men. Says they was just defendin' theirselves."

"That's a lie!" shouted Rebecca. "We've driven these cows all the way from the Trinity River brakes and spent two days fishing them out of quicksand in this wretched Pecos River!"

"Six of us and eleven of them," said McCaleb. "Do

we look fierce enough or foolish enough to buck those odds? If you looked at some of those cows, you saw at least three trail brands, not one of them Mexican. Now take a look at the horses this bunch is forking. Nothing but Mex brands. Don't you reckon that's a mite unusual?"

"Like I said," replied Judge Bean, "wanted t' git your side of it. Now that we got all th' evidence, we can conduct th' trial. Mendoza, you an' your boys face th' bench."

None of the eleven moved. Judge Bean's rifle spoke once and Mendoza's hat was snatched from his head. Without further delay the eleven turned their horses to face the wagon. Mendoza rode a big Bayo Coyote with silver-mounted saddle. He wore a short red jacket trimmed with gold braid and a buscadero rig, each holster tied down. The sun glinted off silver-roweled spurs.

"Mendoza," said Judge Bean, "it strikes me a mite odd that them cows—like Mr. McCaleb pointed out—is all wearin' trail brands. U.S. of A. brands. Ever' horse in your outfit is got Mexican brands. Are you Texans or Mexicans?"

"We are Texican, señor," said Mendoza.

"McCaleb's sayin' these cows—*vacas*—come from right here in Texas. Where are you sayin' they come from?"

"They are *Mejicano*."

"Then how come they're wearin' Texas brands?"

"Because they're part of our herd," interrupted McCaleb.

"You're out of order, McCaleb," snapped Judge Bean, pounding his fist against the wagon seat.

He continued. "Mendoza, there ain't nothin' separatin' Texas from Mexico ceptin' a spring branch, so I ain't sure if yer Mexicans er Texans. I got only yer word, so t' be fair, I'm givin' you th' benefit of th' doubt. Considerin' you boys is Texans, it's my duty t' inform you that all Texas is under th' Reconstruction Act of 1865. Leavin' th' state is agin th' law. Since you been t' Mexico after them cows, I'm imposin' a fine. As unrecon-structed Texans, I'm finin' you however many cows is in that bunch at th' crossing. Th' Reconstruction Act also forbids you t' carry firearms; that's even more serious, 'cause you already broke th' law onct. I'm takin' yer guns in th' name of th' U.S. of A."

Mendoza went for his Colt, but the slug plowed harmlessly into the dirt as the shot from Judge Bean's Henry rifle caught him in the chest. He toppled back-ward off his horse and lay motionless on the ground.

"I'm holdin' him in contempt of court," said Judge Bean, "an' finin' him a horse an' saddle. Next man pullin' a gun gits th' same sentence and th' same fine. Now shuck them guns! Unlatch yer belts an' drop th' whole rig. Keep them hands away from th' gun butts!"

To a man, they unfastened their belts and dropped them carefully to the ground. But Judge Bean wasn't finished with them.

"Now th' saddle guns," he said. "Let 'em down easy, butt first."

More reluctantly than ever, rifles were withdrawn from saddle boots and lowered to the ground. Judge Bean lifted the muzzle of the Henry, pointing south.

"*Pronto*," he said.

The ten trotted their horses in the direction Judge Bean had pointed, not looking back. Following a com-mand from Bean in Spanish, the outriders dismounted and began gathering the abandoned pistols and rifles. One of them stripped the dead Mendoza's buscadero rig and then went through the Mexican's pockets.

"Now that we're rid of *them*," said McCaleb, "what are we expected to pay the 'court' for our cattle?"

"Nothin'," said Bean, "less'n yer of a mind t' pay th' court costs."

"You've got a horse, a silver-mounted saddle, and four hundred dollars' worth of weapons," said McCaleb. "That should be enough."

He kicked the bay into a lope and the others followed,

riding to Horsehead Crossing to recover their long-horns.

"That's the strangest thing I've ever seen," said Rebecca. "Can he *do* that—hold court out on the prairie, impose fines and *shoot* people?"

"He can," said McCaleb, "and he does. I've heard of him. On the western frontier a man who can *talk* like the law, *act* like the law, and then back it all up with a gun, he can *be* the law."

"I ain't sure I like his methods," said Will. "We should of took that bunch of thieves to the nearest cottonwood and stretched their necks. That always cures 'em of rustling."

"I'm satisfied," said McCaleb. "We didn't lose any of our herd, and if Bean hadn't taken that outfit by surprise, we'd have burnt an almighty lot of powder rootin' 'em out. Besides, they might've shot some of us. I reckon he didn't do them any favors, turning 'em loose unarmed."

Brazos chuckled. "Amen. This is Comanche country."

They found the stampeded remnant of their herd grazing peacefully, and by mid-afternoon McCaleb's outfit had caught up with the drive. Goodnight and Loving rode out to meet them. They seemed a bit surprised at the quick recovery without apparent injury to any of the outfit.

"Have any trouble?" inquired Goodnight.

"No," said McCaleb with a straight face. "We took 'em to court and they lost."

CHAPTER 17

*F*rom Horsehead to Pope's Crossing—just south of the Texas-New Mexico line—they saw not a single living thing except rattlesnakes. It was the most desolate country McCaleb had ever seen, and though they were always within sight of the Pecos, there wasn't always access to the water. With the treachery of the river constantly in mind, Goodnight ranged far ahead, seeking bed grounds where the banks were low enough to safely water the herd. Finding such a location, he must then be sure the river wasn't alive with quicksand.

Without serious incident they forded the Pecos again at Pope's Crossing and continued north, crossing the Delaware and Black River. They kept wary eyes on the Guadalupe Mountains to the west, a favorite rendezvous of the Mescalero Apaches. They drove past Comanche Springs, bedding down the herd on a lush, wooded range the Spanish had named Bosque Grande—the big timbers. On the first day of July, near sunset, they bedded the herd on a ridge overlooking Fort Sumner.

"*That's* a fort? Looks more like an Indian camp with a stockade in the middle," said Brazos.

"From what I've been told," said Oliver Loving, "that's about the extent of it. Established in 'sixty-three, mostly through Kit Carson's efforts. I don't understand how a plainsman with Carson's savvy could have been so shortsighted. It's possibly the world's worst location for a reservation. Even if Indians had any desire to farm —which they don't—this soil is unsuited to anything except buffalo grass. As for the Indians themselves, I'm not sure that's Carson's fault. It sounds like a typical Washington blunder. There's close to nine thousand Indians here, a mix of Navajo and Mescalero Apache. Their tribal customs are as different as night and day. While that would have been problem enough, the tribes are bitter enemies of long standing. From the very start there's been fighting and killings. Last fall, the government agent was run out of here, literally riding for his life. He had been in cahoots with a crooked beef contractor, and the two of them had been falsifying purchase orders. The cattle they were buying to feed the Indians existed only on paper, and those scoundrels were pocketing the money. The Mescaleros jumped the reservation and were lured back with the assignment of a new Indian agent and the promise of honest beef rations."

Since the herd was within sight of the fort, only half a dozen riders were left on watch. The others—with the exception of Goodnight, Loving, and McCaleb—would wander about, observing Sumner's limited attractions. Wisely, McCaleb had left Goose with the herd. He had no idea how the Indian might react in the midst of nine thousand Mescaleros and Navajos, or how they might react to Goose. Monte and Rebecca Nance had decided to go with Will and Brazos.

For the most part, Fort Sumner was barren and depressing. Hundreds of Indians sat before their teepees, hunched in their blankets, expressionless faces turned to the morning sun.

"I feel so sorry for them," said Rebecca. "Their eyes are so empty, it's like they're looking into . . . into tomorrow, and seeing nothing."

"That's the kind of feeling I get," said Brazos, "but I couldn't explain it that well. This regimentation's made blanket Injuns of them forever; not worth a damn to themselves or anybody else."

Finally they came upon two squat log huts a dozen yards apart. In front of each stood a sentry in Union blue, his rifle at parade rest. Will spoke to the nearest one.

"This is the Navajo guardhouse," said the sentry. "The other is for the Mescaleros. Impossible to mix the tribes. That's why most of 'em are in there—for tryin' to kill one another, bein' drunk, or both."

Goodnight, Loving, and McCaleb spent almost an hour in the agent's office negotiating the sale of the herd, and then were unable to sell it all. When McCaleb returned to the outfit, he told them what had been agreed upon.

"They're buying all the beeves, two-year-olds and up, eight cents a pound. They're taking delivery in the morning and we'll be paid in gold."

"That's goin' to leave us with three hundred unsold cows," said Brazos. "Not much of a herd to trail all the way to Colorado Territory."

"With Goodnight's and Loving's cut-outs," said McCaleb, "there'll be at least eight hundred, if not more. Loving believes John Iliff—a former Texan ranching in northern Colorado—might buy the whole bunch."

"Don't need three outfits to drive eight hundred trail-broke cows," said Will. "One outfit can do it."

"One outfit's going to," said McCaleb. "Soon as Goodnight and Loving talk it over, I'll be gettin' with them. We'll decide then who takes the rest of the herd to Colorado."

"Tell them *we'll* finish the drive," said Rebecca. "I want to go on to Colorado. It's got to be better than Texas."

But McCaleb didn't meet with Goodnight and Loving. Goodnight rode into their camp after supper. He seemed a little reluctant to talk with everybody gathered around.

"Go ahead, Charlie," said McCaleb. "None of these folks are thirty-a-month riders. Our stake's about equal."

"Bent," said Goodnight, "I think highly of all of you. Because of that, Mr. Loving wanted me to talk to you. We've decided to go into the cattle business together, and one of us is going back to Texas to raise a bigger, better herd while prices are rock bottom. It would be a waste of time and money for *all* of us to drive eight hundred cows to Colorado. Tomorrow, when we've concluded the sale and collected our money, you're free to take what's left of your herd and head for Colorado. However, Mr. Loving is making you what I feel is a generous offer. He will take what's left of *everybody's* herd to Colorado and sell for the best price he can get. You and I and our riders will immediately return to Texas, using our money from this sale to build a bigger, better herd."

"Since you and Loving are partners," said McCaleb, "I can understand him driving the rest of your herd to Colorado. But why ours? That leaves us owing him. We've ridden a lot of trails together, Charlie, but I'm not one to lean on my friends when I can do for myself."

"You'll be repaying Mr. Loving in kind," said Goodnight. "I aim to buy one thousand big steers for him and another thousand for myself. Buy a thousand of your own. You've got six riders and I have eight, including myself. Somewhere between here and Fort Belknap we'll pick up Bill Wilson. That'll give us fifteen riders. Without your outfit, I'd have to hire riders. Together, we can pay Mr. Loving back by helping trail his herd back here to Fort Sumner while he drives the rest of ours to Colorado. When Loving has sold the rest of our stock, he'll return here and wait for us to bring the new cattle."

"Maybe I'm talkin' out of turn, Charlie," said Will, "but by the time we get back to Texas, round up three thousand steers, and drive 'em back to here, there'll be snow in the high country. Deep snow."

"True," said Goodnight, "but we won't be going to the Colorado high country until spring, assuming that we have to go to Colorado at all. We're talking about a herd of big steers—three thousand strong—two-year-olds and up. This is good cattle country. If we don't sell them all at Sumner, we could establish a temporary ranch near here, grazing them until spring, and *then* drive them to Colorado. Why not winter here in New Mexico?"

"Charlie," said McCaleb, "we need to study this awhile. When will Mr. Loving head out for Colorado and when will you start back to Texas?"

"We'll wait until after July fourth and have a good feed. I figure we'll move out on the fifth or sixth."

"By the fourth," said McCaleb, "we'll know what we aim to do."

After Goodnight departed, there was a long silence. McCaleb spoke first.

"The gold we collect for today's sale won't last forever; neither will the trail drives. I aim to eventually take a herd to Colorado, but when I do, I want the biggest and best steers; animals that could bring thirty dollars a head in the mining towns. If there's one of you—or all of you—that's had enough of trail driving, then we'll divvy up after the sale."

"Leave my share in the pot," said Monte. "I want to be around for that big drive to the mining towns. I'd as soon be dead and in Hell as to go back to the nothin' life I had before this drive."

"Charlie made some good points," said Brazos. "There ain't nothin' in Texas to hold us. I spent four years in the Rangers and come out with sixty dollars, and that was 'fore the state was broke. I'll stick around."

"I'll stay," said Will. "I reckon the sooner we can get back to Texas and trail out another herd, the better off we'll be. The time's coming—and soon—when the trails will be glutted with herds. There's already trouble in Kansas because of tick fever. The Shawnee trail will be closed by the end of this year. We'd best cash out while we can."

"Brazos," said McCaleb, "talk to Goose and see how he feels, if you can get through to him."

"Oh, all right!" snapped Rebecca. "I'll go along. It's

just that I don't want to be stuck in this godforsaken part of New Mexico forever."

The following day, they met with the beef contractor and left his office with eighteen thousand dollars in gold, roughly a third of it in McCaleb's saddlebag.

"Mr. Loving will take the chuck wagon," said Goodnight. "It would slow us down. I'm told we can get saddle mules at Santa Rosa, forty miles northwest of here. You ride the mule for endurance. In case of Indian attack, you swap the mule for your fastest horse—which is on a lead rope—and outrun the red devils."

Oliver Loving moved out at dawn. The Goodnight and McCaleb outfits would depart at dusk, traveling at night.

They had but one minor skirmish with the Comanches and lost one pack mule. July 22, seventeen days after leaving Fort Sumner, they were back on Elm Creek range.

"Now," said Goodnight, "we'll go to Weatherford, settle up with Moon and get the supplies we need. Then we'll pitch camp near Belknap and begin buying big steers. I want to head out to Fort Sumner by mid-August."

That night, One-Armed Bill Wilson rode into their camp. Bill was an older version of his brother Charlie. McCaleb expected Wilson to regale the outfit with details of his escape from the Federals, but the one-armed rider kept his silence. He greeted Rebecca as though he'd never seen her before. Goodnight had no questions; Wilson's presence attested to the success of his escape.

McCaleb bought a dozen horses and a 1025 steers, most of them two-year-olds. They used a simple 6 trail brand. Despite Goodnight's enthusiasm for eventual wintering in New Mexico, he limited his and Loving's herd to twelve hundred head. It was a move he wouldn't regret.

August 10, 1866, they lined them out to the southwest, toward the Upper Concho, determined that this drive would be less costly than the first.

Emilio lamented the chuck wagon's absence, and after a few biscuitless days, so did everybody else. They were dependent on pack mules. Five of the hardy little beasts they had brought from New Mexico now carried their provisions and extra ammunition, while a sixth mule bore two water kegs. The rest of the saddle mules traveled with the horse remuda.

"We should have bought more steers," said Rebecca, "while they're only seven dollars a head."

"We'd need to hire more riders," said McCaleb, "and we don't know what market's ahead of us at Fort Sumner. I feel better having some of our stake in gold."

"I've never seen a more skittish bunch of brutes in my life," said Will, a week southwest of Fort Belknap.

"Me neither," said Brazos. "No thunder, no lightning, no rain, not even a dust devil, but we've had a stampede every night. These damn fools are gonna run themselves down to skin and bones. We'll need all winter to put some meat on 'em."

Not only did the nightly stampedes continue, but in the middle of the afternoon a miles-long herd of buffalo split the drive. Terrified, half the cattle went pounding along the back trail, hell-bent for Fort Belknap, while the rest lit a shuck toward Horsehead Crossing. The trail riders spent the rest of that day and part of the next recovering their herd. Some of the bison mixed with the steers and had to be driven out. A pair of particularly troublesome young buffalo bulls refused to leave, and Will shot them, providing hump steak and broiled tongue for supper.

"Boys," said Goodnight, "we've made history. Bill and Charlie Wilson just run a tally and we didn't lose a steer!"

Reaching the Staked Plain—the dread Llano Estacado —they drove the cattle only at night. They reached and crossed the Pecos in record time, avoiding the devastating loss they had suffered on the first drive. They reached Pope's Crossing, again fording the Pecos without difficulty.

"I wish we could just take our herd on to Colorado," said Rebecca. "Once we reach Fort Sumner, we'll have done our part in helping to deliver Loving's herd."

"There'll be snow in Colorado by the time we reach Sumner," said McCaleb, "but I don't aim to *give* these steers away, even if we have to dig in and hold every blasted one until spring. Like I told you, I've never had a better friend than Charles Goodnight, but when it's time to cut the cards, I aim to draw my own, play my own hand. Will and Brazos will side me, if it comes to that."

"So will I," said the girl, "and so will Monte. I suppose Goose would be the only one in question. I haven't been able to figure him out."

"I have," said McCaleb, grinning in the darkness. "He's left-handed."

September 15, 1866—after thirty-five days on the trail—they reached Fort Sumner. Oliver Loving anxiously awaited them with good news. He had sold the remnants of their previous herd to J. W. Iliff, a rancher on the South Platte river, in eastern Colorado. Again they had been paid in gold. But things had changed drastically at Fort Sumner and they faced a long winter with virtually no market for their beef. Rebecca sneaked a furtive look at McCaleb, but he appeared not to even see her. He looked grim, but no more so than Charles Goodnight. . . .

For the first time, McCaleb began to see why Oliver Loving had taken it upon himself to trail the remnants of the first drive to Colorado. In August government beef contracts were let at Fort Sumner, and Loving had wanted to be present from the start. While he couldn't bid, he wanted to be the first to dicker with whomever became the beef contractor for the next twelve months.

"Roberts and the Patterson boys lost out," said Loving. "They were cut down like dogs by some jasper named Andrews. He's agreed to supply Sumner with beef at two-and-a-half cents a pound, on the hoof."

"Why that's . . . that's impossible," roared Goodnight.

"It's quite possible," said Loving. "From what Roberts and the Pattersons have told me, these are cattle driven over the *comanchero* trail, cattle stolen in Texas by the Comanches and sold to New Mexican traders along the Canadian."

"That," said Goodnight, "is an insult to every Texas cattleman. These Union scoundrels won't buy from Rebs, but they'll cut our throats by accepting our very own Texas cattle, stolen by the Comanches and run through a swindling middleman!"

"It's not *all* bad news," said Loving. "There are more honest buyers at Lincoln and Fort Bascom. They're still paying eight cents a pound. Trouble is, we'll have to *share* their contract with three other herds. The Patterson boys, Jacob Roberts, and Franklin Wilburn all got their tails in the same crack as we do. Once a month, for six months, we can send a hundred head to Lincoln and a hundred head to Bascom; twelve hundred head in all. We'll make our first delivery October first and our last on March first, freeing us to return to Texas for a larger herd."

He had forgotten about McCaleb's outfit, but Goodnight hadn't. He was very much aware of the murderous looks directed at Oliver Loving. McCaleb was the first to speak, and his words were directed more to his own outfit than to Goodnight or Loving.

"Charlie, we've about decided to just dig in until spring and trail our herd on to Colorado. I don't aim to be at the mercy of somebody else's beef contract, and I reckon I'm talkin' for the rest of the outfit."

Loving, aware that Goodnight had been embarrassed by his apparent callousness, tried to lessen the impact, but only made it worse.

"There's a new beef contractor at Fort Union, near Santa Fe," said Loving. "He might be interested."

It was 140 miles to Santa Fe, nearly twice as far as either of the locations Loving had arranged for himself and Goodnight. For a long minute nobody said anything; again it was McCaleb who broke the uncomfortable silence.

"Maybe we'll ride over there and look into it. It won't displease me if we graze these cows right here until spring. This is good range; these steers will be fatter and in better condition than they are now."

When Goodnight and Loving rode away, McCaleb's outfit decided they weren't all that put out over the possibility of wintering in New Mexico and then driving north in the spring. Brazos summed it up.

"I reckon we're somewhat beholden to Loving for selling the rest of last year's herd in Colorado, but from here on, I'd as soon not have him making any deals for us. We got more'n a thousand big steers, there's plenty of grass and water, the river's full of fish, we got plenty of grub, with more to be had, and we ain't broke. Once we get settled, why don't we ride to Santa Fe? I've heard it's some kind of town."

"I wish we could," said Rebecca, "but what about the herd?"

"Goodnight's and Loving's riders can look out for our herd," said Will, "and when they're driving to Bascom or Lincoln, we'll return the favor."

"That's all that'll make this place bearable," said Rebecca. "When can we go?"

"Let's hold off until Goodnight and Loving return from their deliveries on October first," said McCaleb. "Then they'll *owe* us."

Remembering their hollowed-out wall in the faraway box canyon on the Trinity, they looked for and found a similar campsite on the west bank of the Pecos. An enormous rock ledge overhung the river, and a dozen feet below it was a level surface that extended back into the river bank almost like the mouth of a cave. With tools from Goodnight's chuck wagon, they widened the precipitous trail until they could ascend or descend safely, even in the dark.

"You'd best keep your eyes and ears open for flash floods." Goodnight chuckled. "I've already had to haul your carcass out of one."

McCaleb laughed. "I remembered that, and that's why I checked out the highest level the water's ever reached. It gets high enough to worry us, and your soddy will be just a mud hole with you sittin' in the middle."

The other outfits preparing to winter in New Mexico —including Goodnight's and Loving's—had simply burrowed into hillsides, building crude dugouts with sod roofs.

"I've never seen a soddy in my life that didn't leak," said Will, "when it rained long enough and hard enough. When she starts to leak, you ain't too far from havin' the whole damn roof come down on your head. First good storm and we'll have the lot of 'em grabbing their soggy blankets and tryin' to squeeze in with us."

Goodnight and Loving had made one move that McCaleb's outfit had been quick to follow. They had pitched their winter camps almost fifty miles south of Fort Sumner, seeking the best graze for their stock and avoiding the possibility of overcrowding by those who had settled ahead of them. Charles Goodnight was plainsman enough that he never underestimated the Indian threat. Despite the proximity of the other herds and the nearness of Fort Sumner, he established three watches, with two pairs of night riders circling the herds from dusk to dawn. McCaleb, no less cautious, grazed his herd adjoining theirs, supplying two riders for each watch.

Oliver Loving's outfit, as salty and aloof as ever, kept mostly to themselves. Goodnight's riders, however, were as friendly a bunch of cowboys as McCaleb could recall. Slowly, Emilio and Donato Vasquez established a friendship with Goose, and the Apache's vocabulary— in Spanish and halting English—began to grow. Bill and

Charlie Wilson, flamboyant and inclined to recklessness, were the gamblers in Goodnight's outfit. Their answer to boredom was poker, and they soon found willing converts in young Monte Nance and the Vasquez boys.

"Monte," pleaded Rebecca, "I wish you'd leave the cards alone. You know that was Daddy's weakness. It ruined him."

"He was an old fool who'd gamble with borrowed money," snarled Monte. "He'd bluff or raise on a pair of deuces; that's what ruined him. Now get off my back!"

McCaleb could say nothing, but he secretly agreed with the girl. Never in his life had he known a gambler —honest or otherwise—who hadn't come to a bad end as a result of his dexterity or the lack of it. Monte Nance was rapidly becoming as much a card sharp as either of the Wilson brothers, and they took an obvious delight in the growing skill of their disciple. Bill and Charlie took to riding first watch for Goodnight's outfit, and then spent the rest of the night playing poker. Donato and Emilio Vasquez were adequate poker players themselves, and when the Wilsons weren't playing, the Mexican riders usually were. The game never seemed to end. Monte and Goose continued riding night watch together and the inevitable happened. Goose learned enough words until he began to understand this time-consuming game the other riders seemed to enjoy. Rebecca and McCaleb rode in at dawn, ending the third watch, and found the Apache carefully studying a deck of cards. He had them correctly divided into suits. Rebecca looked hopelessly at McCaleb. What could they do? By the end of the third week in October, to the delight of just about everybody, Goose stumbled into the nightly poker game. Brazos and Will chuckled and even Goodnight was amused.

"That could destroy him quicker than forty-rod whiskey," said McCaleb. "He'll likely end up shootin' his way out of some saloon or die trying. They'll gun him down, not for lack of honesty, but because he's an Indian."

* * *

It was Oliver Loving and four of his riders who made delivery of the first two hundred beeves from the Goodnight-Loving herd. McCaleb's outfit was restless after six weeks of virtually no activity, and he decided it was time for a visit to Santa Fe. On Friday, October 26, as they prepared to ride out, Goodnight had some advice for them.

"You can always take your herd on to Colorado in the spring, but since you'll be that close to Fort Union, why don't you call on the beef contractor and see if there's a market for your herd? Fort Union is headquarters for this military district. You can always go back to Texas in the spring, buy an even larger herd, and trail it to Colorado before snow flies."

"If there's *that* much potential at Fort Union," said McCaleb dryly, "I wonder why Mr. Loving didn't make himself a deal there, instead of dribbling two hundred head each month until spring?"

Goodnight chuckled. "I'll tell you a secret. Mr. Loving wants the beef contract for Fort Union; maybe even for this entire military district. As you know, our glorious Congress, with its Reconstruction Act, has declared that no beef contracts are to be let to Rebs. However, Mr. Loving has learned that early next year there'll be a new head of the quartermaster's department at Fort Union. Colonel Charles McClure, a man Loving knows and has dealt with before, will be in charge. Due to the urgent government need for beef in this district, McClure has had this foolish law set aside. Loving aims to be in Santa Fe next August to bid on those beef contracts. He's confident he'll get them, so we're going back to Texas and raise the largest herd yet; maybe five thousand head. If their need for beef is that great and the price is right, why not dispose of your present herd and buy an even larger one in the spring? Colorado will still be there."

They rode into Santa Fe on Sunday afternoon, and if Saturday night's din had lessened, there was no evidence of it. While there were a few tents—mostly sa-loons—the town had an air of permanence. Some of the buildings were slab-sided with false fronts, but others were brick, including a two-story hotel. There was a main street, several side streets, and even a few cross streets. While the streets were dirt—dusty in dry weather, muddy in wet weather—there were board-walks along most of them. Next to the bank stood the Condor Saloon, and directly across the street was the Five Aces. There was the Broken Spoke, the Snake Head, the Pecos, and others so unpretentious they had only a crude wooden sign reading WHISKEY.

"Goodnight was talking sense," said Brazos. "Maybe we ought to look up this jaybird who's got the Fort Union beef contract *now*."

"I reckon it won't hurt to talk to him," said McCaleb.

"While you're doing that," said Monte, "I aim to visit the saloons and watch some *real* gamblers play."

A dog followed the riders, barking until a chorus of others, unseen, had joined in. They reined up in front of the Ganadero Hotel.

"I aim to sleep in a bed tonight," said McCaleb, "be-fore I forget how."

Goose halted at the door, refusing to enter. Fancy up-holstered chairs lined the lobby and a worn but clean red carpet covered the floor. Winding wooden stairs led to a second floor. Patient as Brazos was, Goose took some convincing.

The desk clerk was a short little man, not even as tall as Rebecca. He had watery blue eyes, wore glasses, a wilted suit, and there wasn't a single hair on his head. He looked right past McCaleb, his eyes fixed on Goose. The Indian returned the stare. Furious, the little man turned on McCaleb.

"Why is he . . . that savage . . . staring at me?"

McCaleb chuckled. "He thinks you've been scalped, and he's wonderin' how you healed so clean, without any scars."

Brazos, Will, and Monte slapped their thighs and

roared. Rebecca laughed until she cried. To McCaleb's everlasting relief, Goose misinterpreted their mirth and grinned. He thought they were laughing at the little man with no hair.

"Rooms for the night," said McCaleb. "We'll need four. Adjoining."

"I, uh . . . we're full," stammered the desk clerk.

McCaleb looked around the lobby. A grizzled old man—probably an ex-cowboy or rancher—was grinning at them.

"Pardner," said McCaleb, "he thinks this place is full. Is it?"

"They ain't a soul on th' secont floor that I know of."

McCaleb turned back to the sweaty little man behind the desk. He spoke softly but his voice had an unmistakably dangerous edge.

"I misunderstood you; I reckon you mean all the rooms on this floor are full. We don't mind the second floor. Four rooms. Adjoining."

Without a word, the clerk took four keys from somewhere beneath the counter and placed them before McCaleb, who gathered them up and signed the register as "McCaleb and outfit." When they reached the second floor, McCaleb looked at the numbers on the keys. He handed one to Rebecca, one to Monte, and a third to Brazos. He had taken the first room for himself and had given the fourth to Will and Brazos. Rebecca's room was next to his own, while Monte and Goose occupied the room adjoining hers. If there was trouble, he looked for it to involve Rebecca or Goose.

Goose was as reluctant to enter the hotel room as he had been to enter the hotel itself. McCaleb kicked his door shut and dropped his saddlebags on the bed. He grinned when it sagged under their weight. Straw tick. He turned back the blankets and sheets, finding them clean. There were two pillows, each with a pillowcase. Unusual for the time and place. The toe of his boot clanked against something under the edge of the bed. A chamber pot with a lid; even more unusual. An ancient dresser set against the wall, its surface scarred by untold years of cigarette burns. Before it was a single ladder-backed, cane-bottom chair, and upon it sat a chipped granite wash pan and an equally chipped granite pitcher full of water. On the wall above the dresser hung an oval mirror, a crack running from top to bottom. Next to the room's only window was the fire escape—a forty-foot length of rope.

Downstairs, despite ancient furnishings, the hotel strove for some degree of elegance in its dining room. McCaleb avoided it, choosing a little place on a side street that proclaimed its business in the simplest of terms. On a footlong piece of lumber, in big black letters was a single word: EATS. They ordered steak, fried potatoes, biscuits, and coffee, completing their supper with dried apple pie. They drew some curious stares but that was all. Goose was on his best behavior. Despite some of his uncivilized customs, the Apache loved food, and in that respect had adapted well to the ways of the white man. They looked out the front window at the courthouse. It stood just across the street from the café, an impressive two-story brick building that also housed the jail.

"My God," said Will, "the Texas state pen at Huntsville ain't forted up like that; it's just plain old adobe. I purely don't trust a town with a fancy brick jail."

"Good planning on somebody's part," said McCaleb. "None of us may live to see it, but one day New Mexico will be a part of the United States. This may become the capital city. There's already talk that the Santa Fe will build a railroad through here, following the old Santa Fe Trail."

"I'd like to visit the stores and shops," said Rebecca. "I need some things and it's nobody's business what they are. How much money can I have?"

"Owoooo," howled Monte. "There goes our stake!"

"Fifty dollar limit on personal things," said McCaleb. "For everybody. But we return to the hotel first. I'm not about to open this saddlebag out here where others can see."

With the state of Texas under carpetbagger domination and the economy on its knees, the only safe place for their gold—still more than $3500—had been in McCaleb's saddlebags. They went wherever he did, and he was careful not to expose or divulge their contents.

"I'm headin' for the first barbershop I can find that offers hot baths," said Will. "Then me and Brazos will likely mosey over to the Five Aces. Sign out front says they got billiard tables, and I'd like to shoot a few games if I ain't forgot how."

McCaleb looked questioningly at Monte. He immediately became defensive and his response was about what McCaleb had expected.

"I aim to watch some of the poker games, if there's any being played. I'll take Goose with me."

They all looked at him in doubtful silence, especially Rebecca. In a burst of anger he flung his hat to the floor.

"Hell's bells," he bawled, "how can I get in trouble just watching?"

He stalked out and down the hall, Goose following. Brazos turned to McCaleb and spoke quietly.

"You want me and Will to follow them?"

"No," said McCaleb, "he'll know why you're there, and we'll never hear the end of his bitching. If he aims to be a man, keep himself forked end down, he's got to start somewhere. In a way, he's facing the same trial as Goose. I'm as concerned as much for one as the other, but I don't aim to wet nurse either of them. Let a man lean on a crutch long enough and he won't be able to walk without one."

It was almost dark when McCaleb and Rebecca returned to the hotel. A sign on the wall behind the desk said BATHS AVAILABLE, and Rebecca asked the clerk. He was an older man, and he replied without even looking up.

"Two dollars. Tub, water, an' towels brought to your room."

She expected a chuckle or a jibe from McCaleb, but he remained silent. The same bath could be had at a barbershop for four bits, but there was no privacy. He suspected the hotel had few takers at two dollars a throw, but a woman had no choice. McCaleb let Rebecca into her room. Before locking his own door, he rapped on the doors of the other two rooms. There was no response. He stretched out on the bed, not even removing his boots. After a while he heard a clanking in the hall and voices. Rebecca's bath—or at least the tub—had arrived. Bored, he got up, stepped out into the hall and knocked on Rebecca's door.

"Go away; I'm taking a bath."

He tried the knob and it wouldn't turn. He put his key into the lock and it clicked open. He turned the knob and went in. Rebecca was lying in an elongated tin tub, a froth of soapsuds in her hair. She sat up and looked at him.

"Do you always walk in on women who are bathing?"

"Only those I've seen bathing before," he said. He closed the door behind him, took the ladder-back chair and tilted it under the knob.

"Some hotel," she snorted. "Why *bother* with locks at all, when one key unlocks every door?"

McCaleb grinned. "Saves a pile of money on locks and keys. I reckon that's what the chair's for. What's that stuff you've got all over your head?"

"Something besides lye soap. The first scented, civilized soap I've seen since leaving Missouri. Take the rest of that bucket of water and pour it over my head. Slowly."

He did. She stood up and he caught his breath. He had almost forgotten just how beautiful she was. Not trusting himself, he turned to the single window. Suddenly, from up the street where he couldn't see, came a trio of shots. He flung the chair away from the door.

"Wait!" shouted Rebecca. "I'm going with you!"

"You're staying right here," he snapped. "This time, put that chair under the knob!" He slammed the door behind him and thundered down the wooden stairs. Brazos and Will came charging out of the Five Aces. Otherwise the street was deserted, attesting to the frequency and acceptance of violence in the town's saloons. They split up, each going to a different saloon. Will discovered the scene of the trouble and with a shout brought Brazos and McCaleb to the Condor Saloon.

"My God," said Brazos, "three men down."

One of them had been slashed across the chest, his white ruffled shirt soaked with blood. A second victim's shirt had been ripped away, revealing a gory slash on his left arm from shoulder to elbow. The third man sat against the wall groaning, his right arm hanging at an uncomfortable angle. Two other men sat hunched in chairs, their heads in their hands. A leather-thonged Bowie lay on the floor, and McCaleb knew it belonged to Goose.

"Keep your hands off that knife!"

The voice belonged to a big man whose most prominent features were the badge pinned to his vest and the cocked Colt he held on Benton McCaleb. McCaleb stepped back, stumbling over one of the broken chairs that had resulted from the brawl.

"The knife belongs to one of my outfit," said McCaleb. "Where is he?"

"On the way to jail, along with his two friends."

"Only two of them belong to my outfit," said McCaleb. "Who's the other?"

"Clay Allison, that troublesome bastard from Las Animas. Too bad your boys don't watch the company they keep."

"I want to talk to my riders," said McCaleb. "Now."

"They been took to jail. You'll hear the charges against them and their testimony in court. Tomorrow mornin', nine o'clock. Now unless you're payin' customers, vamoose."

CHAPTER 18

$\mathcal{N}$o sooner had they stepped out onto the board-walk when down the street, her still-wet hair fly-ing, ran Rebecca. She was also barefoot, not having taken the time to pull on her boots. She didn't bother with questions; she saw the answer in the grim set of their faces and the anger in their eyes.

"Tell me," she pleaded. "Tell me!"

Quickly McCaleb told her the little they knew.

"We must get them out," she cried. "Can't they go to court tomorrow without spending the night in jail?"

"No," said McCaleb. "Somebody's pressing charges. Saloon owner himself, probably. I get the feeling this town don't think too highly of Clay Allison and they're railroading him. Monte and Goose got sucked into it somehow, likely because they sided Allison. From what I saw, five men got hurt, three of them bad."

"I reckon you sized it up pretty well," said Brazos. "That badge-toter was mighty handy, like he knew just when and where hell was going to bust loose. They likely planned to buffalo Allison, drag him into the alley and maybe kill him. When Monte and Goose bought in, that queered their scheme. They might set up one man and murder him, but not three; not when two of them are strangers and the rest of their outfit's in town."

Suddenly McCaleb stiffened. His saddlebags! He had run from Rebecca's room, leaving the door to his own unlocked! He took the stairs two at a time and ran down the hall. He paused, his lungs burning, before his closed door. He drew his Colt, stepped to one side and turned the knob. The door swung open. McCaleb holstered his Colt and stepped inside. The saddlebags—with the remainder of their gold—were gone! There were footsteps in the hall. Disgusted with his negligence and sick at heart, he turned to face them. He hadn't cried since that long ago day in East Texas when he had buried his young wife, but he felt like it now. They saw the misery in his eyes. Rebecca, forgetting—or not caring—that Will and Brazos stood right behind her, threw her arms around him, crying.

"It wasn't your fault, Bent. You were afraid for Monte and Goose. You just forgot. It wasn't your fault!"

There was no condemnation from Will or Brazos. They knew he felt like a prize fool and didn't add to his misery and humiliation. They simply kept their silence, each of them aware of what this might mean. He thought he knew. He pulled himself free of the sobbing Rebecca and turned to the comrades with whom he'd ridden so many trails. His voice choked, he spoke.

"I took out fifty dollars for all of us. They've robbed Monte and Goose. How much do the two of you . . . have left?"

"Somethin' over forty dollars," said Will.

"Same with me," said Brazos. "Maybe a little more."

McCaleb took an eagle and two double eagles from the pocket of his Levi's. Thank God he hadn't spent anything! Suddenly the girl's eyes went wide, her thoughts racing ahead to the trial the next morning.

"Their fines!" she cried. "They'll be fined more than we can pay!"

Will moved into the room taken by Monte and Goose, so Rebecca would have protection on each side. McCaleb doubted that any of them slept. It wasn't even light when he got up to answer a knock on his door.

"I'm going crazy just waiting," said Rebecca. "I have

thirty dollars left; do we dare go to that café across from the courthouse and get coffee?"

"We might as well," said McCaleb. "If we're short, we'll be so *far* short, a little breakfast won't make any difference."

They didn't have to wake Will and Brazos; they were already awake. It was still so early, they had the little café to themselves. McCaleb recognized the old rider doing the cooking as the one who had embarrassed the hotel desk clerk into renting them rooms on the second floor. The wizened old fellow brought their coffee to the table and McCaleb spoke to him.

"How long you been out of the saddle, cowboy?"

"How'd you know? Was ten year this past September." There was a spark of pride in the old eyes, and despite his hunched back, he tried to stand a bit straighter.

"You still walk like a rider," said McCaleb.

"You all havin' breakfast, er just coffee?"

"Just coffee," said McCaleb. "Pair of our riders got in a brawl at the Condor last night. Trial's this morning; I reckon we'll have to dig deep to come up with the fines."

Clearly it was a dangerous subject. The old biscuit shooter clammed up and turned away. McCaleb tried a different approach.

"This Clay Allison, is he the *same* one that once had a ranch here in New Mexico, down near Cimarron?"

"That's him," said the old rider.

"He killed a man in Cimarron," said McCaleb. "That why he left New Mexico?"

"I heard so. That's why he moved to Las Animas, Colorado, I reckon. Him an' a neighbor had a fight over th' location of a fence. Clay dug a grave an' them two fools got down in it an' fought with knives. Winner was t' bury t'other. Clay give his neighbor a fittin' an' proper funeral. Th' marshal of Cimarron went after Clay, plannin' to git to th' bottom of it, but all he got was th' bottom of 'nother grave. Clay shot him dead. Some of his shenanigans wasn't all that bad. Used t' git drunk at Christmas an' shoot up th' town. Onct, he rid through town on that big black, jaybird nekkid. Swore he'd shoot th' ones that peeked, but most o' th' girls took a chanct." He chuckled.

Suddenly the old man slid off the table on which he'd been sitting and hurried behind the counter. The sheriff came in, kicked back a chair, and without a word sat down. The old cook brought him coffee, waiting to see if the lawman wanted anything else. McCaleb's outfit silently sipped their coffee, saying nothing. The sheriff said nothing, and the ex-puncher returned to his counter. McCaleb thought he looked worried, wondering why the town's lawman had singled out his place and was there so early. The nearby courthouse wouldn't open until eight, and court wouldn't convene until nine. McCaleb finished his coffee. He paid, and the others followed him out onto the boardwalk, leaving the silent sheriff looking after them.

"He wanted to watch us squirm," said Rebecca, "to see how worried we might be."

"No," said McCaleb, "he had a better reason than that. He was givin' us a chance to complain about being robbed last night. He wanted to see how desperate we are. Now he's not sure *why* we didn't report the robbery. He just purely don't know if we've got ten dollars or a thousand. What do you think, Will? Your daddy's a lawyer."

"I don't see how they can be charged with anything more serious than disorderly conduct or disturbing the peace," said Will. "They might fine Allison for being drunk *and* disorderly, assuming he *was* drunk. I'd be surprised if anybody's fine is more than twenty-five dollars. *That's* too much, but we'll come off better just paying it, if we can."

They sat on their straw-tick beds at the hotel. McCaleb's door stood open and he heard the big clock in the lobby strike eight. Before they reached the courthouse, McCaleb spoke to Will.

"When we get there, you tell whoever's supposed to know—the judge, the sheriff, somebody—that you're acting as lawyer for Monte and Goose. Lay on enough legal talk to keep them worried. They won't know how much you know; might force 'em to follow the rules a mite closer."

"He *looks* more like a lawyer than a cowboy." Rebecca giggled nervously.

"Thanks," said Will. "Like my old daddy always says, whatever it is, if it pays more than punching cows, *take* it."

He *did* look the part. Although he was within a year or two of McCaleb's age, Will Elliot had some distinguished gray above his ears. The haircut and bath he'd had the day before helped the illusion. He wore a white shirt, a neatly knotted black string tie, and solid black pants; all he owned, as far as McCaleb knew, aside from his Levi's. They found the courtroom surprisingly well laid out. They also found it three quarters full.

"The native Romans are here," said Will, "to observe the visiting Christians being fed to the lions."

He left them grinning at his highfalutin speech and made his way to the front of the courtroom. A little man who could have been the twin of the bald hotel desk clerk strode after him. The spectators hushed so that they might hear what he had to say.

"Hey," he half shouted, "you can't go up there."

"The hell I can't," snapped Will. "I'm counsel for the defense. I am from a prominent family of attorneys in the state of Texas. My name is Will Elliot. See that it's duly recorded in the court's records."

"Never heard of you," said the little man stiffly. "I'm bailiff for this court; George Washington Chandler's the name."

"I never heard of you either," said Will coldly.

McCaleb grinned. He suspected they were about to see a whole new side to Will Elliot.

"Everybody stand," said Chandler. "This court, of the town of Santa Fe, Santa Fe County, New Mexico Territory, is now in session. Judge Jeremiah Wolfe is presiding. Edgar Sutherland is the attorney for the prosecution, and Will Elliot is the attorney for the defense. Sheriff Parker, bring in the defendants."

There were gasps when the three were led into the courtroom. They had been beaten unmercifully. Their noses and mouths were smashed and swollen. Clay Allison came first. His once-white shirt hung in bloody tatters and he seemed barely able to lift his head. When he did, they saw a nasty bloody gash across his forehead and his eyes were swollen shut. The musical chime of his jingle-bob spurs sounded strangely out of place. Monte Nance had dried blood crusted down the left side of his face and his straw-yellow hair was matted brown. The sleeves of his shirt were gone, and when he turned to face the judge, every blow of the lash was marked with a trail of dried blood in the faded denim.

Of the three, Goose's beating seemed the most brutal because he was without his buckskin shirt. Every bloody welt that crisscrossed his chest and back was visible. Fresh blood still oozed from a wicked slash above his left ear, and a similar wound over his right eye had closed it. His wrists were lashed behind his back. Indian though he was, sight of him brought a spark of pity to some eyes. Goose didn't face the judge; instead, he turned, his one good eye sweeping the courtroom. His malevolent gaze settled on a big man in a derby hat and dark suit, with an unlit cigar clenched in his teeth. A gold watch chain snaked across his ample belly. The Indian said nothing but his look said much. The object of his interest cringed visibly.

"You," shouted Chandler, "face the judge. You . . ."

Slowly, Goose turned to face the little bailiff, and Chandler got a dose that was more than he could swallow. His face went white and he stumbled back against the defense attorney's table where Will sat. Will lifted his hand in a way that meant little to anybody except Goose. Even McCaleb did not understand it. The Indian turned his back on the bailiff and faced the judge's bench. The episode had taken but a few seconds. McCaleb sighed in relief. One threatening move out of Goose and somebody would use it as an excuse to kill him. Chandler had regained enough of his dignity to read the charges. He put on his glasses and took a sheet of paper from an inside coat pocket.

"These men," he intoned, "are charged with—"

"Judge," said Will, "one of my clients has been brought here with his hands bound; I respectfully request that his bonds be removed."

"Judge, that Indian's a killer. A savage," said the large, well-dressed man. "He—"

"Mr. Condor," said Judge Wolfe coldly, "you are out of order."

McCaleb verified what he already suspected. It was the portly saloon owner Goose had singled out. On the other side of the room, from behind the prosecuting attorney's table, Edgar Sutherland got to his feet. He was a cadaverous man. He was dressed entirely in black except for his white shirt. In his swallowtail coat he could have been a misplaced undertaker. Or a buzzard, thought McCaleb. Sutherland cleared his throat.

"Your honor, what Mr. Condor, er, my client, means is that this particular defendant—this savage—has proven himself especially dangerous. It required a dozen men to subdue these three. It took six of them just to beat this savage senseless and bind his hands. Prior to that, he cut two of them badly and broke Mr. Tolliver's arm. We object to counsel's request."

"Judge," said Will, "I object to the manner in which the prosecution's judging this man guilty before the charges have even been read."

"The objection is sustained," snapped Judge Wolfe. "The prosecution will refrain from leveling *any* charges based solely on what the attorney for the prosecution *thinks*. Sheriff, loose that man and seat the three defendants at the defense table. Bailiff, prepare to read the charges against these men." Chandler began to read.

"Clay Allison is charged with being drunk and disorderly. He accused Mr. Tolliver of cheating at cards; when asked to leave, he refused, starting a fight. The other two defendants have refused even to reveal their names. They joined in the brawl, going to Mr. Allison's aid, and have been charged, on John Doe warrants, with disturbing the peace."

"You've heard the charges," said Judge Wolfe. "How do you plead?"

"Guilty to bein' drunk," said Allison, "but *not* guilty to disorderly. Since when is it disorderly to call a cheat a cheat?"

"He *was* cheated," bawled Monte. "I *saw* it happen!"

"Silence!" shouted Judge Wolfe. "You're out of order. Another such outburst and I'll declare you in contempt. Your fine will be increased accordingly."

McCaleb would have swapped his horse and saddle for a chance to tell Monte Nance they were within $160 of being broke and in *no* position to pay exorbitant fines resulting from his temper. Judge Wolfe spoke to Monte and Goose.

"You've heard the charges; how do you plead?"

"Not guilty," snapped Monte. "Either of us."

"Let the Indian speak—or make some sign—for himself."

"He can't talk so's you can understand him," said Monte. "He wasn't doin' anything except watchin' the game, like I was. All he done was help me. I'll plead guilty if you'll let him go."

"The prosecution won't accept that, Your Honor," said Sutherland. "We are going to insist that the Indian be punished to the limit of the law. I am prepared to put a dozen witnesses on the stand who can and will testify to the guilt of these three. We are not prepared to bargain; we'll accept nothing less than a guilty plea."

"Counsel for the defense has heard what counsel for the prosecution has proposed," said Judge Wolfe. "Unless defense has witnesses or wishes to rebut, I have no choice but to render a guilty verdict and impose sentence."

They had played out the string. Will got to his feet.

"Judge, we don't have any witnesses. We have legitimate business here and planned to leave today. In return for some reasonable fine, we'll go along with the prosecution's demand for a guilty plea."

Sutherland got to his feet. He had the flush of victory in his sallow cheeks, and the enthusiasm, McCaleb thought, of a stalking mountain lion about to pounce on three helpless and unwary calves. He cleared his throat.

"This is the third time Mr. Allison has visited our town. It is also the third time he's gotten drunk, gambled away his money, and then accused someone of cheating him. I will agree to defense's proposal on just two conditions. The first, that his fine be set high enough to discourage his coming here in the future, and the second, that he leave town immediately with his, ah . . . friends."

"We'll accept that," said Will.

"Very well," said Judge Wolfe. "Mr. Allison, I have heard something of your penchant for hoorawing towns. While I doubt we can stop you, we *can* make it almighty expensive. The court fines you seventy-five dollars."

The palms of McCaleb's hands were sweating. They *had* to take Allison with them to satisfy the court, but suppose similar fines were levied on Monte and Goose? They couldn't pay!

". . . John Does, the court fines you each twenty-five dollars."

McCaleb laid out $125 and they left the courtroom in silence. Allison walked ahead of them, passing Condor and Sutherland. Condor was chuckling at something Sutherland had said, but his laughter died when he saw Goose. The Indian looked at the saloon owner and spoke just three words in Spanish:

"Busardo bastardo. Matar."

Somberly, silently, they made their way to the livery, and when the hostler brought out their horses, McCaleb paid the bill from their dwindling funds. Clay Allison stood there futilely searching his pockets while the liveryman waited impatiently. Even the dried blood and mass of bruises on Allison's face didn't hide the big man's flush of embarrassment. Without a word, McCaleb handed the hostler the money and he passed the reins of the big black horse to Allison. He waited until the man returned to the livery office, then turned to McCaleb.

"That was white of you."

"Why not?" said McCaleb. "We've already got seventy-five dollars tied up in you. Anything else you need before we leave town?"

The big man flinched under the cruel words, and McCaleb felt a stab of remorse. Painfully, Allison grinned.

"I reckon I deserved that. The only thing worse'n knowin' you're a damn fool is havin' everybody else know it too. I'm lucky you didn't gut-shoot me."

"It crossed my mind," said McCaleb, "but it would have pleasured that bunch of thieving coyotes too much."

"They cheated him," said Monte Nance, unrepentant, "and after they beat us, they robbed us. Someday I'm comin' back here and drilling Condor right through the gizzard."

"Kid," said Allison, "when you brace Condor, you'd better have some good men to side you. He's got money and he owns half this town. He'll take some killing."

"His day will come," said McCaleb, "but this isn't it. Mount up; let's shake the dust of this town."

McCaleb needed time to think, to plan. Nothing had ever rankled him as much as the theft of their gold, and he had more in mind than the simple retribution that Clay Allison and Monte Nance yearned for. He aimed to reclaim that gold, with interest, before they departed New Mexico. Loping his horse alongside Allison's, he spoke.

"Do you know the way to Fort Union?"

"Yeah. Twelve miles or so. I got a horse ranch in southern Colorado, and the officers at Union like my horses. They think more highly of me than them pilgrims in Santa Fe. There's a doctor on post; Doc Griffith. He'll patch us up. Feel like I got some busted ribs."

"We have a thousand head of Texas beeves," said McCaleb. "We're asking eight cents a pound on the hoof. I'd aimed to just hold them where they are, south of Sumner, and drive them to Colorado in the spring. But now I wouldn't mind selling this herd and returning to Texas in the spring for a larger one. What are our chances at Fort Union?"

"Good, if you'll split it up into monthly deliveries. Feller named Belton has the beef contract. I know him. He won't cheat you, long as you run a close tally and keep an eye on him."

Will and Brazos had jogged their mounts close enough to hear this conversation. They had known Benton McCaleb long enough to have some idea as to what he planned to do. He would fill in the details when he was ready.

They found Fort Union as hospitable as Clay Allison had promised. They also had Doc Griffith examine Monte and Goose. The two cuts on the Apache's head required stitches, and he accepted the doctor's ministrations without complaint. Despite appearances, Monte's injuries weren't serious, and he seemed more brash than ever. McCaleb wondered if the kid had learned anything from the experience.

They had to wait until the following morning to meet with Hodge Belton. The man was in his fifties, graying, and gone to fat. He dressed well—like a banker—but he had a good-natured affability that belied his appearance. He showed up driving a fancy buckboard, behind a pair of matched grays. He listened carefully to

McCaleb. With a little gold pen knife, he nipped the end off a cigar. He chewed the end of the cigar until he had positioned it to his satisfaction and lighted it. Then he spoke around it.

"Bring me two hundred head before the tenth of each month, and I'll write you a check. That satisfactory?"

"Not entirely," said McCaleb. "We prefer gold."

"So do I. So do scoundrels and outlaws. You can easily ride from here to Santa Fe in less than an hour. My check will be drawn on the bank there. I can arrange for them to honor it in gold."

McCaleb put aside the little nagging doubt that often plagued him when something wasn't just right. He looked to Will, to Brazos, to Rebecca, to Monte. Even to Goose. They would go with his decision. He turned to the buyer.

"You have a deal. Starting November tenth and ending March tenth. The last drive to run maybe fifteen head higher; remnant of the herd."

While they prepared to ride south, Clay Allison was saddling up to ride to his ranch near Las Animas. He had recovered rapidly, and although swathed in bandages to protect some broken ribs, he seemed hardly the worse for his recent ordeal. He wore a black suit, flowing black string tie, and white ruffled shirt. Bloody and bruised as his face had been, he had taken the time to shave. He spoke first to McCaleb.

"Pardner, I drink too much, gamble too much, raise hell too much, but Clay Allison never forgets a kindness. You ever need help—gun help—send for me; I'll side you till Hell freezes, and we'll skate on the ice."

He held out his big hand and McCaleb took it. Allison dug into his pocket, came out with a handful of double eagles and passed four of them to McCaleb.

"That squares us. They still owed me for that last bunch of horses. I never take *all* my money to Santa Fe. Reckon I needn't explain why."

"I reckon not," said McCaleb.

Allison extended his big hand to Will, to Brazos, and Rebecca. Then he turned to Monte.

"Kid, next time you buy into a game, check the odds a little more careful. *Mucho gracias, amigo.*" Finally he turned to Goose, speaking in careful Spanish.

"*Hombre de bien, Ganos. Malo, malo cuchillo! Hasta luego.*"

While their return trip to Fort Sumner and the herd was uneventful and quiet, there was a feeling, a spark, that seemed to ignite their enthusiasm anew. Come hell or high water, they were an outfit, Texans all!

They stopped at Fort Sumner just long enough to rest and water their horses. McCaleb had something on his mind, and before they moved out, he spoke.

"What happened in Santa Fe is our problem and we'll handle it in our own time and in our own way. I'd as soon nothing be said of it to Goodnight, Loving, or any of their riders."

They were silent, content with the knowledge that their case in Santa Fe hadn't been closed. When they had mounted up and ridden out, Rebecca jogged her horse alongside McCaleb's.

"He's some kind of man, isn't he?"

"Allison? I reckon he'll do. One more reason to send you to Colorado."

"Are you jealous of him?"

"I don't know," said McCaleb. "Should I be?"

"Not unless he'd stop drinking and gambling. I hate that!"

"Then I'm not jealous of him. He's the kind who'll be bushwhacked when he's drunk and careless, or gut-shot across a card table."

"I liked the way he warned Monte, about avoiding trouble in Santa Fe, but there's something about him . . ."

"I reckon he's not one to take his own advice," said McCaleb. "He kept his mouth shut and left town with his tail between his legs, but that's not his style. He'll be riding back, getting even."

"Like you plan to do," she said.

He said nothing, allowing her to draw her own conclusions.

CHAPTER 19

*G*oodnight was pleased to learn McCaleb had made arrangements to sell the herd at Fort Union. Oliver Loving offered his congratulations and asked that they pass on to him anything—even rumors—they might hear at Fort Union regarding the letting of beef contracts.

With almost two months of good graze, the big steers were fat and lazy. McCaleb's outfit cut out two hundred head and headed them northwest on November 3. They reached Fort Sumner on the second day and drove almost to Las Vegas on the third. They reached Fort Union on November 9, only to learn that Hodge Belton wouldn't be there until the next day. They pitched camp in some willows near a creek and were up long before dawn. The sun was three hours high when Hodge Belton drove up in his buckboard. Scanning the herd appreciatively, he turned to McCaleb.

"Exceptional animals," he said. "Rest of 'em the equal of these?"

"As good or better," said McCaleb. "Where are your riders?"

"Coming," said Belton. "Can you hold the herd for me until they arrive?"

"I'll leave you three riders," said McCaleb. "The rest of us are riding into town to swap your check for gold."

* * *

McCaleb, Brazos, and Will mounted up and trotted their horses toward Santa Fe. McCaleb had planned to leave Monte and Goose at Fort Union, but Belton's request had allowed him to leave Rebecca behind as well. Without Monte and Goose, he was uncertain as to their reception in town. Tolliver, the gambler, exited the bank just as they reined up. He wore a cast on his right arm that covered most of his hand. He appeared not to recognize them.

"He won't bottom-deal with that hand for a while," Will said, chuckling.

"Whether he knows it or not," said Brazos, "he's the luckiest gambler in the territory. Goose could've spread his guts all over that saloon floor."

"Thank God he didn't," said McCaleb. "Not that he didn't deserve it, but they'd have hung Goose. He's got to learn there are ways of getting your revenge without getting your neck stretched."

The three of them entered the bank and exchanged the check for gold without a hitch. Will had brought his saddlebags, and into them the money went.

"There's a saddle maker up the street," said McCaleb. "Since we're ridin' that way, let's stop for a few minutes. I miss my saddlebags."

The place smelled of oil and leather. There were bridles, pieces of bridles, unfinished saddles, used saddles, and new saddles. There was no ceiling, and across the overhead beams there were whole tanned cowhides tied down with leather thongs. Before an almost-finished fancy saddle with silver trappings sat a little man in leather apron and wire-rimmed glasses.

"I need some saddlebags," said McCaleb.

"Check that rail along th' back wall," said the saddle maker.

Will and Brazos continued to look at the saddles. In a surprisingly short time McCaleb dropped the worn leather saddlebags on the bench before the old saddle maker. He looked up and spoke.

"Two dollars, if'n ye think it ain't too much."

"They're worth it," said McCaleb. "Where'd you get them?"

"Old Pete Donner brought 'em in, needin' some beer money. Said he found 'em in th' alley behind Condor's saloon. He's th' swamper there."

Unmolested, they rode out. So long had they ridden together and so much in harmony was their thinking, each seemed to know the thoughts of his comrades. The town was well behind them when Brazos spoke.

"That's evidence enough for me."

"More than enough for me," said Will. "When?"

"In March," said McCaleb, "when we've sold the rest of the herd and our business in Santa Fe is finished. I aim to talk to Clay Allison again."

To Rebecca's surprise and disgust, McCaleb began taking a real interest in the nightly poker games. Where Monte and Goose were concerned, he was especially watchful, often chuckling at the Indian's growing perception and skill. The players used the cartridges from their shell belts for chips, and there were nights when Goose was the only man in the game with any shells. Of all the Indian had to learn, the most difficult was the fact that—when he left the game—he must return his "winnings" to those who had lost them. He was as unpredictable as he was impassive. McCaleb watched him draw the worst of all hands and win on a bluff. When his comrades, sure he was bluffing again, called him, he was likely to lay down a straight flush.

"If somebody don't kill him," said Brazos, "that Indian's goin' to be the damnedest poker player in the history of the world. He keeps raisin' his bets like he knows the cards still to be drawed."

Will chuckled. "He pretty well does. He has a talent I've seen only a time or two. He remembers the cards that have been played. Knowin' that, he can calculate his odds on the draw, especially when there's fewer and fewer cards to draw from."

* * *

The first week in December, they delivered their two hundred beeves to Fort Union and again converted Belton's check to gold. McCaleb took a pair of pack mules and they bought supplies to last them through January. He bought tins of fruit, tins of condensed milk, a hoop of cheese, and other luxuries to endjoy during Christmas. In mid-December a three-day blizzard howled out of the west, but they were dug in and ready. The cattle sought shelter in the brakes along the Pecos, and while the snow fell, the poker game in the river-bank shelter never ceased.

In the first week of January 1867, they delivered another two hundred head of cattle to Fort Union and found Clay Allison there. He seemed genuinely glad to see them, and it was a while before McCaleb was able to talk to him in private. He listened while McCaleb told him of the humiliating loss they had suffered in Santa Fe in addition to what had been done to Monte and Goose. He nodded grimly when McCaleb told him where the stolen saddlebags had been found.

Finally he spoke. "You ain't the kind of man to take that; what do you aim to do?"

McCaleb told him, and even before Allison had heard it all, he was wringing his hands in delight.

"Benton McCaleb, you're truly a man after my own heart!"

"Are you sure you want a piece of this fight? You could end up being outlawed in New Mexico Territory."

"I've *already* raised enough hell to get myself outlawed in New Mexico, and none of it for any good reason. I wouldn't miss this for all the tea in China. When we take Condor off their backs, the good people of Santa Fe will likely pin medals on us."

"Mr. Condor is a respectable citizen," said McCaleb.

"Respectable, hell! He's everything his name says. Folks in Santa Fe are scared to death he'll run for mayor. He has wealth and power; he can buy or steal enough votes to win. I could name you some people he's got in his pocket."

"Like Sheriff Parker. What about Judge Wolfe?"

"Not him," said Allison. "He's a crusty old bastard, but he's square. He hates Condor because Condor's started a land grab, taking it legal if he can, stealing it if he has to. When the railroad comes through Santa Fe, he aims to bleed the company dry for right-of-way. There's disturbing talk the railroad might build *around* Santa Fe, if Condor tries to rob them."

"The gent that blows out Condor's lamp won't be all *that* unpopular, then," said McCaleb, "and nothing less is going to stop him."

"Long as a rattler's alive, it's goin' to bite anybody that gets close enough. My God, what you've got in mind is dynamite! It'll be risky as hell because Condor's got fifteen gamblers and gunnies that I know of, and he's just hired the Hogue brothers. Brady and Burke are as nasty a pair of pistoleros as I've ever seen. We'll have to cut them both down before we can even get close to the big buzzard himself."

"When Belton takes the last of our herd in March," said McCaleb, "we'll be ready to return to Texas. But before we leave, we're going on a buzzard hunt. I reckon about March fifth."

"Deal me in," said Allison. "I'll be here."

On their return trip they camped just north of Fort Sumner and right after supper, McCaleb told his group of the plan he had outlined to Clay Allison. While he explained the part each of them would play, the growing excitement in Monte Nance's eyes matched the grimness in Rebecca's. When he finished, there was a long silence. Brazos was the first to speak.

"Suppose they won't let Goose into the game?"

"I'll give you odds," said McCaleb, "the devil himself could buy in, if he's got gold. What concerns me the most is that Goose must understand his part in this scheme and hold his temper. I'm countin' on you to help educate him."

"It'll take me a while; the Vasquez boys could do it quicker."

"You try it first," said McCaleb. "I don't want Goodnight and Loving or their outfits involved in this if it can be avoided."

McCaleb left the fire, walking through the starlit night toward where the horses were picketed. Suddenly he stopped, turned and waited. Rebecca had been only a few steps behind.

"I have business in the bushes," he said.

"It's dark," said the girl, "and I won't interfere. I just want to talk to you where the others can't hear."

"You mean where Monte can't hear."

"I don't understand you, McCaleb. Monte's just a kid long on courage and short on common sense. Goose is an ignorant Indian. They were lucky to escape Condor's saloon with their lives, and now you're sending them back into it. Why can't we just take our money from the sale of *this* herd and ride back to Texas?"

"Two reasons. First, I reckon there's enough lawman left in me that I purely can't abide Condor's den of thieves. Second, after the beating they took, Monte and Goose—as well as Clay Allison—deserve satisfaction. I admire your concern for Monte and Goose, but if they're going to survive on the frontier, it's time they reared up on their hind legs and showed everybody they've got sand. Besides, they won't be alone; Allison will side them, and so will I."

"Then I'll be there too; I'm part of this outfit."

"Condor's saloon is no place for a woman."

"I won't *be* a woman. I'll wear one of your shirts; it'll be big enough and baggy enough to hide my front. And when we take the rest of the herd to Fort Union, buy me a new hat in Santa Fe. I'll cut some of my hair and stuff the rest of it into the hat."

"They've *seen* you in Santa Fe," said McCaleb.

"Only once, and not in Condor's saloon."

"I don't *want* you in Condor's saloon."

He expected her to become angry and swear at him,

but she didn't. She resorted instead to the most persuasive argument a woman can use. Throwing her arms around his neck, she clung to him until he began to respond . . .

McCaleb's outfit made the February drive to Fort Union and returned. Brazos took to sitting in on the poker games, watching Goose. Carefully he began explaining to the Indian what they planned to do. When he first mentioned Condor's saloon, Goose seemed to lose all concentration, a look of madness veiling his obsidian eyes. Slowly, Brazos conquered even that, and McCaleb breathed easier.

February 27, Oliver Loving and four riders headed out all that remained of the Goodnight-Loving herd. Goodnight trotted his big black across the Pecos and up the west bank until he reached McCaleb's camp.

"Well," sighed Goodnight, "that's the end of it. When do you aim to deliver the rest of your herd to Fort Union?"

"We'll move 'em out the day after tomorrow," said McCaleb. "Allowing five days for the drive, we should be able to turn them over to Belton and return here by March eighth. You chompin' at the bit to head for Texas?"

Goodnight chuckled. "Not me, but Mr. Loving is. He wants to rush back and have an even larger herd on the trail by the end of May. He's determined to reach Sumner in time to bid on those beef contracts to be let in August."

"He's welcome to them," said McCaleb, "far as we're concerned. We aim to drive our next herd on to Colorado and maybe beyond. If he's in all that much of a hurry, I expect he'll have a galloping case of the fidgits long before we get back. Don't keep him waiting; go ahead and pull out. You'll be slowed down enough with the chuck wagon for us to catch up. But if you do pull out ahead of us, take our extra mules and horse remuda with you."

They bedded down the herd outside Fort Union late in the afternoon of March 5. Rebecca Nance wore a too-large blue flannel shirt and a hat pulled low to further conceal her newly shortened hair. Burned Mex-brown by the relentless sun and wind, she seemed just another dusty young cowboy. The Colt she carried, butt visible above the waist of her Levi's, further added to the illusion. Much to their disgust, they found Hodge Belton wouldn't arrive until sometime the next day. But Clay Allison was there waiting for them.

"It'd be a mite too much coincidence, us all ridin' into Santa Fe in a bunch," said Allison. "I'll start early in the morning, giving me time to visit some other saloons. I need to seem good and drunk, time I get to Condor's place."

"You'll have plenty of time," said McCaleb. "We'll have to wait for Belton. I want to cash his check before we indulge in the questionable pleasures of Mr. Condor's establishment. We might not be welcome in town after that, at the bank or anywhere else."

It was midday when they finally concluded their business with Belton and rode to town. They first went to the bank, and from there to the little eatery across from the courthouse. They had steak and onions, fried potatoes, apple pie, and coffee. Nobody's appetite seemed affected except Rebecca's. She kept her silence, but her eyes had the look of one who's been condemned and is struggling with a final meal. It was Wednesday afternoon, still early, and the town was quiet. Ominously quiet. It seemed to be just waiting. They were finishing their steaks when Judge Jeremiah Wolfe came in, taking a seat at a nearby table. He nodded to them, saying nothing. Minutes later, almost as though he'd been following the judge, Sheriff Parker entered. Instead of seating himself with or near Judge Wolfe, he took the table next to McCaleb's outfit. He said nothing until they had finished their meal and were about to leave.

"You Texas hellions ain't welcome here. I'm warnin' you not to start anything."

McCaleb walked over to where the lawman sat, placed his hands flat on the table and leaned across it, looking the arrogant sheriff in the eye.

"I promise you we won't start anything we can't finish. If you buy into the game, when the finish comes, you just be sure you're on the right side."

They walked out, ignoring the scowl on Parker's face and without seeing the trace of a smile hiding behind Judge Wolfe's coffee mug.

They paused on the boardwalk outside the hotel. McCaleb passed the saddlebags with their gold to Will, along with final instructions.

"You and Brazos stay out of Condor's place. Give us a couple of hours and then split up, one of you covering the front and the other the rear. If there's gun trouble, don't let any of Condor's coyotes swarm in on us from outside."

He then turned to Monte and Goose. "Remember the signals, Monte. If Goose is allowed to play, they'll be watching him close. Keep your bets low or stay out of the game altogether if they're playing draw poker. When you've drawn your first five cards, draw three more, whether you need them or not. Get as much of the deck in play as you can. Follow Allison's lead; raise occasionally, whether you've got the cards or not. We know they're a bunch of cheating coyotes, but we'll have to spend some money to catch them at it. Remember, we don't want Goose getting in too deep, too soon. Five-card stud, six or more players, and the odds are with him."

Monte and Goose drifted leisurely away toward Condor's saloon, half a block down the street. Will and Brazos were nowhere in sight.

"Oh, I want this to be over and done!" cried Rebecca.

"How long do we have to wait before going to Condor's?"

"Couple of hours," said McCaleb. "They'll be all right, I reckon. That's why I wanted Allison with us. I don't look for any serious poker until late. That's why Monte and Goose have been told to avoid any kind of ruckus until I get there. If we're going to fight over a pot, let's wait until it's big enough to justify the fight."

"But why five-card stud, and why must there be so many players?"

"Because six players puts thirty cards in play," said McCaleb, "twenty-four of them face up before the showdown. If my hole card is an ace and I'm dealt two more without that fourth ace showing, then I've got two more cards coming, the final one with half the deck faceup."

"I'm just scared to death for Goose and Monte. It's one thing to play for pistol cartridges with friendly riders, and something else to play for money with cut-throat gamblers."

"Before this day's over," said McCaleb, "that Indian's going to show those gamblers how the cow ate the cabbage. All we have to do is keep him alive to collect his winnings."

The evening sun was only an hour high when McCaleb and Rebecca pushed through the bat-wings into Condor's saloon. For the time and place, it was elegant. The floor was polished oak and the bar mahogany, with a brass foot rail running the length of it. Polished brass spittoons shone gold in the light from suspended, shaded lamps. On the wall behind the bar hung a full-sized painting. The buxom woman was spared total nakedness by filmy bits of lace in critical areas. A winding carpeted staircase led to the second floor. At the very rear of the long room was an enormous oak table. One end sat in the corner, and its length extended along the back wall. It would easily accommodate a dozen men. Clay Allison sat at the very end, his back to the wall.

Next to Allison sat Monte Nance, and next to him, Goose. McCaleb nodded approvingly. The dealer for the house sat with his back to the open room, a position most of them avoided. Business was slow, and new arrivals failing to patronize the bar weren't encouraged to linger. McCaleb and Rebecca leaned on the bar near the end, where they could observe the poker game in progress. The barkeep moved up behind them, waiting.

"Two whiskeys," said McCaleb over his shoulder.

They needed a diversion, and McCaleb sighed with relief when it came in the form of the stove-up ex-puncher from the café who had first told them about Clay Allison's violent past. The little man made his way to the bar, nodding to McCaleb.

"Howdy, Salty," said the barkeep. "Beer?"

"Yeah," said Salty, "an' gimme th' rest in chips. Ain't played poker in a spell an' I wanta see kin I sit in on that game."

Rebecca looked at McCaleb. His whiskey glass was empty. He had taken advantage of Salty's arrival and had disposed of his whiskey in a convenient spittoon. Unobtrusively he swapped Rebecca his empty glass for her full one. Salty took his place at the poker table, next to the house man. McCaleb had to suppress a grin at the antics of Clay Allison. The vain bastard ought to have become an actor. He had his chair reared back on its hind legs, a cigar clamped between his teeth, and his big grey Stetson canted over his eyes, the epitome of a drunken cowboy trying to play poker and doing a poor job of it. He slapped his cards on the table in disgust as he lost another pot. McCaleb fed the spittoon another glass of whiskey, and when the barkeep spotted their empty glasses, ordered another round.

It came as no surprise to McCaleb when Sheriff Parker swaggered through the bat-wing doors and backed up to the bar, hooking a boot heel over the rail. He glared at McCaleb long and hard. McCaleb ignored him. What did surprise McCaleb—and apparently Sheriff Parker—was the arrival of Judge Jeremiah Wolfe. It soon became evident he was not a frequent visitor, when Condor himself came out to extend a greeting.

"First drink's on the house, Judge," he said, with all the enthusiasm he could muster. "What'll it be?"

"Nothing, thanks," said Judge Wolfe. "Heard the Indian was sitting in on a poker game. Chips, please." He slid a double eagle across the bar.

The barkeep looked at Condor, shrugged his shoulders, and stacked the chips on the mahogany. Judge Wolfe scooped them up, took them to the poker table, and hooking his boot in the rung of a chair, dragged it back and sat down. It was time. Clay Allison leaned forward, clunking the front legs of the chair and his boots against the floor.

"Hey," he bawled, "had 'nough o' this tea party! Le's play a man's game! Five-card stud!"

Attracted by the increased activity, two more of Condor's gamblers had come downstairs. Condor turned to them.

"Take over, Sutton. Five-card stud. New deck."

Sutton was snake-thin and sallow-faced, with just a trace of a moustache. He had thin, bony fingers and long nails. He wore a derby hat, a white ruffled shirt with sleeve garters, gray pin-striped trousers which had been darned on the seat. There was a gold band on the little finger of his left hand. He pulled out a chair and sat down. In the first game of stud, Allison, Monte, and Goose bet low, failing to raise. Judge Wolfe took the small pot. In the next game, Allison, Monte, and Goose raised, building the pot to respectable proportions and the house won. The next small pot went to Salty, the biscuit shooter. Each time there was a decent pot, the house won. When Goose made his move, it was with the swiftness of a striking rattler. Like magic the Bowie appeared in his left hand, and with his right he snatched Sutton's left wrist. Using the surface of the heavy oak table for a chop block, he severed the gambler's little finger! Sutton tumbled over backward, bawling in pain.

"Nobody move!" snapped Monte Nance. He stood

with his back to the wall, his pale blue eyes cold, the
Colt in his hand rock-steady. Nodding to Goose, he
spoke:

"*Ganos, anillo de oro.*"

Calmly, Goose retrieved the severed finger and
slipped off the gold band. He dropped it on the table,
and it was more than a gold band. The set of the ring
was a tiny mirror, detected by the sharp eyes of the
Apache. Worn palm-out on Sutton's dealing hand, it
had allowed the gambler to know the value of the cards
as he dealt them. Judge Wolfe got up and faced Condor.

"I daresay, Condor, this sort of thing is likely to give
visitors a poor impression of our town in general and
your establishment in particular. Have you a single reason why I shouldn't order the sheriff to close your
doors?"

"Now wait a minute!" bawled Sheriff Parker, coming
to life.

He froze as a slug from Monte's Colt splintered the
bar just inches from the hand hovering above his holster. He lifted his hands shoulder high, and Judge Wolfe
continued as though nothing out of the ordinary had
happened.

"Well, Condor?"

"I had no knowledge of what he was doing," said
Condor suavely. "You're through, Sutton. You know my
rules. Get up and get out of here!"

Sutton lay on the floor clutching his hurt hand against
his belly, the bloody stain blossoming ever larger
against the white of his shirt. He got to his knees and
stumbled to his feet. So savage was the hatred in his
eyes, Condor involuntary backstepped. He watched
Sutton through the bat-wings and turned back to Judge
Wolfe.

"Unfortunate. I'm sorry this happened. You gentlemen are welcome to recover what you lost from what's
on the table. The game's closed."

"I think not," said Judge Wolfe. "You have other deal-
ers, Condor, and I want to see if they're following your

rules any closer than Sutton did. Young man, you can put that pistol away now."

Monte holstered the Colt. Clay Allison cast McCaleb a secret wink. Monte had just taken a giant step toward becoming a man, and Goose, while performing in a totally unpredictable way, had proven himself capable of sound judgment. While he would have been perfectly justified in killing the gambler, it might have caused such a furor, they'd have been forced to leave town with their debt to Condor unsettled. McCaleb had no idea why Judge Wolfe had taken a hand in the game. He suspected the crusty old man sensed a showdown in the making between McCaleb's outfit and Condor.

"Mr. Tolliver will deal for the house," said Condor.

McCaleb was surprised when the gambler took the chair so recently vacated by Sutton. He sat right across the table from Goose; there was no way he could have forgotten the Indian had broken his arm. It was going to be interesting to witness his performance!

Tolliver, whether by choice or upon orders from Condor, dealt an honest game. He lost consistently. Just as consistently, Goose won. Judge Wolfe and Salty seemed to take more interest in Goose than in the game.

"*Levantar*," said Goose, when he wished to raise. The amount was never mentioned; he simply pushed the chips to the center of the table. He had an uncanny knack for drawing the very card he needed.

Tolliver began to sweat. McCaleb saw the man's hands tremble as he dealt the cards. Condor leaned against the bar, occasionally speaking to Sheriff Parker, making no secret of their alliance. The time came when Goose had more than a thousand dollars in chips before him, most of it Condor's. Seeing his last faceup card before the showdown, he pushed five hundred dollars in chips to the center of the table.

"*Levantar*," said Goose.

Tolliver paused and looked forlornly at his final faceup card. His hesitation was evidence enough that his hole card didn't measure up and that he dared not match the Indian's raise. He was finished. He folded. When he looked at Condor, the saloon man nodded him out of the game. Condor then said something to Sheriff Parker and the sheriff left the saloon. Without a word, Tolliver relinquished his chair and Condor took over, dealing for the house. He was slick. He fanned the cards from one hand to the other, spiraling them out in a graceful flow. He lost several large pots to Goose. While the others won occasionally, it had become a showdown between Condor and the Indian. Goose was calm, his hands steady. He had discovered a new and far more painful method of scalping his enemy!

By the time Goose had accumulated $2500, McCaleb knew Condor's move must come soon. McCaleb caught Clay Allison's eye and the big man touched the brim of his hat. McCaleb nodded. They would make their move on this hand. Suddenly, as Condor began dealing the cards, McCaleb knew what was coming. Condor dealt each player two cards, one of them a hole card, face down. He dealt Goose a faceup king and himself a faceup ace. McCaleb's suspicions were confirmed when Condor dealt Goose a second faceup king and himself a faceup jack. McCaleb was certain the Indian's hole card was a king, allowing him two more chances to draw the fourth king. Good odds in an honest game, but this wasn't an honest game. Condor's hole card was almost certainly an ace, and if he dealt himself another ace on the next-to-last draw, Allison would stop the game.

Again Condor dealt the cards around the table. There was a gasp from Rebecca when Goose was dealt a *third* faceup king! McCaleb stole a glance at Allison. The big man had eased his chair forward, all its legs resting on the floor. Condor dealt himself a *second* faceup ace, and McCaleb tensed as Goose did exactly what Condor had expected. The Indian swept all his winnings to the center of the table.

"*Levantar,*" he said.

"I'll cover that," said Condor. Slowly, dramatically, he began dealing the last hand. Goose drew a faceup nine of clubs. But before Condor could deal the last faceup card—his own—Clay Allison reached out and caught his wrist.

"Put them down, Condor," said Allison grimly. "Flat on the table."

Condor released what remained of the deck.

"Now," said Allison, "I want Judge Wolfe to draw that last card for you. From the *top* of the deck. Go ahead, Judge."

Carefully Judge Wolfe slid the top card off and turned it, revealing the queen of hearts.

"Now let's have a look at Mr. Condor's hole card. Judge?"

Judge Wolfe turned Condor's hole card. It was the ace of clubs.

"Now," said Allison, "let's see what's on the very *bottom* of the deck; the last card. Judge?"

Judge Wolfe drew the last card—the ace of spades.

"You can't prove a thing!" shouted Condor.

"We don't have to," said McCaleb. "We're settling the ownership of that last pot. Then maybe we'll have another look at your rules."

Clay Allison turned the Indian's hole card face up, placing the fourth king with the other three. Condor's face paled but he sat there in silence.

"Judge," said McCaleb, "I'd appreciate it if you'd tally the pot."

It was the ultimate insult, but Condor kept his silence. There wasn't the slightest doubt in McCaleb's mind that Condor had cold-decked Goose, dealing him a four-of-a-kind, next-to-best hand. Then on the final draw—the showdown—the saloon owner would have dealt himself a fourth ace. From the bottom of the deck! It was brazen cheating, the very brazenness of it accounting for its occasional success. It was difficult to challenge a slick dealer, but McCaleb had seen some good ones. He could have stopped the game himself, but Clay Allison had wanted the satisfaction of exposing Condor's crooked operation.

"I count five thousand three hundred dollars," said Judge Wolfe.

"All right, Condor," said McCaleb. "Ante up, in gold."

"I'll have to get it from the safe," said Condor sullenly. "Upstairs."

"I'll go with you," said McCaleb, "just to be sure you find your way back. Come on."

Condor got up and headed for the stairs.

"Hold it, Condor," said McCaleb. He turned to Judge Wolfe. "Judge, you and Salty had best be gettin' out of here while you can. I can promise you we'll be riding out just as soon as we finish our business with Mr. Condor. The rest of you, cover the front and back doors of this place until I return."

Slowly they ascended the spiral stairs, Condor walking ahead. McCaleb drew his Colt. How many of Condor's men might be awaiting them on the second floor? McCaleb waited until they were near enough to the top of the stairs for him to see the length of the hall. He prodded Condor in the back with the muzzle of his Colt.

"Not a sound out of you," said McCaleb softly. "Where's the office?"

"Third door on the left," said Condor.

They paused before the door, McCaleb waiting impatiently with gun in hand while Condor fumbled for the key. The door swung open on oiled hinges and McCaleb waited until the saloon owner had entered the room. McCaleb followed, closing the door quietly behind him. There was a rolltop desk, a swivel chair, a pair of ladder-back cane-bottoms, and the squat, black gold-lettered safe. Condor knelt before it, turning the combination dial. He swung the door open, took a canvas bag, and began filling it.

"Pile it on the floor," said McCaleb. "When I'm satisfied it's all there, *then* you can sack it."

They left the office, Condor walking ahead. Suddenly

a door opened just ahead of them and McCaleb found himself looking into the startled eyes of a near-naked girl. She slammed the door and Condor used the distraction to his advantage. He dropped the heavy canvas sack, turned on McCaleb, and they fought for the Colt. The saloon man was bull-strong, and as he drove McCaleb's arm upward, the Colt blasted a slug into the ceiling. Other doors opened and other men were on him, one of them from behind. A brawny arm encircled his throat, cutting off his wind. He caught one of his attackers in the groin with his knee, but there were too many of them. A blow to the back of his head sent him to his knees, and one of them slammed a boot heel into his ribs. Somewhere far away he thought he heard pistol shots. With a crash, one of his assailants went to the floor, and there was the sound of booted feet pounding down the hall behind him. McCaleb shook his head and through blurred vision saw Rebecca Nance at the head of the stairs, a Colt in her hand. He got up, stumbling against the wall.

"Thanks," he mumbled. "Condor—"

"He went down the hall toward the back stairs," said Rebecca. "I shot this one, but the rest of them went with him. We'd better get downstairs; there's been shooting outside, front and back of the saloon."

Clay Allison stood next to the back door leading to the alley, a Colt in his hand. Monte Nance covered the front door, while Brazos stood beside a front window, peering around the heavy drapes. The right sleeve of his shirt was bloody from shoulder to elbow. He turned to McCaleb.

"They've got a pair of dead-eyes coverin' the front and back with rifles. They nailed me before I could get in here, and I don't know where Will is. He was coverin' the back door, and it sounded like all hell busted loose in the alley. Soon as the judge and the others got out, they cut down on us."

"Condor and a couple of his men went down the back

stairs," said McCaleb. "With that rifleman already out there, I hope they didn't catch Will in a cross-fire. Where's Goose?"

"He lit out the front door," said Allison, "soon as he heard the fight upstairs. He knew somethin' was wrong, and I'd say he's gone looking for Condor."

"The Hogue boys are out there somewhere," said Brazos. "That's why they let Goose out; they aim to kill him."

"Keep firing," said McCaleb. "I want to see where those sharpshooters are holed up. I'm going out there and take them out of the fight. Then we can maybe give Goose a fighting chance. Come on, Rebecca; I need your help."

He took the stairs two at a time, Rebecca right behind him. He went to the door of the near-naked girl who had made Condor's escape possible. It was locked. He lunged at it, splintering the door frame above and below the lock. The girl, clad only in her underwear, came off the bed screaming.

"Put a stop to that," snapped McCaleb, "any way you can."

Rebecca brought a right all the way from her knees, connecting with the saloon girl's chin. The girl slammed against the wall, slid down to a sitting position against it and was quiet.

"Find something to tie her with," said McCaleb. "Gag her too."

He set about ripping the sheets off the bed. He tied two together and dragged the bed over next to the window. He hoped they had positioned men to cover the front and rear of the saloon and hadn't surrounded it. He tied one end of the pair of sheets to the bed frame and raised the window. He turned to find that Rebecca had stripped the woman of her undergarments and had used them to bind and gag her.

"I want to go with you."

"No," he said. "This is a one-man job. It'll be dangerous enough when I dispose of these snipers. At least wait until I do that."

Without another word he eased himself out the window, slid down the length of the knotted sheets and dropped the last few feet to the ground at the west side of the saloon. He ran to the corner of the building facing the street. Suddenly there was a burst of gunfire from the saloon. From the rooftop of a vacant false-fronted building across the street came the return fire. The street seemed deserted. The only light was from the open door and the front windows of Condor's saloon. He waited for the next volley from the saloon. When it came, with the answering fire, he sprinted across the street. He found a window in the rear of the old building from which the shutters had either rotted or been torn away. There was a crude ladder to the roof, some of the rungs missing. He tested each of them before trusting them to his weight. He came off the old ladder on his knees and there was an audible crunch as something broke under his weight. The rifleman fired first, the slug grazing McCaleb's neck above his shirt collar. McCaleb fired once. He retrieved the rifle and stood looking down at the dead man. He spoke quietly, in disgust.

"You should have stuck to slick-dealing, Tolliver."

From the rooftop McCaleb could see the hotel. Next to it was another saloon, and directly across the street from that was the Five Aces. There was lamplight streaming from open doors of both saloons and from the hotel doors and windows. Goose stood in the street—in the shadows—in front of the Five Aces. Across the street, on the boardwalk in front of the other saloon, stood a big gunman, his hands on his hips. One of the Hogues! McCaleb jacked a shell into the chamber of Tolliver's Spencer and leaned over the false front facing the street. If one of the Hogues was facing Goose, the other would be staked out somewhere to the rear, preparing to back-shoot the Indian if possible. That would put the other Hogue on McCaleb's side of the street, out of his reach! McCaleb could only watch it happen, preparing to defend the Indian as best he could. He kept his eyes on the gunman. It was Goose's play, and it began when Hogue went for his Colt. He was fast. Almighty fast! But not fast enough. Goose fired first and Hogue's half-drawn Colt blasted a slug into the boardwalk. On the heels of that came another shot. McCaleb's eyes went to Goose in time to see the Indian driven to his knees. But he didn't stop there. He twisted to his right and from flat on his back in the dusty street fired once. McCaleb fired three quick blasts from Tolliver's Spencer to get attention and then shouted a warning into the night.

"You men from Condor's place, it's finished. Tolliver's dead; so are the Hogues. We're going after Condor. Stay out of our way!"

By the time McCaleb reached the street, the rest of his outfit was on the boardwalk waiting for him. Will Elliot limped, the leg of his Levi's slit to the knee, a bandage knotted about his right calf.

"Where's Allison?" McCaleb asked.

"He went out to side Goose," said Brazos, "but not soon enough."

"Goose took both of them," said McCaleb, "but the second one wounded him from behind. Let's go!"

There was the sound of boots on the boardwalk, coming toward them, and Salty, ex-cowboy turned cook, limped out of the darkness.

"Condor . . ." he panted. "Condor's upstairs in th' hotel, locked in his room. Sutton, th' gambler he run off, is up there lookin' fer him. With a shotgun!"

They reached Allison and Goose, finding the left shoulder of the Indian's buckskin shirt bloody.

"He'll live to draw another four-of-a-kind," said Allison.

By the time they got to the hotel, a crowd had gathered. Some of them, now unarmed, were gamblers from Condor's place. Judge Wolfe came out of the hotel.

"Stay out of the hotel," he warned. "Sutton's gone crazy and he's armed."

"If he's after Condor," said McCaleb, "he's got cause."

"Nevertheless," sighed the judge, "he must be stopped. It's ironic that the man representing the law has made a mockery of it, but at least this one time Sheriff Parker's going to earn his pay."

Parker arrived, taking the stairs slowly, his Colt in his hand. Judge Wolfe returned to the lobby. McCaleb and his outfit followed, along with Allison and most of the other curious. Suddenly there was the resonant bellow of a shotgun and the splintering of wood.

"No!" screeched Condor, in mortal terror. "No! Please, no . . ."

A second blast from the shotgun ended his pleading. Parker had paused at the head of the stairs. He fired once, twice. A third time the shotgun roared, and as though by an unseen hand, Parker was lifted off the landing and flung halfway down the stairs. Before anyone could speak, Sutton, hard-hit, lurched to the head of the stairs. He tried to speak but couldn't. The shotgun clattered to the floor and the gambler fell face down. Slowly, McCaleb, Allison, and Judge Wolfe climbed the stairs. They had no trouble finding Condor's room. The door had been blown off the hinges. The second blast from the shotgun had caught the saloon owner in the chest and flung him against the wall.

"My God," breathed Judge Wolfe. "My God!"

McCaleb found their gold in a canvas bag in a closet. They followed Judge Wolfe to the stairs, where he paused long enough to rip the badge from the dead sheriff's shirt. Reaching the lobby, Judge Wolfe spoke.

"Condor's finished. Those of you who worked for him, it's time to move on." He then turned to McCaleb.

"At the risk of seeming inhospitable, I'm asking you folks to ride out. Immediately."

Salty was waiting outside the hotel. McCaleb shook the old cook's hand.

"*Hasta luego*, cowboy; you're a man to ride the river with."

"Tarnation," said Will as they mounted. "At least the judge could have given us time to see a doc and get ourselves patched up."

"Better doc at Fort Union," said Allison.

CHAPTER 20

They remained at Fort Union just long enough for the post physician to see to the wounds of Will, Brazos, and Goose. There was a peculiar wistfulness in Rebecca's eyes when they parted with Clay Allison. He shook hands with everybody except Rebecca. When she threw her arms around him, Allison actually blushed.

"Why don't you throw in with us," invited McCaleb, "and ride to Texas for another herd? We'll be returning to southern Colorado in the fall."

"They'd hang me in Texas on general principles," said Allison.

He rode away on his big black, resplendent in his solid black suit, ruffled white shirt, and flowing black tie. Before he rode out of sight, he turned and waved his big gray Stetson.

"There goes a *man*," said Brazos. "A *bueno hombre* with the bark on."

"He's considerably more than just another gun-thrower," said Will. "I doubt he'll cash in during some saloon shootout."

McCaleb said nothing. From the look in Rebecca's eyes, he counted himself lucky that Clay Allison had returned to Colorado. They rode south for what might be the last time, their saddlebags heavy with gold.

* * *

March 9, 1867, they reached their old camp south of Fort Sumner, finding that Goodnight and Loving had departed for Fort Belknap. Goodnight had taken their horse remuda and extra mules.

"With them taking the chuck wagon and extra stock," said Will, "we'll catch them before they reach the Llano."

On March 12 they caught up with Goodnight and Loving at Horsehead Crossing. While Goodnight seemed happy to see them, Loving showed little interest. On April 1 they reached Elm Creek range, south of Fort Belknap. There they split up. Goodnight moved fifteen miles south to set up his camp. Loving returned to Palo Pinto County. McCaleb took his outfit forty miles east, toward the headwaters of the Trinity. The three outfits were to meet at the Elm Creek tributary of the Clear Fork of the Brazos in two months: June 1, 1867.

"This time," said McCaleb, "we'll shoot for two thousand head. Since we plan to drive all the way to Colorado, let's make it something to remember."

"Last time," said Rebecca dryly, "you said we only had enough riders to handle a thousand head."

"This time," said McCaleb just as dryly, "our riders are experienced and we know the trail; at least as far as Fort Sumner. Most trail bosses allow one rider for every four hundred cows."

"Let's buy two thousand and five, then," said Will. "With two thousand even, each of us will be responsible for three hundred thirty-three and one-sixth cows. It's hell trackin' one sixth of a cow after a stampede."

"We're not *having* any stampedes on this next drive," said Rebecca. "I have been involved in enough stampedes to last me a lifetime. Like McCaleb said, we're experienced riders."

They found more and more Texas cattlemen planning their own drives, but for those who could pay, big steers were still available at seven dollars a head. They bought and branded two 2015 steers, and by mid-May were camped on the Brazos, twenty-five miles south of old Fort Belknap.

"I hate to leave Charlie," said Will, "but I'll purely be glad when we get to Fort Sumner and leave Mr. Loving behind. This same time last year we was sittin' on our hunkers, waitin' on him."

"We're waitin' for Goodnight too," said McCaleb. "I'm hoping he'll get here ahead of Loving or that Loving will arrive ahead of him. Some of us need to ride to Weatherford for more supplies, and I don't dare leave the herd short-handed. When one or the other of them show up, there'll be enough riders to discourage any Comanche mischief."

As McCaleb had expected, Goodnight arrived early; a week ahead of their planned departure. He would drive the chuck wagon to Weatherford for his own supplies, and a pair of McCaleb's riders could accompany him. He brought with him twenty-five hundred head of trail-branded steers.

McCaleb sent Will and Brazos to the trading post with Goodnight and the trip was uneventful. Oliver Loving rode into camp on May 31, trailing a herd of twenty-five hundred. Combining the three outfits, they had twenty-six riders and 7025 steers. Charlie Wilson eyed the sea of bawling, milling cattle skeptically.

"Mix this many critters together an' toss in a few stampedes, and we'll be till Christmas roundin' 'em up."

They moved out on June 1, 1867, on schedule. Two days west of Elm Creek range, Indians attacked during the night, stampeding most of the herd. With recent rain, tracks were plentiful. McCaleb's outfit joined Goodnight's at dawn, ready to ride. Goodnight had some instructions for Oliver Loving.

"Mr. Loving, these Comanches are likely headed for the chaparral along the Clear Fork bottom. I won't be surprised if they hit us again tonight. Drive the rest of the herd into the valley west of here. At least there's some hope of defense."

They avoided a confrontation with the Comanches, seeking only to recover their cattle. They spent the day chasing the animals out of the brush, and darkness overtook them.

"We'll have to take a loss on the rest," said Goodnight, "or spend more time beatin' the brush."

"Let's beat the brush some more, then," said McCaleb. "We can't afford a loss like this, two days on the trail."

It was dark when they reined up on the hill above the valley where Loving had bedded down the rest of the herd. They stared, incredulous, and Goodnight swore. Near the end of the valley, Oliver Loving's campfire blazed brightly, snapping sparks into the starlit sky. Impulsive and quick to anger, Charlie Wilson nudged his mount alongside Goodnight's. Bitterly, he said what the rest of them were thinking.

"If there's a Comanche within fifty mile that didn't know we was here, he does now. How'n hell has *that* pilgrim rode so many trails an' managed to keep his hair?"

"Mr. Loving is a religious man," said Goodnight. "He knows no fear."

"He will when the Comanches get done with him," said Brazos. "If he's got no worry for his *own* hide, he could show some for *ours*."

Goodnight kicked his big black into a lope, leaving them to move the recovered cattle into the valley with the rest of the herd. They had no idea what Goodnight might have said to Loving, but within minutes the fire was out.

Shortly before dawn, despite their precautions, the Comanche struck again. Their only warning was a frightened nicker from the horse remuda.

"Roll out," shouted McCaleb. "They're after the horses!"

There was a mix of arrows and gunfire from the attackers, and while the outfits rode frantically to head off the threatened remuda, a second party of Comanches stampeded the newly assembled herd. Nobody had been hit, but they were an impatient and angry lot as they gathered to wait for first light. There were still cattle missing from the stampede the night before. Now the herd was off and running again, taking the horse remuda with it. Will Elliot echoed the sentiments of them all.

"I just hope Mr. Loving don't get *too* impatient with the delay."

Mr. Loving didn't. Nor did he ever build another fire after dark. After two days of hard riding, they were still missing two hundred head and five horses. In the afternoon of the second wasted day, McCaleb sent Goose to scout the Clear Fork bottom. The Apache's report was not good.

"*Mucho Comanch'*," said Goose, shaking his head. "*Malo medicina.*"

The risk was too great. With all his hatred for the Comanches, Goose was no fool. Neither was Charles Goodnight.

"Goose is right," said Goodnight. "Too many Comanches is *always* bad medicine. Our scalps are worth two hundred steers and five horses. We'll graze 'em till dark and then move out."

During the night a storm struck and the already skittish herd stampeded again. Nobody slept. Night after night the herd ran, the worst stampede of all taking place after they'd passed through Buffalo Gap. In predawn darkness the herd overran the camp. Only by flapping the blankets under which they'd been sleeping just seconds before were the riders able to turn the herd and avoid being trampled.

"Damn it," growled Bill Wilson, "I never seen such a spooky herd. We've spent ever' blasted day huntin' the critters that's run off durin' the night. Much more of this, an' I'll find me a little town somewhere and start me a saloon."

"Starting today," said Goodnight, "we'll drive them at least twenty miles a day. Normally I wouldn't; thins 'em down. But not as much as a stampede. From here on when we bed 'em down, they'll be too tired to run."

"We *must* make better time," said Oliver Loving irritably. "I intend to be in Santa Fe on August first for the letting of those beef contracts."

"*You* may be there on August first," said McCaleb, "but this herd won't be at Fort Sumner. This is a spooked bunch, and we'll spend more time rounding them up than driving them."

It wasn't what Loving wanted to hear, but the prediction proved very, very accurate. Despite the long days and exhausting drives, the herd continued to stampede night after night. They didn't reach Horsehead Crossing until mid-July. No sooner had they crossed the Pecos than a storm again sent the herd on the run. At dawn Goodnight took Bill and Charlie Wilson, Red Alford, and Wes Sheek in pursuit of the missing cattle. Twenty-five miles later they found their cattle in the possession of a band of Comanches. A *large* band. They barely escaped with their lives, losing the redskins in the high, thick mesquite.

When they left Horsehead Crossing, their unbelievable run of bad luck changed. Whatever demons had possessed the herd seemed to have quietly departed. But for Oliver Loving, time had run out.

"I'm riding on to Santa Fe," said Loving. "I intend to reach Fort Union in time for the letting of those beef contracts."

"No beef contract's worth the risk of being murdered by the Comanches," said Goodnight. "I say don't chance it."

"I am going," said Loving. "If God intends for me to die at the hands of Indians, then I will. Otherwise, I won't. I have faith."

"In Indian country," said McCaleb, "you also need common sense."

"You're entitled to your beliefs and I to mine," said

Loving. "I'm perfectly capable of making my own decisions, so I am not asking permission. I am simply informing the rest of you as to my intentions."

"If you insist," said Goodnight, "let me offer some suggestions. I'll send Bill Wilson with you. Don't, under *any* circumstances, travel in the daytime. Travel only at night, and when you hide out during the day, do so with an eye for defense."

"Very well," said Loving.

McCaleb had the feeling that Loving would soon forget Goodnight's words of caution. Nor did he have that much confidence in One-Armed Bill Wilson. While Wilson wasn't likely influenced by Loving's religion and consummate faith, he was brash and reckless in his own right. They rode out at dawn, the start of the last week in July.

"Mr. Loving purely hates riding at night," said Goodnight.

"He'll hate bein' scalped by the Comanches a hell of a lot worse," said Charlie Wilson. "I just hope Bill's got sense enough to hold him to your advice."

But Loving detested riding at night, and when he chose to abandon it, he got no argument from Bill Wilson. Just north of Pope's Crossing, in the afternoon of their first day of daylight travel, they were sighted by a large band of Comanches. Desperately they rode for the Pecos, taking refuge on a sandbar among weeds and scrub oak.

Just below the Texas–New Mexico line, Goodnight halted the herd for a two-day rest. There was plenty of water, good graze, and everybody needed a chance to wash clothes and blankets.

"I suppose there's no hurry now," said Goodnight, "with Mr. Loving on his way to Fort Union."

Oliver Loving lay in the cool darkness, weak from loss of blood and feverish from his wounds. Shortly after being trapped by the Comanches in a sandy bend of the Pecos, Loving had been shot in the wrist and in the side.

"Bill," Loving whispered weakly. "Bill."

Bill Wilson eased over next to the wounded man. The Comanches were out there, content to wait.

"Bill," said Loving, "I'm a goner. I want my family in Texas to know—want Charlie to know—what happened. Leave me here. Ease into the water and drift downriver . . . until you're free. Charlie—and the herd —can't be more than forty miles south. . . ."

Bill Wilson stripped off everything except his drawers, undershirt, and hat. He left all the weapons with Loving except for Loving's Henry rifle; its metallic cartridges wouldn't be harmed by the water of the Pecos. When the moon set, he crept into the water and allowed the current to carry him downstream. He believed he could last the day and a half it would take him to reach the herd. It was just as well that neither he or Loving knew of Goodnight's two-day rest; that help, instead of being just forty miles away, was closer to a hundred.

"Hombre," said Goose, pointing.

McCaleb and Goodnight shaded their eyes, barely able to discern the apparition partially obscured by shimmering heat waves and distance.

"My God," exclaimed Goodnight, *"that's* Bill Wilson! What's left of him! He's alone. I was afraid of this!"

He kicked his big black into a gallop, followed by McCaleb and Goose. Wilson's drawers and undershirt— and even his skin—was red with sediment of the Pecos. He staggered and fell before they reached him. Unable to speak, he lay in the sand, extending his hand like a drowning man begging rescue. His eyes were bloodshot, touched with madness, his feet swollen and bloody. The few words he spoke were unintelligible. They lifted him onto Goodnight's horse and took him to the chuck wagon. He could swallow only a little food and water, and it was an hour before he was able to tell them his story. Goodnight rode out at sundown, taking five men with him.

From Wilson's description, Goodnight found the scene of the attack, but no sign of Oliver Loving. But the wounded man, fearful that Bill Wilson had been captured or killed, had slipped into the red waters of the Pecos under the cover of darkness. Found on the bank of the river by a trio of Mexicans, he offered them $250 to take him the 150 miles to Fort Sumner.

McCaleb continued north with the herd. The recuperating Bill Wilson still rode in the chuck wagon. Goodnight, not knowing what else to do, had rejoined the herd at Comanche Springs. So it was Goodnight, scouting ahead, who encountered the rider from Fort Sumner.

"Oliver Loving's at Fort Sumner," he said, "and he's hurt; wants to see you just as quick as you c'n git there."

Taking a saddle mule for endurance, Goodnight rode to Fort Sumner, only stopping to water and rest the mule. He found Loving up and about, but with his wounded arm unhealed. The post doctor had been called to Santa Fe, but Loving refused to allow a young doctor, newly arrived from the East, to amputate the limb. Goodnight sent a rider to Las Vegas for another doctor, but two days before the doctor arrived, a crisis arose. Loving's arm *had* to be amputated to save his life. The young post doctor performed the operation, but it was too late. The tied-off artery broke and Loving went into shock. His condition worsened. . . .

The herd reached Fort Sumner and Goodnight rode out to meet it. Fully recovered, Bill Wilson rode point. Goodnight rode back to drag, and McCaleb's outfit jogged their horses to meet him.

"I'll be going on to Colorado," said Goodnight. "There'll be no more beef contracts. I'll join you on the trail, as soon as I've fulfilled my promise to Mr. Loving."

Oliver Loving lived for twenty-two days, rational to the end. He died on September 25, 1867. . . .

September 26, the day after Oliver Loving was buried at Fort Sumner, Charles Goodnight set out to join the herd. Five days later, at sundown, he rode into camp. They were a hundred miles north of the Canadian River, in northeastern New Mexico. Goodnight called his own outfit, McCaleb's outfit, and Loving's riders together.

"We're pushing on to Colorado," he said, "and those of you who rode for Mr. Loving will be paid just as though he were alive and with us. I aim to start a ranch in southern Colorado and I'll need some of you to ride for me there. You'll see to my affairs while I am away. When the worst of winter's behind us—the snow—I'm riding back to Texas, and I'll want some of you with me. We'll build another herd and drive it north in the spring. We'll be stopping at Fort Sumner long enough to exhume Mr. Loving's body. I have promised to take him back to Texas and see that he's buried in the churchyard with his kin."

It was a somber group that gathered around the supper fire. The first of October was upon them and a chill wind came off the Rockies, carrying the bite of winter. Tomorrow the drive would swing to the northwest and Raton Pass, the gateway between New Mexico and Colorado.

"My God," said Rebecca, "that's spooky. Digging up a dead body and hauling it a thousand miles."

"That's Charles Goodnight," said McCaleb. "He'd do the same for any one of us, even if it was ten thousand miles. He's a man who keeps his promises, whatever it costs him."

"It's going feel almighty strange," said Will, "when he pulls out for Texas, leavin' us in Colorado. We've trailed with him so long, it'll seem like we ought to be ridin' with him."

Brazos chuckled. "Charlie has that effect on people. That's why I'd never be pardners with him. He's such a force, I'd find myself lookin' to him for permission before I'd fork my horse. I'd be just another cowboy, trapped in his shadow and never seein' the sun."

"I knew Will was a philosopher disguised as a cowboy," said McCaleb, "but I'm surprised at *you*. That sounded like something Will might have said. Have you coyotes been readin' the same books?"

"He's pretty well roped and branded my concept of Charlie," said Will. "He's too much his own man to follow anybody's lead. Even with Mr. Loving alive and pursuing them, I doubt those New Mexican beef contracts would've held Charlie's interest for long. He's hankering for Colorado range."

"We know what Goodnight's going to do," said Rebecca, "but what are *we* going to do? Will we start a ranch in Colorado?"

"Why don't we wait until we get there," said McCaleb. "These steers are trail-thin. We'll loose them on some good range, fatten them until spring, and then decide what to do with them."

"I want to go on to Denver," said Monte. "I'd like to ride the train to St. Louis and take a steamboat south to New Orleans. Goose can go with me. We'll be a pair of *malo hombres;* riverboat gamblers."

"Over *my* dead body!" shouted Rebecca.

Monte swatted his hat against the ground and laughed delightedly.

Still ahead of the snow, they drove the herd through the high mesa country, pointed it up the Raton Range, and crossed over the divide into Colorado. There they came upon "Uncle Dick" Wootton's toll station. It was a brazen but legal toll road established by Wootton in 1866. He had applied for and received charters a year earlier from the legislatures of New Mexico and Colorado to build a toll road through the pass of the range dividing the territories. It was virtually the only pass used by mountain travelers from north to south. Wootton demanded and received a toll of ten cents per animal for passage and use of the twenty-seven mile road.

"I see that *all* the thieves in these parts aren't Comancheros and Indians," growled Goodnight. "This is thievery pure and simple, Wootton. We won't pay to use this pass."

Wootton chuckled. "You got no choice. There ain't no *other* pass, an' I got this 'un sewed up legal and proper. Now pay an' move on!"

They paid, Goodnight vowing it would be the first and last time. Amid Wootton's laughter, Goodnight swore he would find another pass and blaze another trail. They moved on toward Trinidad.

McCaleb reined up, struck with the beauty and majesty of Colorado. From Raton Pass he could see far to the north. To the east the mountains leveled down to a vast plateau that stretched, mile upon mile, in virgin grasslands to the faraway valley of the Arkansas. To the west, the Rockies marched majestically northward with Spanish Peaks, the Greenhorns, Pike's Peak, and a procession of others. There were streams breaking from the north side of the Raton Range, flowing north and northwest, eating their way through the plateau to the Arkansas. It was one of these river canyons that Goodnight chose for the first cattle ranch in southern Colorado.

Apishapa Canyon was more than twenty miles long, a stream running the length of it, lined with box elders. While the canyon wasn't very deep, it was virtually inaccessible except at the ends. The graze appeared fresh and untouched.

"This is grand, Charlie," said McCaleb. "For you. But I reckon we'd better cut out our stuff and move north a ways. No point in our steers bein' loosed on your graze when there's so much more, just for the taking."

"I'd take it as a favor if you'd stick around until spring," said Goodnight. "Right after the first of the year, weather permitting, I aim to start back to Texas. I'll leave as many men here as I can, but this is new country, and I'd like to have you here as long as you'll stay. I'm going to throw up a cabin and some outbuildings, and the more hands we have, the sooner we can have shelter."

"We'll stick around until April first, then," said McCaleb. "My outfit has an urge to see Denver, and I'm wondering if cattle prices there might not be the best yet."

"Since you'll have the winter ahead of you," said Goodnight, "and your herd will be safe here, I want to pass on some information to you that I got from Mr. Loving before he passed on. Almost due north of here, maybe a hundred and fifty miles, is the biggest, wealthiest ranch in Colorado. It's owned, as far as anybody knows, by a Britisher named Jonathan Wickliffe. His brand is the Crown W, and Mr. Loving said he's rich enough to buy every cow in Texas. His spread begins at the western border of Kansas, following the Republican River more than a hundred miles into eastern Colorado. Why don't you ride up there before the weather gets too bad and talk to him?"

"I just might do that," said McCaleb.

The first week in December, the weather was fair but cold. Goodnight approached McCaleb with a suggestion.

"We're pretty well dug in here, and the weather seems to be holding. Why don't you ride to the Crown W and palaver with Wickliffe? I'm afraid it's going to be a long, dull winter. You can take your outfit with you."

"That won't be fair to your riders," said McCaleb.

Goodnight chuckled. "That's what you think. We're taking advantage of you. Christmas is coming up and I aim to throw a big feed for everybody. Most of my boys are needin' things like tobacco, some sweets, and something to read. I want you to take half a dozen mules with you and come back through Denver. I'll provide you with a list of what we need, and the gold."

"You got a deal," said McCaleb.

McCaleb got no argument from the outfit. After the dangers and hardships of the trail, the tranquility of the canyon—with shelter, regular meals, and enough sleep —was heaven on earth. And profoundly boring.

"Let's go to Denver *first*," said Monte. "Me and Goose can stay there and mosey around while the rest of you ride to Wickliffe's place."

"I'm having second thoughts about all of us leaving here at the same time," said McCaleb. "Maybe I ought to leave a pair of *malo hombres* behind; you and Goose, for instance."

"I reckon you're right," said Monte. "We'd best go to Wickliffe's first and come back through Denver."

They rode out, each of them leading a pack mule. In addition to Goodnight's list, they had a list of individual needs from the riders. There were requests for everything from chewing or smoking tobacco to long-handled underwear. Facing winter in the secluded canyon, the riders hungered for something to read, even a mail order catalog.

McCaleb estimated they were still a day's ride south of the Wickliffe spread when they began seeing Crown W cattle. It was an unusual brand, the points of the W shaping the upper portion of the "Crown." When they reached the Republican, found a shallow place and forded it, three riders trotted their horses out of an elder thicket. The lead rider wasn't range-dressed. He wore solid black trousers, a sheepskin-lined coat, and polished black cowman's boots. A wide-brimmed, high-crowned black hat was tilted over his eyes. He was astride a big gray horse, and his saddle had silver trappings. He reined up, sweeping back his coat with a flourish, revealing a Colt on each hip. His companions wore Levi's, run-over boots, and older, worn sheepskin jackets which remained buttoned. Their weapons, if they had any, were concealed.

"You're on Crown W range," said the buscadera-belted rider. "Why?"

"We're here to see Wickliffe," said McCaleb.

"You don't see *Mister* Wickliffe unless you first satisfy *me* as to your reason. Who are you and what do you want?"

McCaleb strove to hold his temper.

"We have two thousand head of Texas cows. I'm Benton McCaleb and this is my outfit. Now who are *you*?"

"Dobie Hobbs, the segundo for the Crown W. Keep ridin' the way you're goin'; we get to the house, I'll see if Mr. Wickliffe will talk to you."

It was a hostile move. Hobbs and his companions intended to bring up the rear. Goose might not have understood the words, but he picked up the arrogance and hostility of the voice. He remained where he was, his eyes on Hobbs. The foreman rode closer.

"I said *ride* on!"

Brazos lifted his hand, and without a word, Goose kicked his horse into a lope.

The ranch house was impressive. It was log; long, low, rambling. The windows were real glass. Half a mile west was a similar building that might have been a bunkhouse. There were two barns, each with a six-rail-high corral fence. Hobbs ignored western custom and didn't invite them to dismount. He and his companions swung out of their saddles and Hobbs walked to the house alone. The other two riders stood beside their horses rolling quirlys. McCaleb and his outfit might not have existed. They watched as Hobbs pounded on the door and apparently received permission to enter. When he returned, he was accompanied by a slender man who didn't wear western clothes. McCaleb had little knowledge of or appreciation for eastern attire, but he knew wealth when he saw it. Wickliffe's suit was expensive brown tweed and his ruffle-fronted white shirt sported diamond links at the cuffs. While he wore no tie, there was a yellow scarf about his throat that looked like pure silk. His hair was light sorrel with prominent streaks of gray at the temples. Although neatly cut, it extended to his collar and swept down over his ears. His thin face was clean-shaven and he had deep-set brown eyes. There was a diamond ring on his left hand, and his perfectly manicured nails were the longest McCaleb had ever seen on a man. Wickliffe wore no gun. It was highly unusual for the time and place.

"Step down," said Wickliffe, "and come in."

Enormous logs hewn flat on one side created steps that led to the long front porch on which Wickliffe stood. Hitching rails on each side of the wide steps extended all the way to the end of the porch. McCaleb swung out of his saddle, the others following. They half-hitched the reins of their horses and the lead ropes of the pack mules to the rail and turned to the steps. Dobie Hobbs stood behind Wickliffe, his hard blue eyes hostile. McCaleb mounted the steps, ignored Hobbs and extended his hand to Wickliffe.

"I'm Benton McCaleb and this is my outfit. We have two thousand head of Texas steers at the Charles Goodnight ranch, in Apishapa Canyon, in the valley of the Arkansas. Would you be interested in all or part of them?"

"Perhaps," said Wickliffe. He spoke to McCaleb, but his eyes were on Rebecca.

McCaleb found himself standing alone. The decidedly cool reception had kept the rest of the outfit in the yard. Wickliffe didn't seem to take any real interest in anything that had been said. Dobie Hobbs stepped forward, confronting McCaleb. As hostile and arrogant as ever, he spoke.

"The rest of you can come in, but the Indian stays in the yard, so's we can keep an eye on him."

"He's part of my outfit," said McCaleb coldly, "and if he's not welcome, than neither am I."

Hobbs took another step and his jaw collided with McCaleb's right. It set the foreman back on his heels, slamming him against the wall. He hung there, glassy-eyed.

"Dobie," snapped Wickliffe, "you may go. Return to your duties at once." He then turned to McCaleb, a bit more friendliness in his eyes. "Dobie's prejudices aren't my own, Mr. McCaleb. You and your outfit may come in; each of you are welcome, including the Indian."

He swung the massive front door open and McCaleb beckoned to the others. But Goose remained with his horse, his eyes on the departing Dobie Hobbs. They followed Wickliffe down the long hall to a living room with a fireplace of such proportions it occupied most of one wall. A fire blazed cheerfully. Lamps hung from a beamed ceiling, Navajo rugs covered the wooden floor, and paintings adorned the walls. The furniture, some of it antique, had been brought from the East. But at the far end of the long room stood the most striking object of all. It was a grand piano, its polished surface glowing in the flickering firelight. Rebecca approached it reverently. So fascinated was she that Wickliffe spoke from directly behind her before she was aware of his presence.

"Do you play?"

"N-No," she stammered. "I was admiring it. It's so . . . beautiful."

"So are you," he murmured, so that the others couldn't hear.

"Do you . . . do *you* play?" she asked, moving away.

"No," he said. "My wife did. Once."

The others, amazed at the interplay between the two, said nothing. The tension was broken when an Indian woman brought in a silver tea service, placing it on a low table situated near the fireplace.

"Please be seated," said Wickliffe. "I could offer you tea, but most cattlemen prefer coffee. So do I."

McCaleb introduced the rest of the outfit. He didn't like the way Wickliffe's eyes lighted when Rebecca's name was mentioned. He was further disturbed by the fact the girl hadn't taken her eyes off the rancher since he had spoken to her.

"We're aimin' to drive the herd to Denver in the

spring," said McCaleb. "That might be a good time for you to take a look at them and make us your best offer."

"I am an impulsive man, Mr. McCaleb. I don't believe in putting things off. After Christmas, perhaps I shall visit your camp in the valley of the Arkansas. I have heard much of your friend Charles Goodnight and I would welcome the chance to meet him. For the time being, you are welcome to enjoy the hospitality of my ranch. I have more than enough room for you to stay the night. The Indian is welcome as well."

"The Indian," said Brazos, speaking for the first time, "is just a mite particular about the company he keeps."

Brazos's voice fairly dripped sarcasm, but it was a point well-taken, and McCaleb said nothing. It was a deliberate insult to Wickliffe, and Rebecca's eyes were ablaze with anger. Wickliffe said nothing, enjoying the girl's reaction.

Jonathan Wickliffe was an enigma. McCaleb sensed the man wore two faces and that somewhere beyond this pleasant exterior there lurked a devious, cruel counterpart. McCaleb had no desire to stay the night, but no logical reason not to. It seemed Wickliffe had unlimited help; all Indian, all Ute. The man was resourceful as well as diplomatic. He sent an Indian hostler to stall, rub down and feed their animals. The Ute, apparently upon instructions from Wickliffe, established communication with Goose and lured him into the house. But it was a limited compromise. Goose refused to enter the huge dining room with its chandelier of half a dozen shaded brass lamps, a polished oak dining table that would have seated twenty, real cloth napkins, and genuine silver. The Ute woman who brought the food to the dining room served Goose his supper in the kitchen. McCaleb never learned where the Apache spent the night.

Wickliffe did most of the talking, pausing occasionally to partake of some food or to sip his coffee. His conversation consisted almost entirely of inconsequential things of no possible interest to any of them except possibly Rebecca. To McCaleb's disgust, she hung onto every word.

"You gentlemen must excuse me," said Wickliffe, smiling. "It is seldom I have so charming a guest; I have been neglecting the rest of you. Please, you must have questions or comments."

"I have," said Will, looking him square in the eye. "Is it just *our* Indian your segundo hates, or is it *all* Indians? You don't strike me as a man to take chances."

Rebecca glared at Will and he ignored her. Wickliffe was silent for a moment and then he laughed.

"You are a perceptive man, Mr. Elliot, and very blunt. I presume your question is prompted by my employing Ute help. I have found them faithful and dependable. In all honesty, I'd have to say that Dobie Hobbs has nothing against your Indian rider. I suspect he's taken a dislike to some or all of you and his remark was intended to antagonize you."

"We don't take well to bein' antagonized," said McCaleb, "when we're here to talk business. You used considerably better judgment in choosing your house help than you did when you hired your segundo."

Wickliffe's cordiality vanished and his eyes frosted. When he spoke, his voice was flat, cold.

"I do not employ Dobie Hobbs for his charm or his tactfulness, McCaleb. Were he weighed in the balance, I am sure he would be found wanting on both counts. There have been some indiscretions on his part, but he serves me well. I find the frontier exciting, but barbaric and uncivilized. So I use Dobie as a buffer. He has none of my reservations against sinking into the mire and violence of this land. Now I have bared as much of my soul as I intend to. Come. I'll show you to your rooms."

Having beheld the opulence of the living and dining rooms, McCaleb found the bedrooms unsurprising. He pulled off his boots and stretched out fully clothed. He blew out the lamp and lay in darkness. Rebecca's room was next to his and he didn't have long to wait. He heard the door close softly. He rolled to the edge of the bed, got to his feet and crept to the door. He listened, and hearing nothing, eased the door open. The house, but for the flickering firelight in the living room, was dark. He closed the door quietly and set off down the long hall toward the enormous living room. It occupied one shoulder of a T, the dining room and kitchen the other. He reached the end of the hall and found the living room in shadows. The fire had burned low; the long sofa had its back to him and he could see nothing. But he could hear. There was the pleasant drone of Wickliffe's voice, but he couldn't understand the words. Then Rebecca laughed. It was a mischievous giggle. Pursuing his advantage, Wickliffe continued, and the girl laughed again. McCaleb fisted his hands so hard the nails dug into his palms. His head pounded, bile rose in his throat, and he longed to beat Jonathan Wickliffe within an inch of his life. Common sense came to his rescue. Rebecca Nance was a grown woman. Trembling, he forced himself to swallow his anger and quietly made his way back to his darkened room. He didn't sleep until he heard Rebecca's door open and close.

McCaleb was up before daylight and found the house ablaze with light. The dining table was being set for breakfast. He didn't like the excitement in Rebecca's eyes, and he liked what she had to say even less.

"Jon's going to Denver with us. He's asked me to ride in his buckboard."

"You have a horse to ride and a mule to lead," said McCaleb.

"Dobie Hobbs is going with us," said Wickliffe with a self-satisfied smile. "He can lead both animals."

Breakfast was a silent meal. Once McCaleb caught Monte's eye and the kid tried to grin, but it didn't come off. That old premonition that warned McCaleb of impending disaster began to stir.

CHAPTER 21

They departed Wickliffe's ranch before daylight, and it was after dark before they saw the lights of Denver. They had paused only to rest and water the horses. It was hard on horse and rider, a far lengthier journey than should have been attempted in a day, but they pushed on. McCaleb was anxious for the ordeal to end. Wickliffe's buckboard often fell behind, but Dobie Hobbs—leading Rebecca's horse and one of the mules—kept pace with it. Once the lights of town were in view, McCaleb reined up, waiting for Wickliffe's buckboard to catch up. But Wickliffe sensed what was coming and spoke first.

"The Tremont House is Denver's finest hotel. The ranch has reservations there and I have offered Rebecca the use of one of the rooms. There is an adequate hostelry—the Vasquez House—at Eleventh and Ferry."

With that, he flicked the reins, urging the horses into a trot. There was little McCaleb and the others could do except follow. They came first to the Tremont House, at Sixteenth and Wazee streets. It was elegant, probably the most expensive hotel in town, but McCaleb resented Wickliffe's implication it was more than they could afford. To the rear, across an alley, the hotel had its own livery, and they rode in behind Wickliffe's buckboard. He handed his reins to a stableman, swung off the seat, and helped Rebecca down. The girl seemed self-conscious, averting her eyes as they rode past. Goose, having accepted the hotel in Santa Fe, didn't balk at this one. By the time they reached the desk, Wickliffe and Rebecca had already started down the hall. The clerk, well-dressed in suit and tie, studied them. He fixed his gaze on Goose, and the Indian stared back, unblinking.

"Three rooms for the night," said McCaleb.

"Thirty dollars," said the man, still glaring at Goose.

Seldom was payment demanded in advance unless one's ability to pay was questionable. McCaleb ignored the insult and produced the outrageous sum of money.

"Third floor," said the clerk, dropping three keys on the counter.

"You put that dude in the Yankee suit on the *first* floor," growled Monte. "Ain't we as good as he is?"

"Mr. Wickliffe has standing reservations." The man sniffed. "I can guarantee you the first floor only if you make similar arrangements with the hotel. Otherwise, you take what's available."

McCaleb took a room for himself, assigned the second to Monte and Goose, and the third to Will and Brazos. They hadn't eaten since breakfast and the hotel dining room was closed. Two blocks down the street they found a café.

"Thank God," sighed Brazos. "I'm near dead; nothin' short of steak, onions, fried potatoes, pie, and coffee will save me."

While McCaleb's belly was lank, his mind wasn't on food. He wanted only to have this day—and this night—done with. He longed to make their purchases, to extricate Rebecca from Wickliffe's grasp, and to return to the solitude of Apishapa Canyon. They found a confectioner's shop that sold ice cream. Brazos, Will, and Monte insisted that Goose have some. Despite his anxiety, McCaleb chuckled at the Indian's first experience with the frozen treat. When they returned to the hotel, McCaleb stopped at the front desk.

"I need the room number of the lady who arrived with Jonathan Wickliffe."

The clerk lifted his eyebrows as though this were the most outrageous request he'd ever heard in his life. Finally, with all the indignation he could muster, he spoke.

"Sorry. I am not permitted to divulge that information."

"I wouldn't want you to break any rules," said McCaleb. "She's on this floor somewhere; I'll just knock on doors until I get to hers."

"I can't permit that," said the man stiffly. "If you disturb our other guests, I shall be forced to call the sheriff."

"Friend," said McCaleb coldly, "maybe there's something you *can* do. I have business with Wickliffe; which room is *he* in?"

"Eleven. Now if there's trouble—"

"There won't be," said McCaleb. "At least not in here."

McCaleb turned to the rest of his outfit.

"Best get what sleep you can; we'll be leaving early. I need to find Rebecca and tell her."

"I need to talk to you, McCaleb," said Monte, "after you talk to her."

McCaleb rapped on the door. Wickliffe took his time answering it. McCaleb was blunt and to the point.

"Which is Rebecca's room? I need to talk to her."

"Let it wait until morning; it's late and I'm sure she's exhausted."

"No," said McCaleb. "Tonight."

That was as far as he got. McCaleb saw the desk clerk coming swiftly down the hall. Suddenly the door of the room next to Wickliffe's opened and Rebecca emerged.

"Please, McCaleb," she begged, "don't start any trouble."

"I have no intention of starting trouble," said McCaleb. "We're leaving early in the morning; if you're riding with us, be ready."

"I'll be ready. Jon wants—"

"I don't give a damn *what* Jon wants," gritted McCaleb. "We leave tomorrow. Be ready."

Without another word, he turned and walked down the hall past the angry desk clerk. He mounted the stairs and went to the room shared by Monte and Goose. He knocked once, turned the knob and entered. Monte was stretched out on the bed, minus only his boots and hat. Goose lay on the floor by the open window, without even a blanket or pillow.

"She'll be ready to pull out in the morning," said McCaleb.

"That's not all that's botherin' me," said Monte. "This bastard's slick as calf slobber, McCaleb."

"Except for gettin' her out of town, out of this lobo's clutches," said McCaleb, "what can we do?"

"Tell the skunk we ain't interested in sellin' him the herd," said Monte. "Then he won't have any cause to come ridin' into camp after Christmas, like he's promised to do."

"Kid, I wish it was easy as that. I made the mistake of telling him Goodnight's started a ranch there. That gives him all the excuse he needs to ride down and get acquainted with Charlie."

"When we get back, let's round up the herd and head 'em out."

"Head 'em where? Back to Texas? There's no place to go except north or west, and there's been no real snow yet. First norther that blows in, you'd be in snow over your head, with you sittin' your saddle. It'll be the end of March before we can go without fear of bein' trapped in a blizzard."

"Then what are you going to do . . . when he shows up?"

"I don't know," said McCaleb. "It depends on Rebecca."

They were up by daylight. Rebecca was waiting in the lobby, seated in a red plush chair near the door. There was no sign of Wickliffe. Without a word, she followed them to the hotel livery. Wickliffe's buckboard team was being led out. Dobie Hobbs stood beside his saddled horse, a half smile on his cruel lips. He tossed his cigarette butt at McCaleb's feet. McCaleb stopped, meeting Hobbs's gaze with one just as cold.

"I ain't forgot, bucko. Nobody pushes Dobie Hobbs around. *Nobody!*"

"Then I won't turn my back," said McCaleb, "until you ride on."

Hobbs said no more. Wickliffe crossed the alley and, without so much as a glance at any of them, climbed to the seat of his buckboard. Only then did he speak, and then only to Rebecca.

"I'll see you after Christmas, Rebecca."

He clucked to the horses, sending them cantering down the alley toward the street. Without a backward glance, Dobie Hobbs kicked his mount into a lope and followed.

Once their horses were saddled, they rode out, the pack mules trailing on lead ropes. They reined up at the café where they had eaten the night before. It was as though a pall had fallen over them. Not until they left the café was there a light moment when Rebecca smiled. Goose positioned himself before the confectioner's shop, refusing to leave until he'd had more ice cream. From there they went to Denver Mercantile, the largest general store in town. The pack mules loaded, they headed south, pausing only to rest and water the mules and horses. They rode until well after dark, and immediately after supper rolled into their blankets.

They moved out at dawn. The pack mules slowed them down. They were still a day's ride from Apishapa Canyon when the weather began to change. The Rockies disappeared behind a rolling mass of gray clouds. Within an hour the snow was upon them, riding a rising wind out of the northwest, whitening the ground in minutes. Securing their hats with rawhide thongs, they bowed their heads and rode on. Gray-black snow clouds had seemingly dropped to treetop level, and though it wasn't quite two o'clock, they rode through deepening twilight. McCaleb rode alongside Goose, having to shout to make himself heard above the wind.

"Abrigo, Goose. Cuerda, mula de carga."

Silently, Goose passed him the mule's lead rope and kicked his horse into a trot. He was soon lost in the swirling snow. Facing impending darkness, at the mercy of a worsening storm, they must immediately seek shelter. Goose well understood the urgency of his task; in unfamiliar country one could ill afford to pass up *any* sanctuary. He might ride for miles without finding another, until he was trapped in an eerie world of darkness and freezing wind-driven snow.

Time dragged and still Goose didn't return. The distance he had to ride, unencumbered with a pack mule, would take them twice as long. Lost in somber thought, McCaleb almost didn't hear the shot. It told him that Goose had found shelter, but it wasn't along the southeasterly trail they rode. Then, cutting into the foot of the ridge they'd just descended, McCaleb saw the beginning of a coulee. It ran due south, only a few inches deep at the upper end. Without the warning shot from Goose, they might easily have missed it. It grew wider and deeper as they rode, shutting out the howling wind until the day seemed calm. Brightening the gloom ahead of them was a high-blazing fire. Goose had set fire to a resinous log and was busily adding dry wood from a windfall that had toppled down the slope and into the coulee. Trees on the ridge above them, aided by the ridge itself, had lessened the force of the storm until only a little snow found its way into their shelter. The horses and mules moved closer to the fire, snorting their appreciation. Quickly everyone unsaddled the horses and freed the mules of their burdens.

"Even if we're snowed in for a week," said Will, "we won't starve."

"I reckon not," said Brazos, "but we'll be crazy as a bunch of cows that's been into loco weed. Apishapa

Canyon's dead enough, but it can't hold a candle to this."

"Won't bother me and Goose," said Monte. "I got three decks of cards."

McCaleb said nothing. Rebecca hadn't spoken to him all day and was now breaking out their provisions for supper. He was tempted to help, or at least offer to, but he'd had enough of her sulking. He hoped Wickliffe *did* show up at Apishapa Canyon; once and for all, this fickle girl could make up her mind. Some things—and Rebecca Nance might be one of them—weren't worth the price a man had to pay for them.

Supper finished, Monte inveigled Will and Brazos into a poker game. It wasn't difficult, there being nothing else to do. Rebecca rolled in her blankets and slept, or pretended to. McCaleb watched the others play poker until he was weary enough to sleep. It was a night fraught with nightmares. Jonathan Wickliffe wore Dobie Hobbs's buscadera rig. McCaleb drew, painfully slow, and found himself facing the vindictive Wickliffe, who held a flaming Colt in each hand.

In his horrible dream, gut-shot and dying, McCaleb heard Rebecca laughing. . . . Sweating, he awoke, finding he'd rolled too close to the fire. The poker game continued unabated.

Dawn broke gray and dismal, the snow continuing. They had nothing going for them, McCaleb thought gloomily, except an abundance of snow which could be melted for their own use and to water the mules and horses. Before the end of the second day, trying to save his sanity, McCaleb had taken a hand in the poker game.

"We're getting out of here tomorrow," he growled, "unless the snow's over our heads. This is bad as bein' in jail."

Will chuckled. "No it ain't. The grub's better here."

"While you got time to think on it," said Brazos,

"Goose wants to know why we didn't bring a load of ice cream with us. I told him you'd explain."

"Thanks," said McCaleb. He sneaked a look at Rebecca, but the humor was lost on her. She continued staring glumly into the fire.

The storm blew itself out sometime during the second night, but drifts were deep and they had to pick their way carefully. McCaleb took the lead, breaking trail for the others. Lead ropes must be kept taut, lest the led animals wander out of the narrow, beaten trail into drifts. Once, looking back, he caught Rebecca's rope slack.

"Keep the lead ropes tight," he shouted.

Suddenly there was a commotion behind him and he reined up. Rebecca's mule had bogged down in a drift and stood there braying its misery. McCaleb said nothing; just handed his reins and lead rope to Goose and dismounted.

The mule couldn't, or wouldn't, move. Digging away the snow, they found the animal's left foreleg trapped in a narrow crevice. Forward movement had snapped the bone just above the fetlock.

"Damn it all!" Monte roared, turning to the still-mounted Rebecca. "Have you been so tooken with that slick-talkin' buzzard that you ain't even got sense enough to lead a mule?"

The others were silent; he had expressed their sentiments perfectly. While westerners didn't hold with reviling a woman, neither did they condone the neglect or abuse of an animal. It was a peculiar situation. McCaleb's options were limited.

"Let's unload the mule," he said.

When the mule had been unloaded, McCaleb drew his Colt and shot the suffering animal between the eyes. Rebecca flinched, biting her lower lip. Without a word, the others began helping McCaleb break down the extra goods into five extra bundles. Pointedly ignoring Rebecca Nance, each of them tied a fifth of the dead mule's burden behind their saddles. The extra load would slow them even more, but McCaleb refused to push the horses, even if it meant another night on the trail.

They reached Apishapa Canyon after dark. In their absence, Goodnight's men had built a second cabin, a log bunkhouse, and shelter for the horses and mules. It was a gala evening as the cowboys excitedly gathered around to receive their eagerly awaited goods. McCaleb had brought a couple dozen copies of the *Rocky Mountain News,* including some back issues.

"Well," inquired Goodnight, "are you selling to Wickliffe?"

"I doubt it," said McCaleb. "He said he'd ride down and look at them after Christmas."

Less than a week before Christmas, a mixed herd of twenty-two hundred head came up the trail from Fort Sumner. Willard Burleson and three of his outfit rode into Apishapa Canyon. Burleson was one of half a dozen strapped Texas cattlemen who had witnessed Goodnight's success and hoped to emulate it.

"Surprised you got over Raton Pass," said Goodnight. "Snow was deep enough here; must've been somethin' else in the mountains."

"Was," said Burleson. "We set over yonder t'other side of Wootton's toll road and waited her out. Injuns had already stampeded an' stole some of our cows. Couldn't afford t' lose no more."

"Where you aim to go from here?" asked McCaleb.

"Jist far enough t' find a canyon the equal of this, where the snow don't cover up th' graze. Come spring, I'll cast about for a buyer."

"If the price is right," said McCaleb, "I might be interested in some of the she-stuff and the under-two-year-olds."

It was something McCaleb knew he had yet to discuss with the rest of the outfit, and that he had to do so before Wickliffe arrived. He had little enthusiasm for discussing the future of the outfit with Rebecca moody and on the prod, yet he could hardly pursue what he had in mind without including her. He would wait a few more days. Perhaps the Christmas festivities would put the girl in a better frame of mind.

The day after Christmas, McCaleb told the outfit what he had in mind and that he wanted to buy some of Burleson's she-stuff and under-two-year-olds.

"From what I've read in the Denver paper," he said, "there's the makings of a cattle empire in Wyoming. There's a railroad from Cheyenne to Omaha to Chicago. Once we've sold the steers we have, why not grab ourselves a piece of Wyoming range and build us another herd?"

"You mean our own ranch, then," said Monte. "Like Goodnight's doing."

"That's it," said McCaleb. "From there, we can trail to Montana and beyond. We'll need some more riders."

Their enthusiasm was all McCaleb had hoped for and more. Except for Rebecca. She remained silent, lost to him.

The year 1868 blew in just a few jumps ahead of a blizzard that subsided only to make way for another. Goodnight was restless because his return to Texas was being delayed.

"We could make it on horses," he lamented, "but with all this snow, we'd never get the chuck wagon over the mountains and through Raton Pass."

There was little to do in the secluded canyon except break the ice for the cattle to drink. Even Monte and Goose began to tire of the neverending poker games, leaving them to Bill and Charlie Wilson, the Vasquez boys, and a few others. Rebecca kept to herself.

January came and went without a break in the weather. February brought more of the same, each new snowfall adding to the frozen mass that remained. McCaleb was thankful for the miserable weather. Once it broke, he had little doubt that Jonathan Wickliffe would ride in. Taking advantage of the quiet before the probable storm, he met with Burleson and persuaded the old rancher to sell part of his mixed herd.

"Four hunnert an' seventy-five head, McCaleb. She-stuff and th' less'n two-year-olds. I reckon Goodnight's thinkin' straight, goin' back t' Texas for another herd. 'Fore long, this trail'll be as glutted as th' trails to Kansas. I aim t' leave my boys with the rest of this herd an' hightail it back to Texas with Charlie. I'll use your gold to buy me fifteen hunnert big steers 'fore th' price goes up."

While McCaleb's outfit seemed satisfied with the buy, it posed somewhat of a problem. McCaleb waited until Will brought it up.

"That's twenty-four hundred head; a mixed herd means slower trailing. I doubt we got enough riders to handle 'em any farther than Denver."

"I expect to sell our main herd in Denver," said McCaleb. "If we don't, then I expect you're right; we'll need some more riders."

"Wickliffe might make us an offer," said Brazos.

"It'd better be a good one," said McCaleb. "In a town the size of Denver, we'll play him against other buyers."

Surprisingly, Rebecca spoke. "If he makes anything like a decent offer, McCaleb, sell."

There was a shocked silence. Monte responded bitterly. "Why don't we just tie red ribbons around the necks of the cows and give them to him? I don't like that slick-tongued bastard; I wouldn't sell to him at fifty dollars a head."

The weather finally broke during the first week in March, and for the first time since Christmas, they saw the sun. Goodnight, four of his riders, and Burleson prepared to leave for Texas before yet another blizzard descended on them. It was an emotional parting, especially for McCaleb's outfit. They well knew, amid the dangers and uncertainties of the frontier, it might be the last time they'd see the generous, big bear of a man,

Charles Goodnight. Rebecca briefly came to life, throwing her arms around him and shedding some tears. Goodnight had warm words for them all. He saved Goose until last, bringing something from beneath his heavy coat. McCaleb saw it was the silver-plated Colt—or one just like it—that Goose had once dropped in the dust at Goodnight's feet. Both men remembered. Goose's expression didn't change. His obsidian eyes met Goodnight's as the big man extended the Colt, butt first. The Indian took the pistol, deftly slipping its muzzle in the waist of his buckskins. Slowly he extended his hand —his *left* hand—and Goodnight took it. Not a word was spoken. Goodnight mounted his big black, waiting for his riders to say their farewells.

Emilio and Donato Vasquez spoke to Goose in Spanish. Bill and Charlie Wilson, hot-tempered to a fault, shook hands all around and seemed genuinely sorrowful. Never once had Bill Wilson so much as spoken to Rebecca, so far as McCaleb recalled, but he did now. The girl flamed scarlet to the collar of her shirt. McCaleb would have given a handful of double eagles to know what One-Armed Bill had said.

Emilio led out with the chuck wagon. Goodnight, Donato Vasquez, and Bill and Charlie Wilson swung in behind it. McCaleb's outfit and the rest of the Goodnight riders watched in silence as Goodnight, his accompanying riders and the chuck wagon, grew smaller and smaller. Finally they were lost to distance.

Two days after Goodnight's departure, Jonathan Wickliffe, followed by Dobie Hobbs on horseback, drove his buckboard into Apishapa Canyon. McCaleb greeted him as courteously as he could. While Wickliffe responded in kind, an underlying smugness belied his sincerity. He seemed pleased by some impending event that he expected McCaleb to find proportionally distasteful. Without being asked, he stepped down from the buckboard. He swept off his hat, bowing elaborately and kissing Rebecca's hand. As furiously as she was blushing,

McCaleb noted she didn't withdraw her hand. The arrival of two strangers had aroused the curiosity of the others, and every rider in the canyon stood there gawking. Wickliffe had his back to them all, but McCaleb forced him to take his eyes off Rebecca and turn around.

"Men," said McCaleb, "this is Jonathan Wickliffe and Dobie Hobbs, of the Crown W ranch. They're here, I believe, to have a look at our herd."

"Among other things," said Wickliffe. "I'd also like to meet Goodnight, since we're virtually neighbors."

"He's left for Texas," said McCaleb brusquely. "This might be a good time for you to look at the herd, if you're still interested."

"Your hospitality leaves something to be desired, McCaleb. But perhaps you're right; if Goodnight's gone, I doubt there's any reason for me to tarry here."

With that, he turned to Rebecca.

"I trust you're familiar enough with the herd to show me around."

Without waiting for her consent, he hoisted her to the seat of the buckboard. He then took the reins—which he had half-hitched to the brake handle—and swung up beside her. He flicked the reins and they swept off down the canyon. McCaleb hoped he didn't look as much the fool as he felt. But that wasn't the worst of it. He cut his eyes to the still-mounted Hobbs, who chuckled as he looked after the buckboard. Gloating, he turned his insolent grin on McCaleb and said exactly the wrong thing.

"Nice little piece of baggage you *had*, bucko. Must've been fun to trail with, but that's done. Mr. Wickliffe's used to gettin' what he wants. Don't take it personal if she comes back with her britches on wrong side out."

McCaleb launched himself like a lobo wolf, sweeping the burly segundo out of the saddle and to the half-frozen ground. McCaleb was on top, but Hobbs quickly reversed the position. Straddling McCaleb, Hobbs began beating his head against the hard ground. With all his strength, McCaleb bowed his lower body backward, then upward, locking his legs around Hobbs's neck. He flung the man flat on his back, but Hobbs was cat-quick. He got McCaleb with a thrust of his boots, partially in the lower belly, partially in the groin. McCaleb gave in to the force, hoping to lessen the devastating effect. Now on his feet, McCaleb stumbled backward, trying to avoid Hobbs. He needed a few precious seconds in which he might overcome the sickening throb in his belly. But Hobbs was up and at him. The man had the strength of a bull, the adroitness and speed of a cat.

Hobbs charged and they clinched. Hobbs tried the groin gouge again, but McCaleb beat him to it. Involuntarily, Hobbs bent from the force of the blow, and McCaleb, stepping back, brought his right practically from the ground. The resulting *thunk* had the satisfying sound of an ax biting deep into a log. Numbing pain shot up McCaleb's arm all the way to his shoulder. Hobbs, his eyes glazed, slammed against the log wall of the barn. He bounced away, falling on his face. But he wasn't finished. He struggled, getting to his hands and knees. Bleeding from nose and mouth, he lifted his head to glare at McCaleb.

"You ready," gasped McCaleb, "to mount and ride out? While you can?"

"Make me . . . you Texas bastard. If you're man enough."

He lunged, and McCaleb was ready. He brought up his right knee, caught Hobbs in the face, and Hobbs flopped on his back. McCaleb felt like he'd dislocated his knee. Unbelievably, Hobbs had his forearms against the ground, trying to get up. Seeing that he couldn't, he fumbled at his twin holsters. His left-hand Colt was missing, but he curled his fingers around the butt of the other. But the toe of McCaleb's boot caught his wrist and the Colt went flying. McCaleb caught Hobbs by the front of his shirt and heard the back of it rip. He flung the burly foreman against the log wall of the barn and was killing the man with his fists when they pulled him away. Hobbs just crumpled like an empty feed sack and didn't move again.

McCaleb leaned against the log wall of the barn, breathing like a ruptured bellows. He felt the back of his head and found it matted with blood, bits of gravel having lacerated his scalp. His belly still ached, his knee throbbed, and his arms felt like lead, hurting all the way to his shoulders. But the worst was yet to come.

"They're comin' back," said one of the riders.

Wickliffe drew the buckboard up next to the barn. Rebecca's face went white when she saw the inert body of Dobie Hobbs. Wickliffe spoke to McCaleb.

"You should have killed him, my friend, because when he's able, he'll kill you."

"Better men have tried," said McCaleb.

"I'll pay you ten dollars a head for your cattle, McCaleb. Delivered to the Denver stockyards."

"Why you skinflint old bastard," shouted Monte Nance. "I'd shoot every damn cow before I'd see you get them. At any price."

"Is he speaking for the outfit, McCaleb?" Wickliffe asked.

"He is," gritted McCaleb. "Seein' as how we got nothing else to talk about, pile what's left of that back-shootin' coyote in your wagon and get out of here."

"I have nothing more to say to you," said Wickliffe pleasantly, "but I believe Rebecca does. Tell him, my dear."

She kept her head down, unable to look him—or any of them—in the eye. When she finally spoke, McCaleb couldn't hear her.

"Speak up!" snapped McCaleb. "If you're goin' to talk when this old man pulls the string, then do it loud enough to be heard!"

"All right," snapped Rebecca, her temper flaring. "Jonathan has invited me to ride back to Denver with him. He wants to show me the town. I'll stay at the Tremont House until you get there with the herd."

"So *that's* what you've had on your mind," said

McCaleb. "You and your daddy cooked up this little trip in December, didn't you? *That's* what's been eatin' at you, givin' you the whim-whams. You haven't been quite sure how to break the news, have you?"

"*You* made up my mind, McCaleb! You! Just because you don't like Jonathan, you picked a fight with Dobie Hobbs and beat the man half to death! Maybe it's time I got away from this drive for a while, where men don't behave like . . . like animals. I'll see you in Denver, and where we go from there depends on you!"

Grim and defiant, she said no more. Wickliffe got down and managed to get the unconscious Hobbs into the back of the buckboard. Brazos brought Hobbs's horse. Monte walked to the buckboard, put one booted foot on the wheel hub and glared at Rebecca.

" 'Be good, Monte,' " he simpered. " 'Stay away from cards, Monte. Leave the women alone, Monte. Don't go to hell like your daddy did, Monte. Leave the whiskey alone, Monte.' You're a *fine* one, tellin' *me* what to do with *my* life! You're goin' off to live in a hotel with a silly old man with enough wrinkles on his horns to be your daddy. A suck-egg dude with lace on his drawers—"

She hit him so hard he would have fallen if he hadn't caught the upper side of the wagon wheel. McCaleb thought at first that Monte was going to return the blow, but the kid fooled him. Without a word he turned and walked away. By then Wickliffe had climbed to the seat. Flicking the reins, he sent the team trotting away to the north. To Denver. McCaleb thought Rebecca was crying, but he couldn't be sure, since he could see only her back. Perhaps it was only the jolting of the buckboard that caused her shoulders to shake.

McCaleb had all the sympathy he could have asked for. To a man, they had heard Dobie Hobbs degrade Rebecca Nance and then they had witnessed Hobbs, beaten in a fair fight, go for his gun. Even the grizzled old Texans from Oliver Loving's original outfit—standoffish and shy—believed McCaleb had done what any man worthy of the term would have done. But their understanding and acceptance did nothing to soothe the ache in McCaleb's heart. She had promised to see him in Denver, but what effect might the town—with its nightlife—have on her? He had promised Goodnight he would remain here in Apishapa Canyon until April 1, but could he? The drive to Denver would take two weeks. With Denver as a backdrop, he felt himself pitted against Wickliffe's charm, position, and money. He would have five weeks to isolate Rebecca, to disenchant her with McCaleb and the life she'd been living. While he feared the chasm might become so wide and so deep it could never again be bridged, he refused to start the herd for Denver any sooner than he had planned. His own outfit seemed to understand his dilemma. Monte Nance became his staunchest ally, flatly refusing to begin the drive until April 1. Since that strange night in Santa Fe, in Condor's saloon, the kid had done a lot of growing up. He was fast becoming a *bueno hombre*.

"I got me a *malo* feelin' about Denver," said Brazos. "Wickliffe knows we're goin' there with the herd. If there's all that much need for beef, then how can he make us an offer he knows we'll refuse? Why, we ought to be able to ask—and get—three times what he offered us for them big steers!"

"You should've read those newspapers we brought from Denver," said Will. "Mr. Wickliffe makes some big tracks; there's talk that he'll be the next governor of the territory. When he says the word, I'd not be surprised if everybody in Denver jumps. He has powerful friends; I expect he'll arrange it so there'll *be* no better offer than his."

"If he's that powerful," said Monte, "he could force us out of Denver; maybe even out of Colorado."

They were nearing the same conclusion that McCaleb had already reached. What better way to widen the rift between Rebecca and McCaleb than to force them to trail the herd north to Wyoming or Montana? If they sold the herd in Denver, there would be no immediate need for them to move on. McCaleb could—and might —remain indefinitely. Wickliffe wouldn't expect them, given a choice, to leave Colorado without Rebecca. When—if—she learned of this nefarious scheme, would she care? For the first time in his life Benton McCaleb felt himself at a disadvantage, as though he were headed for a showdown whose outcome was in doubt.

It was just as well they had not begun the drive to Denver sooner than they had planned. Four days after Rebecca had departed with Wickliffe, another blizzard laid almost two feet of new snow across the high plains, with drifts over a man's head.

They rounded up their enlarged herd and headed it northwest on April 1. The ground was still frozen, snow remaining in shaded areas where the sun hadn't reached it. Despite patches of blue sky and occasional sun, there was a chill north wind. They wore wool-lined gloves, heavy mackinaws over woolen shirts, and wool scarves to protect their ears. Even Goose, used to milder South Texas winters, wore a heavy white man's coat over his buckskin shirt. Gradually the temperature crept higher, and as the snow began to melt, streams abounded. Every little gully, most always dry, now ran bank-full. The valleys where they bedded down the herd offered graze that was untouched. Creeks, lined with willow and box elder, boasted speckled trout aplenty.

"This is almighty fine country," said Will, "but I miss Texas. Grass is greening there. I won't ever forget the meadows with oceans of blue bonnets that just seem to roll on forever."

"I wish you hadn't said that." Brazos grinned. "I never thought I'd miss Texas, but I reckon I do. Long as we was goin' back for another herd, I didn't think much about it, but this seems kind of . . . final."

"I never had a state, or any place, I could miss," said Monte. "The old man was always in trouble with somebody; usually the neighbors. We'd end up sneaking out of town during the night. Folks called us 'them no-account Nances.' ''

For McCaleb, already morose and silent, it brought to mind Rebecca and the things she had told him about her heart-breaking childhood. The talk had taken a negative turn and Will sought to change the subject.

"I wonder what Goose misses the most about Texas?"

Brazos caught the Apache's eye and waved. Goose trotted his horse alongside and Brazos spoke to him. Suddenly the Indian grinned.

"*Comanch'*," he said. "*Comanch' bastardos.*"

They all laughed. Even McCaleb.

In mid-April they bedded down the herd ten miles south of Denver, on Cherry Creek.

"This is where they found the first gold," said Will, "back in 'fifty-eight. If you got an early start and worked hard all day, you could clear seventy cents, easy."

"I'm riding into town," said McCaleb, "and I want Monte to go with me. I want some idea as to what we're facing when it comes to selling the herd, and I need to know what Rebecca aims to do. Part of this herd is hers."

Will and Brazos said nothing. While they doubted Monte could say or do anything to influence the girl, his riding with McCaleb was proof of McCaleb's desperation.

They dismounted before the Tremont House, half-hitched their horses to the rail, and made their way into the lobby. To McCaleb's disgust, the same stuffy, uncooperative clerk with whom he had tangled horns before was again at the front desk. He now wore a black and gold lapel pin that said his name was Wilkerson. McCaleb didn't waste time on formalities.

"I have business with Jonathan Wickliffe. Is he in his usual room?"

"Mr. Wickliffe is not here, period."

"Then where *is* he?" gritted McCaleb.

"I don't interest myself in Mr. Wickliffe's where-abouts *or* his business," said Wilkerson stiffly. "How-ever," he continued with obvious relish, "I do not feel I'm intruding upon Mr. Wickliffe's privacy or violating a confidence by telling you what seems to be common knowledge about the town. Mr. Wickliffe and his fiancée took the train to St. Louis last week. They planned to be married there, I believe."

His smirk vanished and his face paled as McCaleb caught him by his red necktie and hoisted him halfway across the desk.

"*What did you say?*" shouted McCaleb.

Abruptly aware that he was choking the man, McCaleb released him. Wilkerson stumbled back against the wall. McCaleb stood there breathing hard, his fists clenched.

Wilkerson straightened his tie. Finally, regaining some of his old arrogance, he spoke. "Get a copy of the newspaper and read it for yourself; *if* you can read."

Ignoring the insult, McCaleb made his way outside and stood on the boardwalk staring dumbly at the toes of his boots.

Shaken, Monte said, "Damn her, McCaleb, if she's gone and done *that*, I'd as soon kill *her* as him! Why, he's old enough to be her daddy!"

McCaleb's initial fury had begun to subside, and Monte's anger reached him. He spoke with far more calmness than he felt.

"We don't know for sure, kid. Before we kill anybody, I reckon we ought to get a newspaper and see if what we've been told is anything more than a nasty rumor. She's done some fool things, but surely not this."

They bought two papers, seated themselves in a café and ordered coffee. They eventually found eight lines that neither confirmed or denied what Wilkerson had told them. The writer hadn't mentioned Rebecca by name, referring to her with tongue-in-cheek style as

Wickliffe's "current fiancée." He had merely posed a question regarding the trip to St. Louis. Would a single *lady* accompany a single gentleman on a journey as far as St. Louis for anything less serious than marriage?

"Current fiancée?" said McCaleb. "No newspaper would dare print that without a reason. Wickliffe's planted this story and encouraged the gossip. He aims for us to bog down in this up to our ears. Suppose we take this for the truth and give Rebecca hell; what do you reckon she'll do?"

"Marry the sonofabitch," said Monte, "just to prove she can."

"That's why we're not goin' to let this light our fuse," said McCaleb. "We'll congratulate her and smile, if it kills us."

Feeling a little better, they left the café. Despite his misgivings as to their prospects, McCaleb intended to try and sell their main herd. Then, just ahead of them, Dobie Hobbs stepped out of a saloon and stood on the boardwalk, waiting. His thumbs were hooked in his belt near the butts of his twin Colts. With a sneer he spoke.

"Soon as Mr. Wickliffe gits back, bucko, I aim to kill you. I want his new bride to have a front-row seat when I gut-shoot you. Nobody does what you done to Dobie Hobbs and goes on livin'. *Nobody!*"

CHAPTER 22

Word of the enmity between McCaleb and Hobbs had obviously spread, and as though by magic, men appeared in doorways and at windows. The boardwalk cleared as passersby removed themselves from a possible line of fire. Relaxed and ready, McCaleb said nothing. But Hobbs grinned, and apparently for the benefit of the spectators, swaggered back into the saloon from which he had come. A thin young man with a tablet under his arm and a pencil behind his ear approached McCaleb. He wore wire-rimmed spectacles, an old blue serge suit, string tie, and a white shirt that had seen too many washings. But none recently. He halted a dozen feet from McCaleb, as though uncertain of his welcome.

"I'm Bascom, with the *Rocky Mountain News*. You're McCaleb?"

McCaleb nodded.

"What can you tell me about this, ah, feud between you and Hobbs?"

"Nothing," said McCaleb.

"Hobbs claims it started over a woman; to be specific, the young woman who is the current companion of Jonathan Wickliffe. Hobbs says he's been forced into this running fight with you because of your vendetta against Wickliffe. Have you anything to say in your own defense?"

"No," said McCaleb. Without another word, he continued along the boardwalk, Monte following.

"That Hobbs is a lyin' bastard," said Monte. "Why didn't you say so?"

"This is Wickliffe's town, and Hobbs is Wickliffe's man. Nothing I could say would make two bits worth of difference. Hobbs aims to bring this to a head when Wickliffe returns, and I reckon I'll have to kill him. Or he'll kill me."

They had reached the Tremont House. Wilkerson was still on duty and exhibited little enthusiasm for another encounter with McCaleb.

"I want a room on the first floor," said McCaleb.

"I told you I don't have—"

"You also told me Jonathan Wickliffe's out of town," said McCaleb. "You have at least two rooms reserved for him. I want one of them; I'll give it up when he returns."

McCaleb didn't offer to pay in advance, and so perturbed was Wilkerson that he failed to demand it. Sullenly he produced a key, and McCaleb took it. He unlocked the door to the room Rebecca had occupied and handed the key to Monte.

"You'll be staying in town the rest of today and tonight," said McCaleb. "I'll send Will or Brazos to take over tomorrow. Stay out of the saloons. Be there in the morning when the train arrives from the east. Should Wickliffe and Rebecca be on it, ride back to the herd and get me."

"She's my sister and I—"

"You'll have your say. Just don't start anything on your own. This is Wickliffe's town. You start a ruckus, sister or not, and you'll end up in the *juzgado*. Wickliffe's likely countin' on us making fools of ourselves, so don't do anything foolish."

"But if she's married that—"

"Then gettin' yourself jailed or killed won't change a thing. If she steps off that train wearin' a diamond big as a horse apple, then you hightail it to camp and get me. *Comprender?*"

Monte nodded and McCaleb left the hotel. He walked to the outskirts of town, to the Kansas Pacific railroad tracks, along which a dozen stock pens had been built. He entered a barnlike building with a single word in foot-high block letters across its front: LIVESTOCK. A fat man, his booted feet on a scarred desk, sat tilted back in an old swivel chair. With agonized creaking of the chair, he dragged his feet off the desk and stubbed out his cigar in a coffee mug before him. He was blunt and his response was not unexpected.

"Wouldn't be interested. I understand Mr. Wickliffe's got an option."

"Wickliffe made an offer," said McCaleb, "which has been refused."

"In that case, ten dollars a head."

McCaleb didn't even dignify that with a refusal. He rode past whorehouses on Market and Larimer streets and met an approaching column of heavy freight wagons arriving from the south.

"Hey, Texas!"

The whacker slowed one of the wagons and the little man who had been riding with him scrambled down. It was Salty, the stove-up ex-cowboy cook from Santa Fe. McCaleb reined up and waited for the limping old fellow to reach him.

"Salty, what'n tarnation are you doin' here?"

"Things was gittin' a mite too civilized in Santa Fe. Th' railroad's comin' through fer shore. Th' town's come up with what they calls a Chamber of Commerce, an' it's sendin' letters back East, invitin' folks t' settle in an' around Santa Fe. Nex' thing you know, they'll be sodbusters a-plowin' an' a-plantin', with not a longhorn cow in a hunnert mile. Some jasper done brung in a mess o' sheep—ten thousant of th' woolly bastards—an' set up a sheep ranch in th' north o' Lincoln County. Some ranchers rimrocked 'bout a thousant woollies, an' th' sheepmen gunned down two cowboys. I might not be aroun' t' see it, but they's gonna be war betwixt cattlemen an' sheepmen. I tell you, th' territory's just gone plumb t' hell, an' I got out whilst I could."

"What are you aimin' to do here?"

"I dunno. I jist hitched on with th' freight outfit 'cause I knew some of th' whackers that'd come in th' café. Reckoned I might tie in with some cow outfit needin' a cook. I ain't wuth a damn on a hoss, but I c'n cook an' drive a chuck wagon. Jist t' be part of a honest-t'-God cow outfit, I'd near 'bout hire on fer grub an' a bunk. Ain't needin' a cook, are ye?"

"Got no chuck wagon," said McCaleb. "Usin' pack mules."

"How *many* mules?" he asked, a calculating gleam in his eyes.

McCaleb grinned. "Enough to pull a chuck wagon, if we *had* one."

"S'pose I could dicker fer one?"

"Then I reckon the outfit would welcome you," said McCaleb. "The herd's bedded down on Cherry Creek, south of here. We'll be in these parts for a few days. We have Room 10 at Tremont House. If I'm not there, one of my outfit will be. We're the Bar Six outfit; I'm Benton McCaleb."

"Reynolds," he said. "Salty Reynolds. Gran'pappy fought in th' Revolution, an' whilst I was too little t' object, they named me George Washington Reynolds. Y'ever call me anything but Salty, I'll pizen yer grub!"

McCaleb rode on, strangely elated over his encounter with the old cook. He knew the outfit would welcome Salty, especially after Rebecca's departure. They had come to depend as much on the girl's cooking as they had on Charles Goodnight's innovative chuck wagon. With or without Rebecca, the addition of a chuck wagon and a gifted, willing, full-time cook would be welcome. He had been touched by the wistfulness in Salty's eyes, his longing for the open range, and his determination to return to it. Even if the old man had to swap his Texas saddle for the hard seat of a jouncing wagon . . .

* * *

The following morning, McCaleb sent Will Elliot to town. When Monte returned to camp, he brought some welcome news.

"The old-timer from Santa Fe—Salty—wants a couple teams of mules. Some outfit in St. Louis is buildin' chuck wagons copied after Goodnight's. One of the wagon yards in town's got a couple of 'em. Salty says they're seventy-five dollars."

"That's a powerful lot for a wagon," said McCaleb innocently. "Can we afford it?"

"My God, yes!" said Brazos. "If it's even *close* to Goodnight's, it'll be cheap at twice that. Especially when we got a cook that's chompin' at the bit to throw in with us. Take the money out of my share of the stake."

When Brazos rode to town to relieve Will, Monte accompanied him, each of them leading a pair of mules. Brazos took with him money to pay for the new wagon, harness for the mules, and sufficient supplies to stock the chuck wagon. Monte and Will would return to camp with Salty. But Brazos and Monte had been gone less than an hour when Will rode in. He swung out of the saddle, his lathered horse attesting to a hard ride. He didn't waste words.

"You'd better saddle and ride. Wickliffe and Rebecca came in on the morning train. I turned in the key at the desk and paid for the room. This may be tough on the kid; her bein' his sister, he's likely to do something foolish."

"Is she . . . ?" McCaleb couldn't say the word, but Will understood.

"I didn't like what I saw. When they stepped off the train . . . my God, I wouldn't have *known* her but for Wickliffe struttin' along. She's done somethin' with her hair; it's different. She wore a long green dress that's just about the color of her eyes. I swear, Bent, the Queen of England couldn't have looked better. . . ."

His voice trailed off, but he had said enough. No decent woman allowed a man to dress her in finery unless she was married to him. Or about to be. McCaleb hurriedly saddled his horse. It was Sunday afternoon, April 24, 1868.

Two or three miles south of town, McCaleb encountered Salty with the chuck wagon. Only Brazos accompanied him. It came as no surprise; McCaleb only hoped he reached town before Monte said or did the wrong thing.

McCaleb reined up before Tremont House, swung down and half-hitched his reins to the rail. The only other horse, a buckskin, bore the 6 brand on its left hip. Monte's horse. McCaleb half expected to hear shots—or *some* kind of commotion—from the hotel, but again the kid surprised him. Monte came out of a café on the corner; he had been watching for McCaleb. But so had others. Some stood in doorways, and faces appeared at windows.

"Look at them," growled Monte. "A flock of buzzards. Dobie Hobbs has been buyin' the drinks, tellin' everybody he'll kill you before sundown."

"What about . . . Rebecca?"

"I kept out of sight when the train come in," said Monte. "Damn him, McCaleb, he's got her all gussied up like he *owns* her. But that ain't the worst of it; she's prancing around like a high-steppin' filly. I heard men sayin' she ain't no better'n a whore, running off with him like that. I'd gut-shoot a man for sayin' that about her if it wasn't the God's truth. I waited for you, like you said. Now what are we goin' to do?"

"Talk to her, I reckon. We're leaving tomorrow, with her or without her. But she's part owner of the herd; we can't just leave without talking to her. It's only fair to reach a settlement of some kind."

They entered the lobby of the Tremont House and, ignoring the front desk, went directly to the room Rebecca had occupied before. McCaleb was not prepared for the vision that answered his knock. It was Rebecca as he'd never seen her before. Her dark hair hung in curls to her shoulders. Her flowing green gown had white lace at the wrists and about the collar. It was everything Will had said it was. And more. She was more beautiful, more desirable, than McCaleb had ever seen her. He drank her in, from her shining hair to the white slippers she wore. She clasped her hands in front of her as though to prevent their trembling, and even in the dim light from the hall there was the unmistakable twinkle of a diamond on her left hand.

"Come in," she said, so softly they barely heard her.

They entered and she closed the door. There were chairs, but such was the state of their minds, none of them thought of sitting. They stood there woodenly, at a loss for words.

Finally Rebecca spoke. "I—I'm sorry I . . . wasn't here when you came. Jon took me to St. Louis to see a play, a melodrama called *Under the Gaslight*. A New York playwright—Augustin Daly—wrote it, and it opened there last summer. . . ."

It was a pathetic attempt at small talk; aware of the futility of it, her voice trembled.

Monte had taken all he could. "For God's sake," he blurted, "what's he *done* to you? Them clothes . . ."

She tried to laugh but it came out a whimper.

"It's—It's not what you think. Oh, it's not. He's been . . . Jon's been a perfect gentleman. This dress and these shoes belonged to his wife. She's dead and he says I'm so much . . . like her."

"So much," said McCaleb, in a voice that hardly sounded like his own, "that you're takin' her place."

She wrung her hands as though in anguish and the tears began. McCaleb and Monte stood there gripping their hats with both hands. When she finally spoke, between sobs, it was in a whisper. Every word seemed torn from her.

"He asked me . . . begged me . . . said he *needed* me. Dear God, I didn't know *what* to do. He already had the . . . the ring. He slipped it on my finger and begged . . . begged me not to take it off. He's already told everybody . . . the newspapers . . . that I . . . I—"

Her sobs again took control and she said no more. She bowed her head and tears rolled off her cheeks onto the bosom of the expensive green gown. It was more than Monte could stand. He grabbed her shoulders and shook her.

"When?" he growled. "When did you promise to *marry* that bastard?"

It was the wrong thing to do. McCaleb had warned him. Rebecca tore herself from his grasp, her green eyes blazing.

"The first Sunday in June," she snapped, "but I'm going to ask him to make it sooner. Maybe *next* Sunday!"

Before Monte could respond with a similar burst of anger, McCaleb took control. He shoved the kid aside and spoke to Rebecca as kindly as he could.

"Rebecca, part of the herd belongs to you. I reckon we won't be able to square it with you until we sell, and nobody in this town will pay us a fair price. . . ."

She responded to his kindness and again tears welled up. For just a second or two there was the old softness he remembered so well, but it faded, leaving only a thousand years of heartache and sorrow. After those few gut-wrenching seconds, she couldn't bear to look into his eyes, nor he into hers. She calmed herself enough to speak, head bowed, in a whisper.

"I don't want any part of the herd. Monte, you . . . they're . . . yours. Please take them."

McCaleb couldn't stand another minute of it. He stumbled to the door, taking Monte with him, but the kid would have none of it. Leaving McCaleb in the dimly lit hall, he turned back.

"I don't want your damn cows," he snarled. "I'll tally 'em out and shoot ever' last one. You've give me hell all my life. You taught me to be honest, walk straight, and I always looked up to you, even when you was the hardest on me. You made *me* somebody because I believed *you* were somebody and I wanted to be as good as you. You're all the family I had, and now you're gone. You've sold out to a slick-tongued old man with money. Daddy would of sold his soul to the devil for a gold eagle and a jug of moonshine, and for all your highfalutin preachin', you ain't no better than he was. He sold his soul and you're sellin' your body."

Monte slammed the door and stalked toward the lobby, McCaleb following. Jonathan Wickliffe stepped out of his room and stood looking down the hall after them. He knocked on Rebecca's door and, getting no response, tried the knob. The door was locked.

When Monte and McCaleb reached the boardwalk, Monte was still white-faced with anger, while McCaleb was sick at heart. The very last person Benton McCaleb wished to meet was that pushy bastard from the newspaper, but there he was. Bascom had seen them enter the Tremont House and had patiently awaited their departure. A spark of excitement in his eyes overcame his reluctance and he approached them.

"Dobie Hobbs swears he'll meet you here at one o'clock, McCaleb. What do you intend to do?"

"Gut-shoot you," snapped McCaleb, "if you don't quit following me."

"They're taking bets in the saloons," said Bascom slyly, "and the odds favor Hobbs. He says if you ride out, he'll follow."

"McCaleb," said Monte, "why *don't* we just ride out? You can outshoot that loudmouth blindfolded. We don't have to prove anything to this town."

McCaleb looked around. Some of the curious had gotten close enough to hear the conversation. Why *didn't* he simply ride away, leaving Hobbs to strut and bluster to his heart's content? Then he became aware that some of the onlookers were staring past him, and he turned. On the boardwalk outside the Tremont House stood Jonathan Wickliffe, arms folded across his chest and a look of satisfaction on his handsome face. McCaleb turned to the eager young reporter and spoke loud enough for everybody—including Wickliffe—to hear.

"One o'clock, then."

Those who had heard hurried away to tell others. From a saloon across the street came the tinkling of a piano and a rising crescendo of voices, like the buzzing of excited bees.

"I'm takin' bets," somebody shouted.

Wickliffe had gone back into the hotel. Bascom fished a dollar watch from his coat pocket.

"Fifteen minutes of one," he said.

McCaleb turned back to the Tremont House, went into the lobby and took a chair near the door. Monte knelt beside the chair, his back to the wall. At the front desk Wilkerson pointedly ignored them.

"I'll side you," said Monte.

"You'll stay out of it," said McCaleb. "I can take Hobbs, but if some of his *compadres* buy in, there's no sense in both of us gettin' shot. If I don't come out of it clean, you'll have to ride back to camp and tell the others."

Monte swallowed hard and said nothing. He was all too aware of the big grandfather clock that slowly, grimly, ticked away the minutes. There was a silence, a waiting; even the piano across the street was still. Somewhere there was a single gunshot, and on the heels of it the grandfather clock chimed once.

"You're sure—" began Monte.

"I'm sure, kid," said McCaleb. "Thanks. I know you've got the sand, but I'll likely need you more when this is finished. However it ends."

He got up, tilted his hat over his eyes and checked his Colt. Pausing at the door, he surveyed the street before stepping out on the boardwalk. Through the swinging doors of the Bull's Head saloon, three hundred yards away, stepped a solitary figure. McCaleb stood in the street before the Tremont House, thumbs hooked in his belt. Monte remained on the hotel porch, out of the line of fire. The town held its breath as Hobbs began his slow walk. So intent was McCaleb on the advancing figure, he never saw Rebecca's frightened, tear-streaked face at an upstairs window, nor was he aware that Jonathan Wickliffe stood on the second-floor balcony of the hotel. Waiting.

Benton McCaleb didn't know—nor would he have approved if he had—that just minutes before his showdown with Dobie Hobbs, Rebecca had made a last desperate appeal to Jonathan Wickliffe.

"Please, Jon," she had cried, "don't let this happen. Can't you stop Dobie Hobbs? He's one of your men. McCaleb won't fight unless he has to, but he's not afraid. Please, please don't make him go through with this!"

"Your compassion for McCaleb is touching," Wickliffe had replied, "but I have no control over Hobbs. I have dismissed the man; if he kills or is killed, it's no concern of mine. I've grown weary of people expecting *me* to muzzle Dobie Hobbs. I would suggest that you remain in your room until the wretched spectacle is over."

However wretched the spectacle, she dared not miss it. Whatever horror she might witness, *not* knowing if McCaleb were alive or dead would be all the more terrible. As the dreaded hour approached, she heard Wickliffe's door open and close. She crept down the hall and found the lobby crowded; people pushed and shoved, seeking favored positions at door or window. She climbed the stairs to the second floor and, to her dismay, found Wickliffe on the balcony overlooking the street. She pushed through the double doors until she stood behind him. So absorbed was he in the unfolding drama below, he didn't know she was there. While she could see Hobbs, she couldn't see McCaleb. Moving closer to the balcony rail brought her to Wickliffe's attention. He turned to her with a grim smile.

"There is a little barbarian in all of us, eh?"

She ignored him. Her eyes were on McCaleb, and so

great was her concern that she wasn't aware that Wick-liffe's attention was focused on neither of the men in the street. Instead, his eyes darted to the roofs and false-fronted saloons and shops that lined the street directly ahead of McCaleb.

Rebecca wondered where Monte was. She had half expected to find the kid in the street, preparing to side McCaleb. Immediately she was ashamed for having had such thoughts. Sure as she was that McCaleb wouldn't run from a fight, she was even more sure that he would neither expect or permit someone else to shoulder a responsibility he regarded as his own.

McCaleb waited as Hobbs approached. To a stranger unfamiliar with the frontier, they might have been old friends, about to meet after a prolonged separation. Hobbs drew nearer. A hundred yards. Ninety. Eighty. Seventy. Fifty. Benton McCaleb's eyes weren't on Hobbs, but on a second-story window to the left of the gunman. It was an insignificant thing, no more than the wink of the westering sun off a windowpane. Or a rifle barrel. Then, to the surprise of everybody—including Hobbs—McCaleb drew and fired once, twice, three times! But he was shooting high, over Hobbs's head, and his first shot took the glass out of a window with a tinkling crash. Before the echo of McCaleb's last shot had died away, Hobbs had a blazing Colt in each hand. The first slug burned its way through the fleshy under-side of McCaleb's upper left arm, the second snatched the hat from his head, and a third took him just below the collarbone. The force of the slug turned McCaleb half around, dropping him on his back in the dusty street.

"No," cried Rebecca. "No, no, no!"

As much as she yearned to go to him, she couldn't move. Heart pounding, she silently prayed for some sign of life. McCaleb lifted himself to his elbows, and two more shots sang over his head, dangerously close. McCaleb fired once. For a long second or two, Dobie Hobbs seemed frozen in place. His reflexes triggered a blast from each of his Colts into the dust at his feet. Then he went down on his back and a playful breeze sent his hat skittering away. He lay there unmoving, a circle of crimson spreading over the breast of his white shirt like the unfurling of a rose.

Freed from the shock that had imprisoned her, Rebecca sprang for the door, only to have Wickliffe grab her about the waist.

"He's alive, my dear, and that's as far as your interest is allowed to go. Our engagement has been announced and I'll not have you down there making a fool of yourself. Or of me. Now let's return to our rooms, shall we?"

In the aftermath of the shooting, the spectators quickly lost interest and drifted away to the saloons, the losers to pay and the winners to collect. Nobody had been more shaken by the fight than Monte Nance. While he was concerned with McCaleb's wounds, something far more troublesome was dogging his mind. McCaleb was lightning quick with a Colt, and never once, that Monte recalled, had he missed. Yet he had drawn first, fired four times, but hit Hobbs only once. Why had he allowed Hobbs to get a slug into him first, and then needed a fourth shot to cut the man down? Unassisted, McCaleb got to his knees and then to his feet. Blood had soaked the left side of his denim shirt from shoulder to waist. Monte looked at him and swallowed hard.

"How bad?"

"Worst one just below the collarbone," said McCaleb. "Another burned off some hide under my left arm. Time for a doc, I reckon."

But the doctor came second; the next man they saw wore a badge. Sheriff Langdon Simmons had a surprise for them. An unpleasant surprise.

"Mr. McCaleb, for your safety, I'm lockin' you up for the night. Now, I ain't chargin' you with nothin', understand. Man's got a right to defend himself, and you done that. But Hobbs had friends, and I ain't puttin' it past them to get juiced up and come after you. Come on; I'll get the doc to come around and patch you up."

"Sheriff," said McCaleb, "while I appreciate your concern, I have an outfit just south of town. Soon as a doc looks me over and plugs this hole, I aim to ride out. I doubt Hobbs's friends will follow me to Wyoming."

"Well," said Sheriff Simmons, "you can't leave until after the hearin' and the inquest. Legal enough, you punchin' Hobbs's ticket, but I got a dead man on my hands. Won't take more'n a few minutes to get the legal part of this took care of, but it can't be done 'fore nine o'clock in th' mornin'."

"You won't settle for anything less than me spendin' the night in jail, then," said McCaleb.

"That's it." Simmons grinned. "It ain't entirely for your benefit. I got my reputation as sheriff at stake. I ain't had a lynchin' yet, and I don't aim for you to be the first. While I can't watch *all* the likkered-up rowdies in town, I *can* keep an eye on you. When you ride out tomorrow, I want you in one piece, without a stretched neck."

The jail—three cells on each side of a long corridor—was in the basement of the courthouse. Three hungover, disconsolate cowboys sat on cots in the first cell on the right, and McCaleb was given the cell next to theirs. Monte was allowed to remain with McCaleb for a few minutes, and as soon as the sheriff left them alone, McCaleb had instructions for him.

"Take my horse to the livery and see that he's cared for. Then ride to camp and tell the others what's happened. I want either Will or Brazos to ride in after dark and stake out the jail, just in case Hobbs *does* have friends with lynching on their minds. And tell Will or Brazos—whoever rides in—to bring me another two hundred dollars for that court appearance in the morning. I'm not sure I won't face some trumped-up charge with a stiff fine. But I only want *one* man in town tonight. I want the rest of you to round up the herd and move them out at dawn. Drive them west of town, then north across the South Platte River, and hold them there. Now get going; they'll be wondering what's happened to us."

Monte had been gone only a few minutes when the doctor arrived. He was a businesslike little man who spoke not a single word. McCaleb peeled off his shirt, ripping the fabric loose where it clung to his wounds, starting them bleeding again. By now he had the undivided attention of the three men in the adjoining cell. In turn, McCaleb studied them while the little doctor cauterized his wounds, setting them afire with some kind of venomous liquid. When the doctor had bandaged his wounds and departed, McCaleb sat there looking at his ruined shirt. Why hadn't he thought to have Monte send him another with Will or Brazos? He felt a bit self-conscious as his captive audience studied his bare torso with its impressive mass of scars. Most of them had resulted from lead, arrows, and knives. But there was one—an ugly gash from a Comanche lance—that began near his navel and half circled his right side.

"Pardner," said one of the admiring trio, "you must be a Texan. Anybody else would of just took the easy way out an' died."

They all chuckled at this macabre cowboy humor, and McCaleb grinned. He reckoned the oldest of the three wasn't more than twenty-five, if that.

"The world's a mite hard on Texans," said McCaleb.

"Amen, brother," said another of the trio. "We heard some Colts a-poppin' a while ago; was you in the midst of that?"

"Considerably," said McCaleb. "Had to shoot an hombre that wouldn't have it any other way. He returned the favor, in part."

"You're in the *calabozo* for defendin' yourself?"

"Just for the night, I reckon," said McCaleb. "There's a hearing and an inquest in the morning. The sheriff thinks this jaybird's friends might invite me to a necktie party just to get even. I'm in here for my own protection."

"Onliest protection you can count on in *this* town, friend, is a loaded-to-the-chamber repeatin' rifle or a hair-trigger Colt six-shooter."

McCaleb was an impulsive man and he liked these affable cowboys. He got up off the cot and put his hand through the bars that separated their cells.

"I'm Benton McCaleb, Red River County, Texas."

"My God," said one of the trio, "no wonder you look like you just come from an Injun war; you near 'bout growed up in the Territory. I'm Pendleton Rhodes. My friends call me Pen. I'm from Waco and part Injun myself."

Rhodes had high cheekbones, jet-black hair, and deep brown eyes. McCaleb shook his hand and then turned his attention to the other cowboys. They were obviously brothers, towheaded and blue-eyed.

"Jediah Vandiver," said the oldest of the two, "and this is my brother, Stoney. We're from San Antone, and my God, how I wish I was there now—even with all the blue bellies and carpetbaggers."

McCaleb shook their hands. These Texans were his kind of people. In his mind an idea was taking hold, and he needed to know more about these cowboys.

"If it ain't too personal," he said, "what are you accused of?"

"Drunk and disorderly conduct," said Jed.

"Disturbin' the peace," said Stoney.

"Destruction of private property," finished Pen.

McCaleb said nothing, waiting for them to continue. Having divulged that much, they proceeded to tell their story.

"We come up the Chisholm Trail with a herd," said Pen. "Had nearly a hundred dollars apiece, never been out of Texas before, never rode a train."

"We should of gone back to Texas," said Stoney, "but we wanted to ride the train. You can't ride the train without goin' *somewheres*, so we come here."

"That was only our *first* mistake," said Jed. "The second was goin' to that whorehouse—Madame X's place

—on Market Street. They give us a drink on the house and robbed us!"

"Loaded drinks," said McCaleb.

"My God, yes," said Pen, "any one of 'em laced with enough stuff to have floored a tribe of Comanches."

"Time we got upstairs," said Stoney, "we was so out of it we couldn't even get our boots off. We was so near dead we didn't come to our senses until this mornin'. They'd picked us clean as Christmas geese and throwed us in the alley."

"We gets ourselves together," said Jed with a wry grin, "goes in there and expresses our dissatisfaction with the service."

"You wrecked the place," said McCaleb.

"Considerable," said Pen, "but we had help. There was this big gent with the body and brains of a grizzly. A bouncer. He follered us upstairs and we throwed him back down. He come back and we throwed him down again. Ever' time he went down, he took somethin' with him. Most of the banister, last time."

"But that wasn't the worst part," said Stoney. "Somebody went and got the sheriff. He brung about sixteen big bastards with him, all of 'em swingin' clubs and gun butts. They trapped us in an upstairs bedroom and it was the Alamo all over again. They nearly kilt us. Ever'time I shake my head, somethin' rattles. My brains, mebbe."

"Can't be *that*," chuckled Jed. "You ain't got any. None of us have."

"The damage is the big thing, then," said McCaleb.

"Didn't break nothin' that can't be fixed," said Pen, "unless it was that gent we throwed out an upstairs window."

"There'll be fines and damages," said McCaleb.

"Won't make no difference to us," said Stoney, "if it's five dollars or five hundred. They picked us so clean, we couldn't raise enough amongst us to buy a sack of Durham."

"Suppose I could get you out of here and into a trail herd," said McCaleb. "What would it be worth to you?"

Clearly they believed he was hoorawing them. He saw resentment, and then anger, in their eyes. Without going into painful detail regarding his loss of Rebecca and his trouble with Hobbs, he told them about the herd. He explained their need for more riders, that there might be greater drives from Texas along the western trail to Wyoming, Montana, and beyond.

"Mr. Benton McCaleb," said Pen Rhodes, "I can't speak for these other two jaybirds, but you get me out of here—give me a shot at this drive—and I will work the first year just for my grub. Not only that, but the next ugly bastard that comes after you with killin' on his mind, he'll have to step over my dead carcass to get to you."

"He's talkin' for us too," said Stoney. "Trouble is, we sold our mounts in Ellsworth so's we could ride the train. We got only our saddles and our saddlebags at the Vasquez House. We owe for a room we never slept in."

"I just lost a . . . a rider," said McCaleb, "so there'll be extra horses in the remuda. We'll need more, though."

"Well, let's don't buy 'em here," said Pen. "The way everything else's turned sour in this town, they'll likely cost a hundred dollars apiece. I hear in the Montana Territory they got wild ones runnin' free."

Will Elliot had kept watch during the night, as McCaleb had requested. He showed up at the jail at eight o'clock and the sheriff brought him back to McCaleb's cell. Monte had remembered and had sent McCaleb a clean shirt. There was a spark of recognition in Pendleton Rhodes's eyes as he shook Will's hand. Pen vaguely remembered Will's family in the days before they had left Waco for Mineral Wells. Will brought the requested two hundred dollars in gold eagles; McCaleb hoped it would be enough to get the three young Texans released.

Sheriff Simmons led them upstairs to the courtroom.

There were no spectators. On one side of the room sat an expensively dressed woman who McCaleb suspected was Madame X. From Pen's description, the huge man beside her had to be the grizzly-brained bouncer. McCaleb's hearing, as he'd hoped, came before the court first. To his surprise, it seemed there was no question as to his exoneration.

"Most of the town," said Sheriff Simmons, "saw Mr. McCaleb take part in this fight with Dobie Hobbs, and everybody knows it was fair. Ever'body is also aware that Hobbs pushed it. McCaleb claims self-defense, and rightly so. From the evidence, he's justified."

The judge was a little man named Hobart Short. His voice was low and raspy, like that of a crow, had a crow been endowed with speech. Glaring at McCaleb with what he considered his sternest judicial manner, he spoke.

"The court accepts your plea of self-defense. However, I have been approached by certain prominent citizens who believe it is in the best interests of the town if you depart immediately."

McCaleb had little doubt as to the identity of at least *one* of those "prominent citizens" who wanted him out of town. Killing him had been the first option; that having failed, he would be banished as an undesirable. The only other business before the court was the disposition of the charges against the three cowboys. More and more, Pendleton Rhodes was reminding McCaleb of Will Elliot. Pen had the same wry, studious manner. He asked for and received permission to plead their case before the court.

"We plead not guilty to being drunk and disorderly," said Pen, "and not guilty to disturbing the peace. We'll plead guilty to the destruction of private property and we'll pay reasonable damages for dismissal of the other two charges."

"No!" shrieked Madame X. "I won't accept that!"

Pen sighed. "I reckon we'll have to file charges of our own, then," he said. "If we were drunk and disorderly, if we disturbed the peace, it was because our drinks were loaded, and while we were unconscious we were robbed. How can a man get drunk on just *one* drink, and why *shouldn't* he get disorderly and disturb the peace when he's been robbed? I reckon we busted up a right smart of the lady's whorehouse while we was disorderly and disturbin' the peace, and when we *pay* for *that*, we're payin' for bein' disorderly and disturbin' the peace. Now we ain't gonna pay *twice*."

"Suppose," snapped Judge Short, "the court does not accept your pleas and finds you guilty on all counts?"

"Then we'll pay *no* damages," said Pen. "We'll squat right here in your jail and eat our heads off, until the court is satisfied we've been punished enough."

The bluff was as logical as it was ridiculous, an argument only a Texas cowboy could have conceived. McCaleb and Will laughed, and even the sheriff looked amused. The sheriff consulted with Madame X and then with Judge Short. The judge cleared his throat.

"In return for a guilty plea in the destruction of private property and compensation for damages in the amount of a hundred dollars, the court will dismiss the other charges."

When McCaleb had paid the money and they'd left the courthouse, he turned to Will.

"Ride to camp and bring three of our extra horses. We'll be in the café across the street from the Vasquez House."

They entered the café and McCaleb ordered coffee for them all. While his new riders talked, McCaleb listened. Or appeared to listen. When Will returned with the horses and had taken the new riders safely out of town, McCaleb had one last painful duty to perform. He had to go to Tremont House and say good-bye to Rebecca. His heart was heavy and he almost wished Hobbs's shot had been dead center, that he had never risen from that dusty Denver street.

* * *

Rebecca's door was locked and when he knocked there was no response. Suddenly the door to the adjoining room opened and Jonathan Wickliffe stepped into the hall.

"I had the doctor give her a sedative, McCaleb. She's asleep. Don't make it difficult for her. She's made her choice. You're finished."

CHAPTER 23

$\mathcal{W}$ ith three new riders, a cook, and a chuck wagon—
but without Rebecca—McCaleb headed the herd
north toward Cheyenne. McCaleb, Will, Brazos, and
Monte were quiet, withdrawn. Goose was as inscrutable
as ever. Jed, Stoney, and Pen—even Salty—sensed there
was something they hadn't been told. In time they
would know, but for now they held their peace. Having
gotten a late start, they bedded down the herd not more
than a dozen miles north of Denver. It was Salty's first
meal as part of the outfit, and the old cook outdid himself. He was duly congratulated by all the riders. They
sat around the fire after supper, drinking coffee and
making feeble attempts to relieve the painful silence.

"There's eight of us now," said Brazos. "How do you
aim to set up night watches? Two riders, two hours
apiece?"

"I reckon," said McCaleb.

Pendleton Rhodes, part Indian himself, established a
budding friendship with Goose. Pen spoke Spanish
even more fluently than Brazos, and Monte gave up—at
least temporarily—his long-standing position with
Goose on night watch so that Goose and Pen might ride
together. McCaleb suspected, however, that Monte
needed to talk, and there was no better—or more private—time than while night-hawking. Jed and Stoney
made a second team, Brazos and Will a third, while

McCaleb and Monte comprised a fourth. When Brazos and Will had finished the third watch, McCaleb still hadn't slept, and he doubted if Monte had. The kid needed somebody to talk to. McCaleb didn't feel like talking, but he had no choice.

"How could you just *leave* her there with that old bastard, McCaleb?"

"*You* blessed her out and left her there too," said McCaleb.

"That's different. She's my sister; I can't marry her. It still ain't too late or too far to ride back, gut-shoot that old fool, hog-tie her and bring her with you."

"Kid," said McCaleb wearily, "she's a grown woman and she's made a choice. If *she* don't want *me*, then killin' Wickliffe—or a hundred like him—won't change a thing."

Their second day on the trail took them another twenty miles. While it was the last week in May, daytime in the high country was crisp and cool. Their winter coats and gloves were welcome when the sun dipped behind the Rockies.

Rebecca groaned and lifted her head. Immediately she sank back to the pillow, half sick. Gradually it came back to her. McCaleb had been shot but he was alive. The doctor had come and given her something to make her sleep. She remembered nothing else. Flinging back the covers, Rebecca found she wore only a nightgown. Otherwise she was stark naked. Had Wickliffe undressed her? Involuntarily she flushed with shame. But why? she wondered. She wore the man's ring. She rolled to the edge of the bed, got her feet on the floor and sat up. She was in dire need of the chamber pot, and when she leaned over to look for it, her head pounded all the more. What had they *done* to her?

She took hold of a bedpost and forced herself to stand. Her legs were weak and trembly and it was a while before she trusted herself to walk. She pushed the curtain aside and found the sun low in the west. Dear

God! She had slept all night and most of the day! How was McCaleb and why hadn't he come to see her? Wildly, she began looking for something to wear. Damn him, what had he done with her clothes? In the closet she found only sheets and blankets. Still unsteady on her feet, she went to the door and looked out into the empty hall. She knocked softly on Wickliffe's door, waited a moment and knocked again. Impatiently she tried the knob, found the door unlocked and stepped into the room. The bed had been made and on a night table next to it was a large bottle. Removing the cork, she sniffed the contents and it almost made her sick. It was the rest of that vile-tasting medicine the doctor had left for her. She knelt on shaky knees beside the bed and emptied the bottle into the chamber pot. Then she began looking for her clothes. The fancy gowns that Wickliffe had given her had been hung neatly in the closet. In a corner, amid old newspapers and other refuse, she found her old hat, run-over boots, and dusty trail clothes.

Suddenly she heard voices in the hall, one of them Wickliffe's. She found herself silently praying he wouldn't look first into her room and find her gone. Strangely, the thought of having him discover her virtually naked in his room was repugnant to her. She slipped quickly into the closet and closed the door behind her. Once they had entered the room, she had no trouble hearing their every word. Wickliffe was furious.

"I owe you *nothing*, Rudd. You botched the job; we have nothing more to discuss. Now get out!"

"We got plenty to discuss, Mr. Wickliffe. I near 'bout got my head shot off, follerin' your orders. You owe me! You says to me, Rudd, don't shoot until Hobbs does, and what does Hobbs do? He don't shoot, damn him, until that Texan has put a slug through my hat and shot off my collar button! If Hobbs hadn't finally decided to draw, that third shot would of been the finish of me!"

"You had the edge, shooting from cover," snapped

Wickliffe, "and you didn't fire a shot. What were *you* doing while McCaleb was killing Hobbs?"

"Savin' my neck, you damn fool! That Texan *knowed* I was up there! He cut down on me before Hobbs ever drawed. When Hobbs finally drilled him, he *still* had his sights on me. You saw how he got up. Even hurt, he was just waitin' for me to show, so's he could cut me down."

"Rudd," said Wickliffe, "you are dismissed. Fired. If you know what's good for you, you will take your belongings and ride. I have informed the sheriff that Hobbs has friends. Suppose the sheriff learned that *one* of those friends—you—was the target of McCaleb's first three shots?"

"You double-crossin' bastard," snarled Rudd, "what if the newspapers was told that the territory's next governor—*you*—had hired me and that loud-mouthed, no-account Hobbs to kill a man so's you could have his woman?"

Rebecca Nance listened in growing horror. Not consciously aware of what she was doing, she slipped the diamond from her finger and let it drop to the floor of the darkened closet. Slowly she sank to her knees, buried her face in her hands and wept silent tears of remorse and shame. Bitter tears for the hurt she had caused those she loved . . .

When they bedded down the herd at the close of the third day, they were fifty miles north of Denver. When supper was over, without a word to anyone, McCaleb walked to a grassy knoll from which he could see the back trail. He would wait there, as he had at the close of the past two days, until the darkness ended his vigil. Every rider, even the newcomers, knew why he was there. Twilight, purple and majestic, had taken the land. Already it was too dark to see, but McCaleb lingered. Suddenly Goose got to his feet, keening the wind like a lobo.

"*Polvo*," he said, pointing south. "*Polvo*."

In a lope, Goose headed for the picketed horses. Not

taking the time to saddle, using only a bridle, he sprang to the back of McCaleb's favorite horse and kicked the animal into a canter. It was still light enough for the rest of the outfit to see the Indian reach McCaleb, dismount, and point to the south. They slapped their hats against their thighs, whooping like Comanches, as McCaleb sent the horse galloping down a back trail slowly vanishing in violet shadow.

McCaleb could smell the dust that had alerted Goose, and the thump of his heart matched the pounding hoofs of the horse. If he lived a thousand years he would never forget his first sight of her galloping over the starlit high plains. Her familiar old hat rode her shoulders by its chin thong, her dark hair streaming in the wind. Run-over boots, Levi's pants, and old blue flannel shirt completed her garb. He swept her out of her saddle, lost his balance and tumbled with her into the buffalo grass. She came down on top of him, and he hardly noticed the pain from his not-quite-healed wound. For a long time there was no sound except her heart-wrenching sobs and the crunch-crunch-crunch of their horses grazing nearby.

"Bent," she finally sobbed, "I have to tell—"

"You don't have to tell me anything."

"But don't you want to know?"

"No," he said. "You're here; that's enough. There's something I want *you* to know. When she died, I . . . I couldn't let her go. I wanted *you* to be *her*, and when I'd look at you, I'd see . . . her. But that day . . . when you left with him . . . something changed. I tried to think of her, to forget you, but she was gone. Your face was all I could see, and I *wanted* it to be you. Part of me was buried with her, back there in Red River County. But that part of me, along with her, is a memory. You're real, Rebecca Nance, and I have a place for you. If you want it."

"I don't begrudge her that small part of you," said Rebecca softly, "if I can have the rest. That's how I'd want you to remember me, if I'd found you first . . . and left you like . . . she did."

"Come on," he said, "and let's head for camp. Salty can round you up a biscuit or two. I bought a chuck wagon, hired a cook and three more riders." He chuckled. "You're almighty hard to replace."

They rode in to the chuck wagon and the welcoming cries of the outfit. Except for Monte Nance. Even in the firelight McCaleb could see the chalk-white of his face and the stubborn set of his jaw. Was the kid going to let pride override his common sense and his heart? Would he spoil it for her? No! He dropped his coffee cup, ran to the girl and lifted her off the ground in a bear hug.

April 28, 1868. They pointed the herd north at dawn, Texans all, bound for Wyoming Territory, for Montana Territory, along the Powder River, beyond the Yellowstone. They followed an uncharted route that history would someday brand *The Western Trail*.

EPILOGUE

*C*harles Goodnight was born in Macoupin County, Illinois, on March 5, 1836. He was brought to Milan County, Texas, in 1846 by his mother and stepfather. In 1857 Goodnight moved to Palo Pinto County, where he was a Texas Ranger and Indian scout. Thus prepared, he performed his Civil War service as scout and guide for a Frontier Regiment.

Prior to his first trail drive to Fort Sumner, New Mexico Territory, in 1866, Goodnight is credited with having designed and built the first chuck wagon. Afterward, no outfit worth its salt took to the trail without a faithful copy of Goodnight's original "chuck wagon."

Despite Goodnight's dream of a cattle empire in Colorado, his most successful year—1871—netted him and a partner only seventeen thousand dollars. It was the year he married Ann Dyer.

In 1876 he moved from Colorado to Palo Duro Canyon in the Texas Panhandle. Just a year later he went into partnership with John G. Adair, and in time the JA ranch ran more than a hundred thousand head of cattle on a million acres of land.

Goodnight developed one of the nation's finest herds by introduction of Hereford bulls. He pioneered the breeding of buffalo to Polled Angus cattle, resulting in the first "cattalo."

In 1880 Goodnight was one of the founders of the

Panhandle Stockmen's Association. In 1887 the Adair ranch was divided between Goodnight and Adair's widow. Three years later Goodnight sold his portion. His last years were spent at his small ranch in Goodnight, Texas, a Panhandle town named for him. His first wife died in 1926, and a year later, at age ninety-one, he married Corrine Goodnight. Charles Goodnight died on December 12, 1929, at his winter home in Tucson, Arizona.

Cullen Montgomery Baker was killed on January 6, 1869, by a group of men that included his father-in-law.

HERE IS AN EXCERPT FROM *THE WESTERN TRAIL* —BOOK 2 IN RALPH COMPTON'S BOLD NEW WESTERN SERIES:

They reached the north fork of the Laramie river, and McCaleb estimated they were thirty-five miles south of Boxelder. The next morning they moved out in the first gray light of dawn, the only water they were sure of being Boxelder Creek, or the North Platte, forty or more miles to the east. In the early afternoon, towering thunderheads began building west of the Rockies, shrouding the sun. The blood-red afterglow fanned out to a dusty rose and then gave way to twilight.

"Not more'n fifteen miles to Boxelder," said McCaleb, "but we won't make it today. It'll mean another dry camp, but not for long, by the looks of those clouds."

Goose said something none of them understood and made swimming motions. There would be water in abundance before morning. A chill wind from the southwest brought the smell of rain.

"Don't shuck anything but your saddles and your hats," said McCaleb. "I've heard these High Plains storms are almighty fierce. Best to take one blanket and throw the rest of your rolls in the chuck wagon."

It was good advice. The herd was restless, cows bawling disconsolately for no apparent reason, except for the discomfort of another dry camp. But McCaleb, born and reared in cow country, knew what was bothering them. He could sense the static electricity in the crisp mountain air and as he lay down, his head on his saddle, he knew he wouldn't rest there for long. Despite his misgivings, he slept.

The storm was contrary to anything McCaleb had ever seen or heard tell of. There was very little thunder.

Lightning came in dazzling blue and green streaks. Suddenly a cow bawled and as if on cue, others joined in. As one, the herd rose to its feet and lit out to the south.

"Roll out!" one of the night-hawks bawled. "They're runnin'!"

Seconds counted. Saddles forgotten, they mounted and struck out hell-for-leather through the rain-swept, lightning-splintered darkness. McCaleb let go and almost fell when, before his eyes, his horse's mane turned to green fire. Sparks leaped from one of the animal's ears to the other, and it fled as much from fear as from his urging. Somewhere ahead, amid the thunder of the herd and the wind-whipped rain, he could hear gunfire. Some of the riders were trying to turn the herd. He was riding parallel to the herd, accomplishing nothing. A horn raked his horse's flank and the animal screamed in pain, bucking wildly. Saddleless, it was all McCaleb could do just to hang on. By the time he had calmed the horse, he was hopelessly outdistanced by the herd. . . .

THE WESTERN TRAIL—AVAILABLE FROM ST. MARTIN'S PAPERBACKS IN AUGUST 1992!